EST
1637

IN VITAM MORTEM

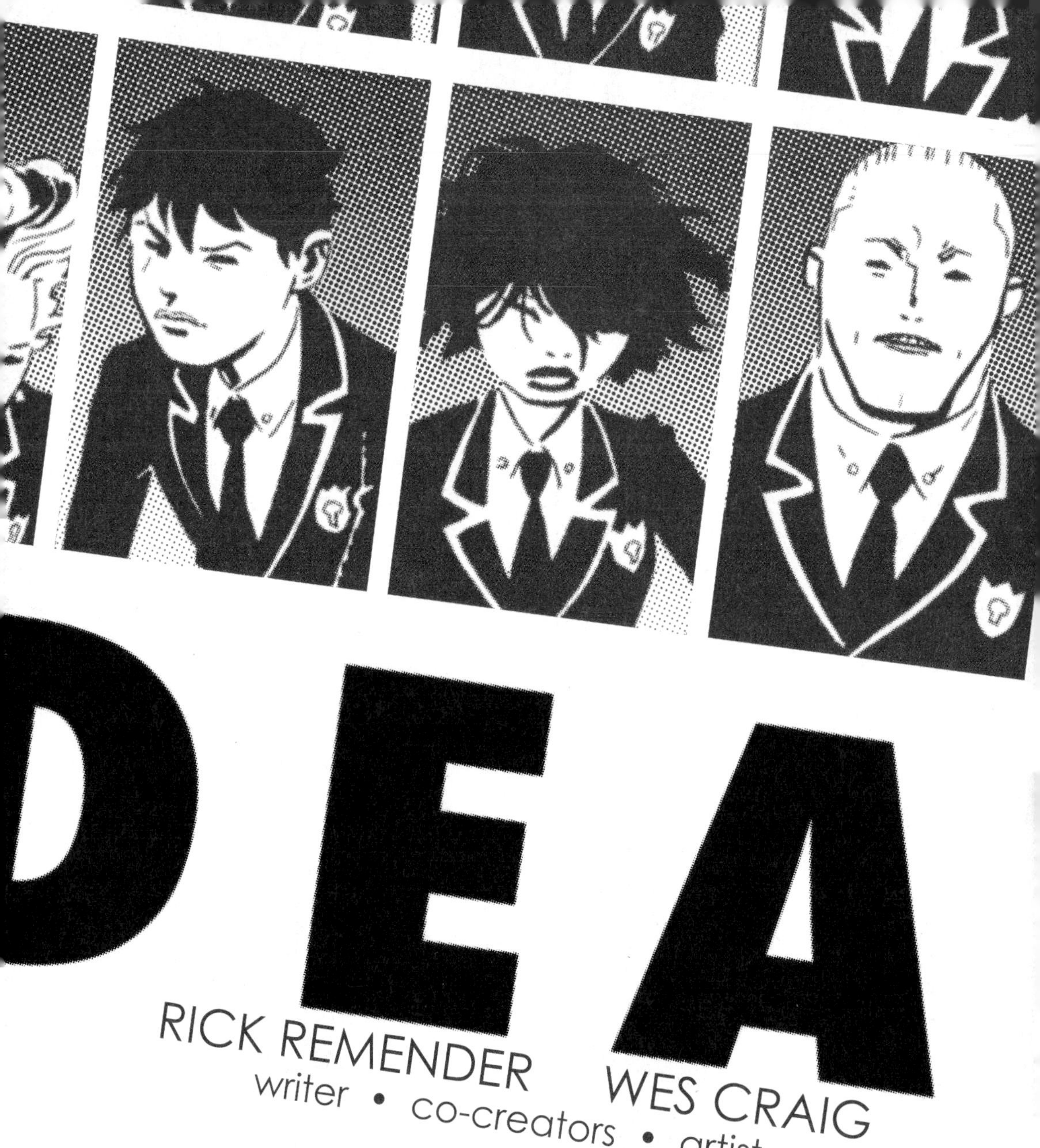

RICK REMENDER writer • co-creators • artist WES CRAIG

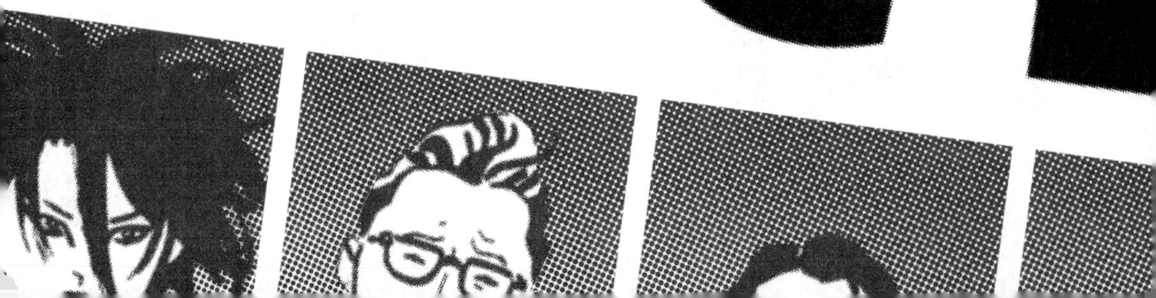

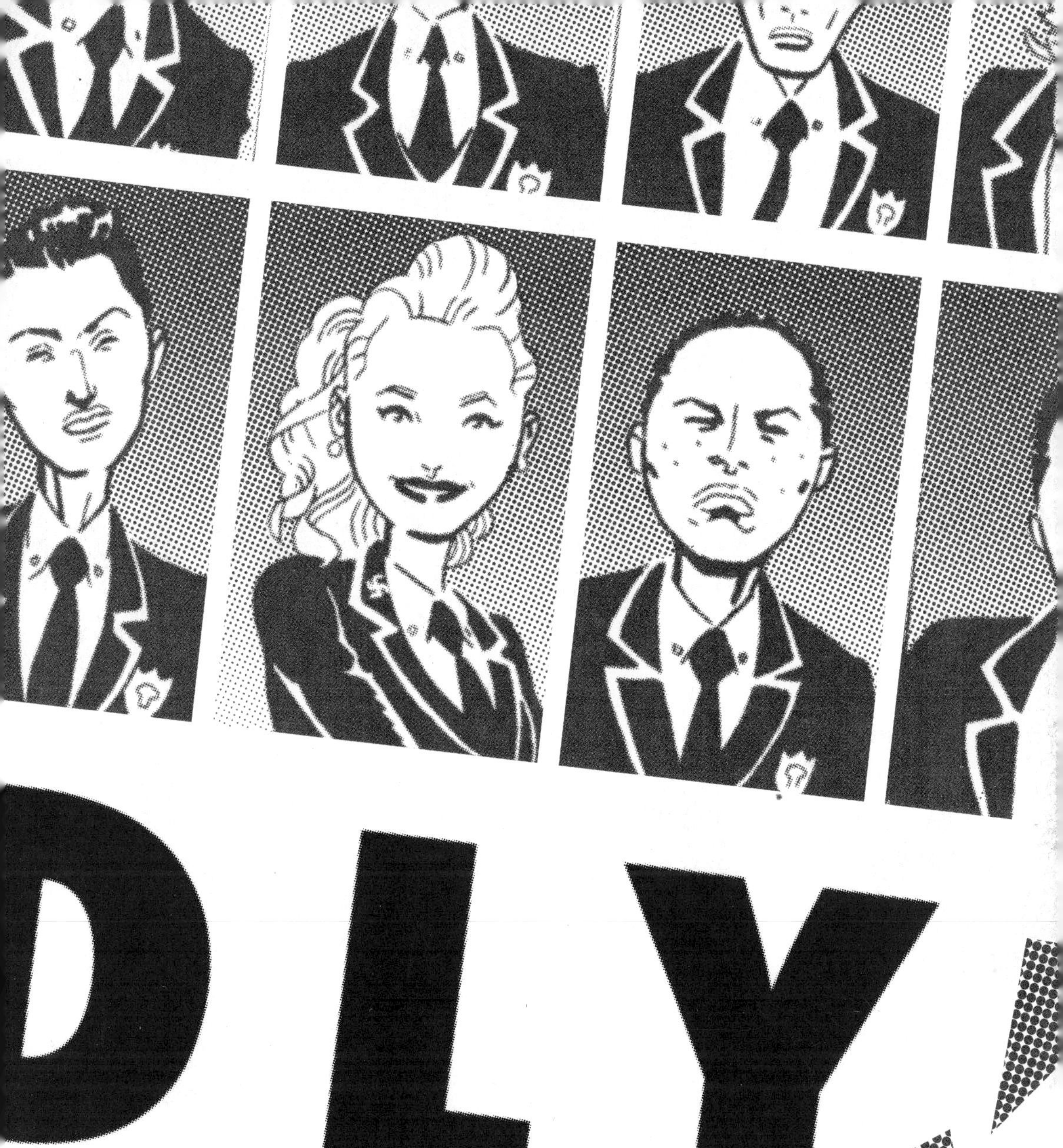

LEE LOUGHRIDGE
colorist

RUS WOOTON
letterer • logo design

WILL DENNIS
editor

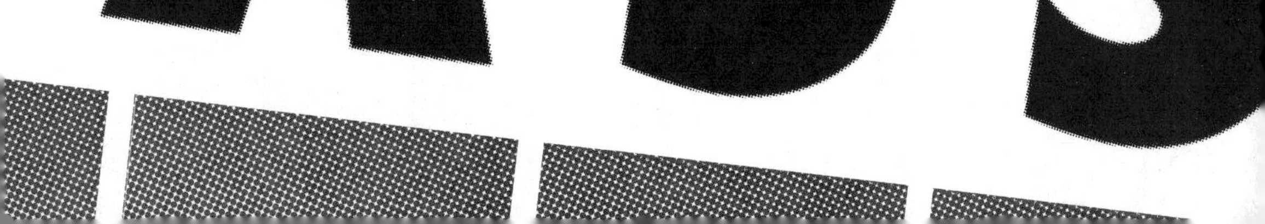

IMAGE COMICS, INC.

Todd McFarlane • President
Jim Valentino • Vice President
Marc Silvestri • Chief Executive Officer
Erik Larsen • Chief Financial Officer
Robert Kirkman • Chief Operating Officer

Eric Stephenson • Publisher / Chief Creative Officer
Nicole Lapalme • Controller
Leanna Caunter • Accounting Analyst
Sue Korpela • Accounting & HR Manager
Marla Eizik • Talent Liaison
Jeff Boison • Director of Sales & Publishing Planning
Dirk Wood • Director of International Sales & Licensing
Alex Cox • Director of Direct Market Sales
Chloe Ramos • Book Market & Library Sales Manager
Emilio Bautista • Digital Sales Coordinator
Jon Schlaffman • Specialty Sales Coordinator
Kat Salazar • Director of PR & Marketing
Drew Fitzgerald • Marketing Content Associate
Heather Doornink • Production Director
Drew Gill • Art Director
Hilary DiLoreto • Print Manager
Tricia Ramos • Traffic Manager
Melissa Gifford • Content Manager
Erika Schnatz • Senior Production Artist
Ryan Brewer • Production Artist
Deanna Phelps • Production Artist

imagecomics.com

TYLER JENNES & GABE DINGER
assistant editors

ERIKA SCHNATZ
production design

DEADLY CLASS VOLUME 10: SAVE YOUR GENERATION. First printing. October 2021. Published by Image Comics, Inc. Office of publication: PO BOX 1445 Portland, OR 97293. Copyright © 2021 Rick Remender & Wes Craig. All rights reserved. Contains material originally published in single magazine form as DEADLY CLASS #45-48. DEADLY CLASS™ (including all prominent characters featured herein), its logo and all character likenesses are trademarks of Rick Remender & Wes Craig, unless otherwise noted. Image Comics® and its logos are registered trademarks of Image Comics, Inc. No part of this publication may be reproduced or transmitted, in any form or by any means (except for short excerpts for journalistic or review purposes), without the express written permission of Rick Remender & Wes Craig, or Image Comics, Inc. All names, characters, events, and locales in this publication are entirely fictional. Any resemblance to actual persons (living or dead), events, or places, without satirical intent, is coincidental. **PRINTED IN THE USA.** For international rights, contact: foreignlicensing@imagecomics.com ISBN: 978-1-5343-1932-5

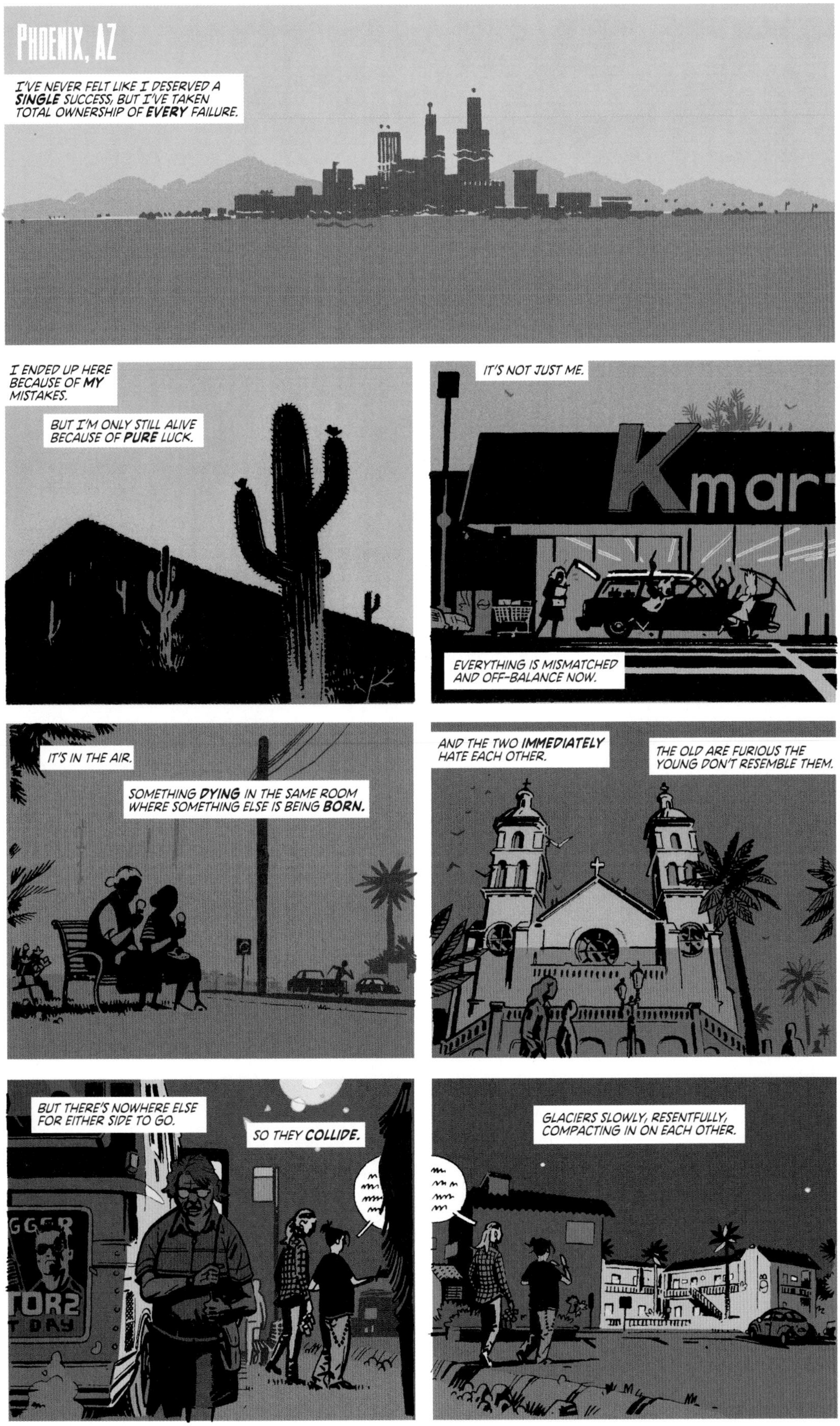
PHOENIX, AZ
I'VE NEVER FELT LIKE I DESERVED A SINGLE SUCCESS, BUT I'VE TAKEN TOTAL OWNERSHIP OF EVERY FAILURE.
I ENDED UP HERE BECAUSE OF MY MISTAKES.
BUT I'M ONLY STILL ALIVE BECAUSE OF PURE LUCK.
IT'S NOT JUST ME.
Kmart
EVERYTHING IS MISMATCHED AND OFF-BALANCE NOW.
IT'S IN THE AIR.
SOMETHING DYING IN THE SAME ROOM WHERE SOMETHING ELSE IS BEING BORN.
AND THE TWO IMMEDIATELY HATE EACH OTHER.
THE OLD ARE FURIOUS THE YOUNG DON'T RESEMBLE THEM.
BUT THERE'S NOWHERE ELSE FOR EITHER SIDE TO GO.
SO THEY COLLIDE.
GLACIERS SLOWLY, RESENTFULLY, COMPACTING IN ON EACH OTHER.

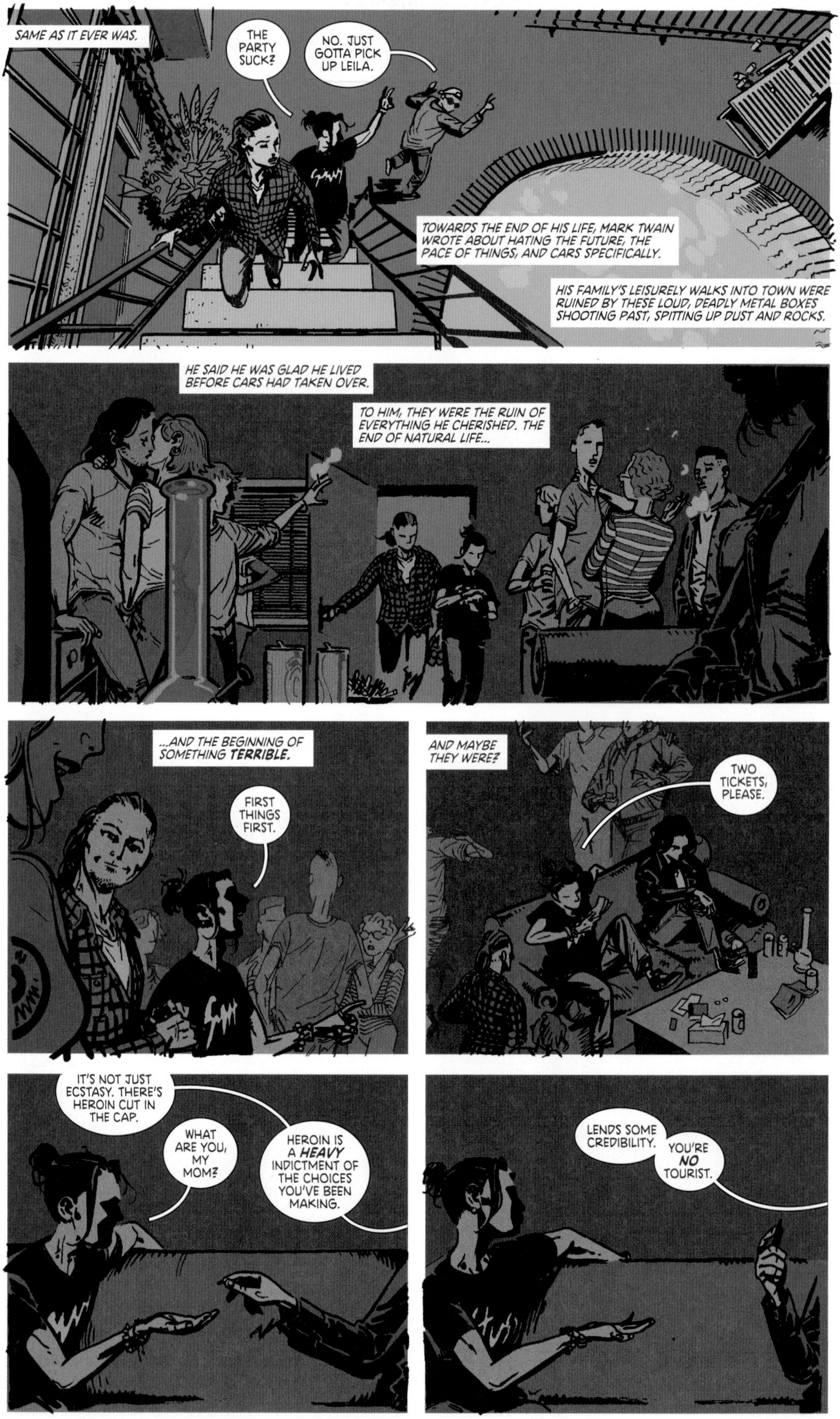
SAME AS IT EVER WAS.
THE PARTY SUCK?
NO. JUST GOTTA PICK UP LEILA.
TOWARDS THE END OF HIS LIFE, MARK TWAIN WROTE ABOUT HATING THE FUTURE, THE PACE OF THINGS, AND CARS SPECIFICALLY.
HIS FAMILY'S LEISURELY WALKS INTO TOWN WERE RUINED BY THESE LOUD, DEADLY METAL BOXES SHOOTING PAST, SPITTING UP DUST AND ROCKS.
HE SAID HE WAS GLAD HE LIVED BEFORE CARS HAD TAKEN OVER.
TO HIM, THEY WERE THE RUIN OF EVERYTHING HE CHERISHED. THE END OF NATURAL LIFE...
...AND THE BEGINNING OF SOMETHING **TERRIBLE.**
FIRST THINGS FIRST.
AND MAYBE THEY WERE?
TWO TICKETS, PLEASE.
IT'S NOT JUST ECSTASY. THERE'S HEROIN CUT IN THE CAP.
WHAT ARE YOU, MY MOM?
HEROIN IS A **HEAVY** INDICTMENT OF THE CHOICES YOU'VE BEEN MAKING.
LENDS SOME CREDIBILITY.
YOU'RE **NO** TOURIST.

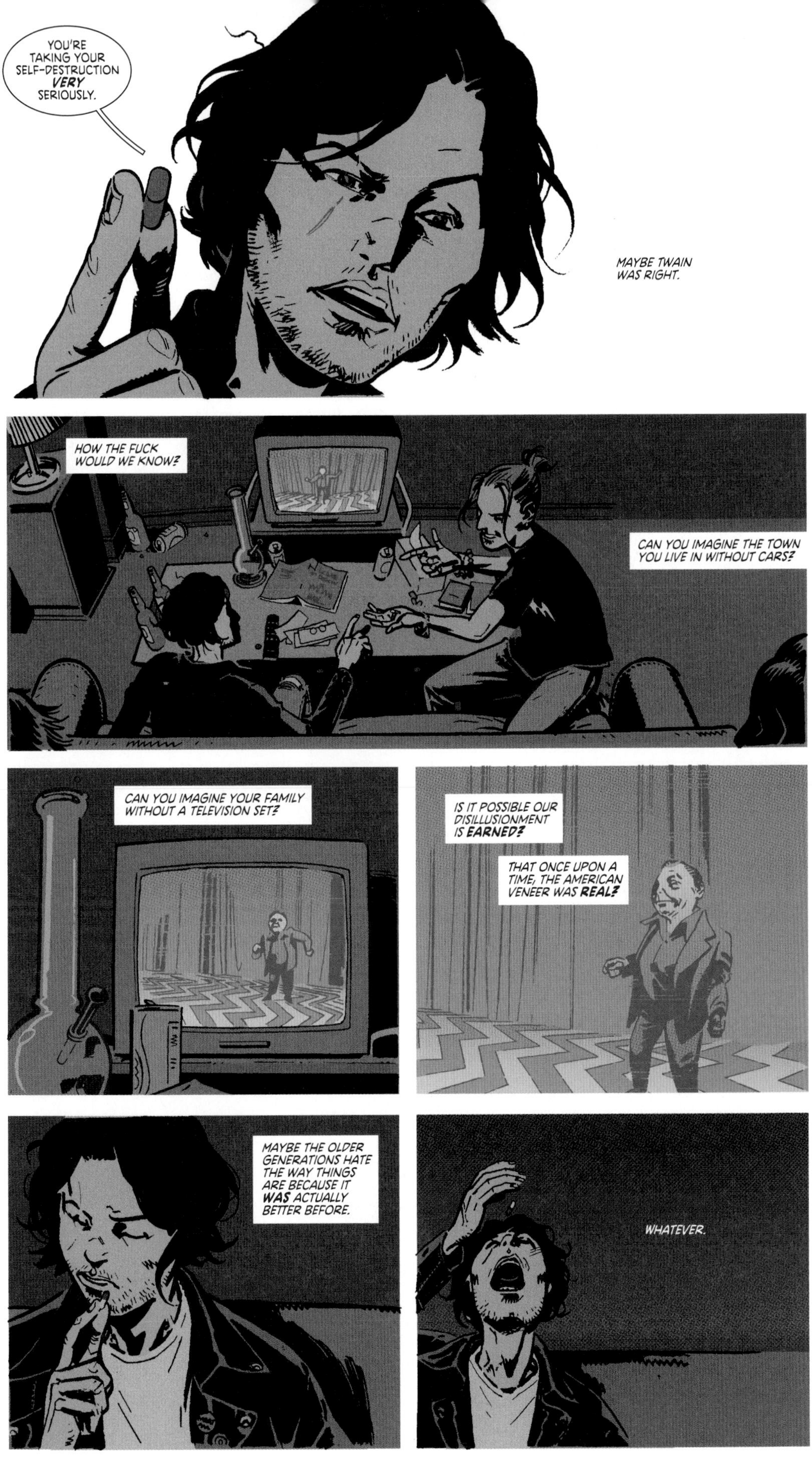

YOU'RE TAKING YOUR SELF-DESTRUCTION **VERY** SERIOUSLY.
MAYBE TWAIN WAS RIGHT.
HOW THE FUCK WOULD WE KNOW?
CAN YOU IMAGINE THE TOWN YOU LIVE IN WITHOUT CARS?
CAN YOU IMAGINE YOUR FAMILY WITHOUT A TELEVISION SET?
IS IT POSSIBLE OUR DISILLUSIONMENT IS **EARNED?**
THAT ONCE UPON A TIME, THE AMERICAN VENEER WAS **REAL?**
MAYBE THE OLDER GENERATIONS HATE THE WAY THINGS ARE BECAUSE IT **WAS** ACTUALLY BETTER BEFORE.
WHATEVER.

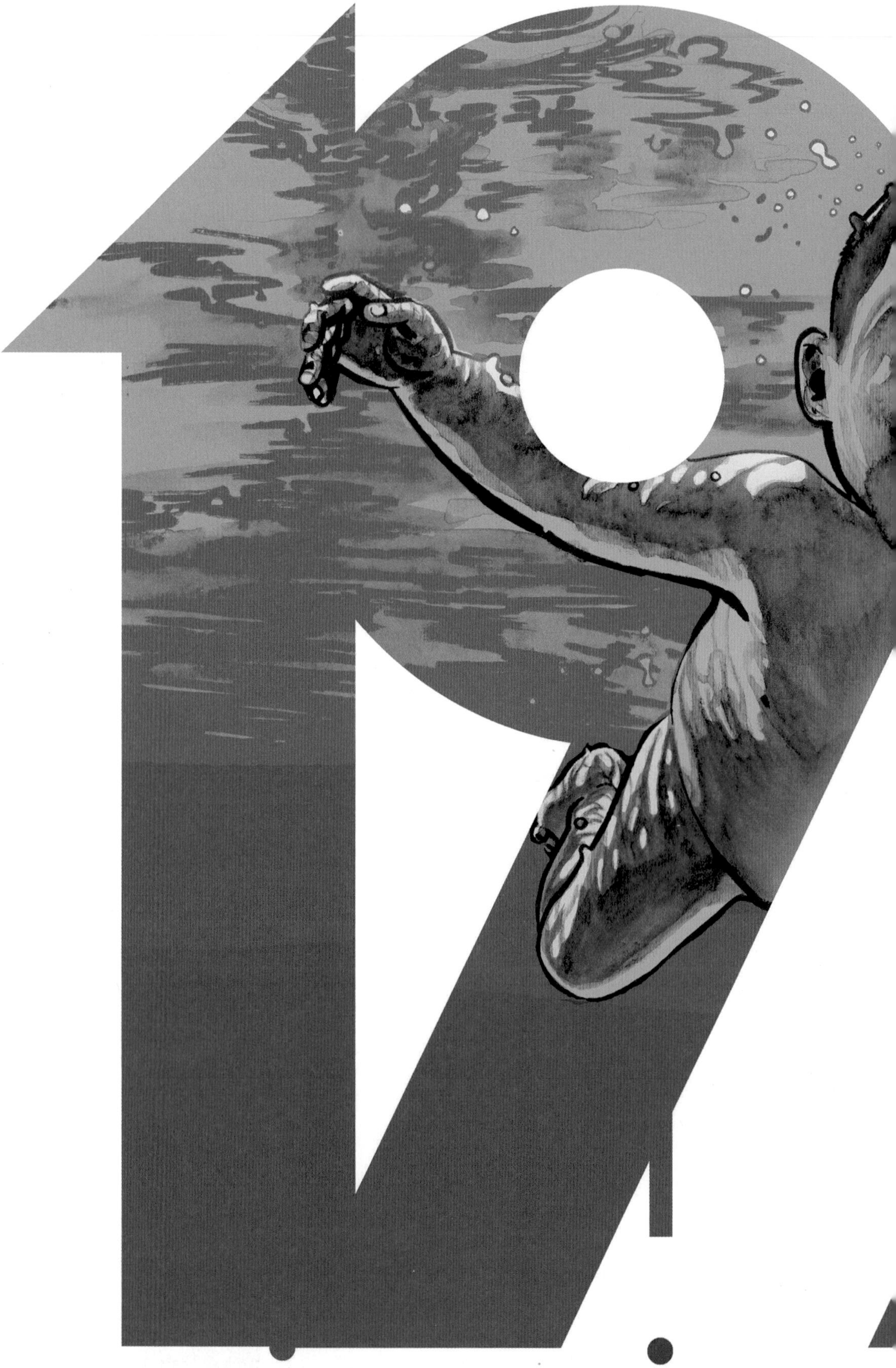

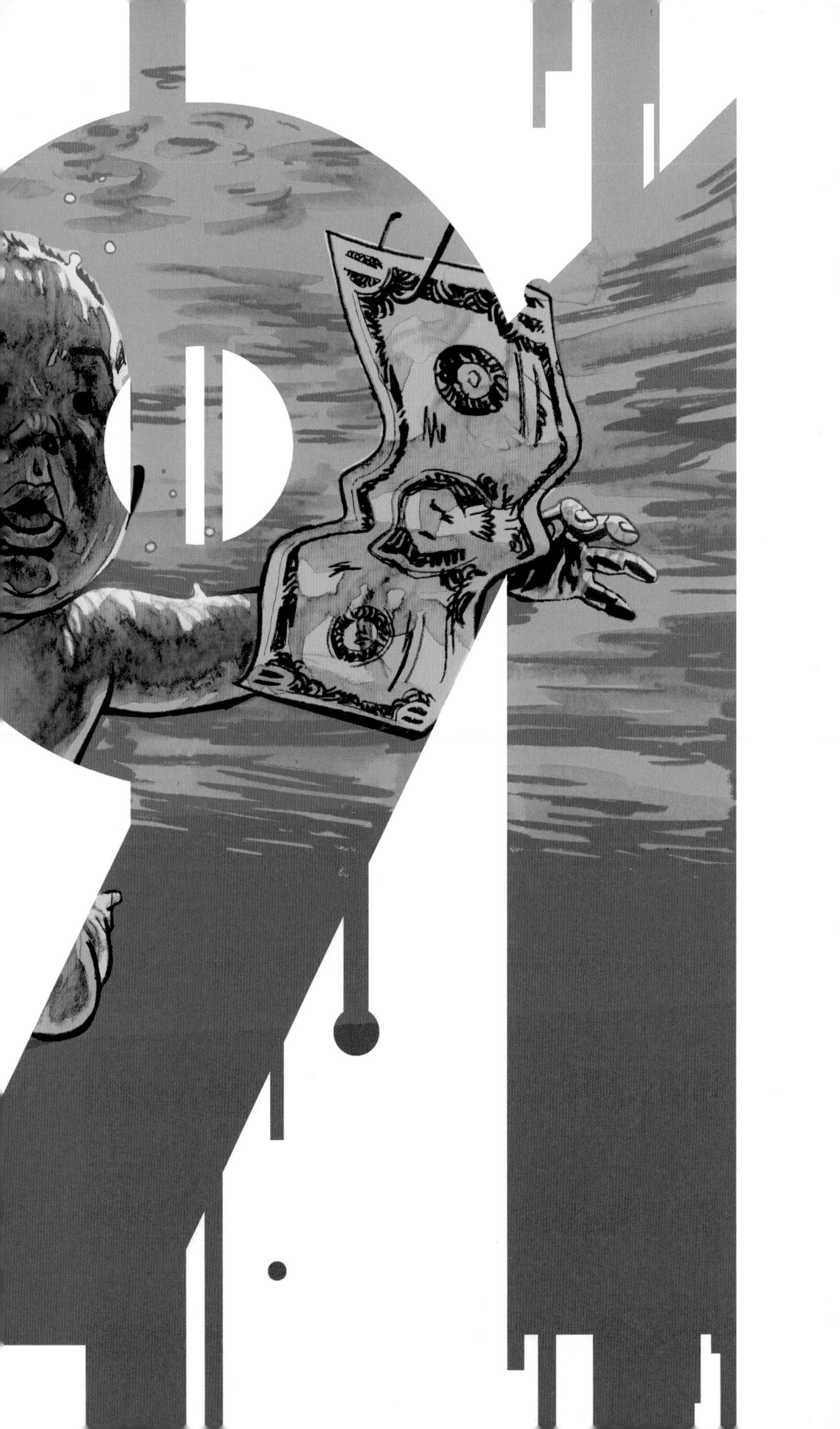

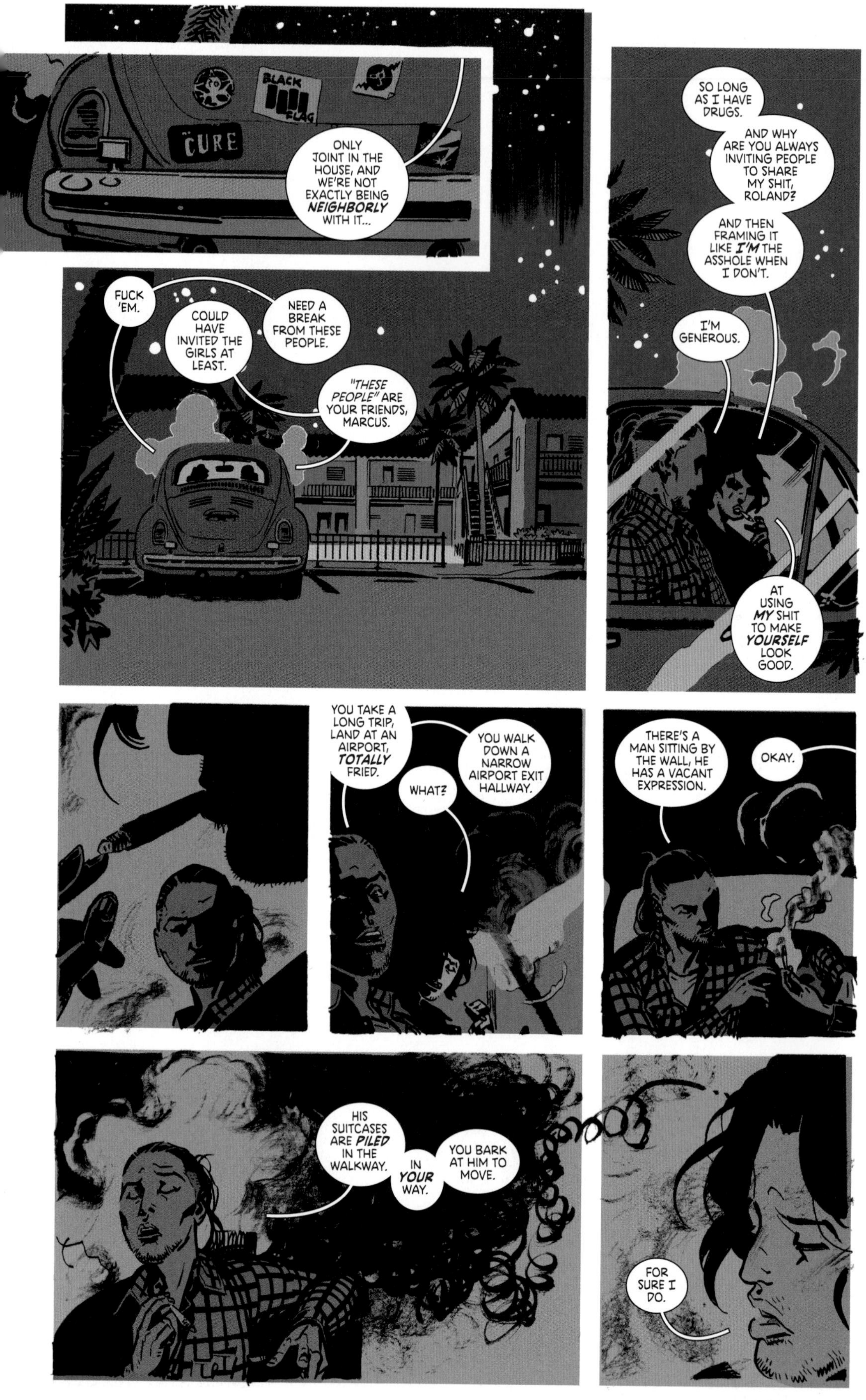
ONLY JOINT IN THE HOUSE, AND WE'RE NOT EXACTLY BEING NEIGHBORLY WITH IT...
CURE
BLACK FLAG
FUCK 'EM.
COULD HAVE INVITED THE GIRLS AT LEAST.
NEED A BREAK FROM THESE PEOPLE.
"THESE PEOPLE" ARE YOUR FRIENDS, MARCUS.
SO LONG AS I HAVE DRUGS.
AND WHY ARE YOU ALWAYS INVITING PEOPLE TO SHARE MY SHIT, ROLAND?
AND THEN FRAMING IT LIKE I'M THE ASSHOLE WHEN I DON'T.
I'M GENEROUS.
AT USING MY SHIT TO MAKE YOURSELF LOOK GOOD.
YOU TAKE A LONG TRIP, LAND AT AN AIRPORT, TOTALLY FRIED.
WHAT?
YOU WALK DOWN A NARROW AIRPORT EXIT HALLWAY.
THERE'S A MAN SITTING BY THE WALL, HE HAS A VACANT EXPRESSION.
OKAY.
HIS SUITCASES ARE PILED IN THE WALKWAY.
IN YOUR WAY.
YOU BARK AT HIM TO MOVE.
FOR SURE I DO.

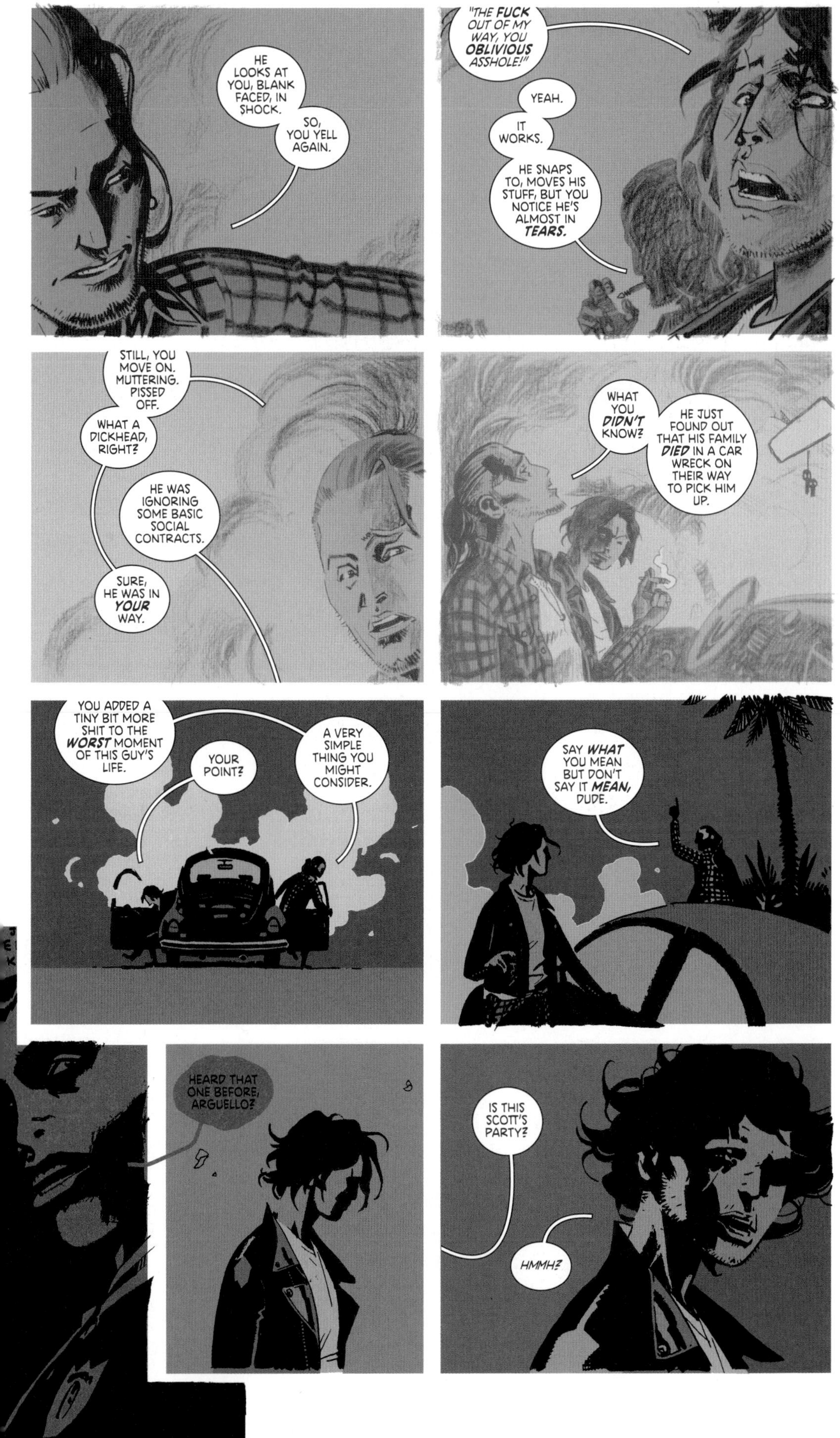
HE LOOKS AT YOU, BLANK FACED, IN SHOCK.
SO, YOU YELL AGAIN.
"THE FUCK OUT OF MY WAY, YOU OBLIVIOUS ASSHOLE!"
YEAH.
IT WORKS.
HE SNAPS TO, MOVES HIS STUFF, BUT YOU NOTICE HE'S ALMOST IN TEARS.
STILL, YOU MOVE ON. MUTTERING. PISSED OFF.
WHAT A DICKHEAD, RIGHT?
HE WAS IGNORING SOME BASIC SOCIAL CONTRACTS.
SURE, HE WAS IN YOUR WAY.
WHAT YOU DIDN'T KNOW?
HE JUST FOUND OUT THAT HIS FAMILY DIED IN A CAR WRECK ON THEIR WAY TO PICK HIM UP.
YOU ADDED A TINY BIT MORE SHIT TO THE WORST MOMENT OF THIS GUY'S LIFE.
YOUR POINT?
A VERY SIMPLE THING YOU MIGHT CONSIDER.
SAY WHAT YOU MEAN BUT DON'T SAY IT MEAN, DUDE.
HEARD THAT ONE BEFORE, ARGUELLO?
IS THIS SCOTT'S PARTY?
HMMH?

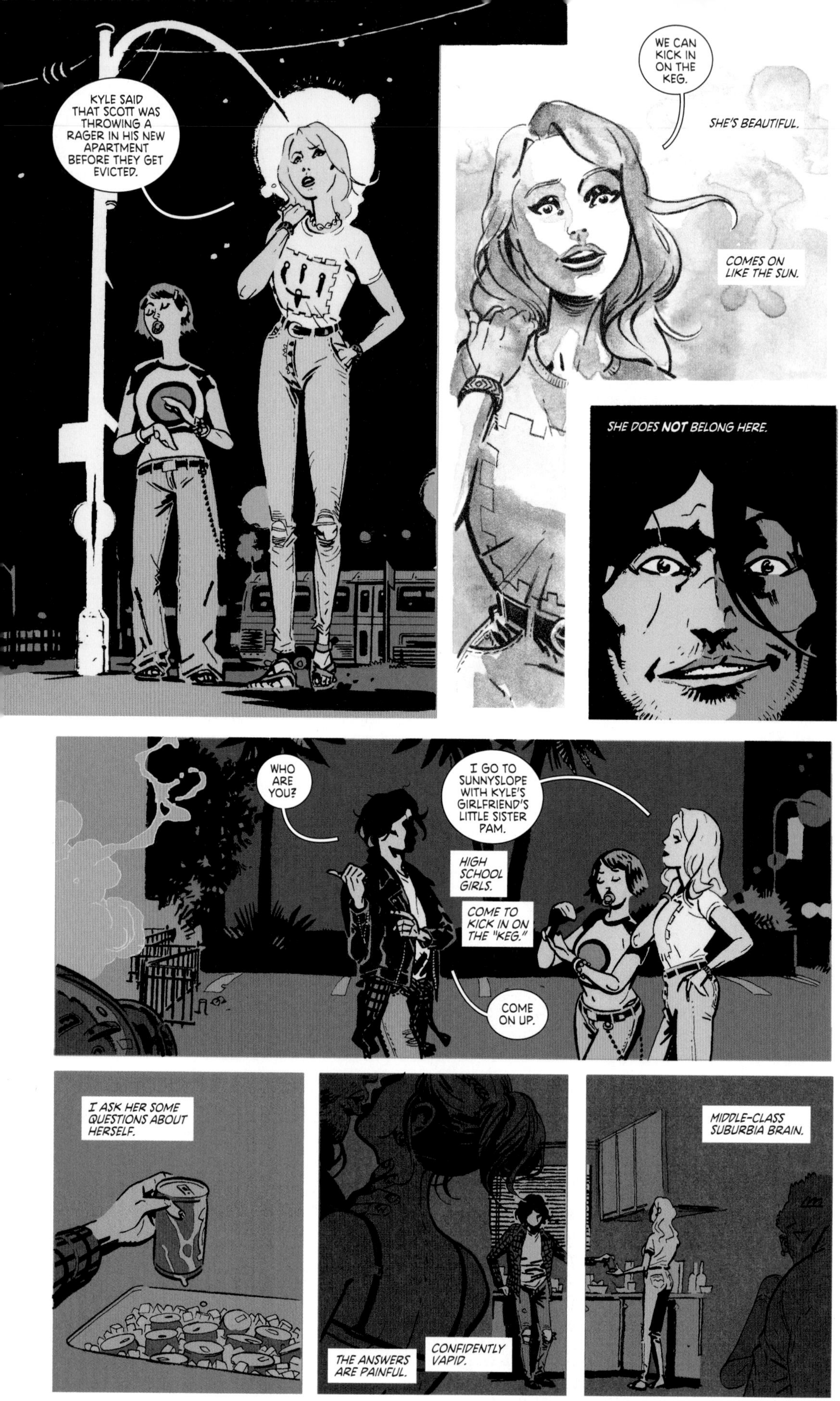
KYLE SAID THAT SCOTT WAS THROWING A RAGER IN HIS NEW APARTMENT BEFORE THEY GET EVICTED.
WE CAN KICK IN ON THE KEG.
SHE'S BEAUTIFUL.
COMES ON LIKE THE SUN.
SHE DOES **NOT** BELONG HERE.
WHO ARE YOU?
I GO TO SUNNYSLOPE WITH KYLE'S GIRLFRIEND'S LITTLE SISTER PAM.
HIGH SCHOOL GIRLS.
COME TO KICK IN ON THE "KEG."
COME ON UP.
I ASK HER SOME QUESTIONS ABOUT HERSELF.
THE ANSWERS ARE PAINFUL.
CONFIDENTLY VAPID.
MIDDLE-CLASS SUBURBIA BRAIN.

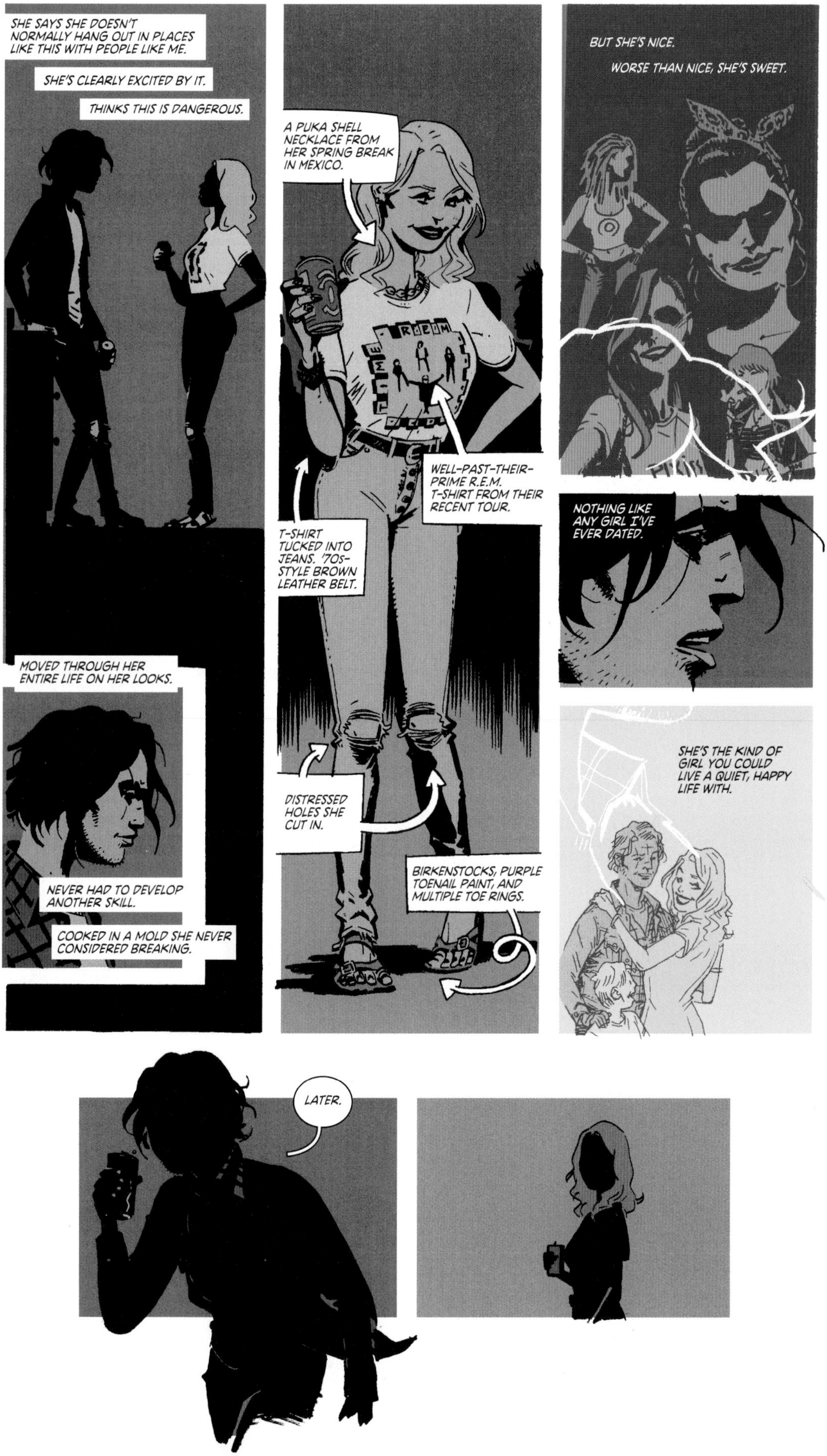
SHE SAYS SHE DOESN'T NORMALLY HANG OUT IN PLACES LIKE THIS WITH PEOPLE LIKE ME.
SHE'S CLEARLY EXCITED BY IT.
THINKS THIS IS DANGEROUS.
A PUKA SHELL NECKLACE FROM HER SPRING BREAK IN MEXICO.
WELL-PAST-THEIR-PRIME R.E.M. T-SHIRT FROM THEIR RECENT TOUR.
T-SHIRT TUCKED INTO JEANS. '70s-STYLE BROWN LEATHER BELT.
DISTRESSED HOLES SHE CUT IN.
BIRKENSTOCKS, PURPLE TOENAIL PAINT, AND MULTIPLE TOE RINGS.
BUT SHE'S NICE.
WORSE THAN NICE, SHE'S SWEET.
NOTHING LIKE ANY GIRL I'VE EVER DATED.
SHE'S THE KIND OF GIRL YOU COULD LIVE A QUIET, HAPPY LIFE WITH.
MOVED THROUGH HER ENTIRE LIFE ON HER LOOKS.
NEVER HAD TO DEVELOP ANOTHER SKILL.
COOKED IN A MOLD SHE NEVER CONSIDERED BREAKING.
LATER.

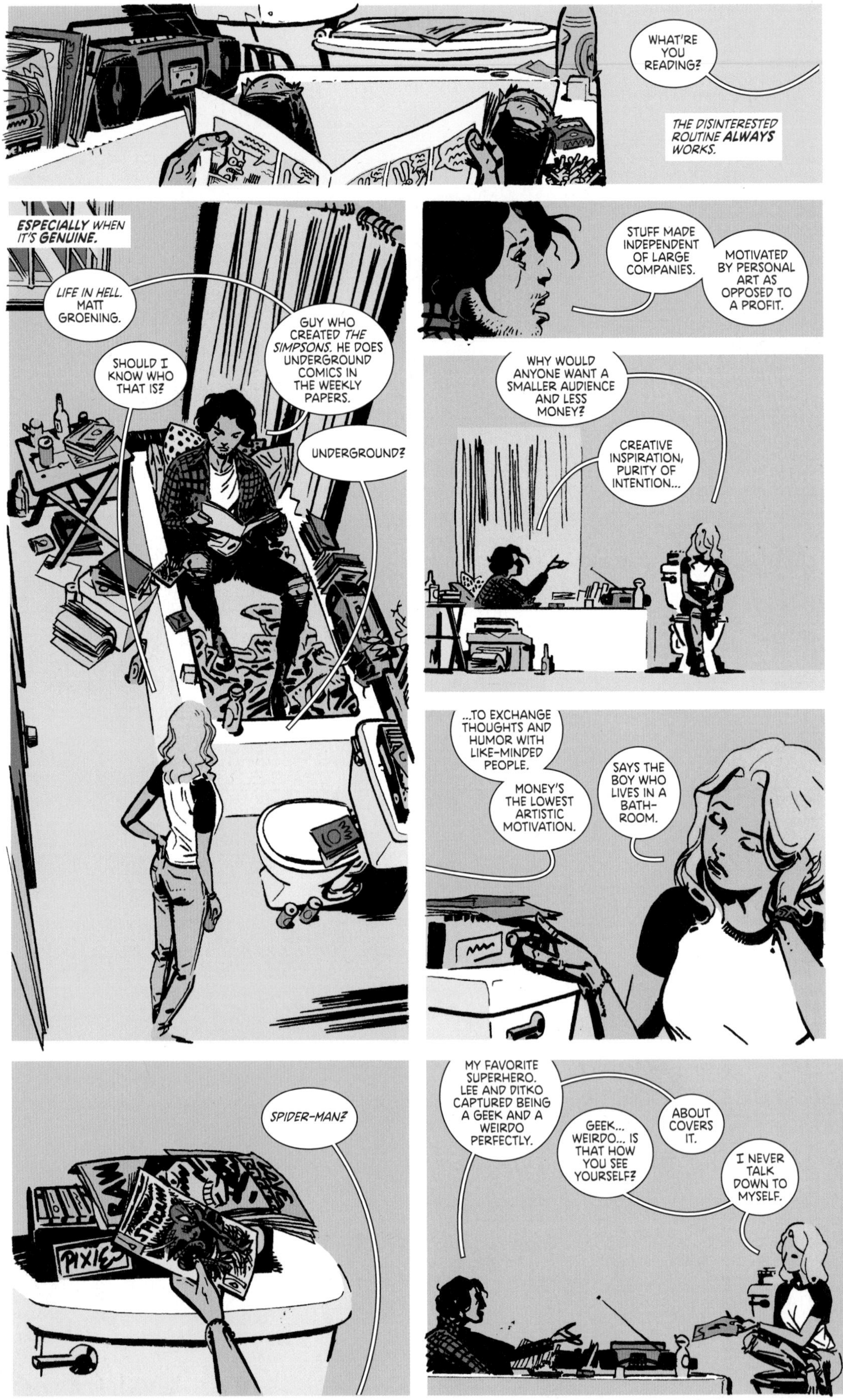
WHAT'RE YOU READING?
THE DISINTERESTED ROUTINE ALWAYS WORKS.
ESPECIALLY WHEN IT'S GENUINE.
LIFE IN HELL. MATT GROENING.
SHOULD I KNOW WHO THAT IS?
GUY WHO CREATED THE SIMPSONS. HE DOES UNDERGROUND COMICS IN THE WEEKLY PAPERS.
UNDERGROUND?
STUFF MADE INDEPENDENT OF LARGE COMPANIES.
MOTIVATED BY PERSONAL ART AS OPPOSED TO A PROFIT.
WHY WOULD ANYONE WANT A SMALLER AUDIENCE AND LESS MONEY?
CREATIVE INSPIRATION, PURITY OF INTENTION...
...TO EXCHANGE THOUGHTS AND HUMOR WITH LIKE-MINDED PEOPLE.
MONEY'S THE LOWEST ARTISTIC MOTIVATION.
SAYS THE BOY WHO LIVES IN A BATH-ROOM.
SPIDER-MAN?
MY FAVORITE SUPERHERO. LEE AND DITKO CAPTURED BEING A GEEK AND A WEIRDO PERFECTLY.
ABOUT COVERS IT.
GEEK... WEIRDO... IS THAT HOW YOU SEE YOURSELF?
I NEVER TALK DOWN TO MYSELF.

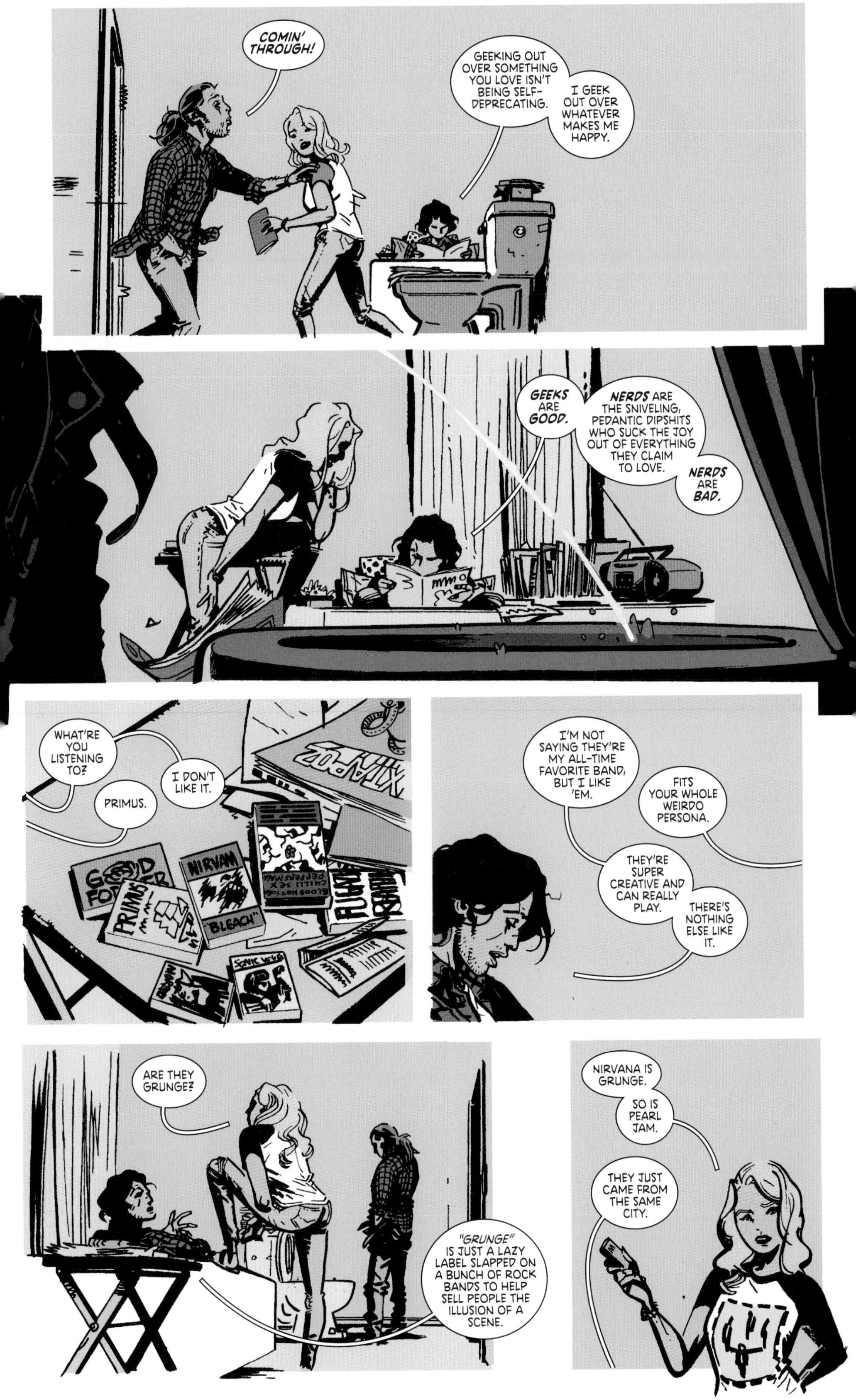

COMIN' THROUGH!
GEEKING OUT OVER SOMETHING YOU LOVE ISN'T BEING SELF-DEPRECATING.
I GEEK OUT OVER WHATEVER MAKES ME HAPPY.
GEEKS ARE GOOD.
NERDS ARE THE SNIVELING, PEDANTIC DIPSHITS WHO SUCK THE JOY OUT OF EVERYTHING THEY CLAIM TO LOVE.
NERDS ARE BAD.
WHAT'RE YOU LISTENING TO?
PRIMUS.
I DON'T LIKE IT.
NIRVANA
"BLEACH"
PRIMUS
SONIC YOUTH
I'M NOT SAYING THEY'RE MY ALL-TIME FAVORITE BAND, BUT I LIKE 'EM.
FITS YOUR WHOLE WEIRDO PERSONA.
THEY'RE SUPER CREATIVE AND CAN REALLY PLAY.
THERE'S NOTHING ELSE LIKE IT.
ARE THEY GRUNGE?
"GRUNGE" IS JUST A LAZY LABEL SLAPPED ON A BUNCH OF ROCK BANDS TO HELP SELL PEOPLE THE ILLUSION OF A SCENE.
NIRVANA IS GRUNGE.
SO IS PEARL JAM.
THEY JUST CAME FROM THE SAME CITY.

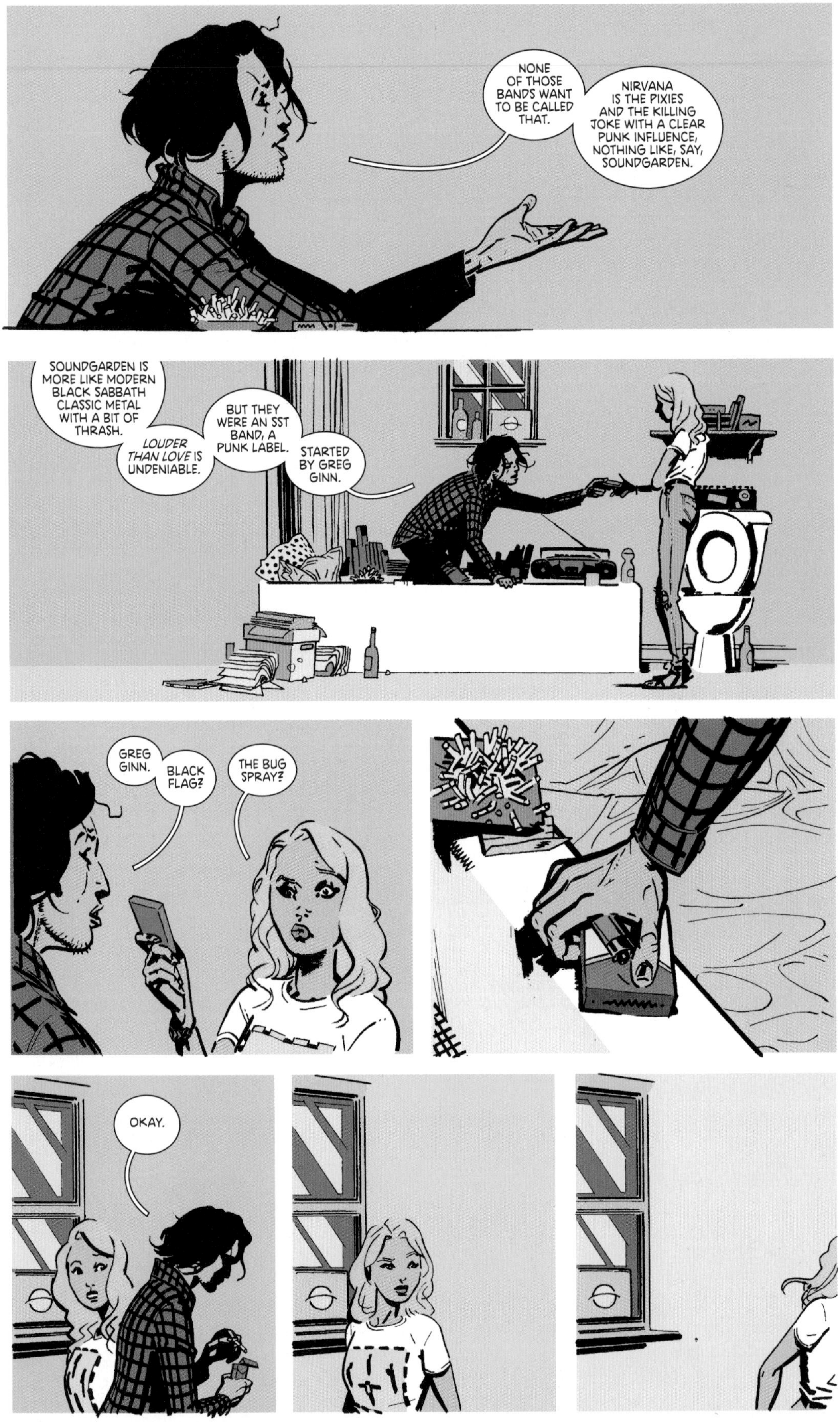
NONE OF THOSE BANDS WANT TO BE CALLED THAT.
NIRVANA IS THE PIXIES AND THE KILLING JOKE WITH A CLEAR PUNK INFLUENCE, NOTHING LIKE, SAY, SOUNDGARDEN.
SOUNDGARDEN IS MORE LIKE MODERN BLACK SABBATH CLASSIC METAL WITH A BIT OF THRASH.
LOUDER THAN LOVE IS UNDENIABLE.
BUT THEY WERE AN SST BAND, A PUNK LABEL.
STARTED BY GREG GINN.
GREG GINN.
BLACK FLAG?
THE BUG SPRAY?
OKAY.

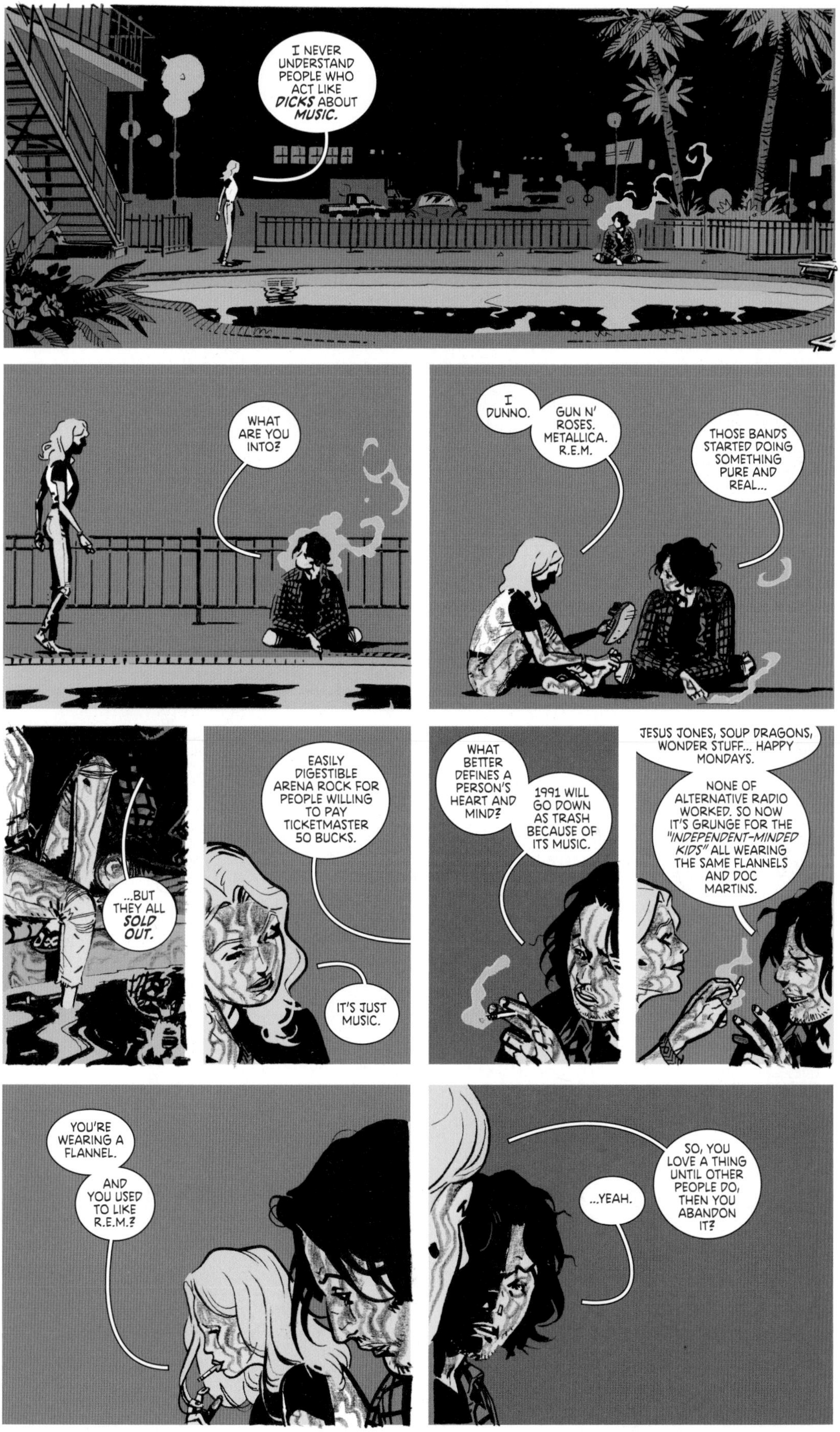
I NEVER UNDERSTAND PEOPLE WHO ACT LIKE DICKS ABOUT MUSIC.
WHAT ARE YOU INTO?
I DUNNO.
GUN N' ROSES. METALLICA. R.E.M.
THOSE BANDS STARTED DOING SOMETHING PURE AND REAL...
...BUT THEY ALL SOLD OUT.
EASILY DIGESTIBLE ARENA ROCK FOR PEOPLE WILLING TO PAY TICKETMASTER 50 BUCKS.
IT'S JUST MUSIC.
WHAT BETTER DEFINES A PERSON'S HEART AND MIND?
1991 WILL GO DOWN AS TRASH BECAUSE OF ITS MUSIC.
JESUS JONES, SOUP DRAGONS, WONDER STUFF... HAPPY MONDAYS.
NONE OF ALTERNATIVE RADIO WORKED. SO NOW IT'S GRUNGE FOR THE "INDEPENDENT-MINDED KIDS" ALL WEARING THE SAME FLANNELS AND DOC MARTINS.
YOU'RE WEARING A FLANNEL.
AND YOU USED TO LIKE R.E.M.?
SO, YOU LOVE A THING UNTIL OTHER PEOPLE DO, THEN YOU ABANDON IT?
...YEAH.

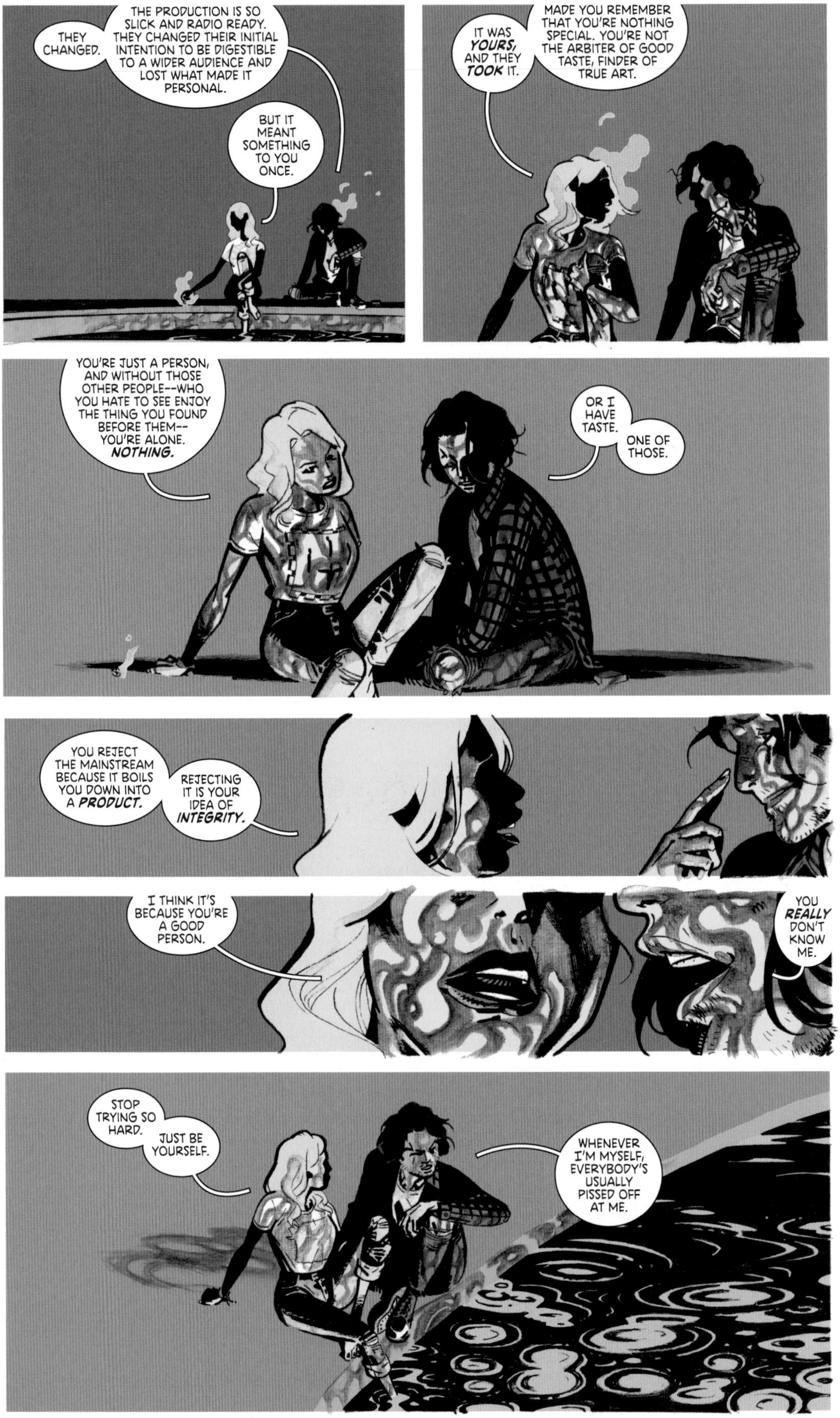
THEY CHANGED.
THE PRODUCTION IS SO SLICK AND RADIO READY. THEY CHANGED THEIR INITIAL INTENTION TO BE DIGESTIBLE TO A WIDER AUDIENCE AND LOST WHAT MADE IT PERSONAL.
BUT IT MEANT SOMETHING TO YOU ONCE.
IT WAS *YOURS,* AND THEY *TOOK* IT.
MADE YOU REMEMBER THAT YOU'RE NOTHING SPECIAL. YOU'RE NOT THE ARBITER OF GOOD TASTE, FINDER OF TRUE ART.
YOU'RE JUST A PERSON, AND WITHOUT THOSE OTHER PEOPLE--WHO YOU HATE TO SEE ENJOY THE THING YOU FOUND BEFORE THEM--YOU'RE ALONE. ***NOTHING.***
OR I HAVE TASTE.
ONE OF THOSE.
YOU REJECT THE MAINSTREAM BECAUSE IT BOILS YOU DOWN INTO A ***PRODUCT.***
REJECTING IT IS YOUR IDEA OF ***INTEGRITY.***
I THINK IT'S BECAUSE YOU'RE A GOOD PERSON.
YOU ***REALLY*** DON'T KNOW ME.
STOP TRYING SO HARD.
JUST BE YOURSELF.
WHENEVER I'M MYSELF, EVERYBODY'S USUALLY PISSED OFF AT ME.

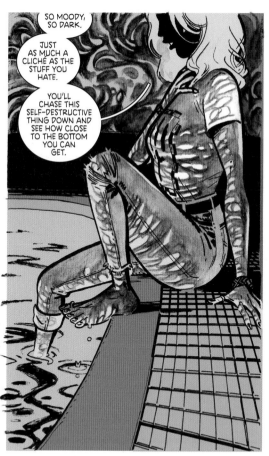

SO MOODY, SO DARK. JUST AS MUCH A CLICHÉ AS THE STUFF YOU HATE.

YOU'LL CHASE THIS SELF-DESTRUCTIVE THING DOWN AND SEE HOW CLOSE TO THE BOTTOM YOU CAN GET.

BUT YOU'LL COURSE CORRECT, MOVE BACK HOME WITH YOUR PARENTS, RESET, AND GET READY FOR LIFE IN THE CUBICLES.

HUH.

YOU *SURE* ABOUT THAT?

IT'LL BE A NARROW ESCAPE--BUT THIS IS JUST A PHASE.

I'LL GROW OUT OF IT?

NOT TONIGHT.

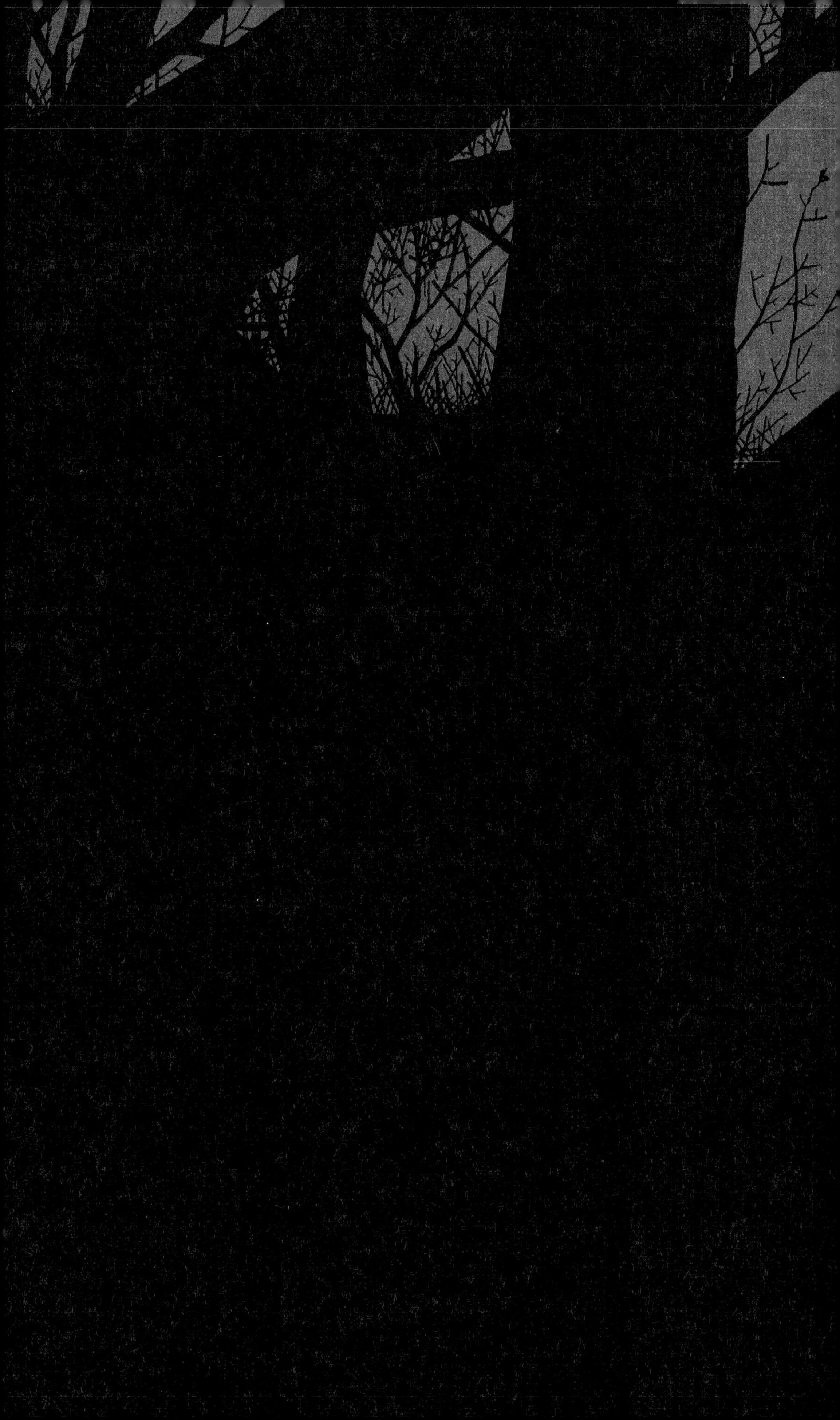

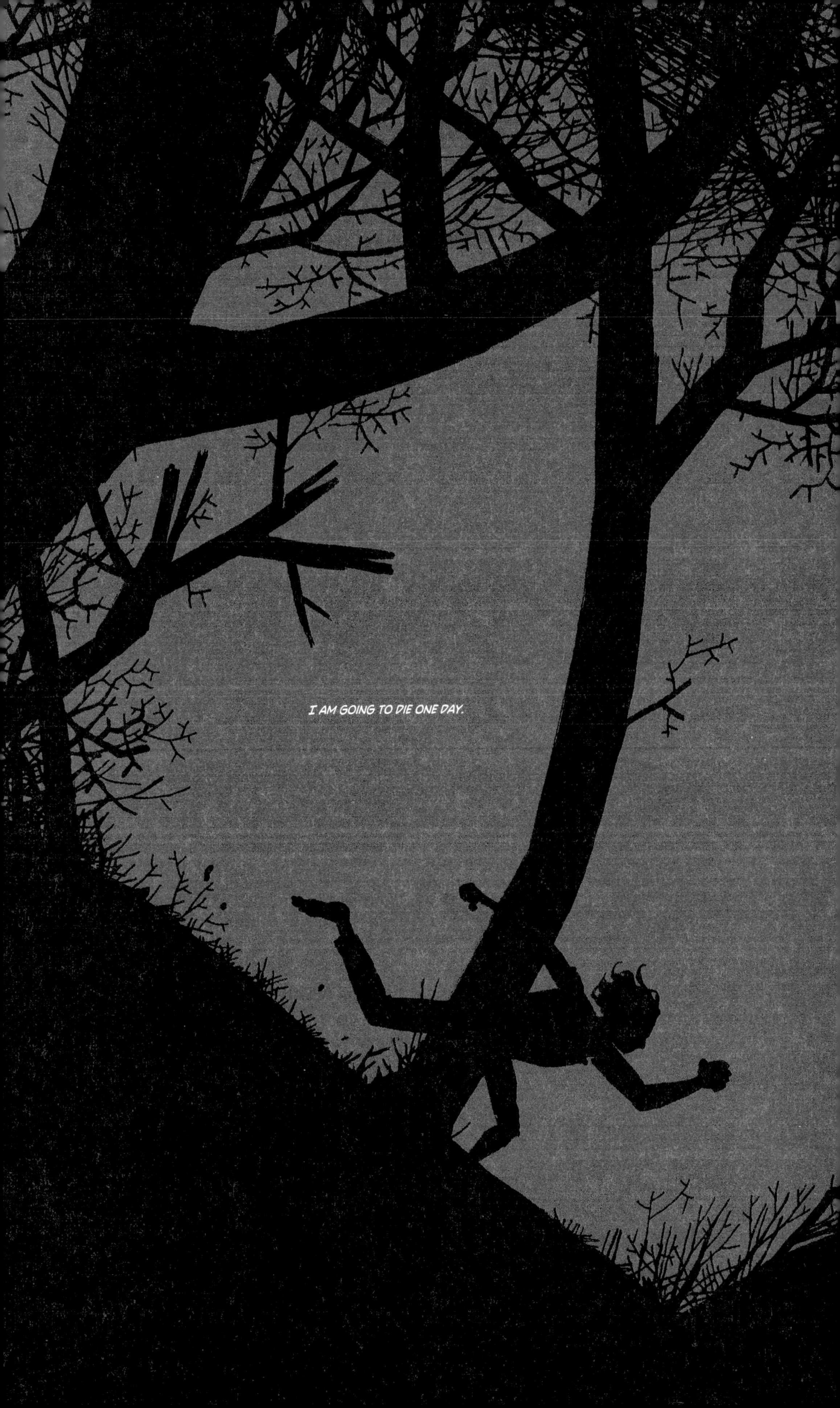
I AM GOING TO DIE ONE DAY.

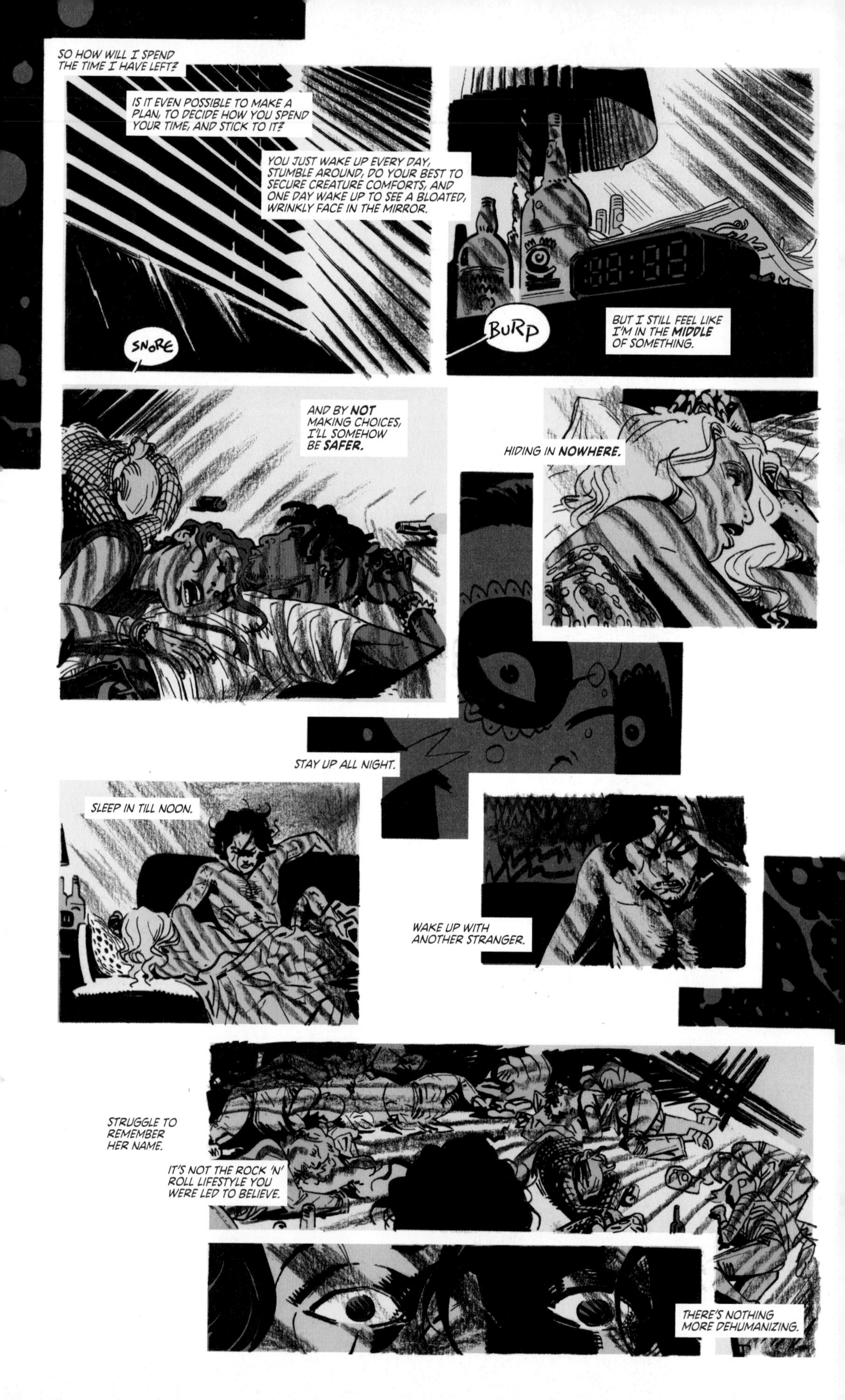
SO HOW WILL I SPEND THE TIME I HAVE LEFT?
IS IT EVEN POSSIBLE TO MAKE A PLAN, TO DECIDE HOW YOU SPEND YOUR TIME, AND STICK TO IT?
YOU JUST WAKE UP EVERY DAY, STUMBLE AROUND, DO YOUR BEST TO SECURE CREATURE COMFORTS, AND ONE DAY WAKE UP TO SEE A BLOATED, WRINKLY FACE IN THE MIRROR.
SNORE
BURP
BUT I STILL FEEL LIKE I'M IN THE MIDDLE OF SOMETHING.
AND BY NOT MAKING CHOICES, I'LL SOMEHOW BE SAFER.
HIDING IN NOWHERE.
STAY UP ALL NIGHT.
SLEEP IN TILL NOON.
WAKE UP WITH ANOTHER STRANGER.
STRUGGLE TO REMEMBER HER NAME.
IT'S NOT THE ROCK 'N' ROLL LIFESTYLE YOU WERE LED TO BELIEVE.
THERE'S NOTHING MORE DEHUMANIZING.

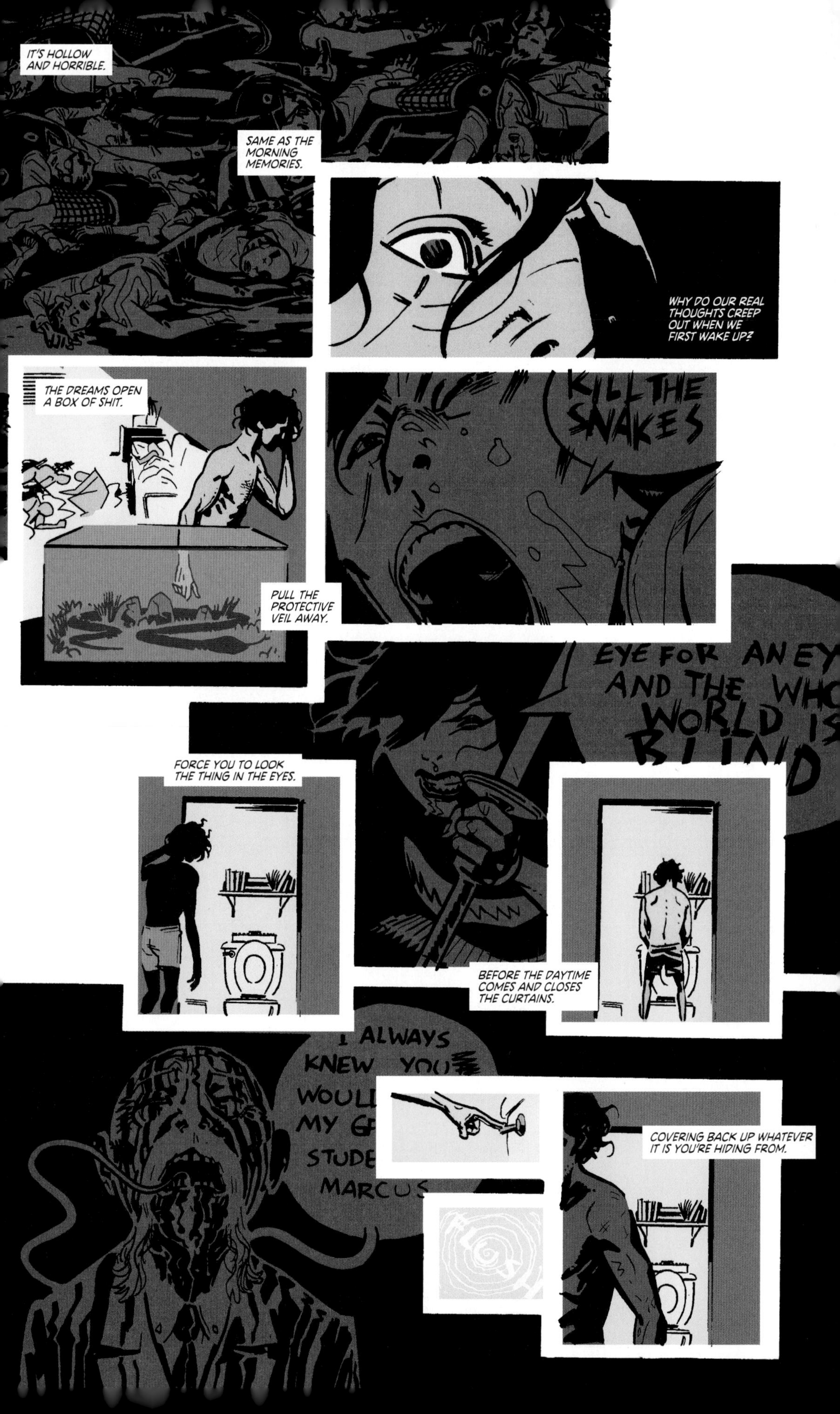
IT'S HOLLOW AND HORRIBLE.
SAME AS THE MORNING MEMORIES.
WHY DO OUR REAL THOUGHTS CREEP OUT WHEN WE FIRST WAKE UP?
THE DREAMS OPEN A BOX OF SHIT.
KILL THE SNAKES
PULL THE PROTECTIVE VEIL AWAY.
EYE FOR AN EY
AND THE WHO
WORLD IS
FORCE YOU TO LOOK THE THING IN THE EYES.
BEFORE THE DAYTIME COMES AND CLOSES THE CURTAINS.
I ALWAYS
KNEW YOU
MARCUS
COVERING BACK UP WHATEVER IT IS YOU'RE HIDING FROM.

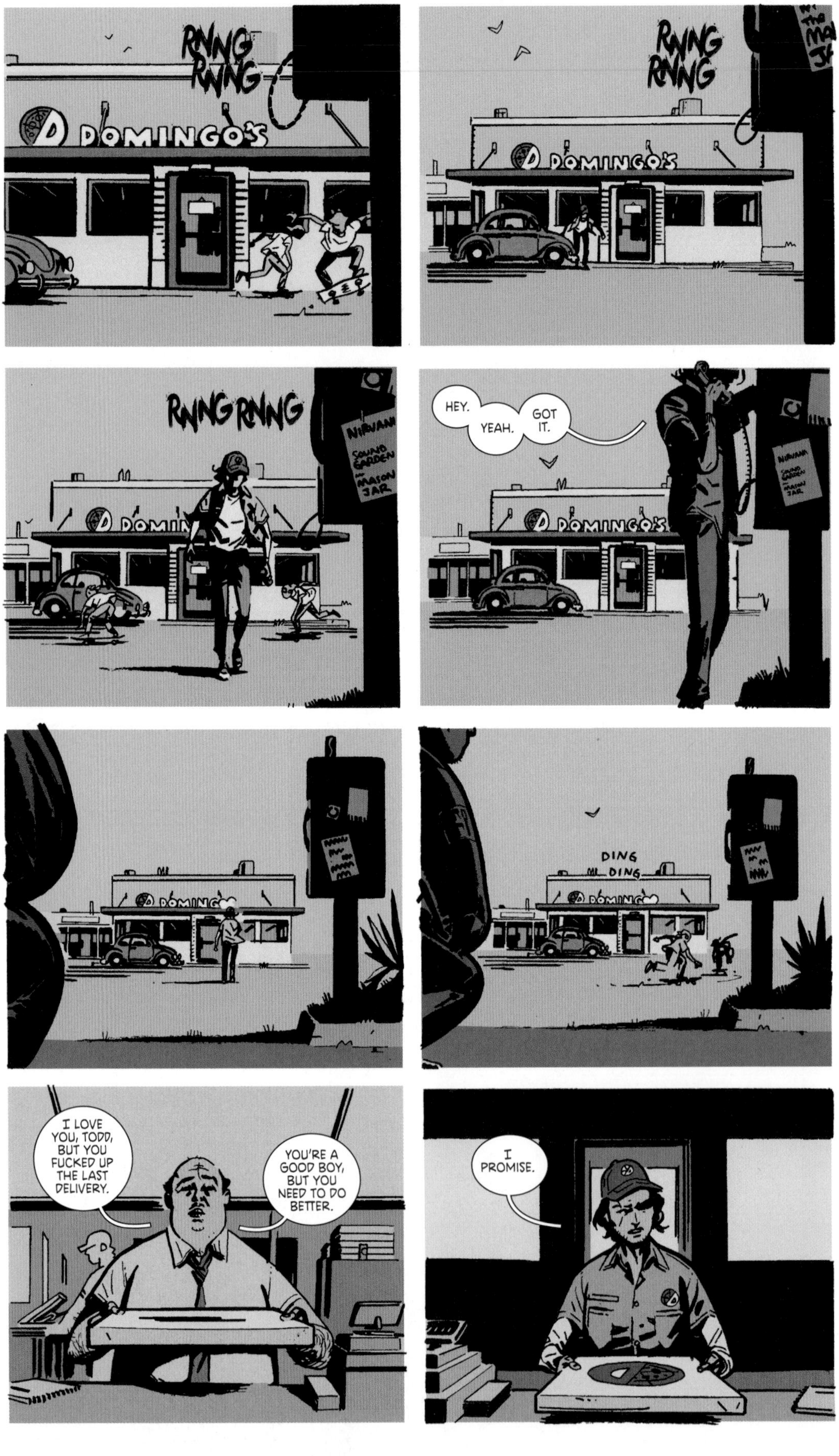
RNNG RNNG
DOMINGO'S
RNNG RNNG
DOMINGO'S
RNNG RNNG
NIRVANA SOUND GARDEN MASON JAR
HEY.
YEAH.
GOT IT.
DING DING
I LOVE YOU, TODD, BUT YOU FUCKED UP THE LAST DELIVERY.
YOU'RE A GOOD BOY, BUT YOU NEED TO DO BETTER.
I PROMISE.

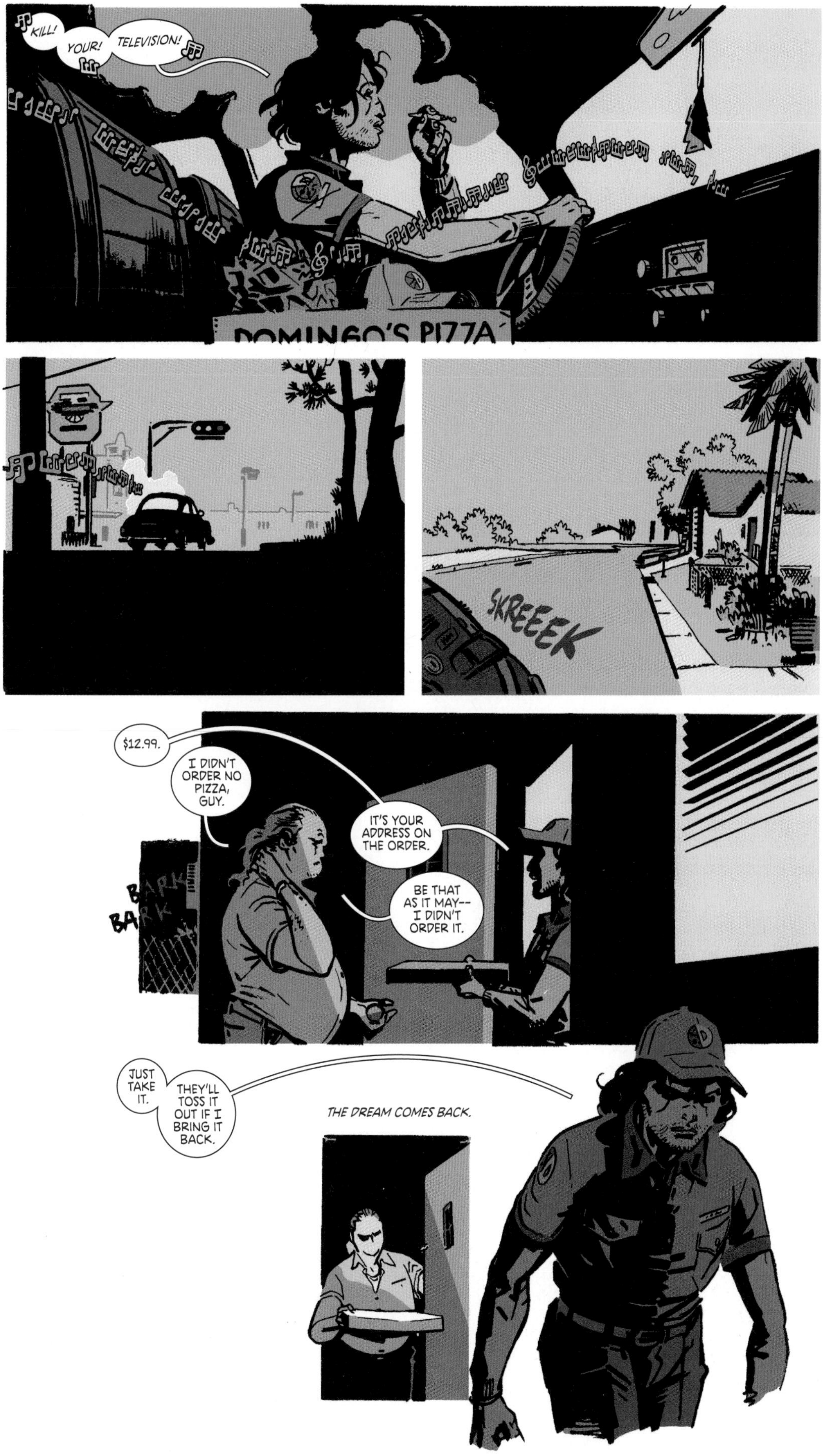
KILL!
YOUR!
TELEVISION!
DOMINGO'S PIZZA
SKREEEK
$12.99.
I DIDN'T ORDER NO PIZZA, GUY.
IT'S YOUR ADDRESS ON THE ORDER.
BE THAT AS IT MAY-- I DIDN'T ORDER IT.
BARK
BARK
JUST TAKE IT.
THEY'LL TOSS IT OUT IF I BRING IT BACK.
THE DREAM COMES BACK.

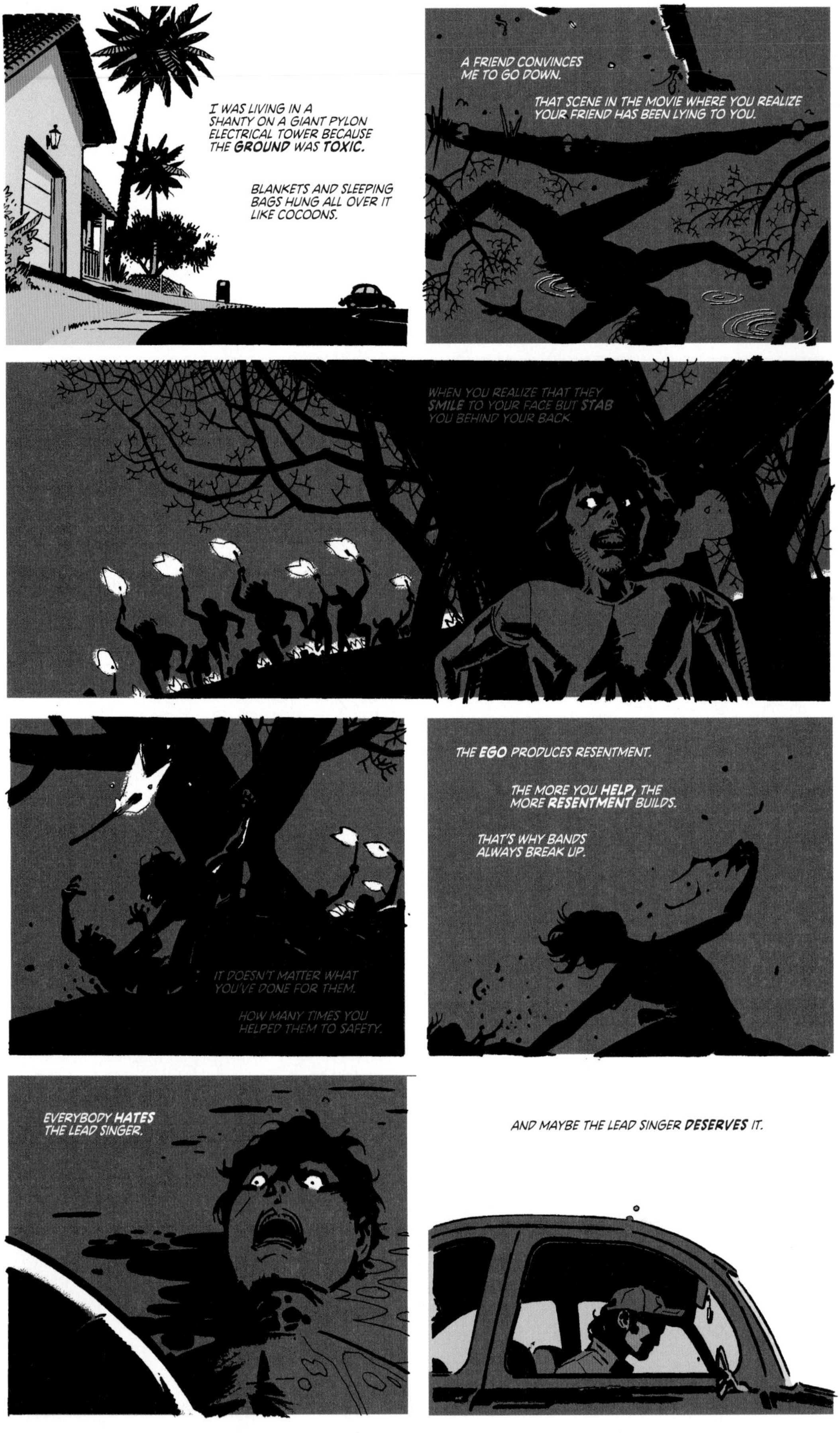
I WAS LIVING IN A SHANTY ON A GIANT PYLON ELECTRICAL TOWER BECAUSE THE GROUND WAS TOXIC.
BLANKETS AND SLEEPING BAGS HUNG ALL OVER IT LIKE COCOONS.
A FRIEND CONVINCES ME TO GO DOWN.
THAT SCENE IN THE MOVIE WHERE YOU REALIZE YOUR FRIEND HAS BEEN LYING TO YOU.
WHEN YOU REALIZE THAT THEY SMILE TO YOUR FACE BUT STAB YOU BEHIND YOUR BACK.
IT DOESN'T MATTER WHAT YOU'VE DONE FOR THEM.
HOW MANY TIMES YOU HELPED THEM TO SAFETY.
THE EGO PRODUCES RESENTMENT.
THE MORE YOU HELP, THE MORE RESENTMENT BUILDS.
THAT'S WHY BANDS ALWAYS BREAK UP.
EVERYBODY HATES THE LEAD SINGER.
AND MAYBE THE LEAD SINGER DESERVES IT.

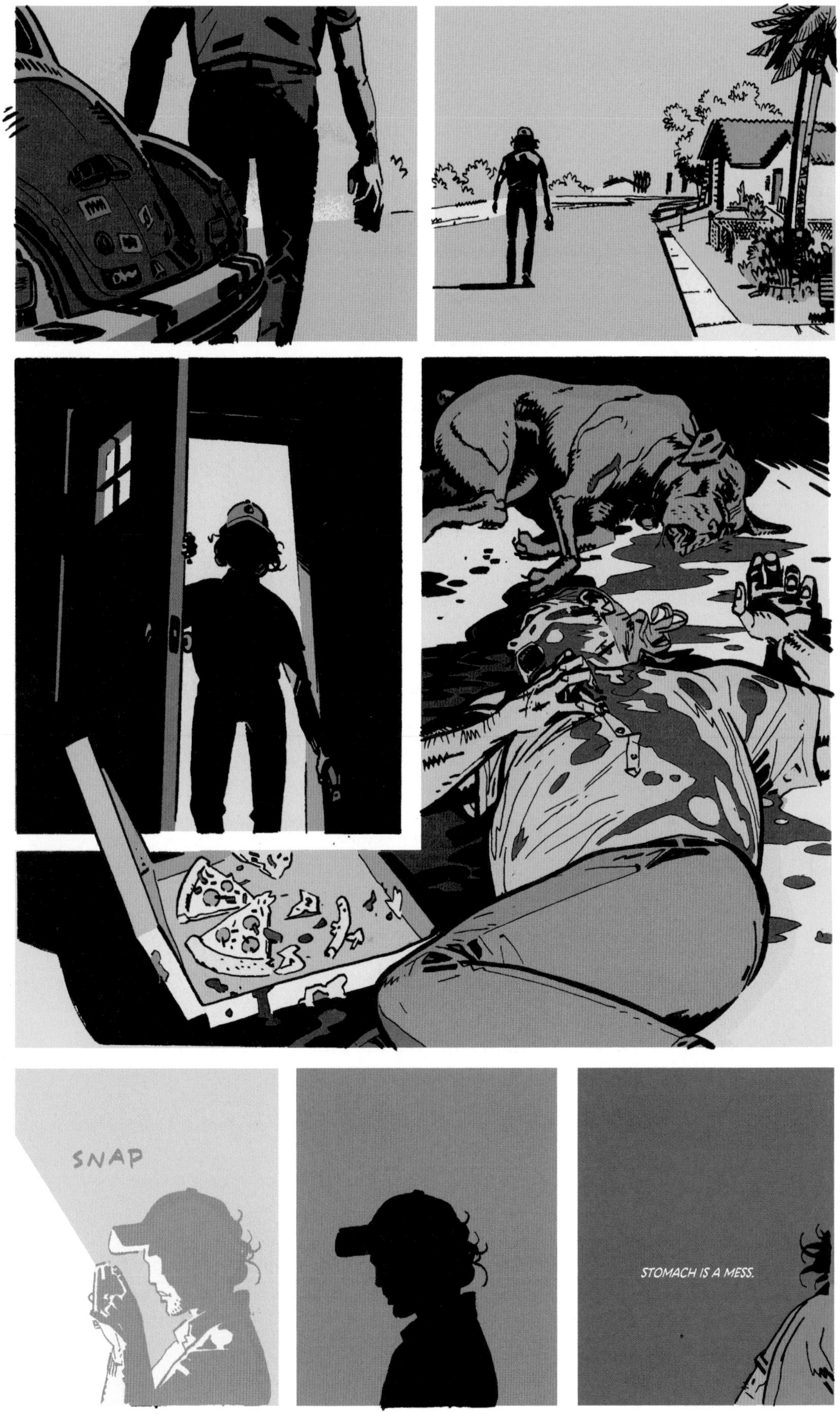
SNAP
STOMACH IS A MESS.

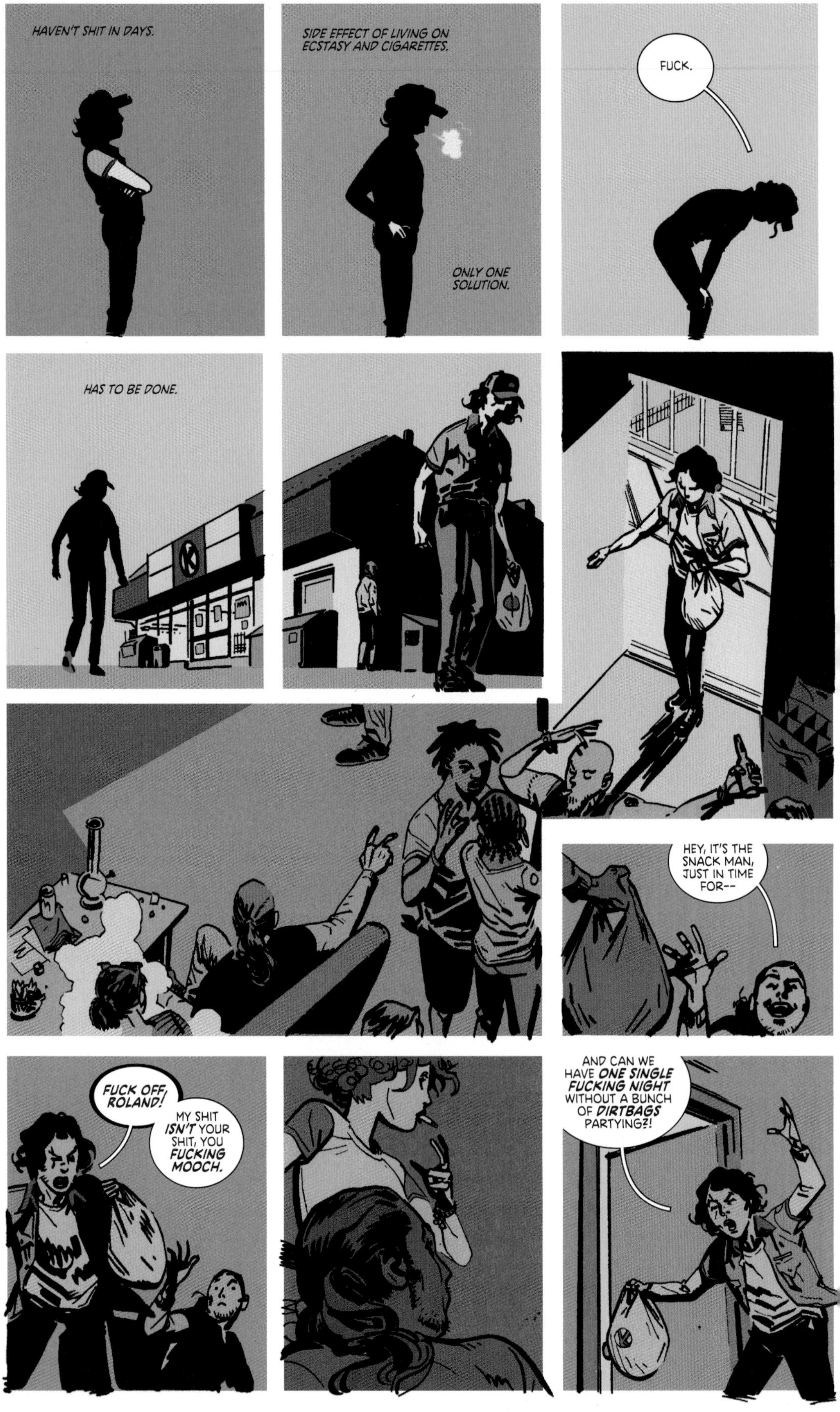
HAVEN'T SHIT IN DAYS.
SIDE EFFECT OF LIVING ON ECSTASY AND CIGARETTES.
ONLY ONE SOLUTION.
FUCK.
HAS TO BE DONE.
HEY, IT'S THE SNACK MAN, JUST IN TIME FOR--
FUCK OFF, ROLAND!
MY SHIT ISN'T YOUR SHIT, YOU FUCKING MOOCH.
AND CAN WE HAVE ONE SINGLE FUCKING NIGHT WITHOUT A BUNCH OF DIRTBAGS PARTYING?!

FUCKING HELL.

PURCHASE THE ENEMA KIT FROM A DRUGSTORE.

DONE.

BUY SOME PETROLEUM JELLY IF YOU THINK YOU'LL NEED LUBRICATION.

UGH.

LAY SOME TOWELS ON THE FLOOR.

KEEP SOME OTHER TOWELS AND WASHCLOTHS WITHIN ARM'S REACH.

DON'T EVEN WANT TO KNOW WHAT THAT'S FOR.

REMOVE THE CAP FROM THE TIP OF THE ENEMA NOZZLE.

IF NEEDED, APPLY SOME PETROLEUM JELLY TO THE ANUS TO EASE THE INSERTION OF THE ENEMA.

LIE ON THE FLOOR ON YOUR RIGHT SIDE WITH THE RIGHT KNEE BENT, PLACING THE ROLLED-UP TOWEL UNDER THE RIGHT KNEE TO SUPPORT IT.

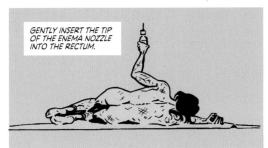

GENTLY INSERT THE TIP OF THE ENEMA NOZZLE INTO THE RECTUM.

THIS MAY BE UNCOMFORTABLE BUT SHOULD NOT CAUSE PAIN.

GHA.

AFTER INSERTION, START SQUEEZING THE ENEMA CONTAINER TO PUSH THE LIQUID INTO THE RECTUM.

PHSH.

A TIP FROM THE MANUFACTURER:

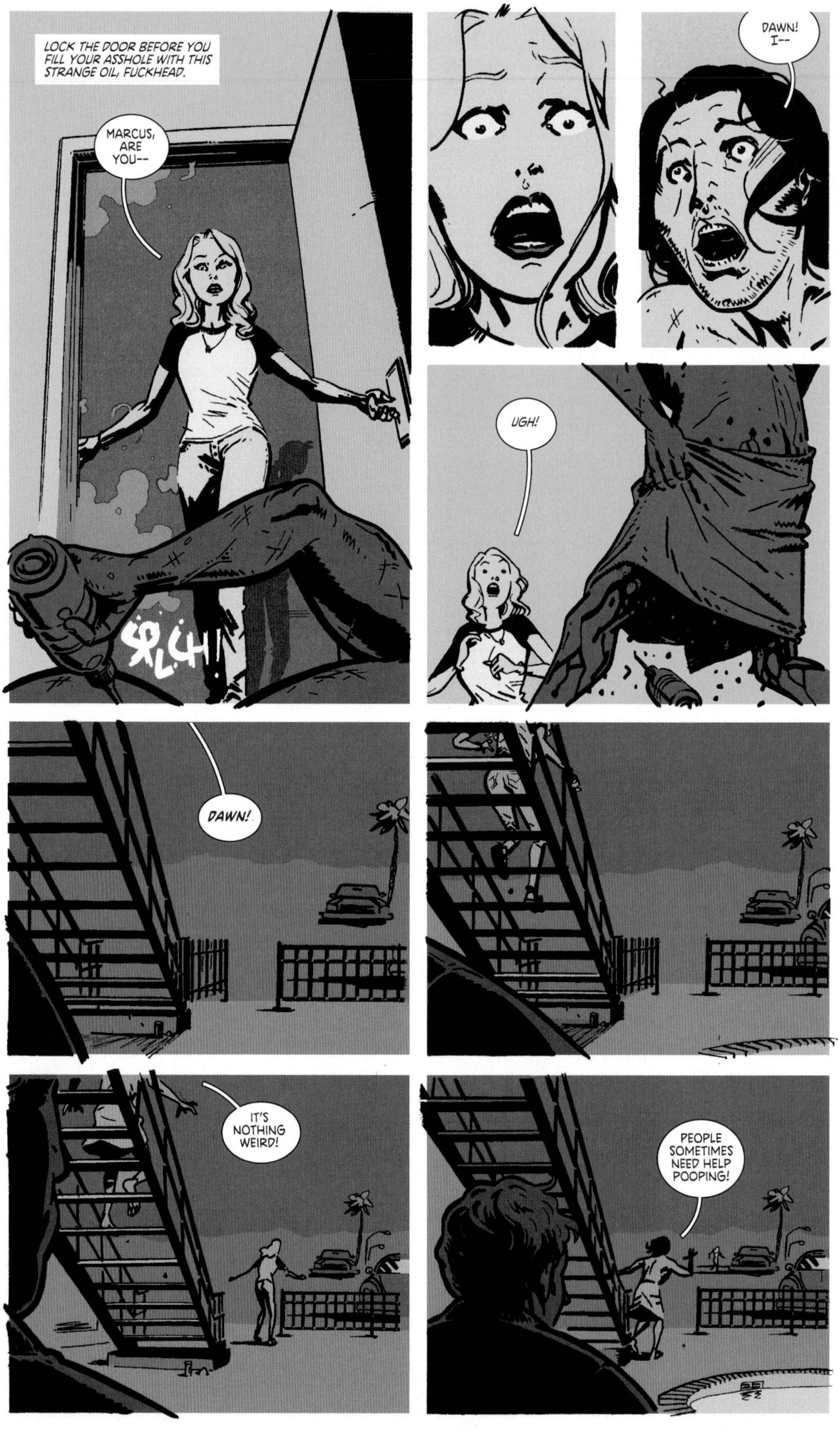
LOCK THE DOOR BEFORE YOU FILL YOUR ASSHOLE WITH THIS STRANGE OIL, FUCKHEAD.
MARCUS, ARE YOU--
SPLCH
DAWN! I--
UGH!
DAWN!
IT'S NOTHING WEIRD!
PEOPLE SOMETIMES NEED HELP POOPING!

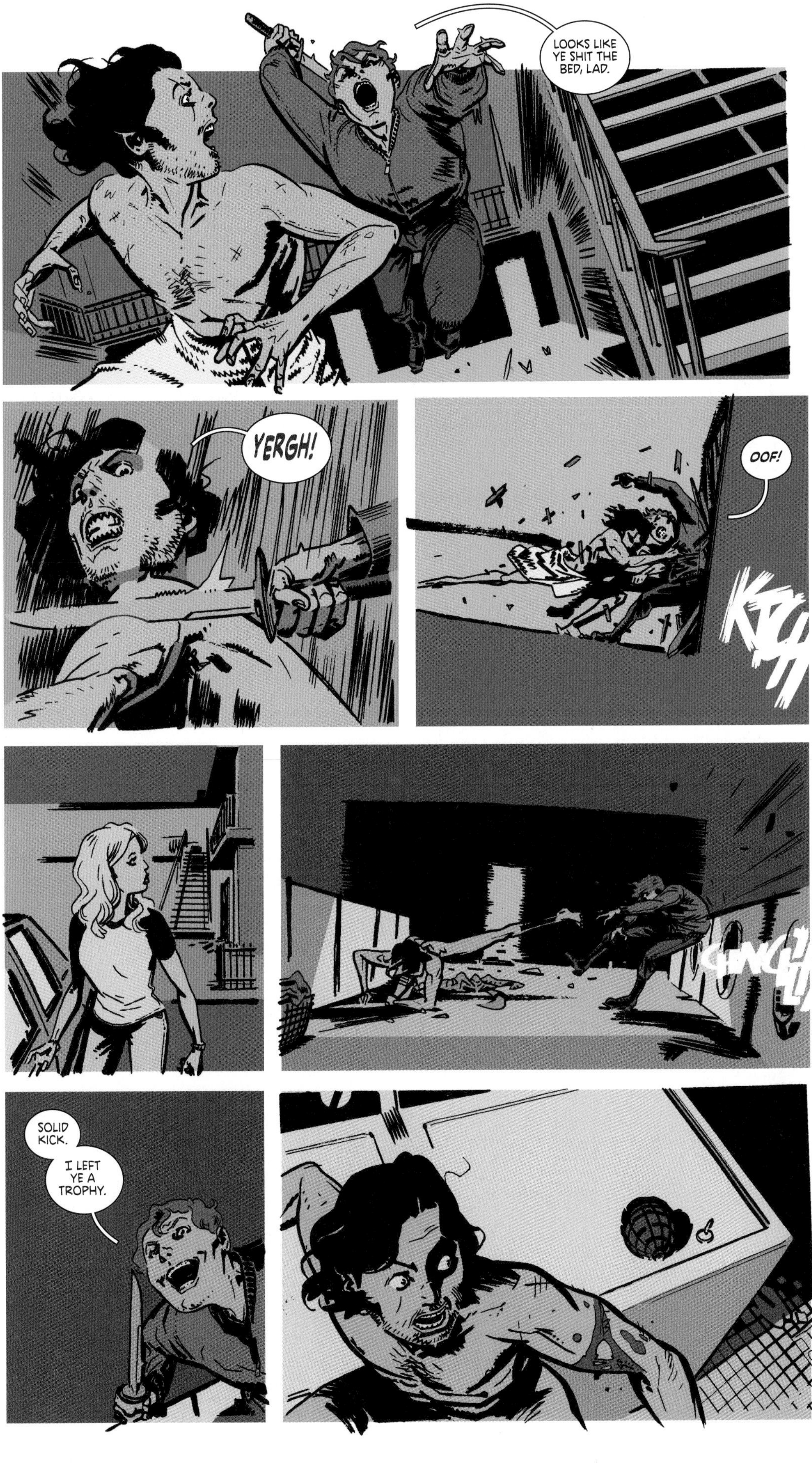
LOOKS LIKE YE SHIT THE BED, LAD.
YERGH!
OOF!
SOLID KICK.
I LEFT YE A TROPHY.

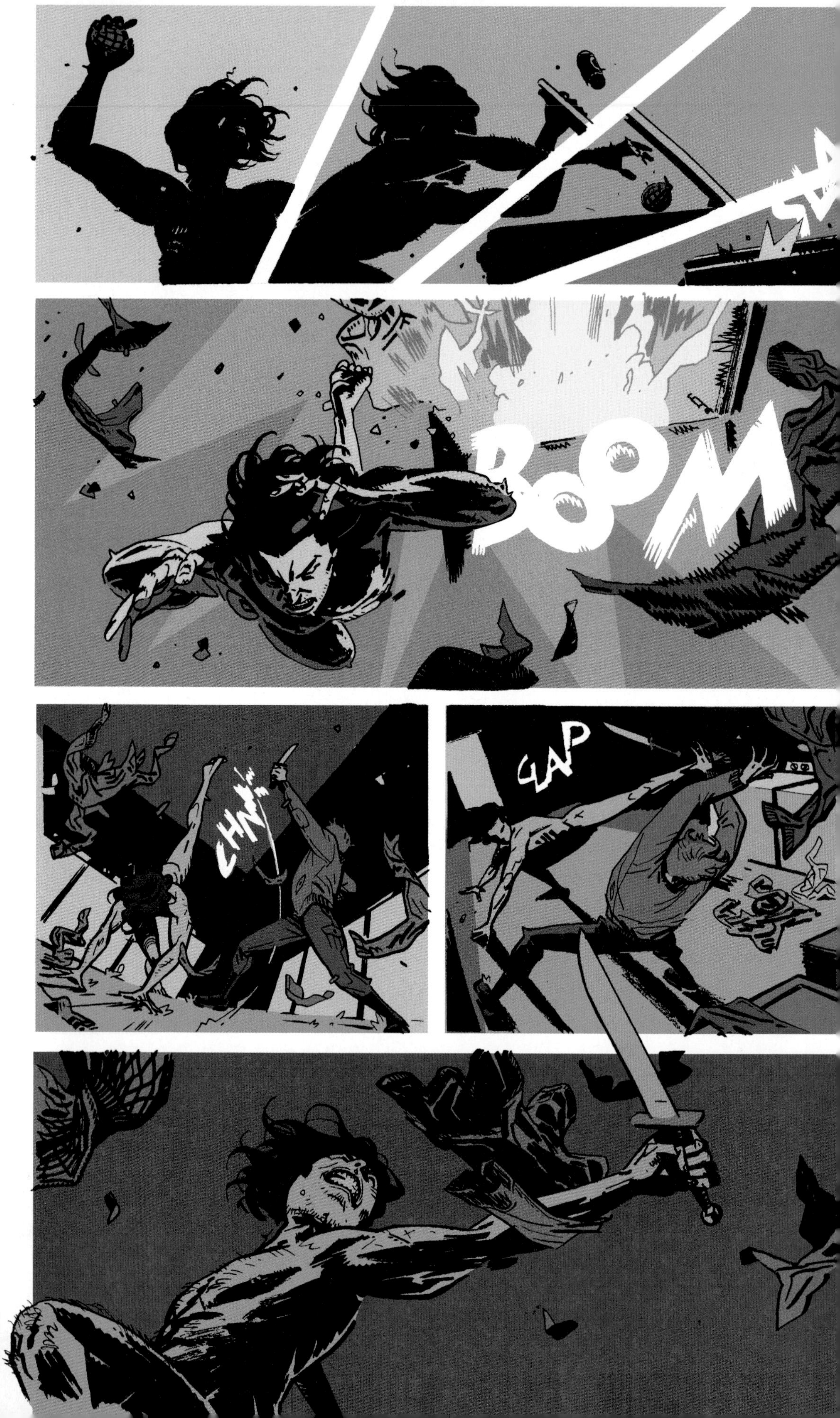
BOOM

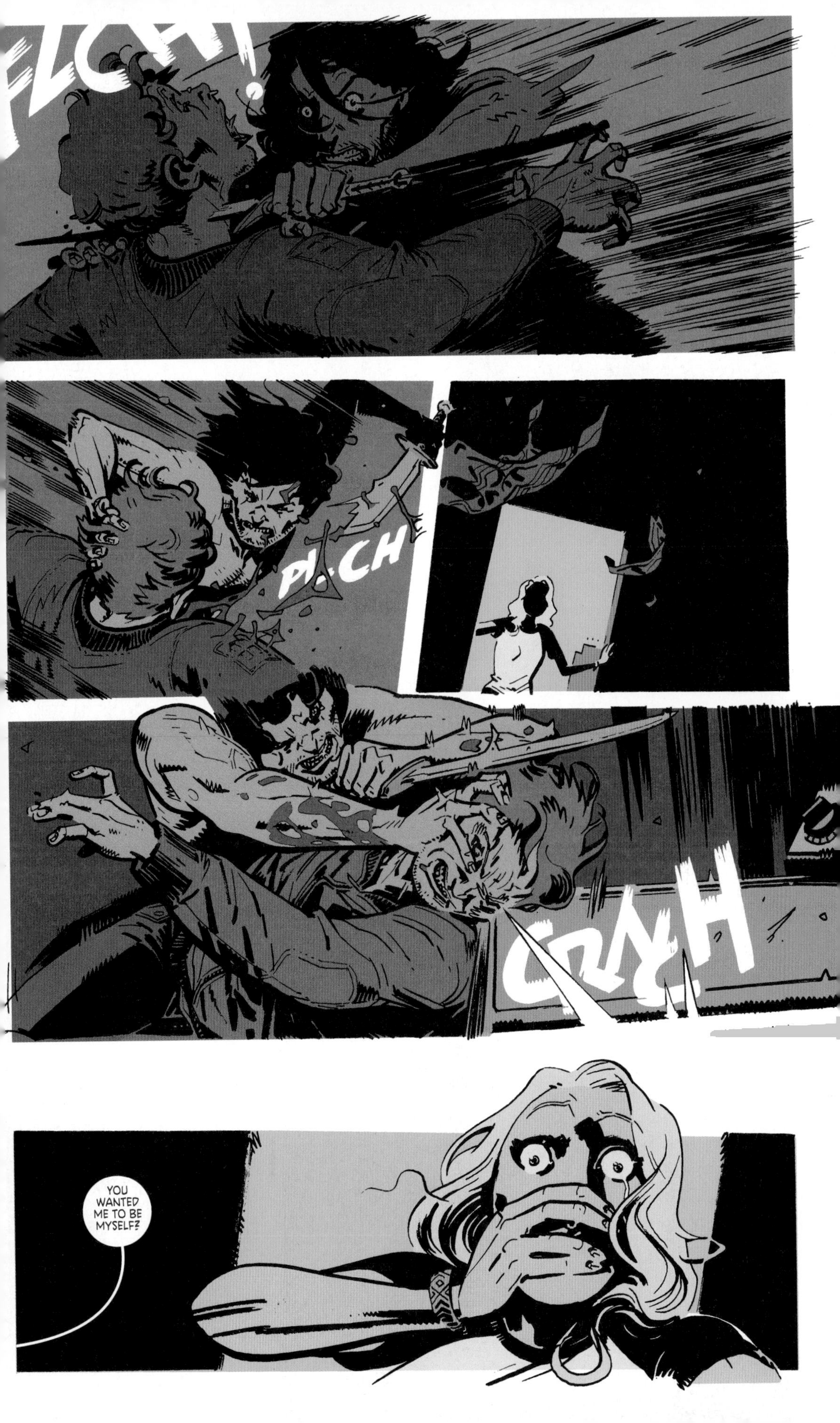
FZCH!
PL.CH
CRAK.H
YOU WANTED ME TO BE MYSELF?

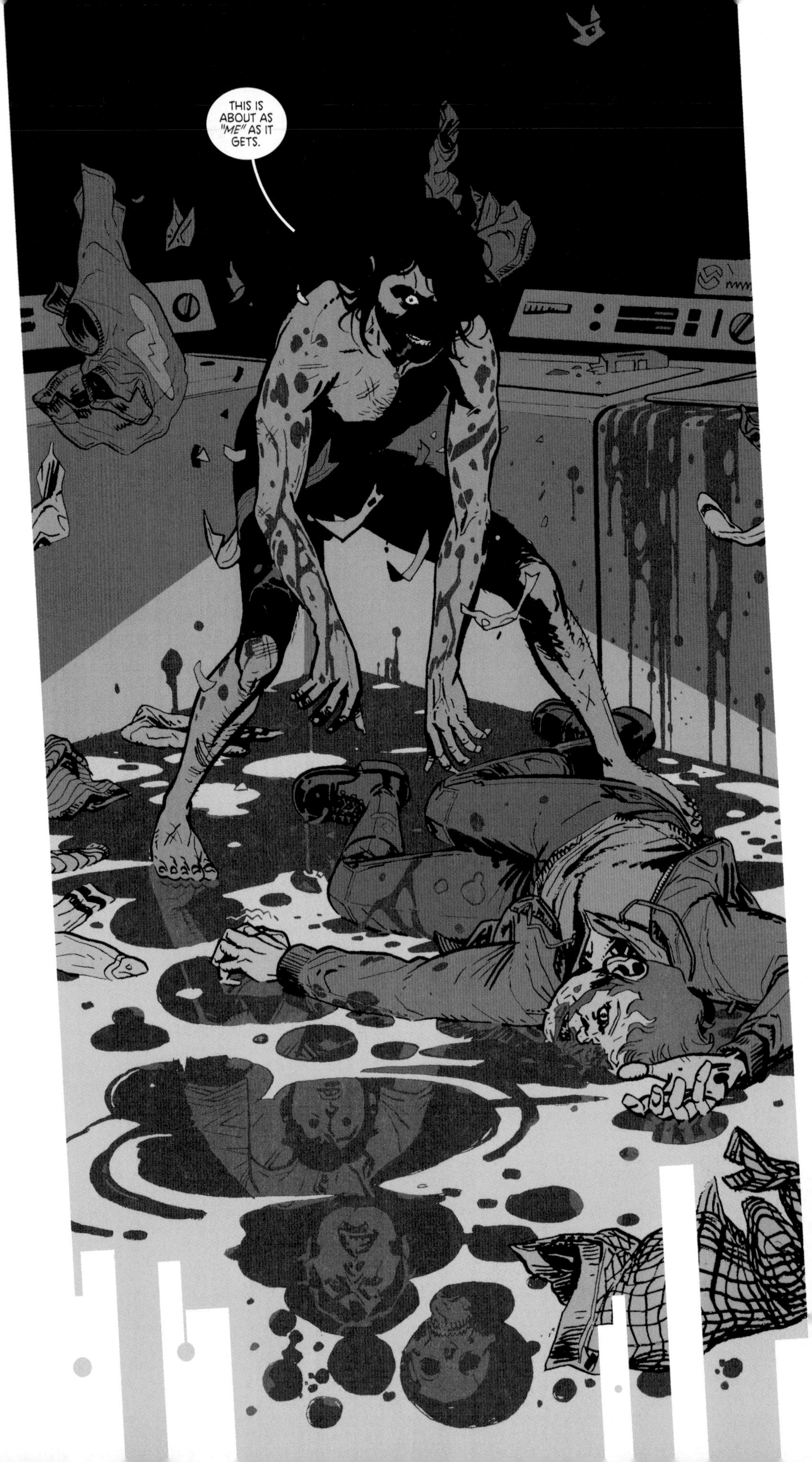
THIS IS ABOUT AS "ME" AS IT GETS.

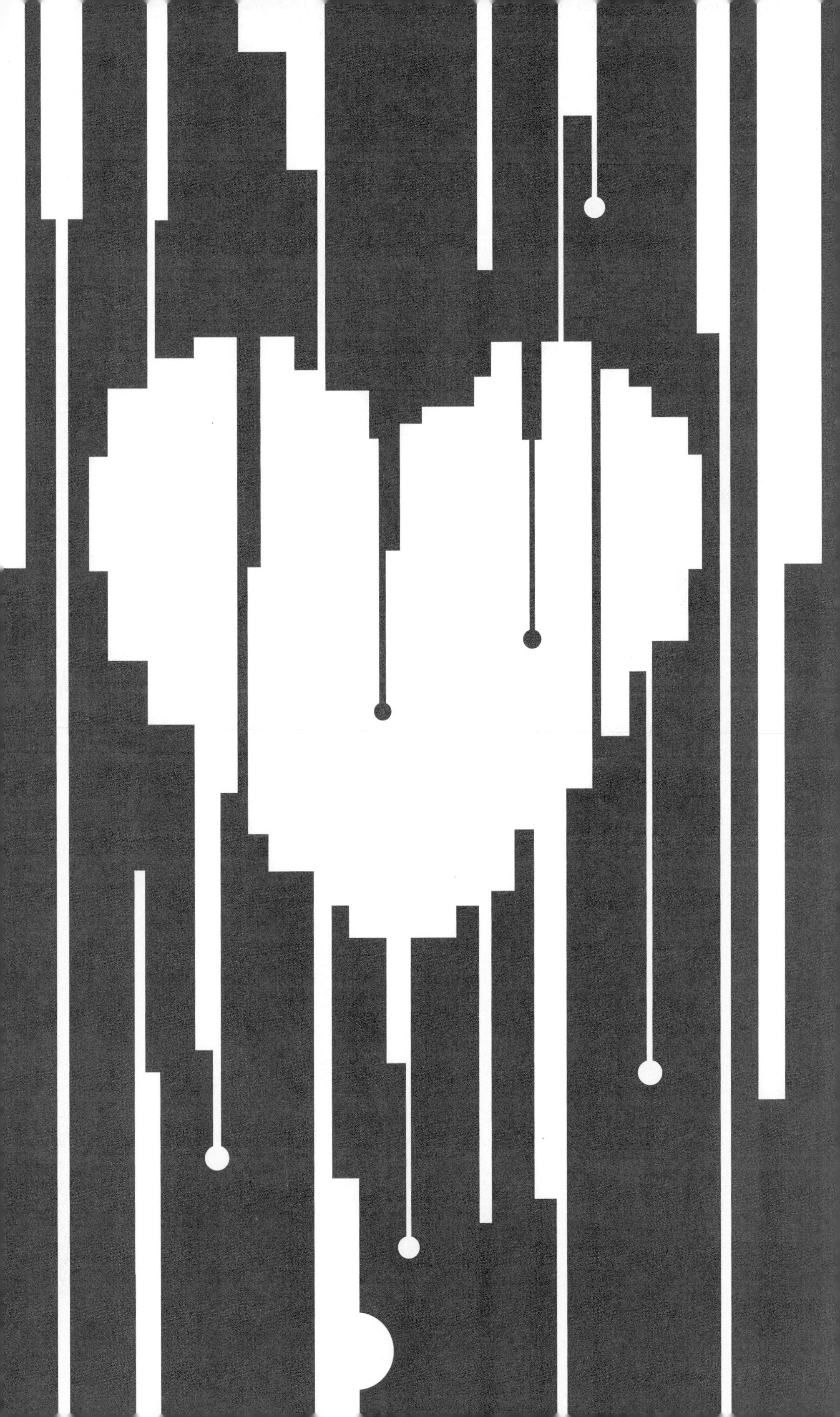

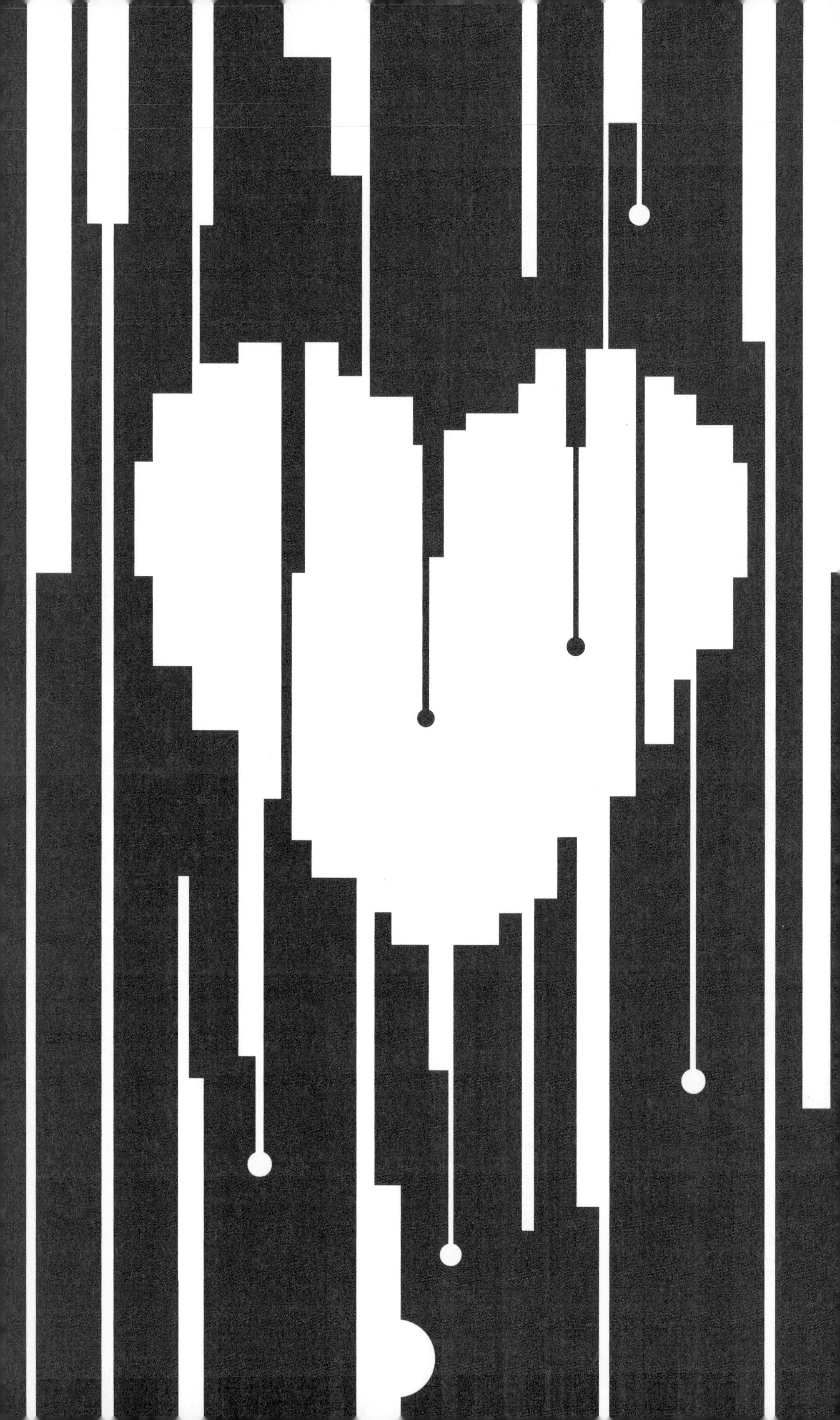

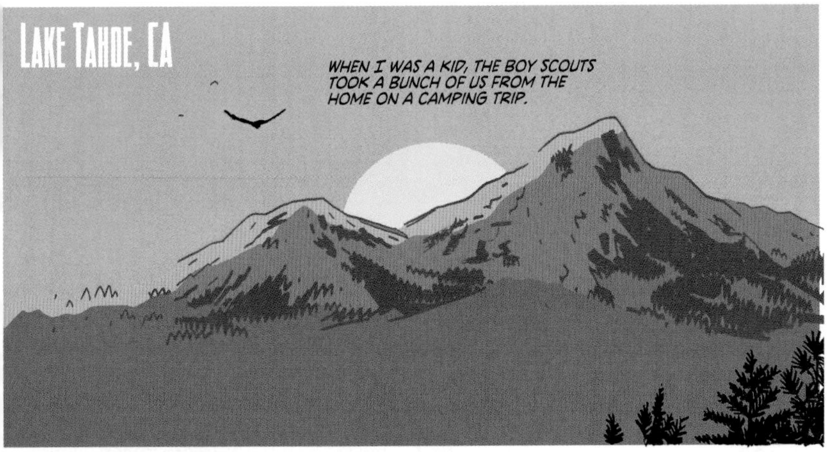
LAKE TAHOE, CA
WHEN I WAS A KID, THE BOY SCOUTS TOOK A BUNCH OF US FROM THE HOME ON A CAMPING TRIP.

IT WAS A THREE-HOUR DRIVE TO THE WOODS UP BY THE OREGON BORDER.

HALFWAY, WE STOPPED AT A GAS STATION TO USE THE BATHROOM AND FUEL UP.

I WALK INTO THE BATHROOM, FIRST THING I SEE, A VENDING MACHINE THAT SELLS CONDOMS AND SPANISH FLY PILLS.

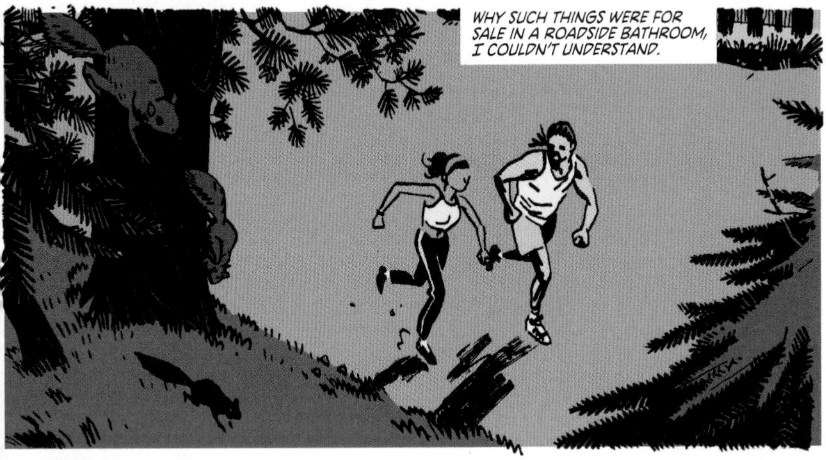
WHY SUCH THINGS WERE FOR SALE IN A ROADSIDE BATHROOM, I COULDN'T UNDERSTAND.

MINUTE LATER, WHILE I'M WASHING MY HANDS, THIS KID, JOHN I THINK, TOTAL GOON, COUPLE YEARS OLDER THAN ME, WALKS IN.

HE SEES THE VENDING MACHINE, APPROACHES IT, WAITS TILL I'M LOOKING, DIGS OUT A FEW QUARTERS FROM HIS POCKET, PLOPS THEM IN, AND BUYS A PACK OF GLOW-IN-THE-DARK CONDOMS.

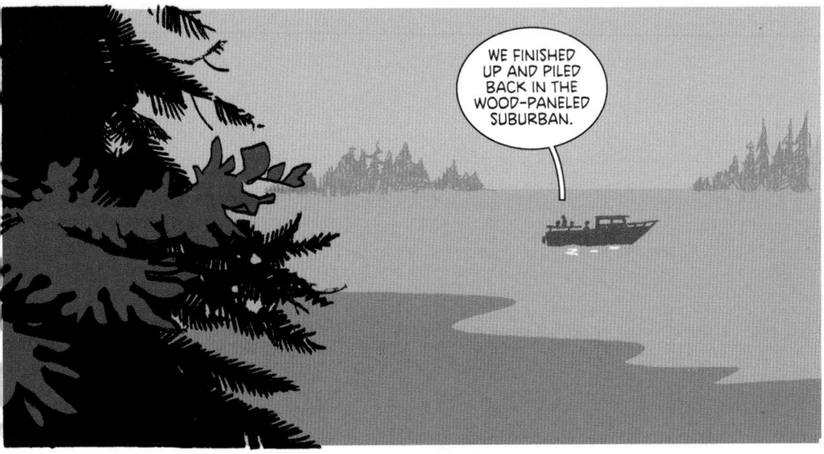
WE FINISHED UP AND PILED BACK IN THE WOOD-PANELED SUBURBAN.

A MILE OR TWO DOWN THE ROAD, JOHN PRODUCES THE GLOW-IN-THE-DARK CONDOMS AND VERY VISIBLY, VERY NOISILY, CRAMS THEM IN HIS VELCRO VAN HALEN WALLET.

LIKE BURT REYNOLDS ON HIS WAY TO THE PLAYBOY MANSION.

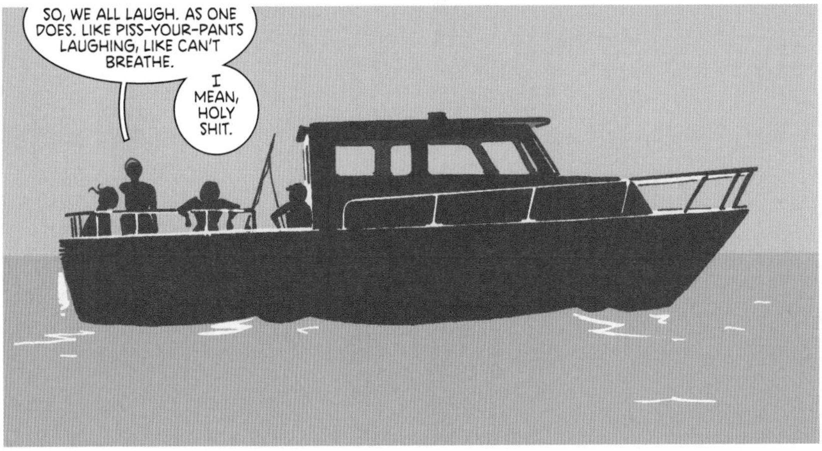
SO, WE ALL LAUGH. AS ONE DOES. LIKE PISS-YOUR-PANTS LAUGHING, LIKE CAN'T BREATHE.
I MEAN, HOLY SHIT.

JOHN, HE ACTS LIKE HE DOESN'T CARE, HE THROWS ON HIS VUARNET SUNGLASSES AND SAYS...

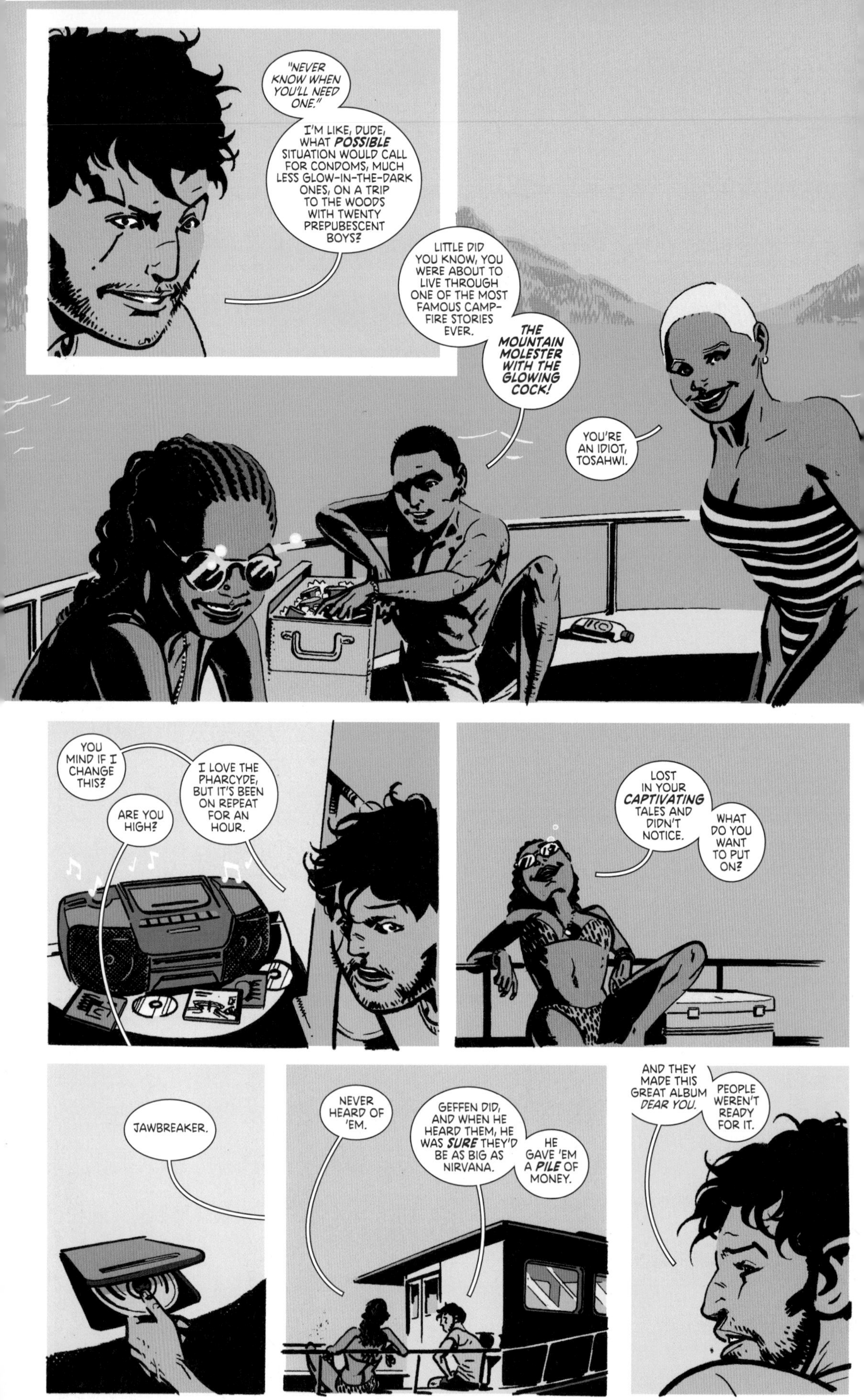
"NEVER KNOW WHEN YOU'LL NEED ONE."
I'M LIKE, DUDE, WHAT POSSIBLE SITUATION WOULD CALL FOR CONDOMS, MUCH LESS GLOW-IN-THE-DARK ONES, ON A TRIP TO THE WOODS WITH TWENTY PREPUBESCENT BOYS?
LITTLE DID YOU KNOW, YOU WERE ABOUT TO LIVE THROUGH ONE OF THE MOST FAMOUS CAMP-FIRE STORIES EVER.
THE MOUNTAIN MOLESTER WITH THE GLOWING COCK!
YOU'RE AN IDIOT, TOSAHWI.
YOU MIND IF I CHANGE THIS?
I LOVE THE PHARCYDE, BUT IT'S BEEN ON REPEAT FOR AN HOUR.
ARE YOU HIGH?
LOST IN YOUR CAPTIVATING TALES AND DIDN'T NOTICE.
WHAT DO YOU WANT TO PUT ON?
JAWBREAKER.
NEVER HEARD OF 'EM.
GEFFEN DID, AND WHEN HE HEARD THEM, HE WAS SURE THEY'D BE AS BIG AS NIRVANA.
HE GAVE 'EM A PILE OF MONEY.
AND THEY MADE THIS GREAT ALBUM DEAR YOU.
PEOPLE WEREN'T READY FOR IT.

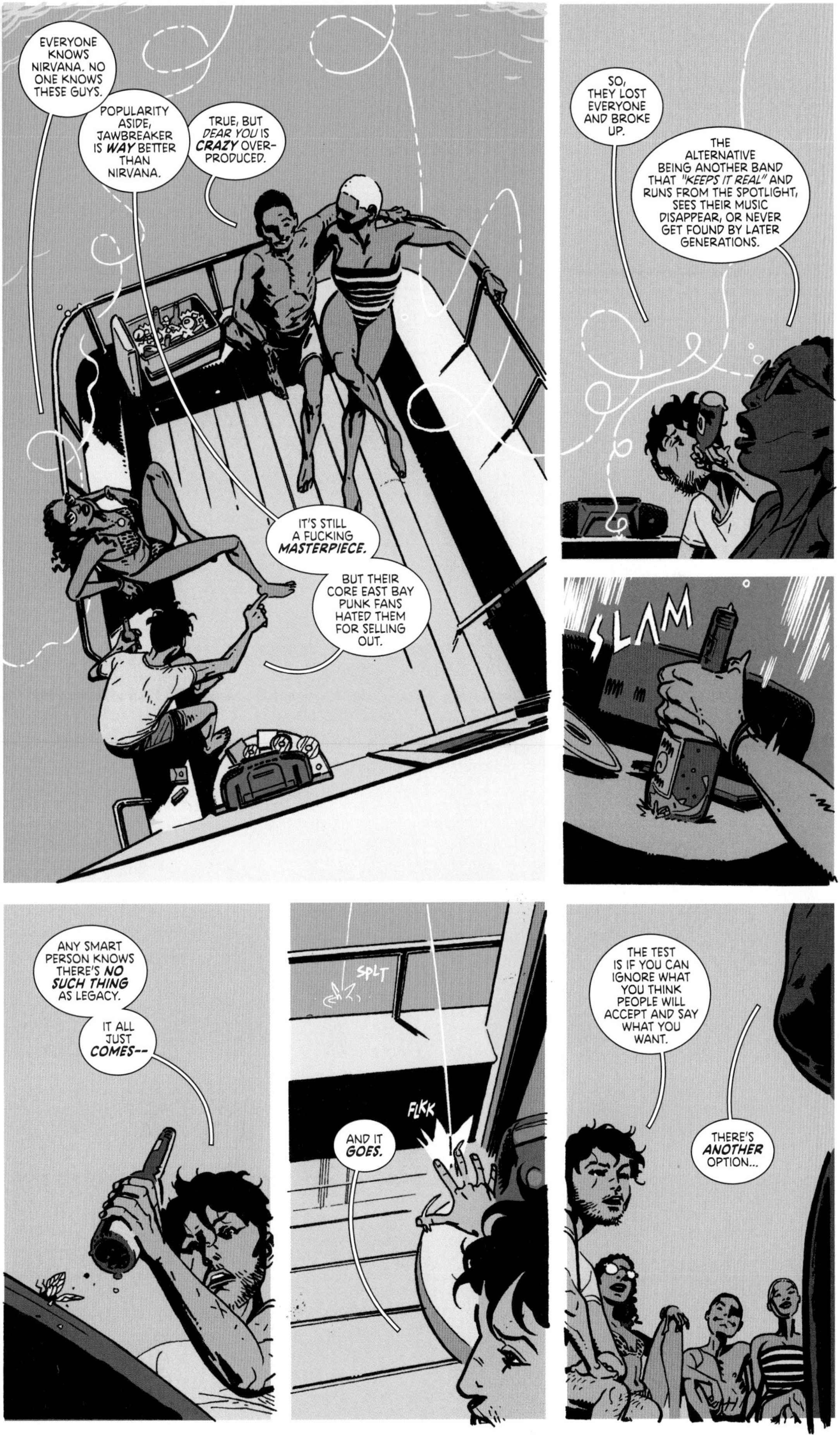
EVERYONE KNOWS NIRVANA. NO ONE KNOWS THESE GUYS.
POPULARITY ASIDE, JAWBREAKER IS **WAY** BETTER THAN NIRVANA.
TRUE, BUT *DEAR YOU* IS **CRAZY** OVER-PRODUCED.
IT'S STILL A FUCKING **MASTERPIECE.**
BUT THEIR CORE EAST BAY PUNK FANS HATED THEM FOR SELLING OUT.
SO, THEY LOST EVERYONE AND BROKE UP.
THE ALTERNATIVE BEING ANOTHER BAND THAT *"KEEPS IT REAL"* AND RUNS FROM THE SPOTLIGHT, SEES THEIR MUSIC DISAPPEAR, OR NEVER GET FOUND BY LATER GENERATIONS.
SLAM
ANY SMART PERSON KNOWS THERE'S **NO SUCH THING** AS LEGACY.
IT ALL JUST **COMES--**
SPLT
FLKK
AND IT **GOES.**
THE TEST IS IF YOU CAN IGNORE WHAT YOU THINK PEOPLE WILL ACCEPT AND SAY WHAT YOU WANT.
THERE'S **ANOTHER** OPTION...

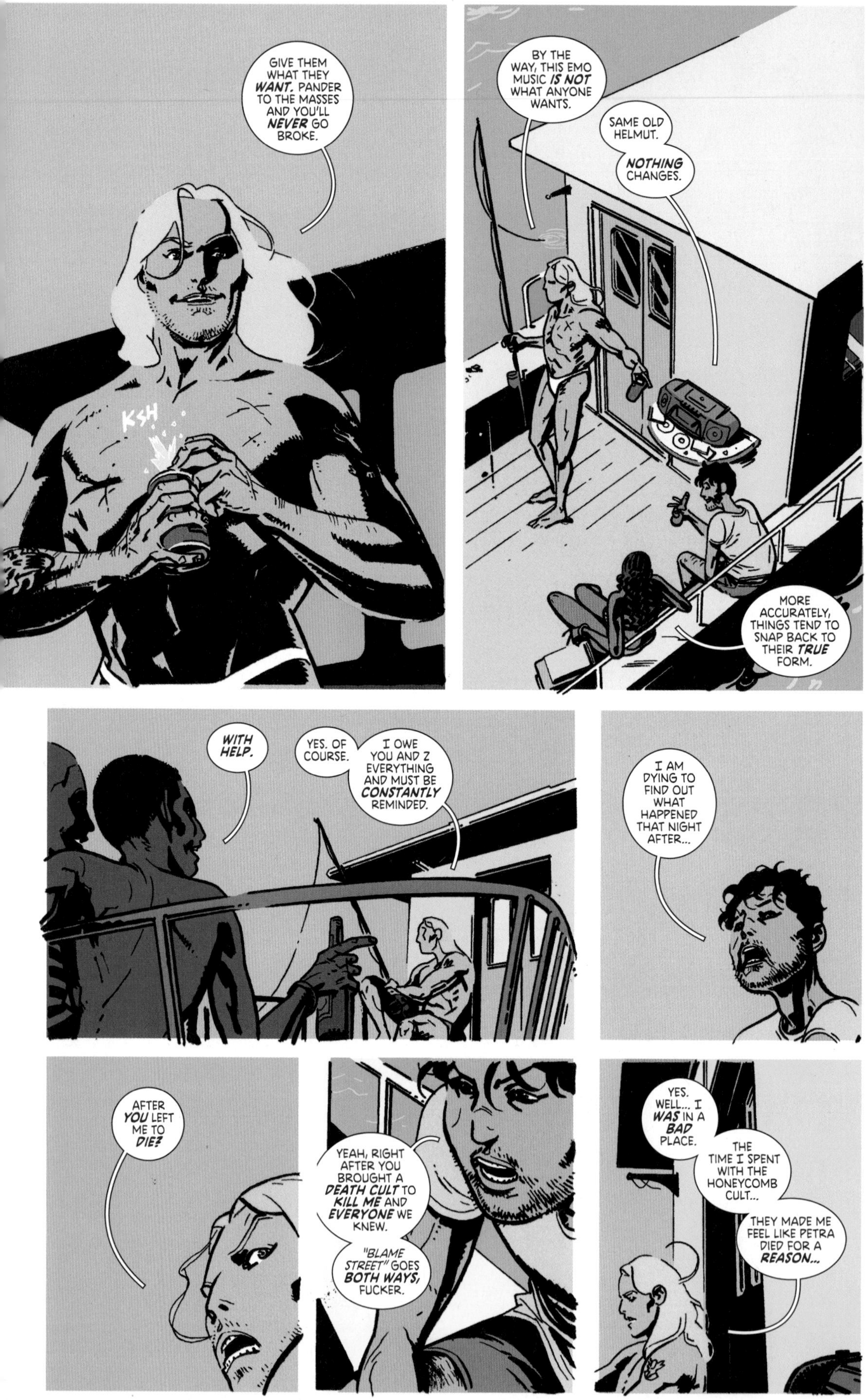
GIVE THEM WHAT THEY WANT. PANDER TO THE MASSES AND YOU'LL NEVER GO BROKE.
KSH
BY THE WAY, THIS EMO MUSIC IS NOT WHAT ANYONE WANTS.
SAME OLD HELMUT.
NOTHING CHANGES.
MORE ACCURATELY, THINGS TEND TO SNAP BACK TO THEIR TRUE FORM.
WITH HELP.
YES. OF COURSE.
I OWE YOU AND Z EVERYTHING AND MUST BE CONSTANTLY REMINDED.
I AM DYING TO FIND OUT WHAT HAPPENED THAT NIGHT AFTER...
AFTER YOU LEFT ME TO DIE?
YEAH, RIGHT AFTER YOU BROUGHT A DEATH CULT TO KILL ME AND EVERYONE WE KNEW.
"BLAME STREET" GOES BOTH WAYS, FUCKER.
YES. WELL... I WAS IN A BAD PLACE.
THE TIME I SPENT WITH THE HONEYCOMB CULT...
THEY MADE ME FEEL LIKE PETRA DIED FOR A REASON...

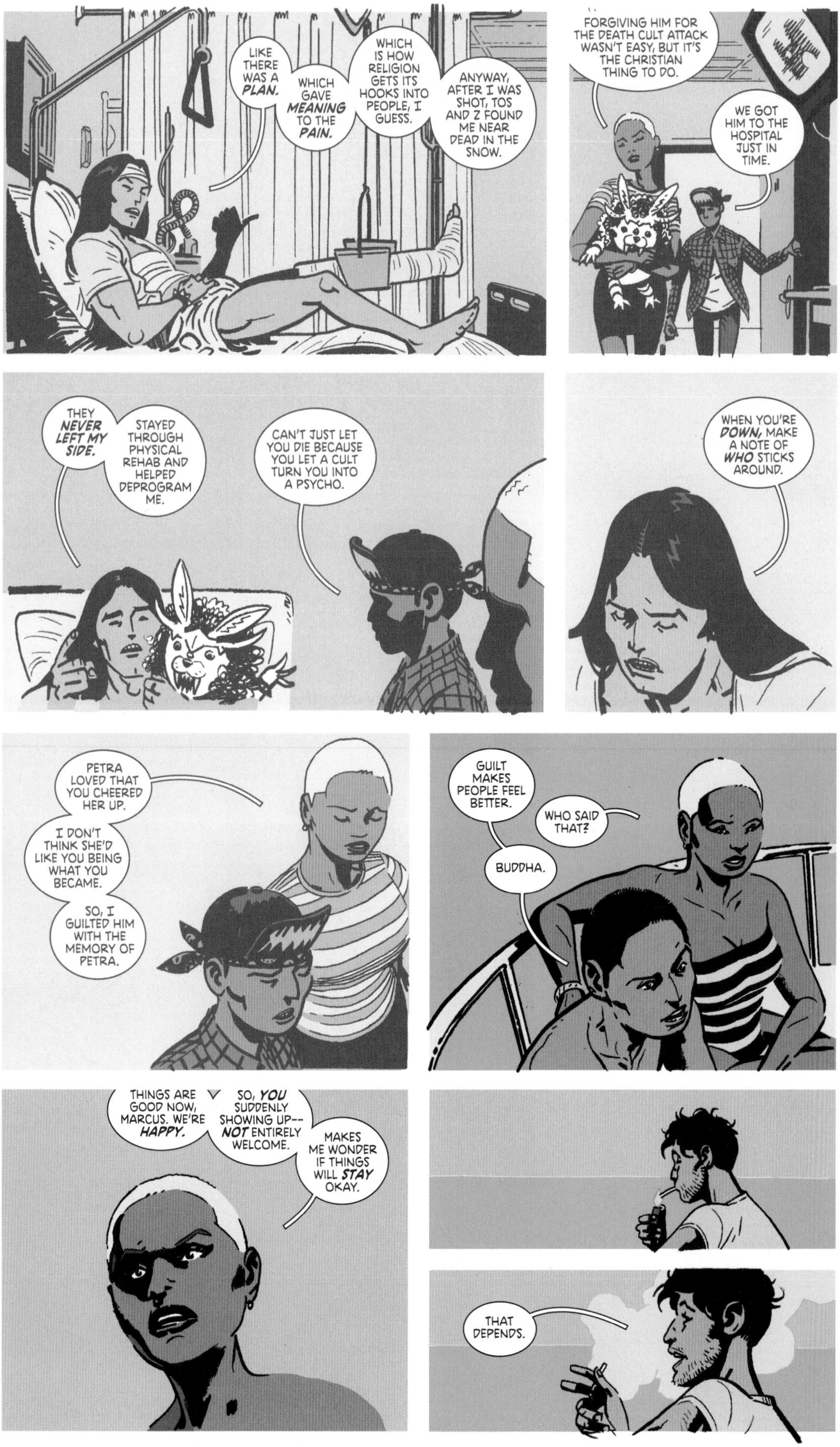
LIKE THERE WAS A PLAN.
WHICH GAVE MEANING TO THE PAIN.
WHICH IS HOW RELIGION GETS ITS HOOKS INTO PEOPLE, I GUESS.
ANYWAY, AFTER I WAS SHOT, TOS AND Z FOUND ME NEAR DEAD IN THE SNOW.
FORGIVING HIM FOR THE DEATH CULT ATTACK WASN'T EASY, BUT IT'S THE CHRISTIAN THING TO DO.
WE GOT HIM TO THE HOSPITAL JUST IN TIME.
THEY NEVER LEFT MY SIDE.
STAYED THROUGH PHYSICAL REHAB AND HELPED DEPROGRAM ME.
CAN'T JUST LET YOU DIE BECAUSE YOU LET A CULT TURN YOU INTO A PSYCHO.
WHEN YOU'RE DOWN, MAKE A NOTE OF WHO STICKS AROUND.
PETRA LOVED THAT YOU CHEERED HER UP.
I DON'T THINK SHE'D LIKE YOU BEING WHAT YOU BECAME.
SO, I GUILTED HIM WITH THE MEMORY OF PETRA.
GUILT MAKES PEOPLE FEEL BETTER.
WHO SAID THAT?
BUDDHA.
THINGS ARE GOOD NOW, MARCUS. WE'RE HAPPY.
SO, YOU SUDDENLY SHOWING UP-- NOT ENTIRELY WELCOME.
MAKES ME WONDER IF THINGS WILL STAY OKAY.
THAT DEPENDS.

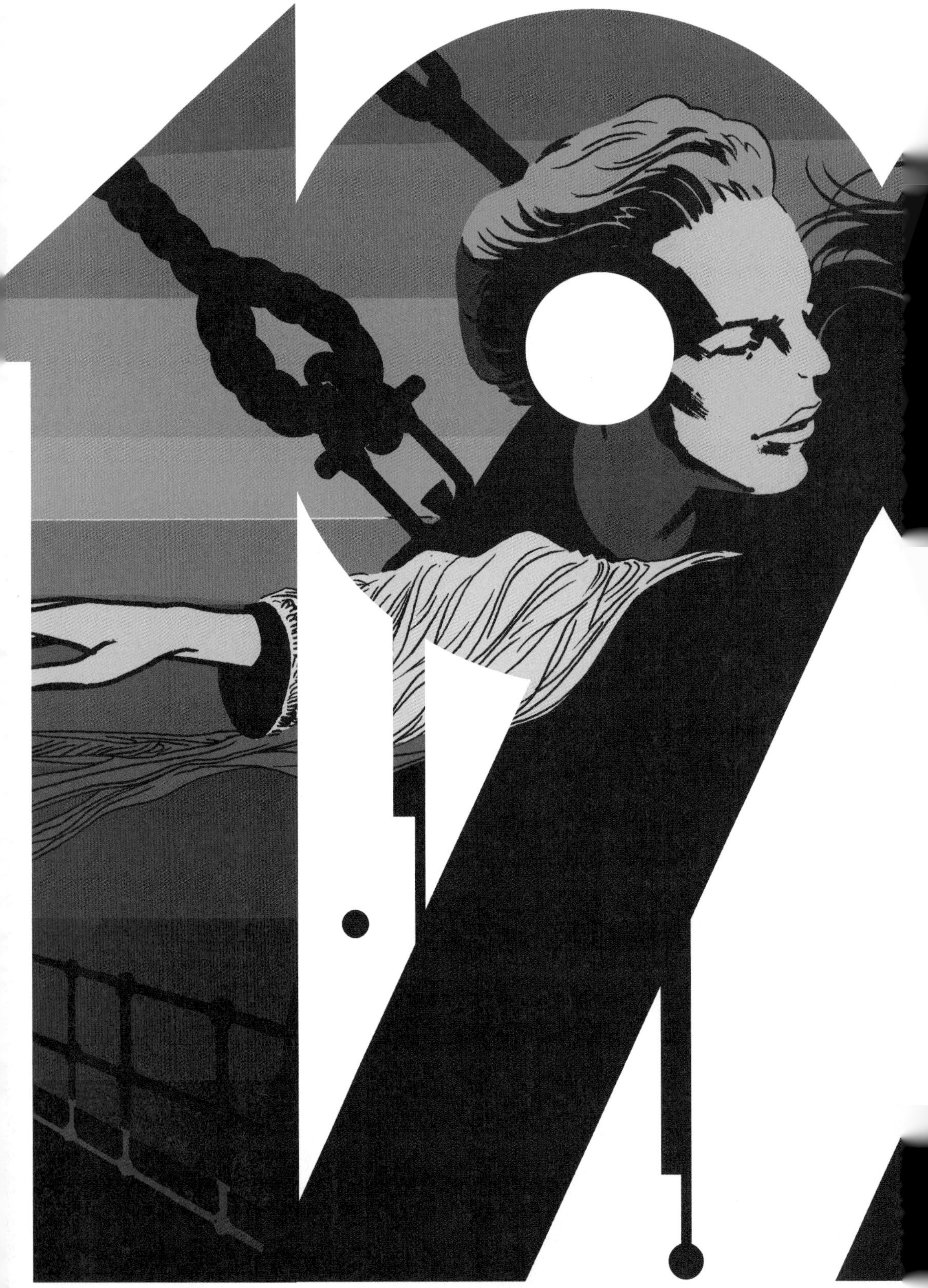

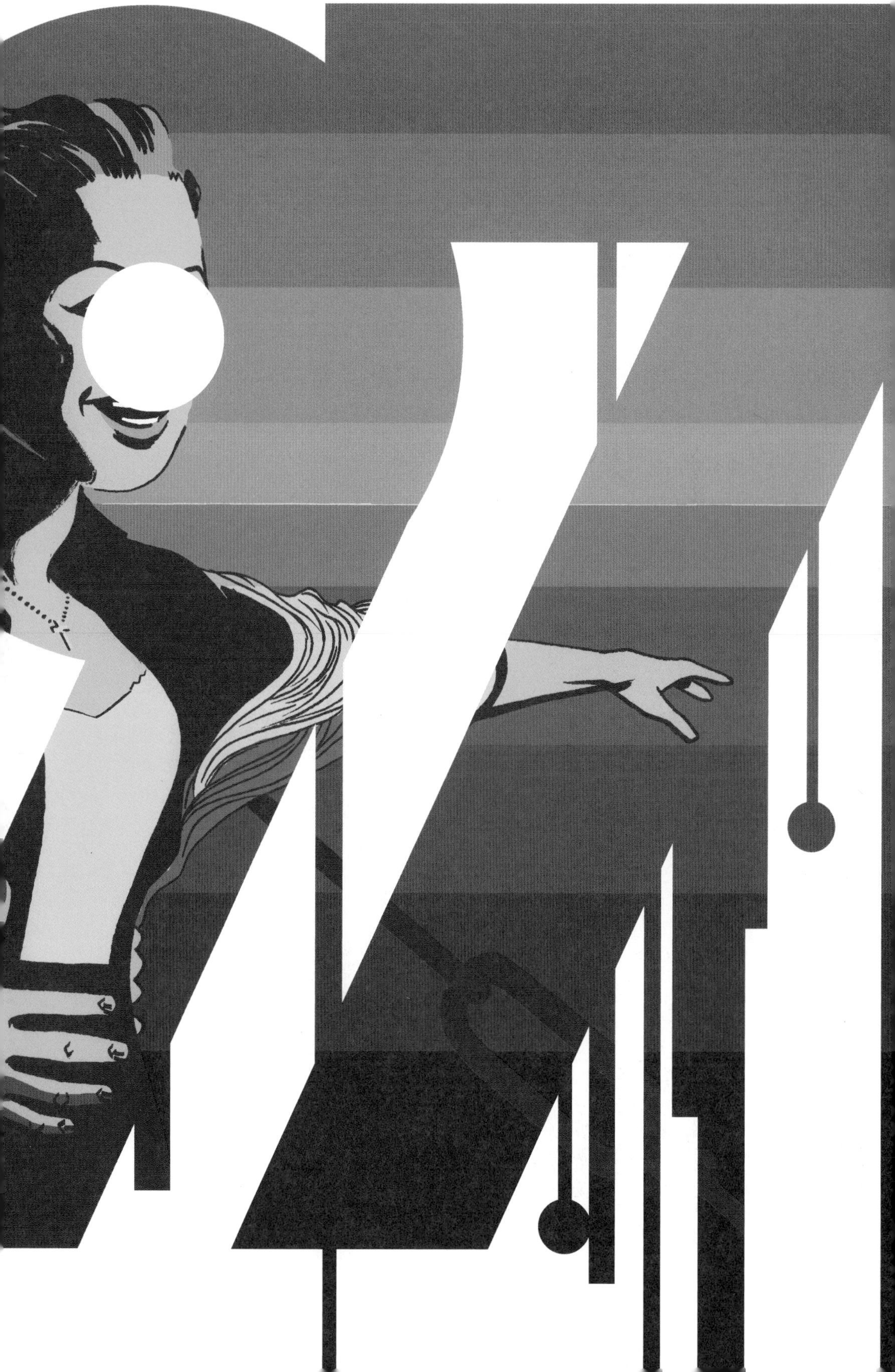

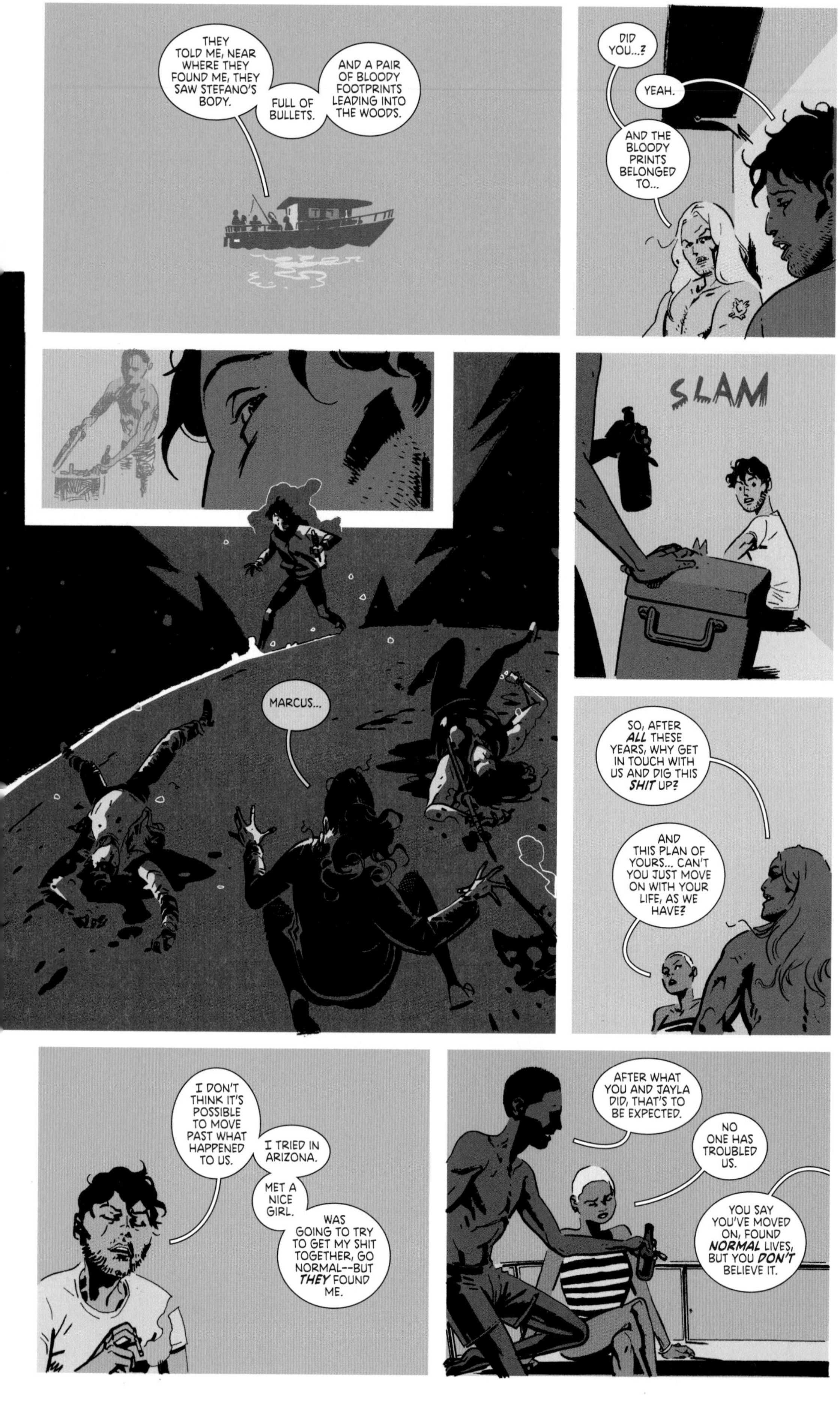
THEY TOLD ME, NEAR WHERE THEY FOUND ME, THEY SAW STEFANO'S BODY.
FULL OF BULLETS.
AND A PAIR OF BLOODY FOOTPRINTS LEADING INTO THE WOODS.
DID YOU...?
YEAH.
AND THE BLOODY PRINTS BELONGED TO...
MARCUS...
SLAM
SO, AFTER ALL THESE YEARS, WHY GET IN TOUCH WITH US AND DIG THIS SHIT UP?
AND THIS PLAN OF YOURS... CAN'T YOU JUST MOVE ON WITH YOUR LIFE, AS WE HAVE?
I DON'T THINK IT'S POSSIBLE TO MOVE PAST WHAT HAPPENED TO US.
I TRIED IN ARIZONA.
MET A NICE GIRL.
WAS GOING TO TRY TO GET MY SHIT TOGETHER, GO NORMAL--BUT THEY FOUND ME.
AFTER WHAT YOU AND JAYLA DID, THAT'S TO BE EXPECTED.
NO ONE HAS TROUBLED US.
YOU SAY YOU'VE MOVED ON, FOUND NORMAL LIVES, BUT YOU DON'T BELIEVE IT.

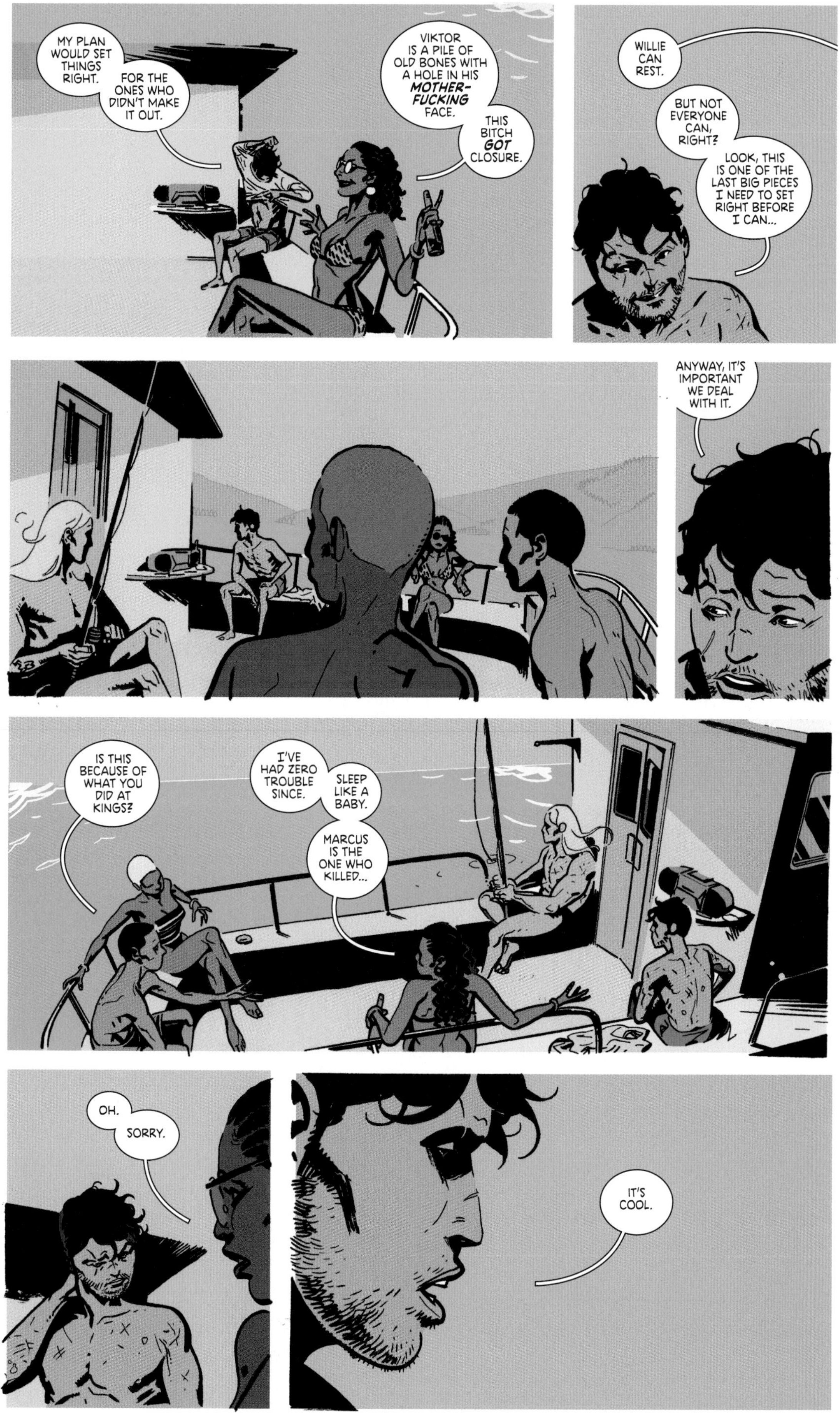
MY PLAN WOULD SET THINGS RIGHT.
FOR THE ONES WHO DIDN'T MAKE IT OUT.
VIKTOR IS A PILE OF OLD BONES WITH A HOLE IN HIS *MOTHER-FUCKING* FACE.
THIS BITCH *GOT* CLOSURE.
WILLIE CAN REST.
BUT NOT EVERYONE CAN, RIGHT?
LOOK, THIS IS ONE OF THE LAST BIG PIECES I NEED TO SET RIGHT BEFORE I CAN...
ANYWAY, IT'S IMPORTANT WE DEAL WITH IT.
IS THIS BECAUSE OF WHAT YOU DID AT KINGS?
I'VE HAD ZERO TROUBLE SINCE.
SLEEP LIKE A BABY.
MARCUS IS THE ONE WHO KILLED...
OH.
SORRY.
IT'S COOL.

EVERYTHING'S FINE.

YOU DON'T WANT TO
LIVE IN THE PAST.

SPLSH

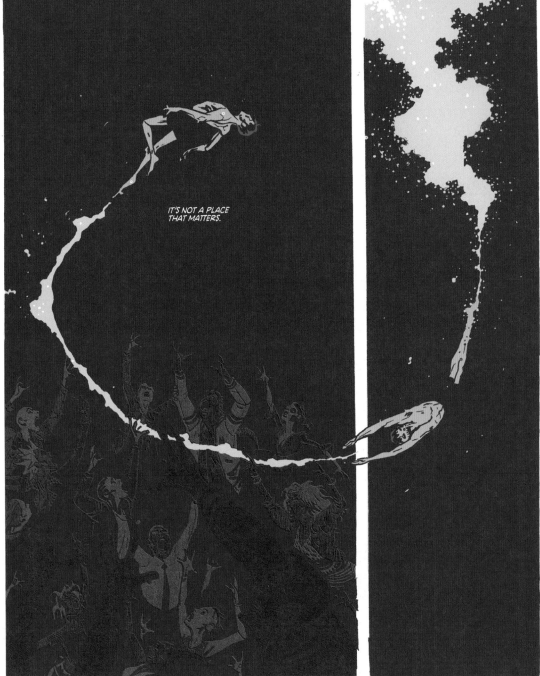
IT'S NOT A PLACE
THAT MATTERS.

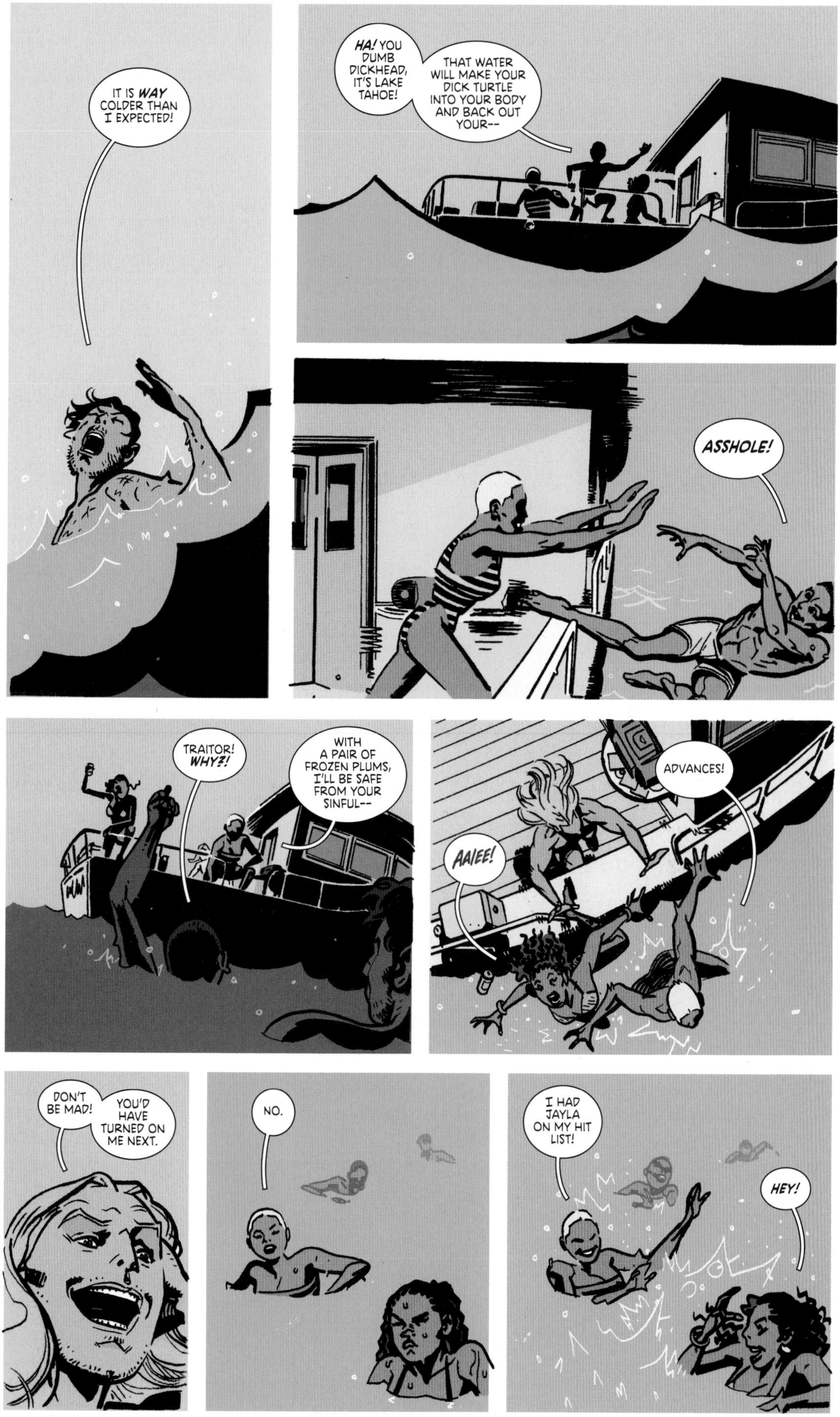
IT IS WAY COLDER THAN I EXPECTED!
HA! YOU DUMB DICKHEAD, IT'S LAKE TAHOE!
THAT WATER WILL MAKE YOUR DICK TURTLE INTO YOUR BODY AND BACK OUT YOUR--
ASSHOLE!
TRAITOR! WHY?!
WITH A PAIR OF FROZEN PLUMS, I'LL BE SAFE FROM YOUR SINFUL--
ADVANCES!
AAIEE!
DON'T BE MAD!
YOU'D HAVE TURNED ON ME NEXT.
NO.
I HAD JAYLA ON MY HIT LIST!
HEY!

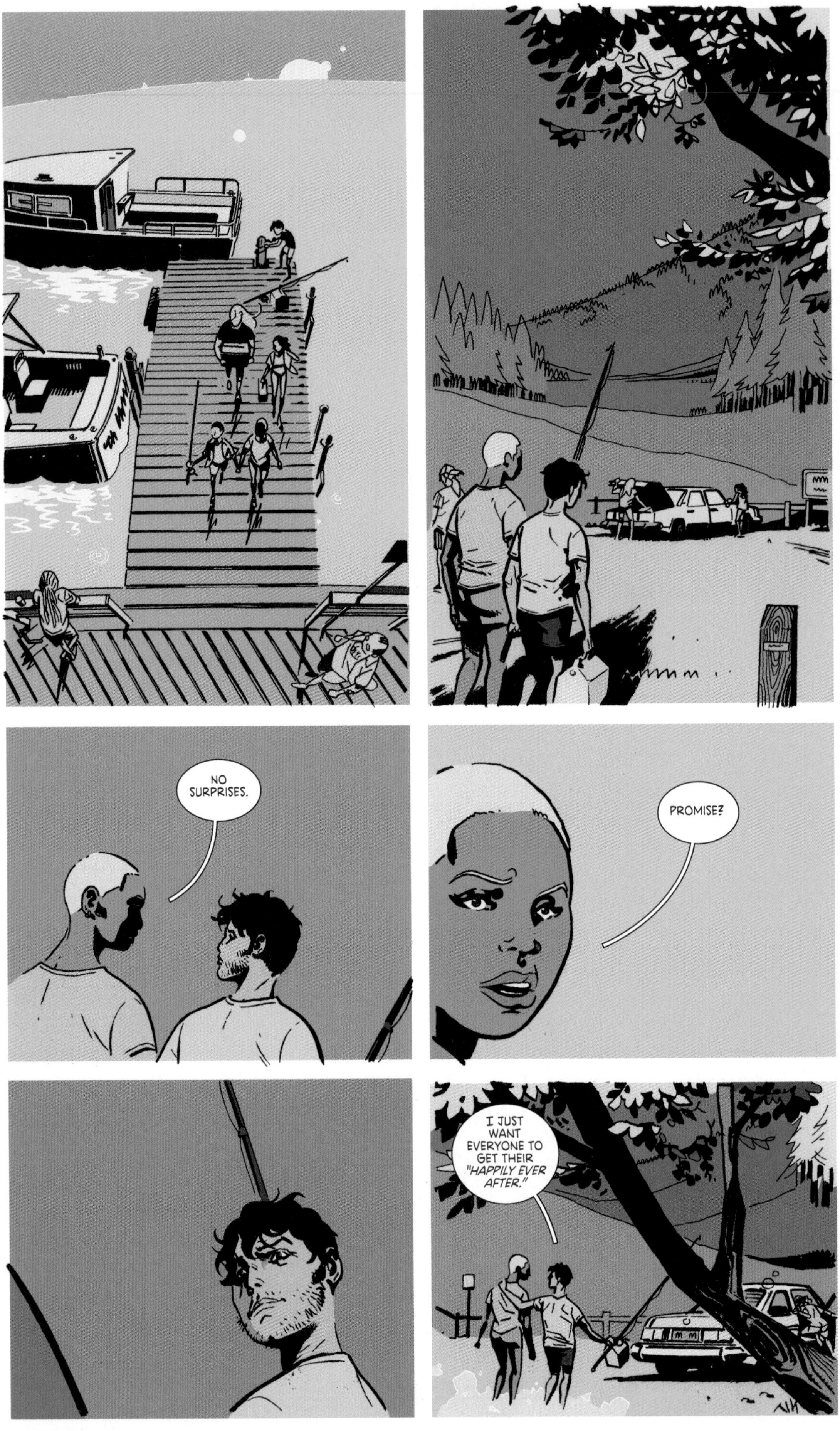
NO SURPRISES.
PROMISE?
I JUST WANT EVERYONE TO GET THEIR *"HAPPILY EVER AFTER."*

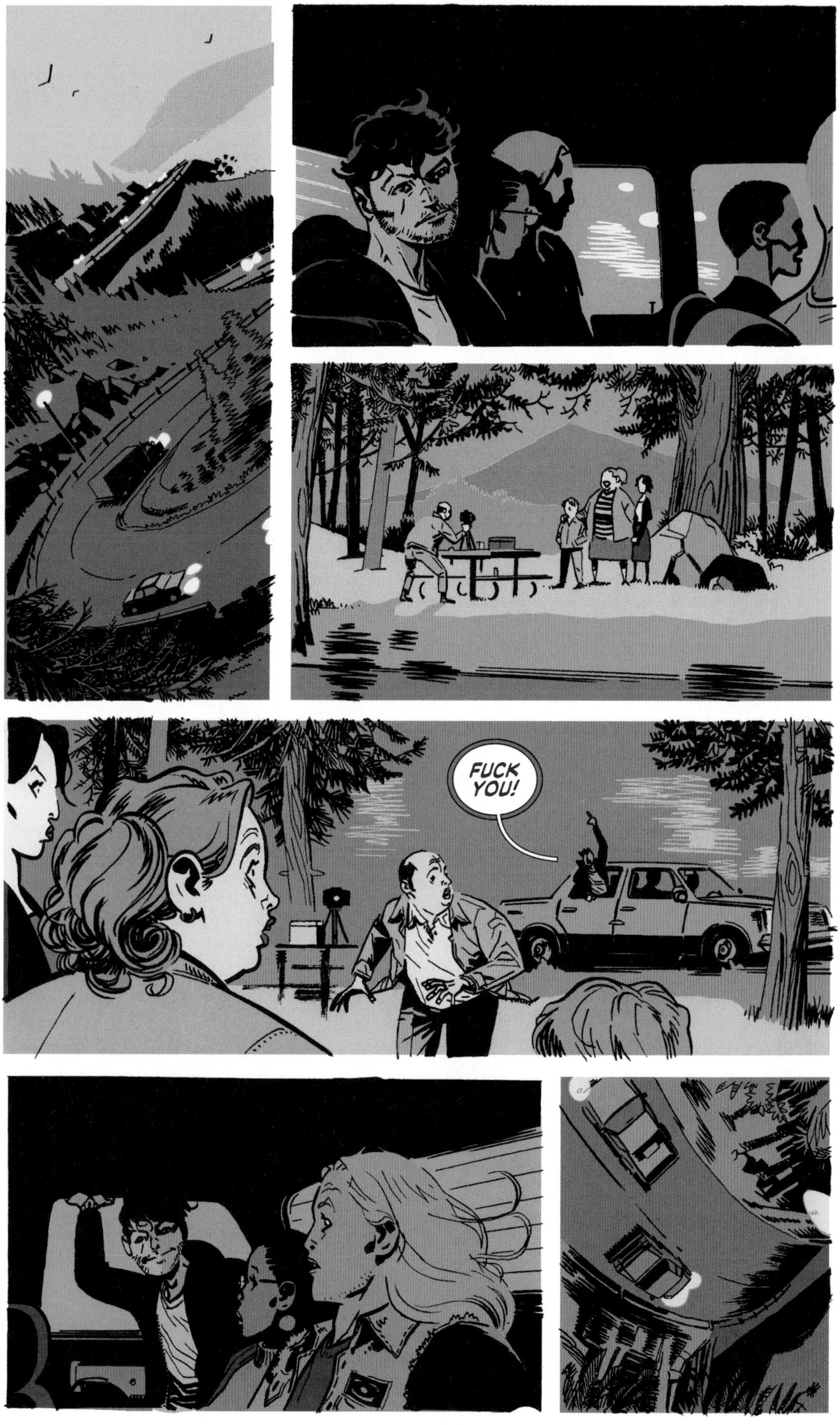
FUCK YOU!

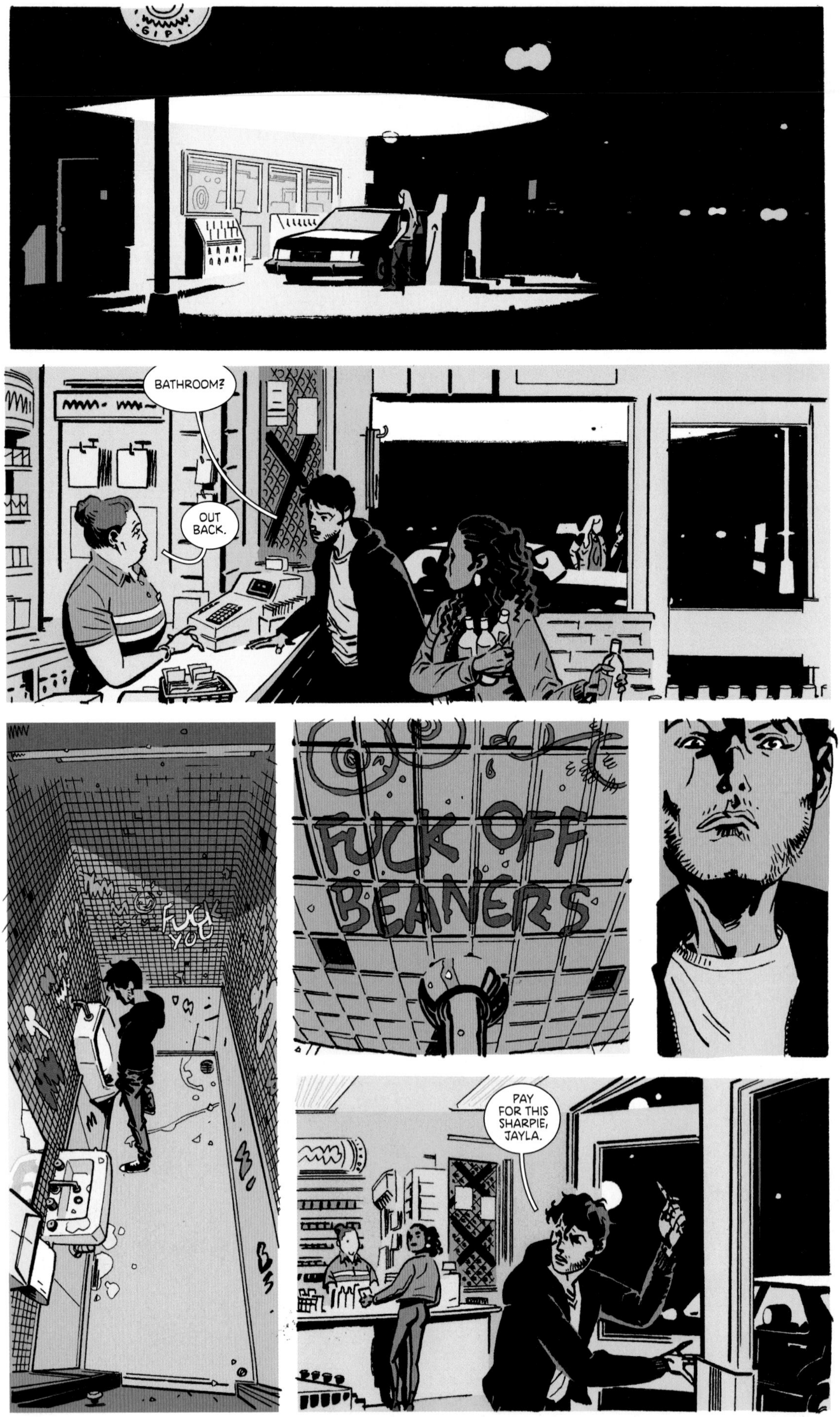
GIPI
BATHROOM?
OUT BACK.
FUCK YOU
FUCK OFF BEANERS
PAY FOR THIS SHARPIE, JAYLA.

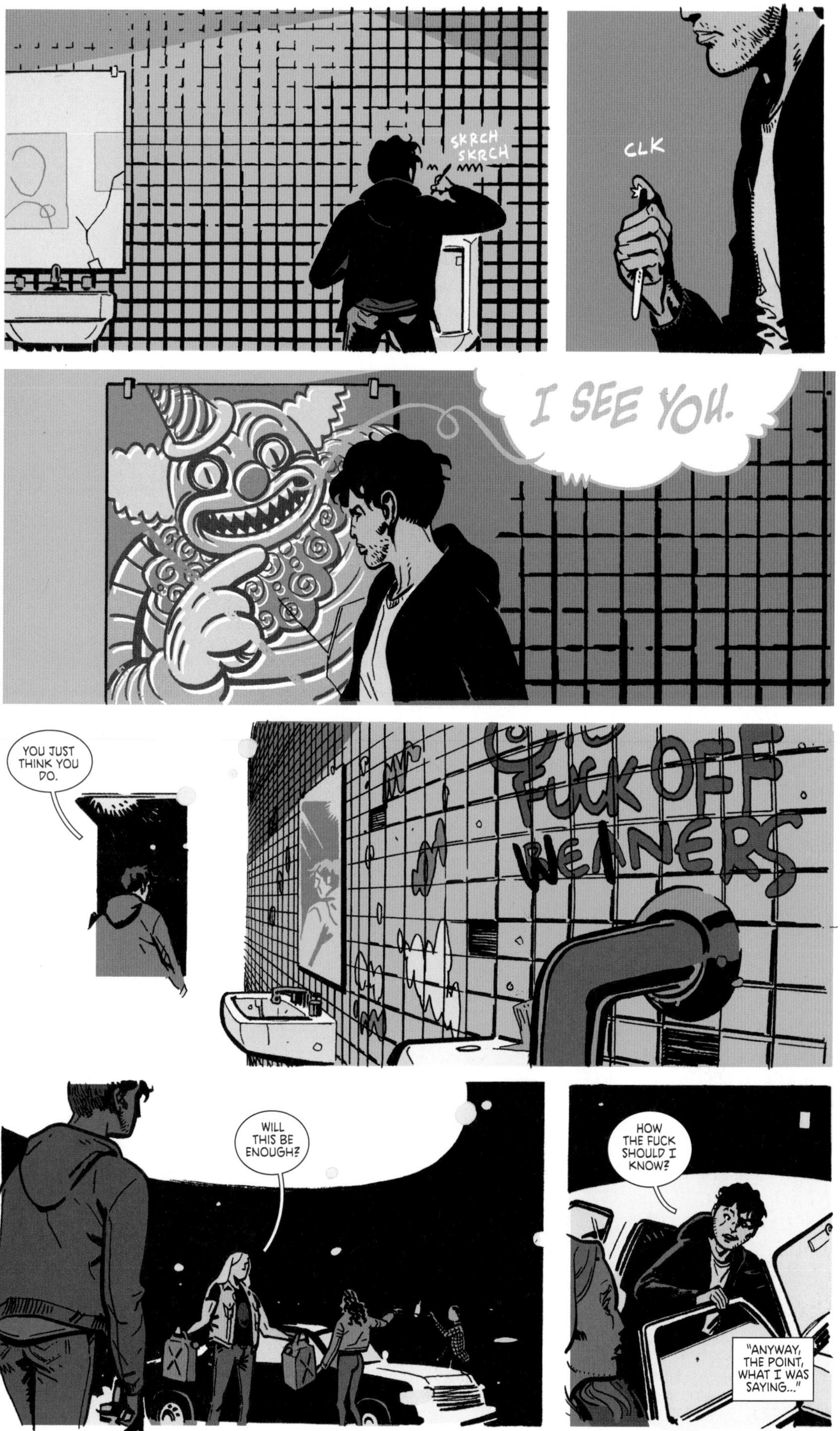
SKRCH SKRCH
CLK
I SEE YOU.
YOU JUST THINK YOU DO.
FUCK OFF WEANERS
WILL THIS BE ENOUGH?
HOW THE FUCK SHOULD I KNOW?
"ANYWAY, THE POINT, WHAT I WAS SAYING..."

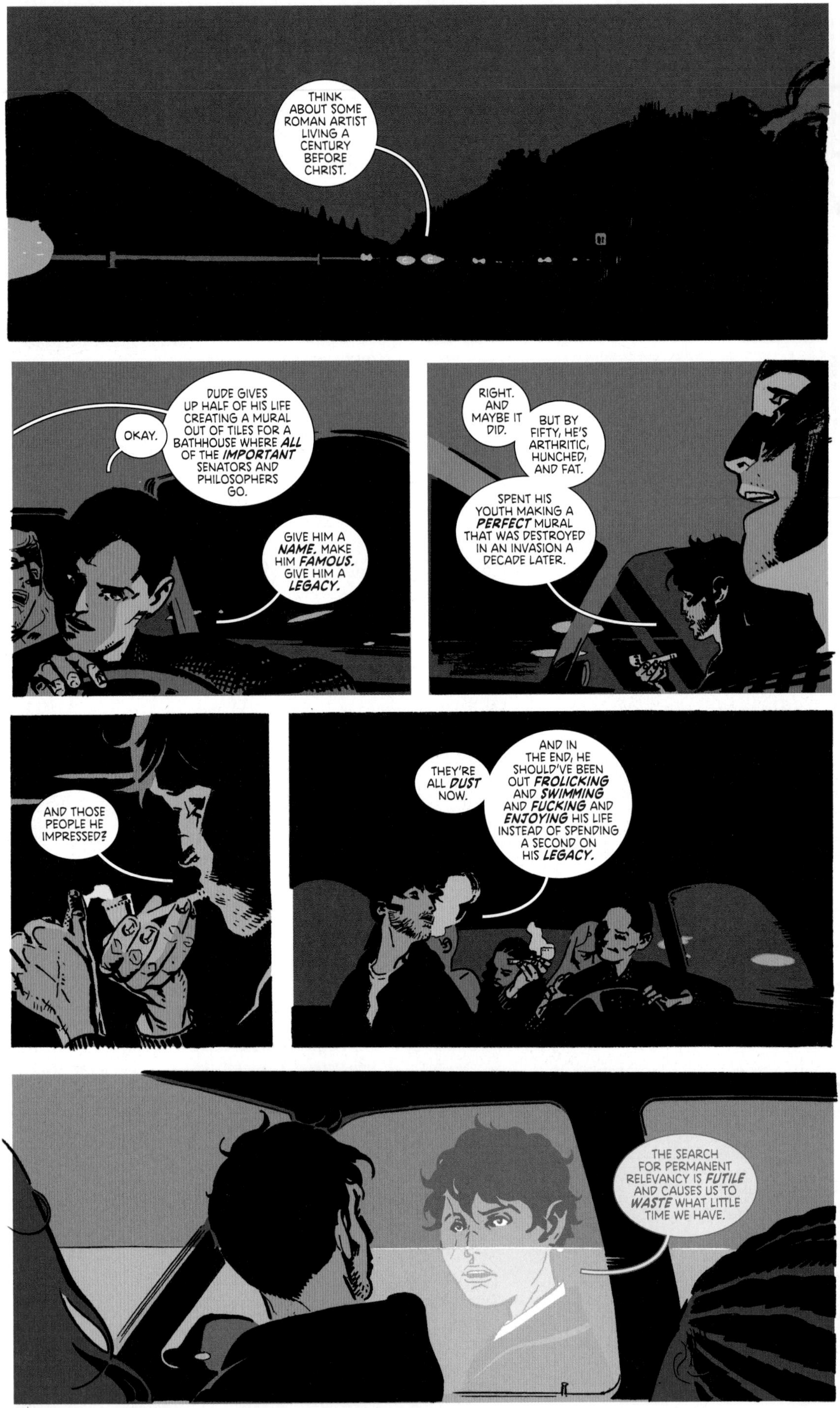
THINK ABOUT SOME ROMAN ARTIST LIVING A CENTURY BEFORE CHRIST.
DUDE GIVES UP HALF OF HIS LIFE CREATING A MURAL OUT OF TILES FOR A BATHHOUSE WHERE *ALL* OF THE *IMPORTANT* SENATORS AND PHILOSOPHERS GO.
OKAY.
GIVE HIM A *NAME.* MAKE HIM *FAMOUS.* GIVE HIM A *LEGACY.*
RIGHT. AND MAYBE IT DID.
BUT BY FIFTY, HE'S ARTHRITIC, HUNCHED, AND FAT.
SPENT HIS YOUTH MAKING A *PERFECT* MURAL THAT WAS DESTROYED IN AN INVASION A DECADE LATER.
AND THOSE PEOPLE HE IMPRESSED?
THEY'RE ALL *DUST* NOW.
AND IN THE END, HE SHOULD'VE BEEN OUT *FROLICKING* AND *SWIMMING* AND *FUCKING* AND *ENJOYING* HIS LIFE INSTEAD OF SPENDING A SECOND ON HIS *LEGACY.*
THE SEARCH FOR PERMANENT RELEVANCY IS *FUTILE* AND CAUSES US TO *WASTE* WHAT LITTLE TIME WE HAVE.

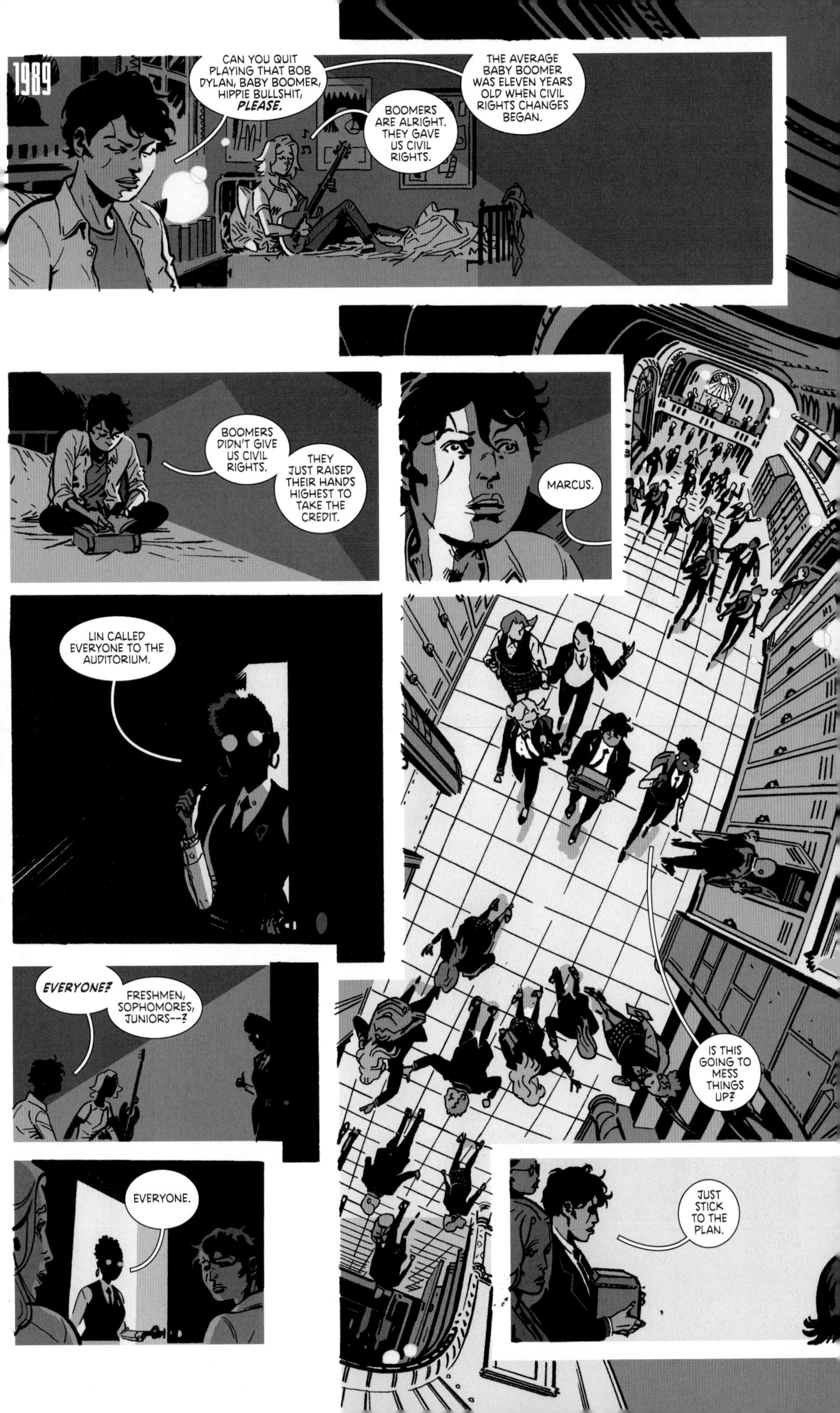
1989
CAN YOU QUIT PLAYING THAT BOB DYLAN, BABY BOOMER, HIPPIE BULLSHIT, *PLEASE.*
BOOMERS ARE ALRIGHT. THEY GAVE US CIVIL RIGHTS.
THE AVERAGE BABY BOOMER WAS ELEVEN YEARS OLD WHEN CIVIL RIGHTS CHANGES BEGAN.
BOOMERS DIDN'T GIVE US CIVIL RIGHTS.
THEY JUST RAISED THEIR HANDS HIGHEST TO TAKE THE CREDIT.
MARCUS.
LIN CALLED EVERYONE TO THE AUDITORIUM.
EVERYONE?
FRESHMEN, SOPHOMORES, JUNIORS--?
EVERYONE.
IS THIS GOING TO MESS THINGS UP?
JUST STICK TO THE PLAN.

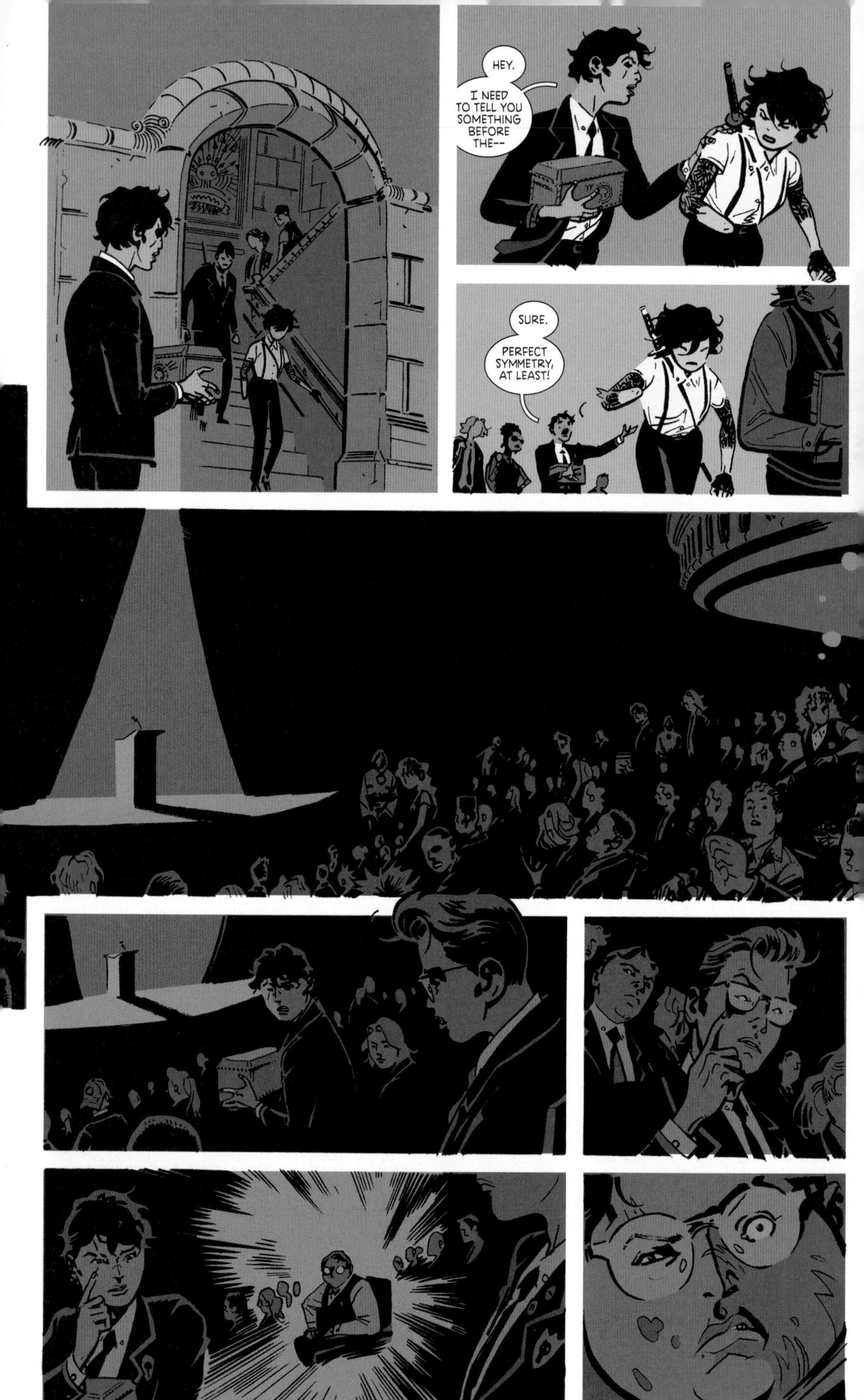
HEY.
I NEED TO TELL YOU SOMETHING BEFORE THE--
SURE.
PERFECT SYMMETRY, AT LEAST!

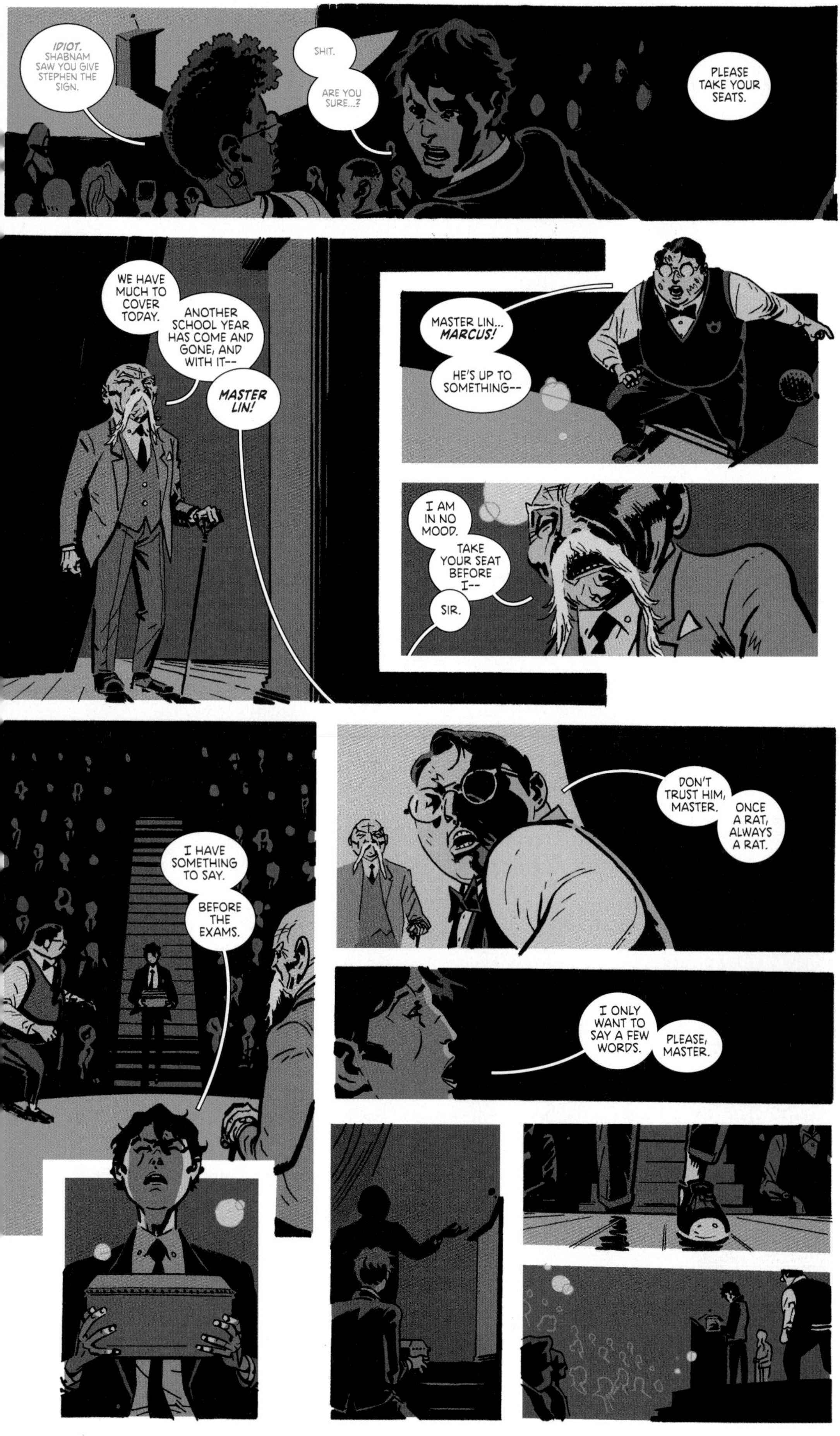

IDIOT. SHABNAM SAW YOU GIVE STEPHEN THE SIGN.
SHIT.
ARE YOU SURE...?
PLEASE TAKE YOUR SEATS.
WE HAVE MUCH TO COVER TODAY.
ANOTHER SCHOOL YEAR HAS COME AND GONE, AND WITH IT--
MASTER LIN!
MASTER LIN... MARCUS!
HE'S UP TO SOMETHING--
I AM IN NO MOOD.
TAKE YOUR SEAT BEFORE I--
SIR.
I HAVE SOMETHING TO SAY.
BEFORE THE EXAMS.
DON'T TRUST HIM, MASTER.
ONCE A RAT, ALWAYS A RAT.
I ONLY WANT TO SAY A FEW WORDS.
PLEASE, MASTER.

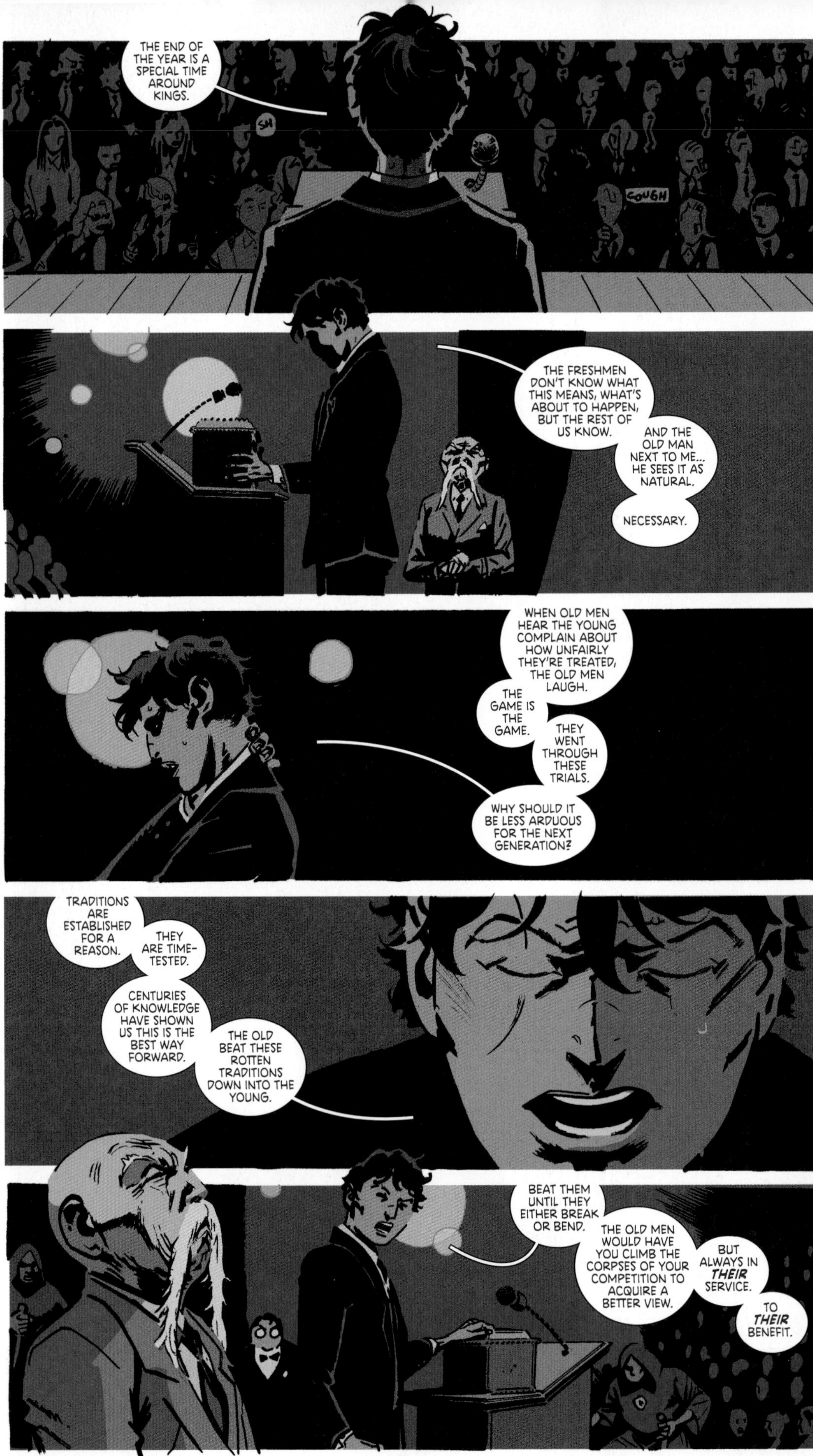
THE END OF THE YEAR IS A SPECIAL TIME AROUND KINGS.
SH
COUGH
THE FRESHMEN DON'T KNOW WHAT THIS MEANS, WHAT'S ABOUT TO HAPPEN, BUT THE REST OF US KNOW.
AND THE OLD MAN NEXT TO ME... HE SEES IT AS NATURAL.
NECESSARY.
WHEN OLD MEN HEAR THE YOUNG COMPLAIN ABOUT HOW UNFAIRLY THEY'RE TREATED, THE OLD MEN LAUGH.
THE GAME IS THE GAME.
THEY WENT THROUGH THESE TRIALS.
WHY SHOULD IT BE LESS ARDUOUS FOR THE NEXT GENERATION?
TRADITIONS ARE ESTABLISHED FOR A REASON.
THEY ARE TIME-TESTED.
CENTURIES OF KNOWLEDGE HAVE SHOWN US THIS IS THE BEST WAY FORWARD.
THE OLD BEAT THESE ROTTEN TRADITIONS DOWN INTO THE YOUNG.
BEAT THEM UNTIL THEY EITHER BREAK OR BEND.
THE OLD MEN WOULD HAVE YOU CLIMB THE CORPSES OF YOUR COMPETITION TO ACQUIRE A BETTER VIEW.
BUT ALWAYS IN *THEIR* SERVICE.
TO *THEIR* BENEFIT.

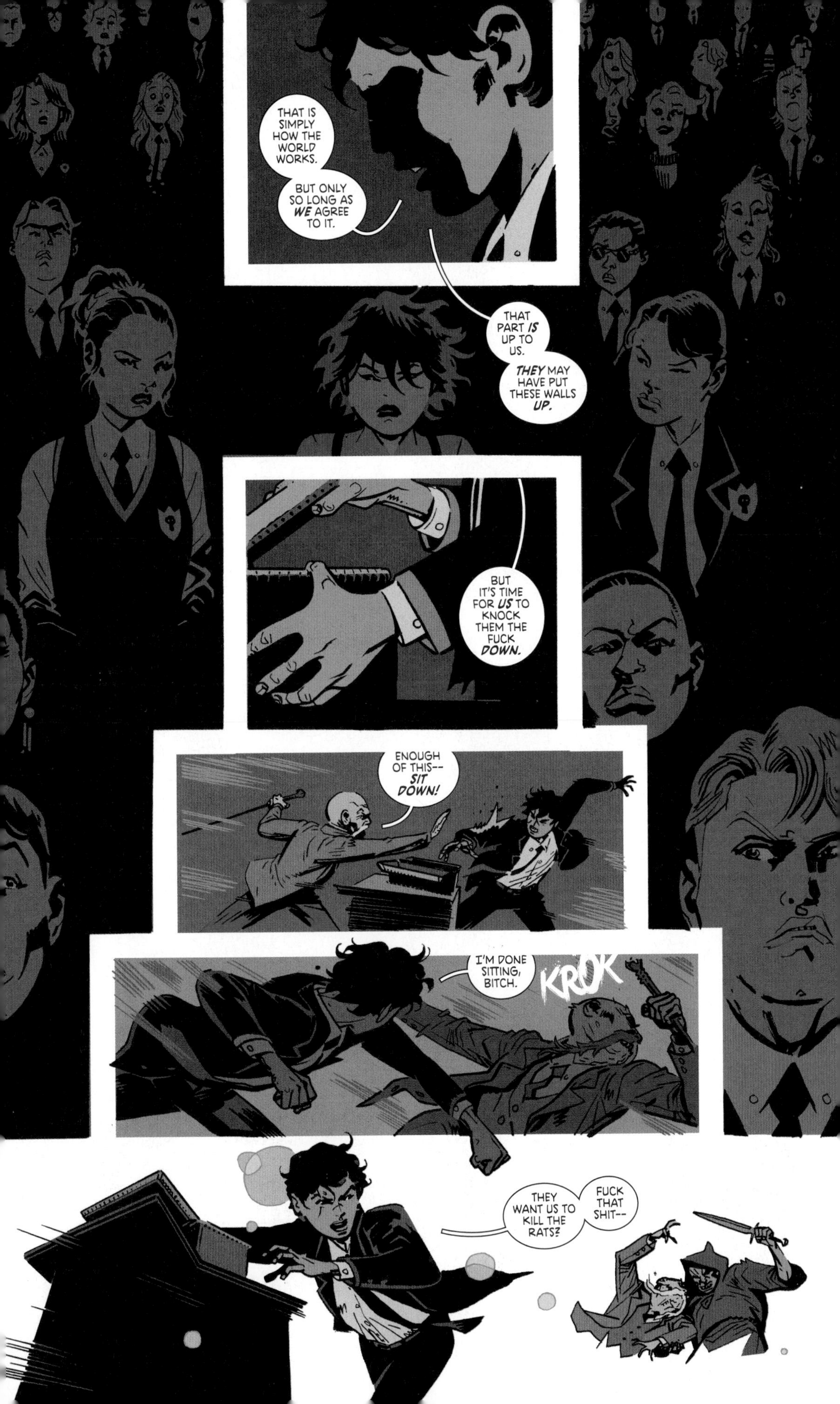

THAT IS SIMPLY HOW THE WORLD WORKS.
BUT ONLY SO LONG AS WE AGREE TO IT.
THAT PART IS UP TO US.
THEY MAY HAVE PUT THESE WALLS UP.
BUT IT'S TIME FOR US TO KNOCK THEM THE FUCK DOWN.
ENOUGH OF THIS-- SIT DOWN!
I'M DONE SITTING, BITCH.
KROK
THEY WANT US TO KILL THE RATS?
FUCK THAT SHIT--

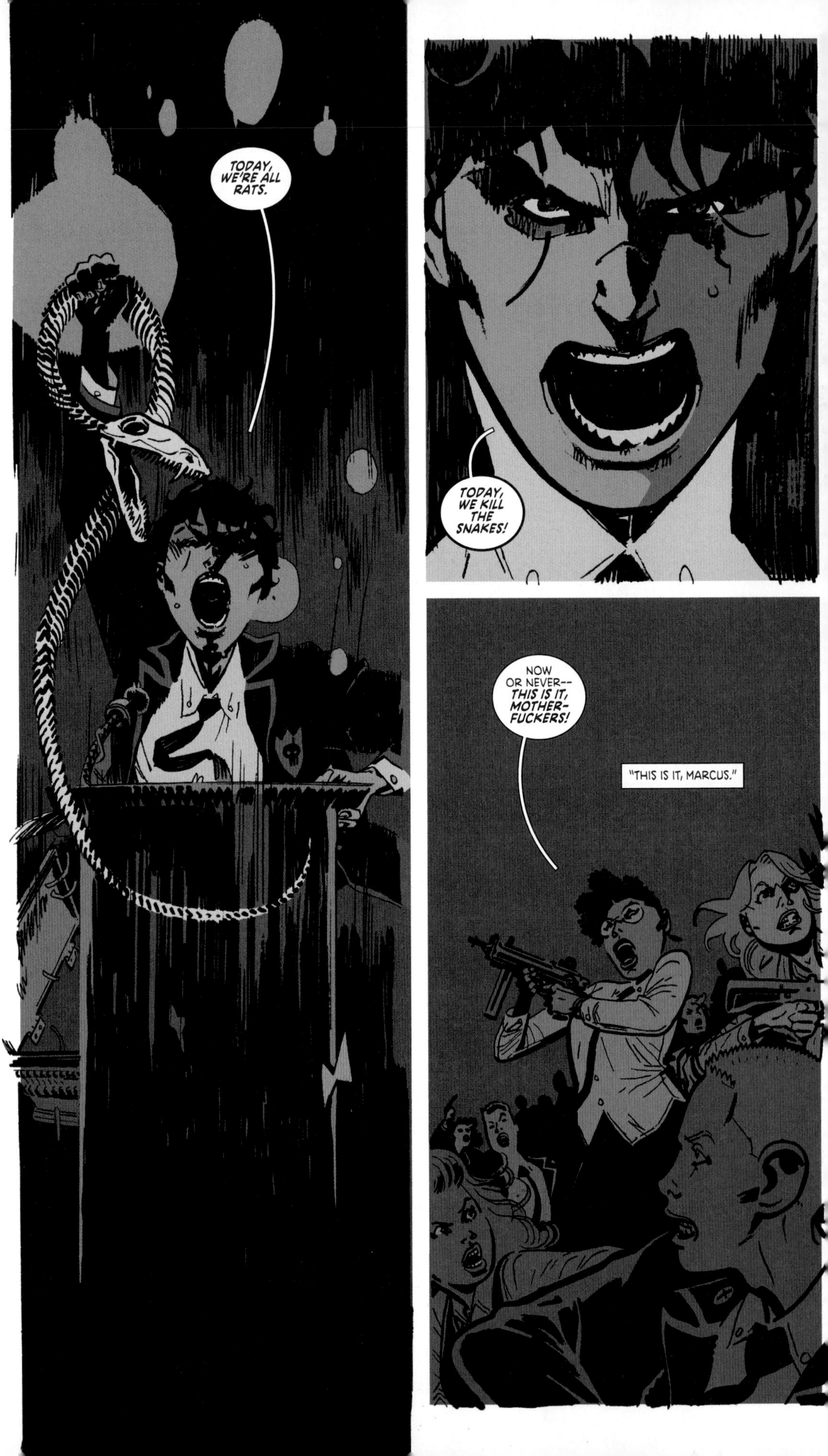
TODAY, WE'RE ALL RATS.
TODAY, WE KILL THE SNAKES!
NOW OR NEVER-- THIS IS IT, MOTHER-FUCKERS!
"THIS IS IT, MARCUS."

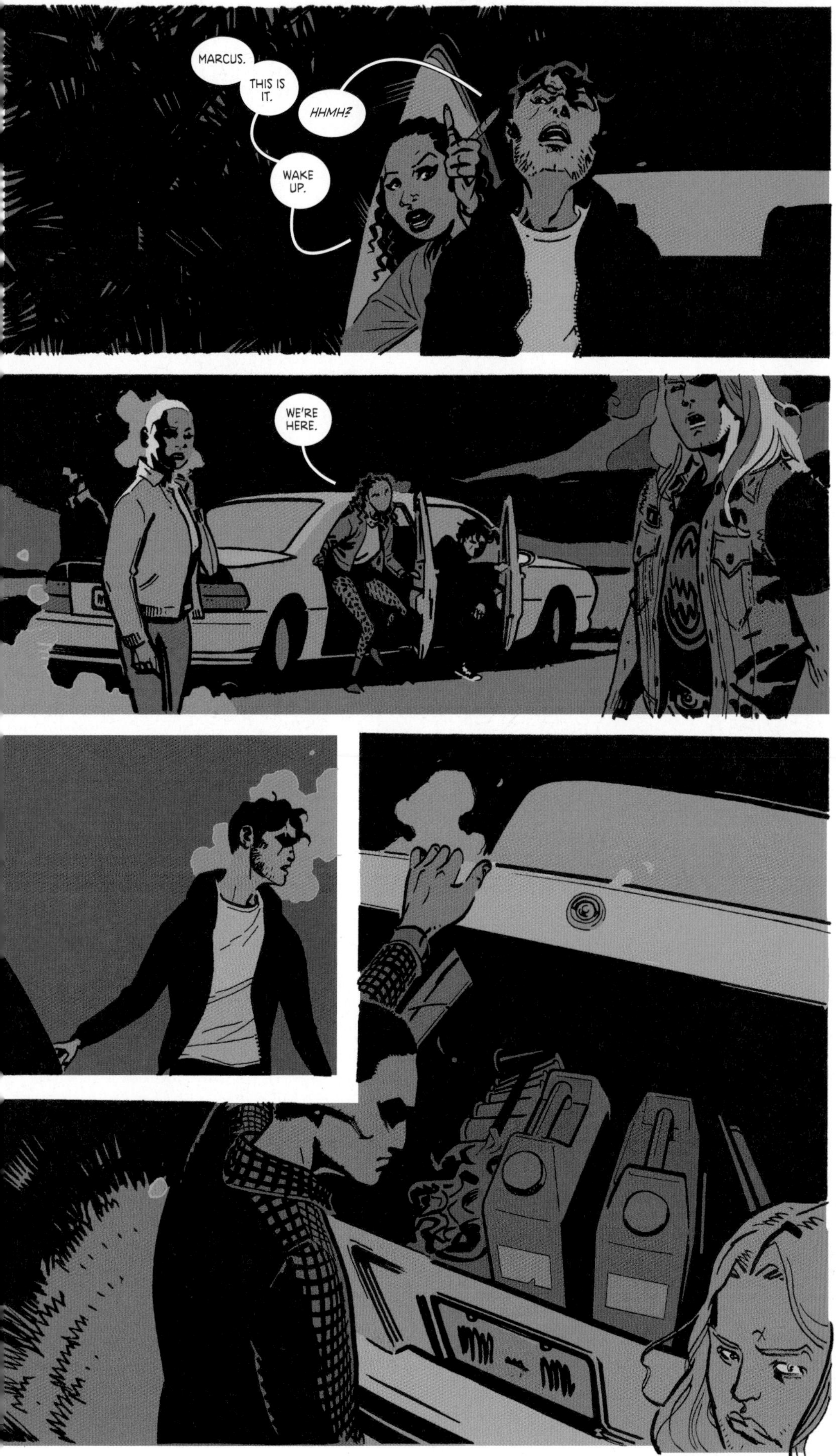
MARCUS.
THIS IS IT.
HHMH?
WAKE UP.
WE'RE HERE.

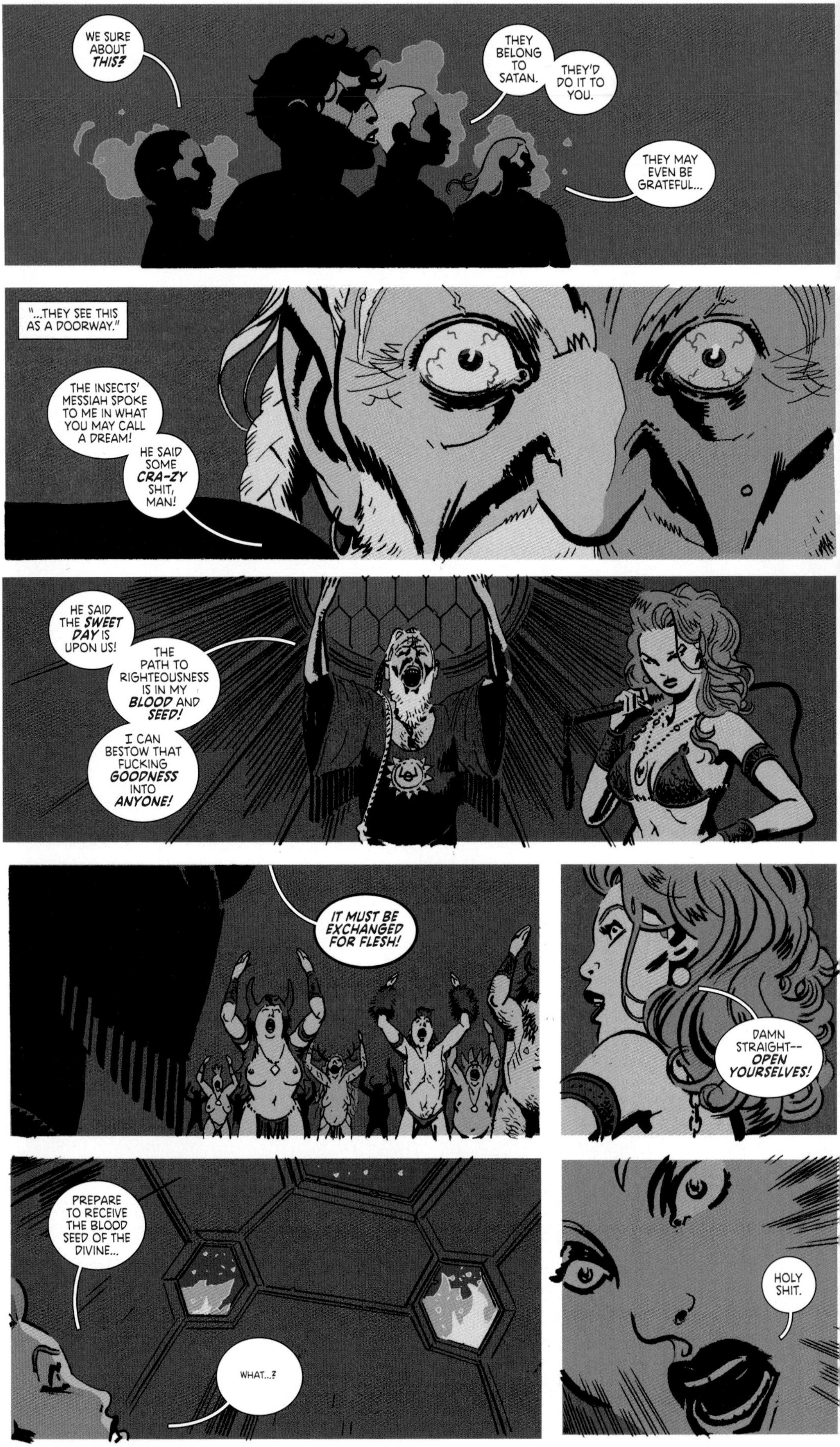
WE SURE ABOUT THIS?
THEY BELONG TO SATAN.
THEY'D DO IT TO YOU.
THEY MAY EVEN BE GRATEFUL...
"...THEY SEE THIS AS A DOORWAY."
THE INSECTS' MESSIAH SPOKE TO ME IN WHAT YOU MAY CALL A DREAM!
HE SAID SOME CRA-ZY SHIT, MAN!
HE SAID THE SWEET DAY IS UPON US!
THE PATH TO RIGHTEOUSNESS IS IN MY BLOOD AND SEED!
I CAN BESTOW THAT FUCKING GOODNESS INTO ANYONE!
IT MUST BE EXCHANGED FOR FLESH!
DAMN STRAIGHT-- OPEN YOURSELVES!
PREPARE TO RECEIVE THE BLOOD SEED OF THE DIVINE...
WHAT...?
HOLY SHIT.

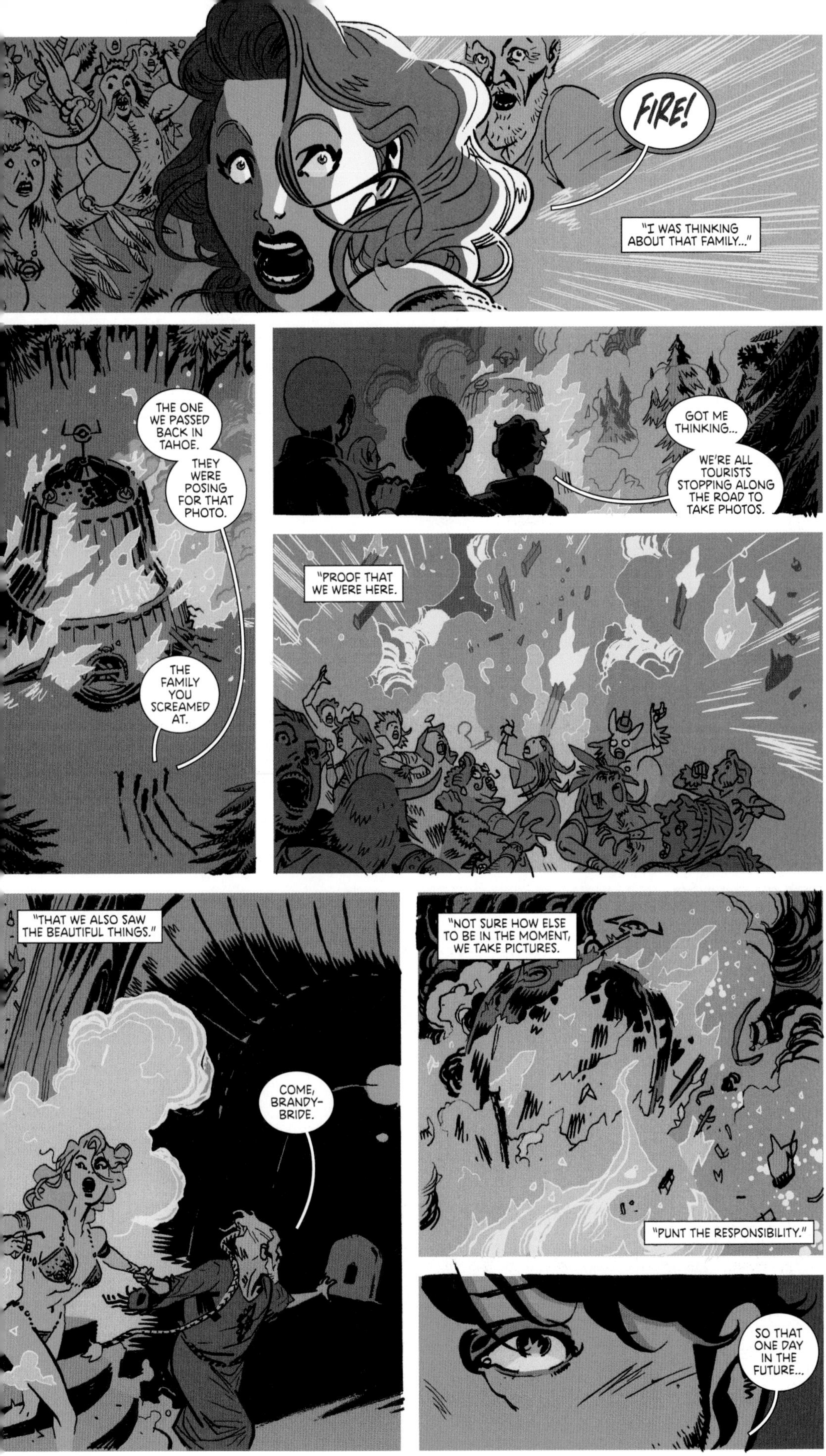
FIRE!
"I WAS THINKING ABOUT THAT FAMILY..."
THE ONE WE PASSED BACK IN TAHOE.
THEY WERE POSING FOR THAT PHOTO.
THE FAMILY YOU SCREAMED AT.
GOT ME THINKING...
WE'RE ALL TOURISTS STOPPING ALONG THE ROAD TO TAKE PHOTOS.
"PROOF THAT WE WERE HERE.
"THAT WE ALSO SAW THE BEAUTIFUL THINGS."
COME, BRANDY-BRIDE.
"NOT SURE HOW ELSE TO BE IN THE MOMENT, WE TAKE PICTURES.
"PUNT THE RESPONSIBILITY."
SO THAT ONE DAY IN THE FUTURE...

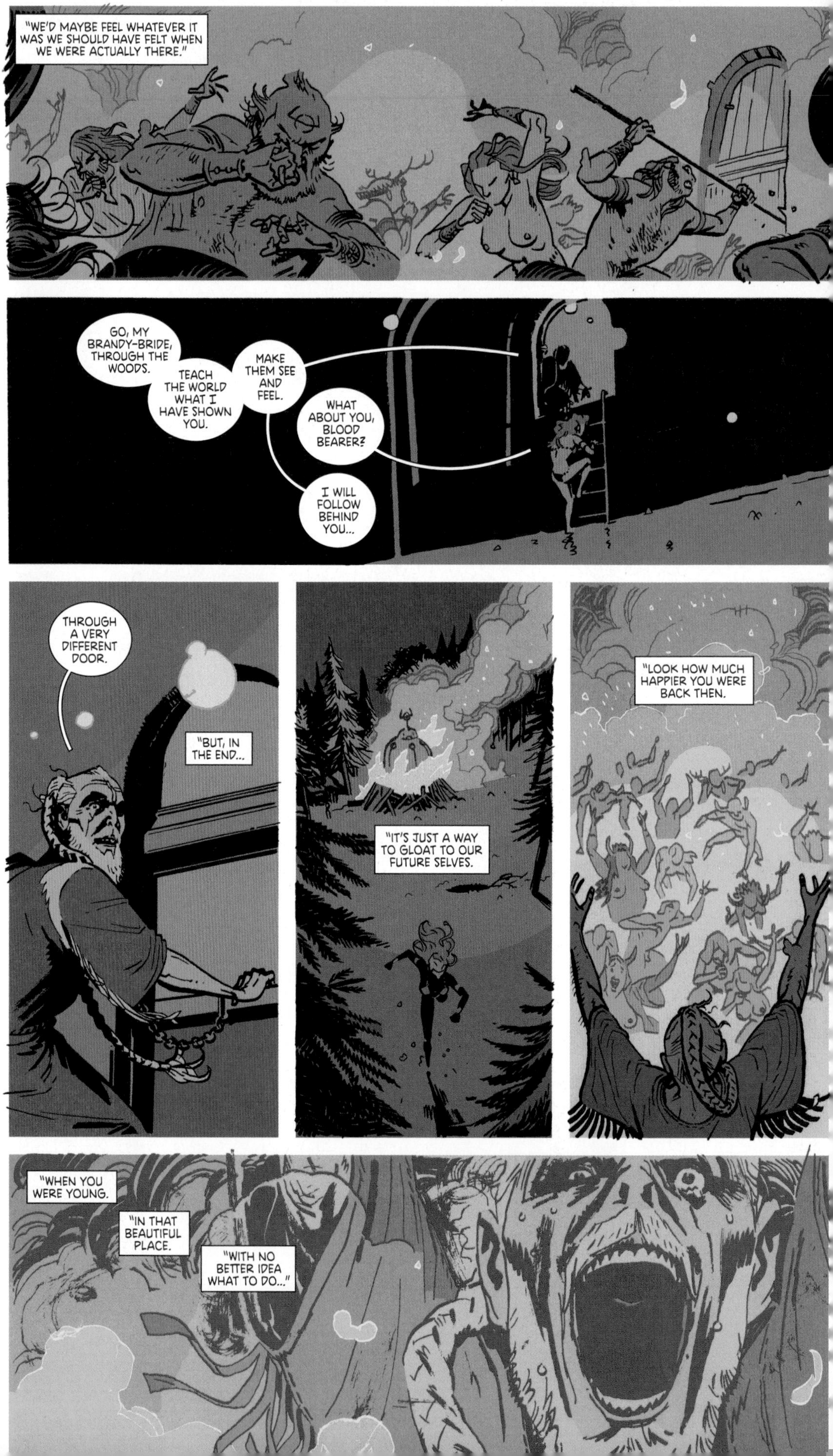
"WE'D MAYBE FEEL WHATEVER IT WAS WE SHOULD HAVE FELT WHEN WE WERE ACTUALLY THERE."
GO, MY BRANDY-BRIDE, THROUGH THE WOODS.
TEACH THE WORLD WHAT I HAVE SHOWN YOU.
MAKE THEM SEE AND FEEL.
WHAT ABOUT YOU, BLOOD BEARER?
I WILL FOLLOW BEHIND YOU...
THROUGH A VERY DIFFERENT DOOR.
"BUT, IN THE END...
"IT'S JUST A WAY TO GLOAT TO OUR FUTURE SELVES.
"LOOK HOW MUCH HAPPIER YOU WERE BACK THEN.
"WHEN YOU WERE YOUNG.
"IN THAT BEAUTIFUL PLACE.
"WITH NO BETTER IDEA WHAT TO DO..."

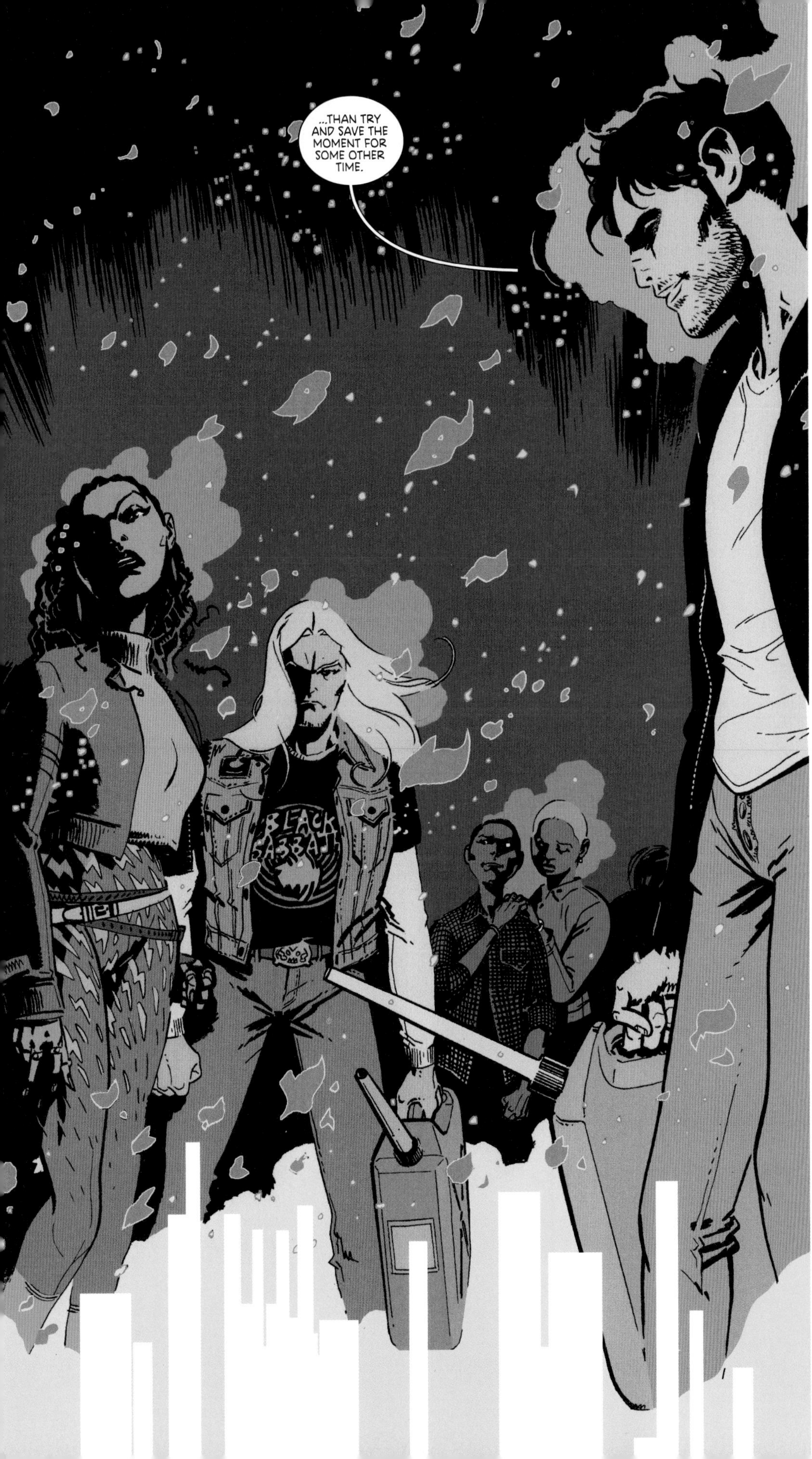
...THAN TRY AND SAVE THE MOMENT FOR SOME OTHER TIME.
BLACK SABBATH

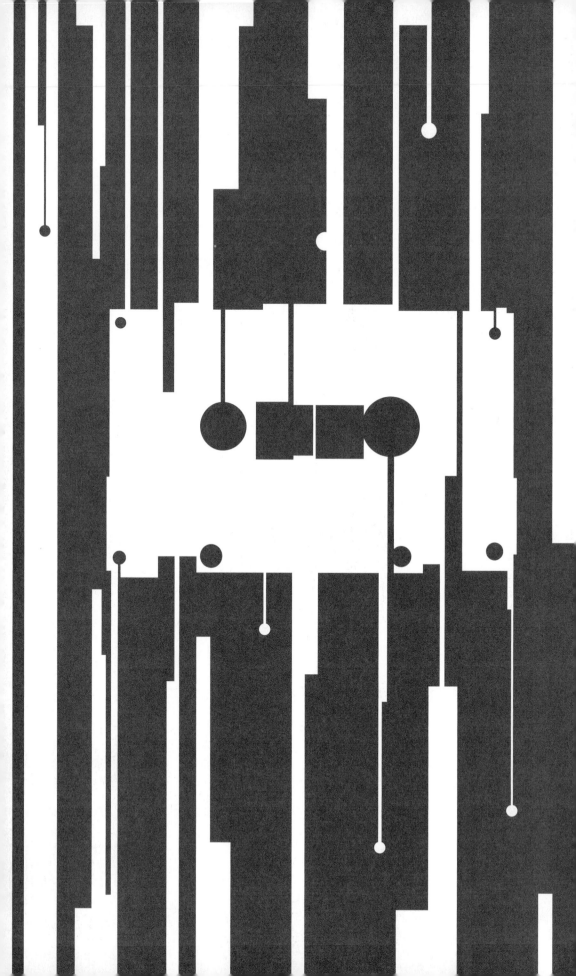

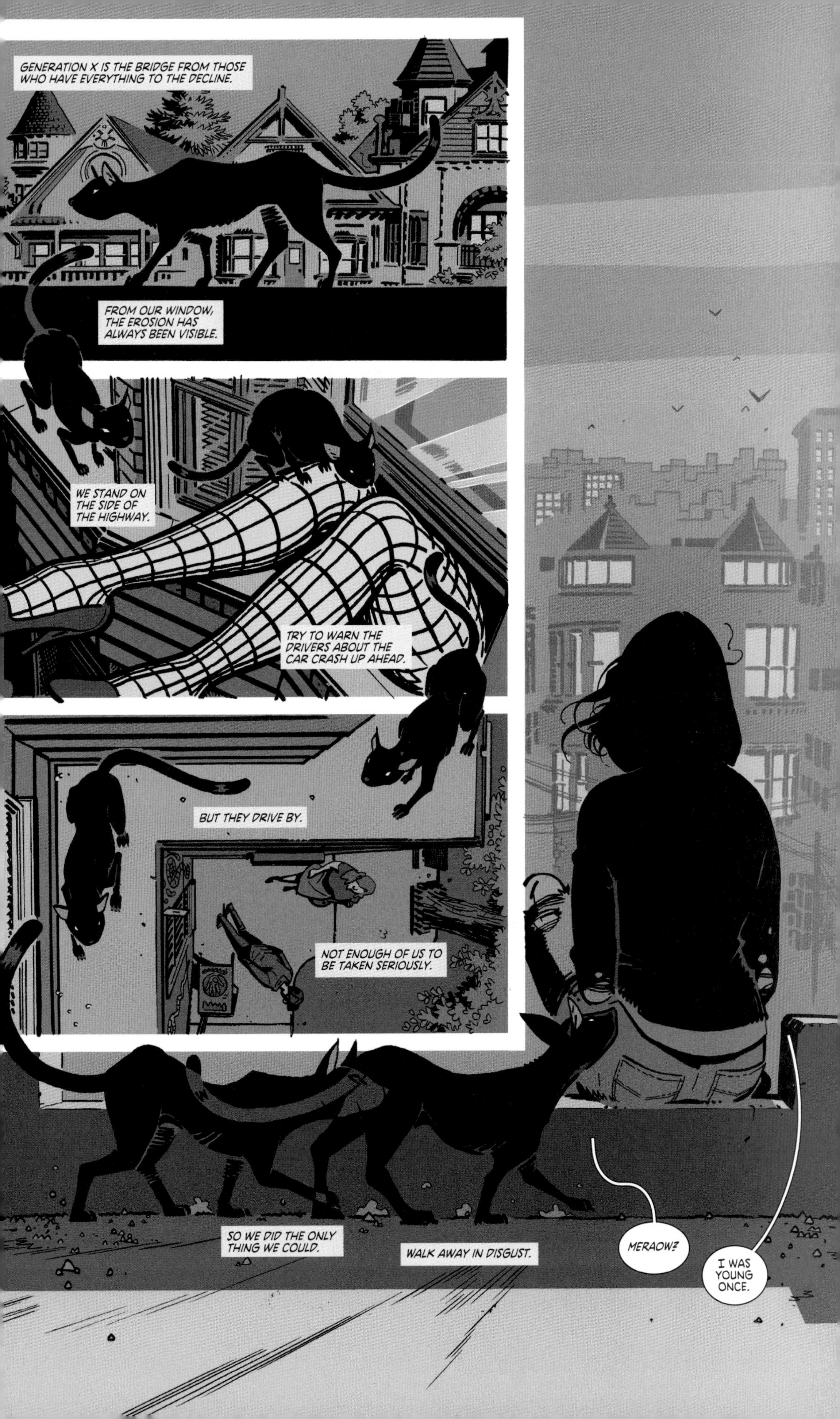
GENERATION X IS THE BRIDGE FROM THOSE WHO HAVE EVERYTHING TO THE DECLINE.
FROM OUR WINDOW, THE EROSION HAS ALWAYS BEEN VISIBLE.
WE STAND ON THE SIDE OF THE HIGHWAY.
TRY TO WARN THE DRIVERS ABOUT THE CAR CRASH UP AHEAD.
BUT THEY DRIVE BY.
NOT ENOUGH OF US TO BE TAKEN SERIOUSLY.
SO WE DID THE ONLY THING WE COULD.
WALK AWAY IN DISGUST.
MERAOW?
I WAS YOUNG ONCE.

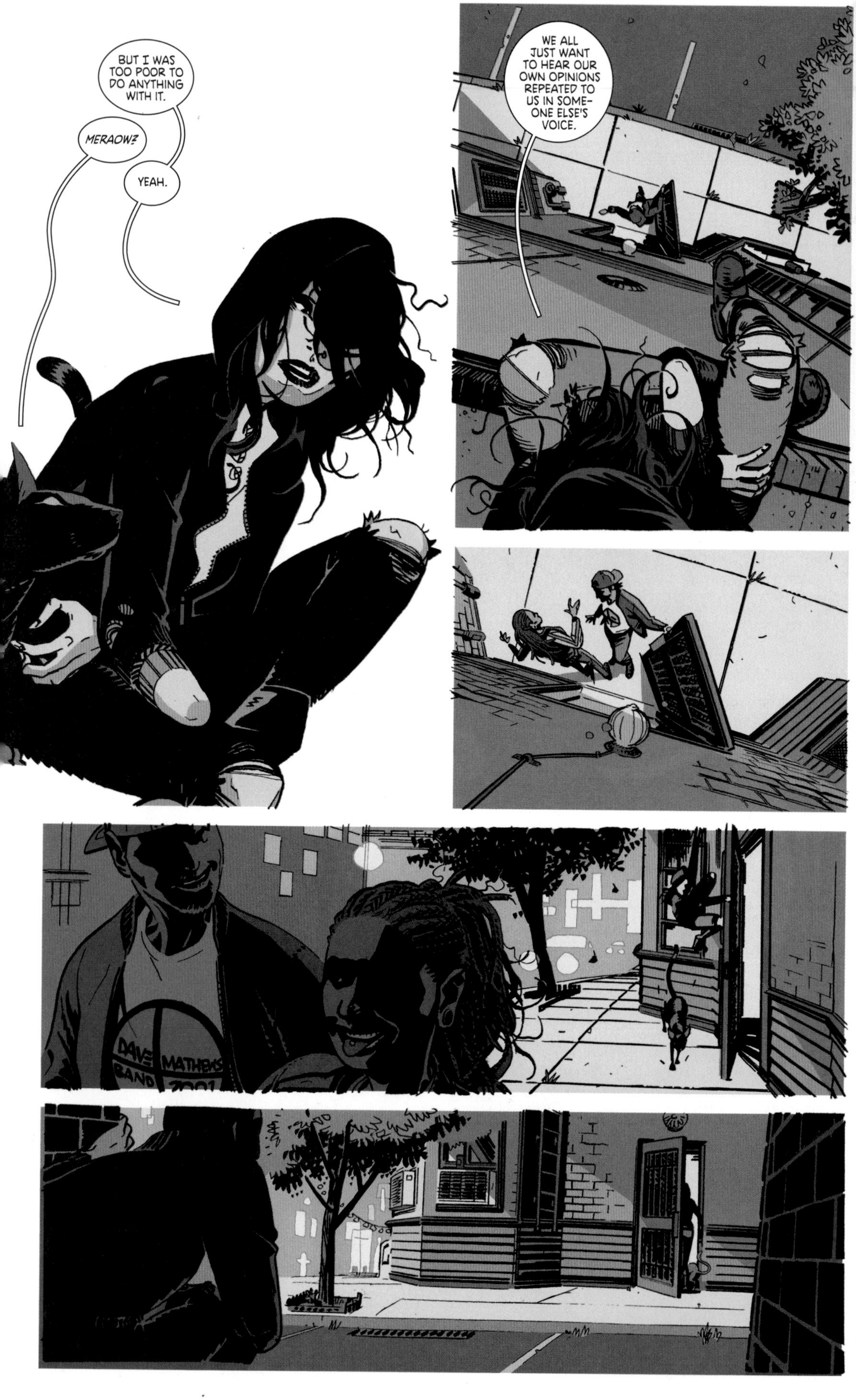

BUT I WAS TOO POOR TO DO ANYTHING WITH IT.
MERAOW?
YEAH.
WE ALL JUST WANT TO HEAR OUR OWN OPINIONS REPEATED TO US IN SOME-ONE ELSE'S VOICE.
DAVE MATHEWS BAND

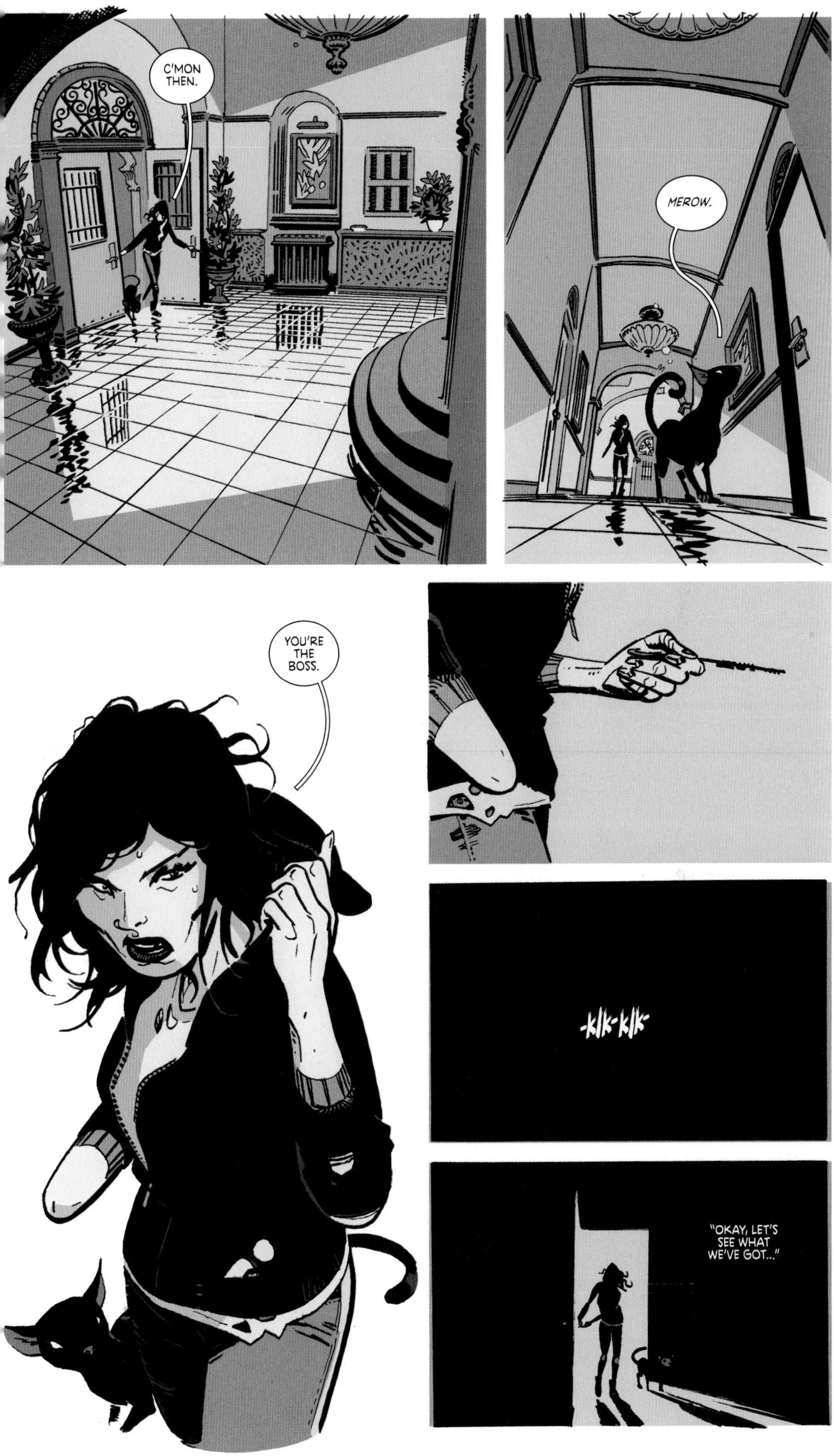
C'MON THEN.
MEROW.
YOU'RE THE BOSS.
-KLK-KLK-
"OKAY, LET'S SEE WHAT WE'VE GOT..."

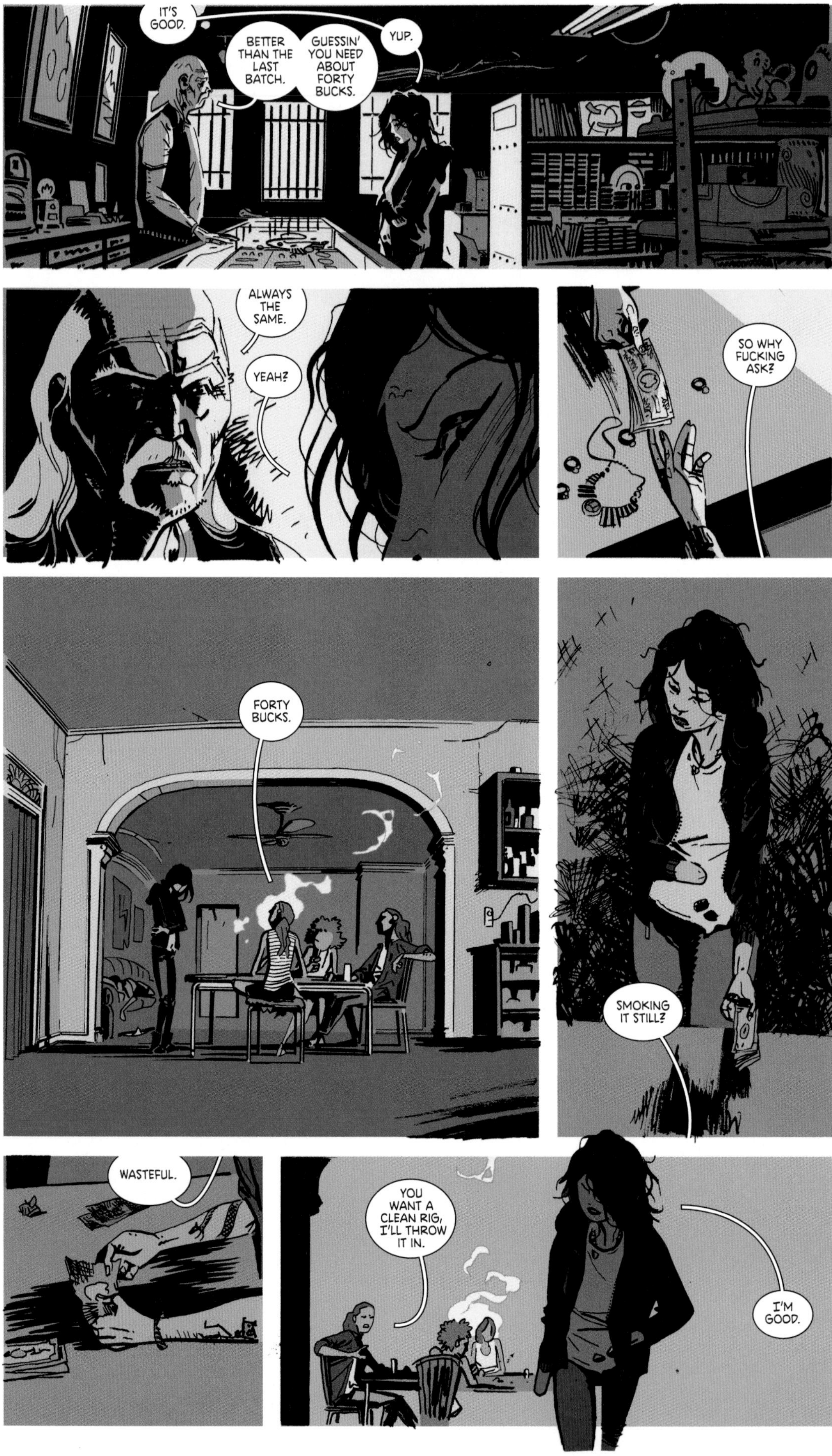
IT'S GOOD.
BETTER THAN THE LAST BATCH.
GUESSIN' YOU NEED ABOUT FORTY BUCKS.
YUP.
ALWAYS THE SAME.
YEAH?
SO WHY FUCKING ASK?
FORTY BUCKS.
SMOKING IT STILL?
WASTEFUL.
YOU WANT A CLEAN RIG, I'LL THROW IT IN.
I'M GOOD.

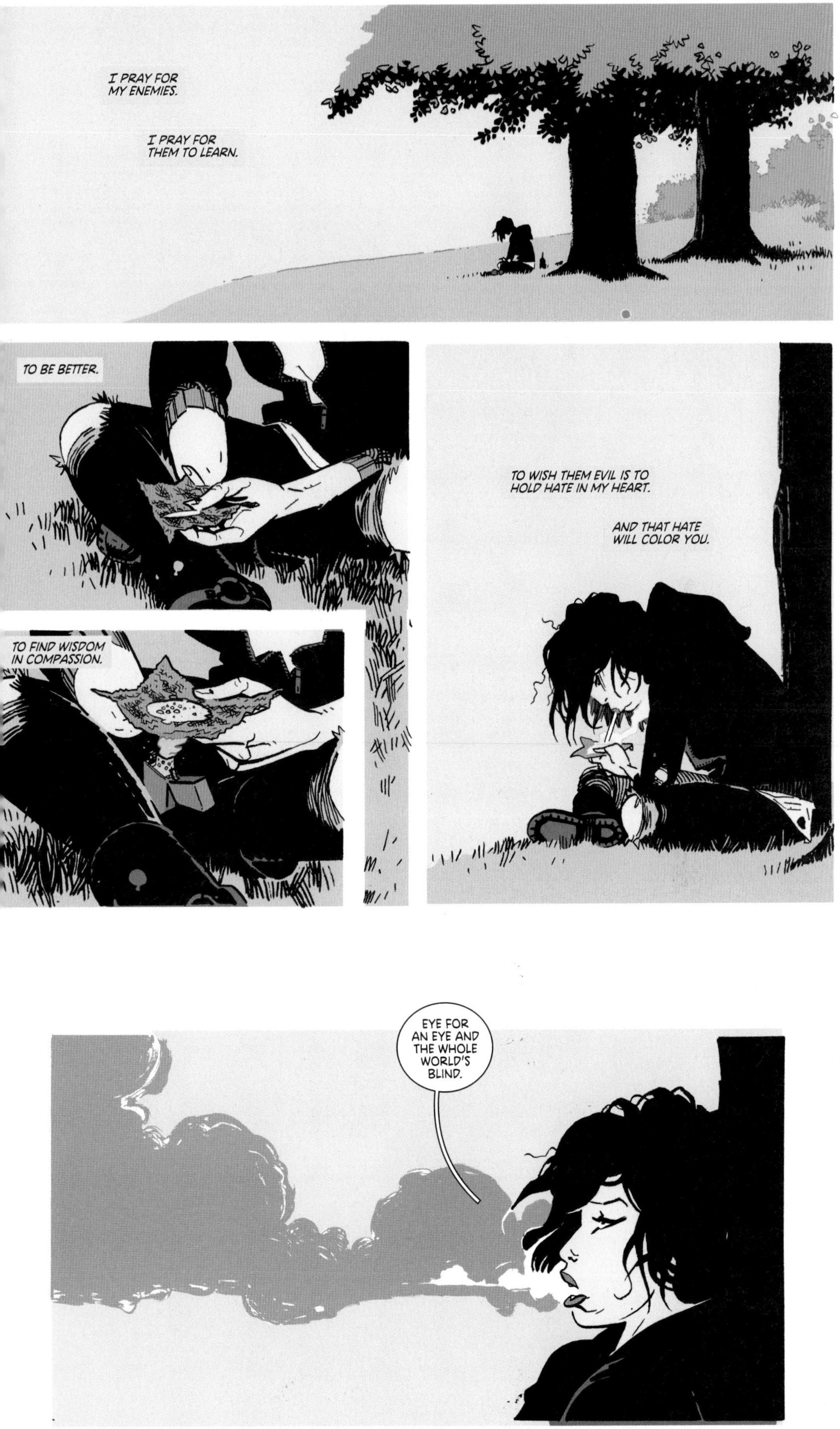
I PRAY FOR MY ENEMIES.
I PRAY FOR THEM TO LEARN.
TO BE BETTER.
TO FIND WISDOM IN COMPASSION.
TO WISH THEM EVIL IS TO HOLD HATE IN MY HEART.
AND THAT HATE WILL COLOR YOU.
EYE FOR AN EYE AND THE WHOLE WORLD'S BLIND.

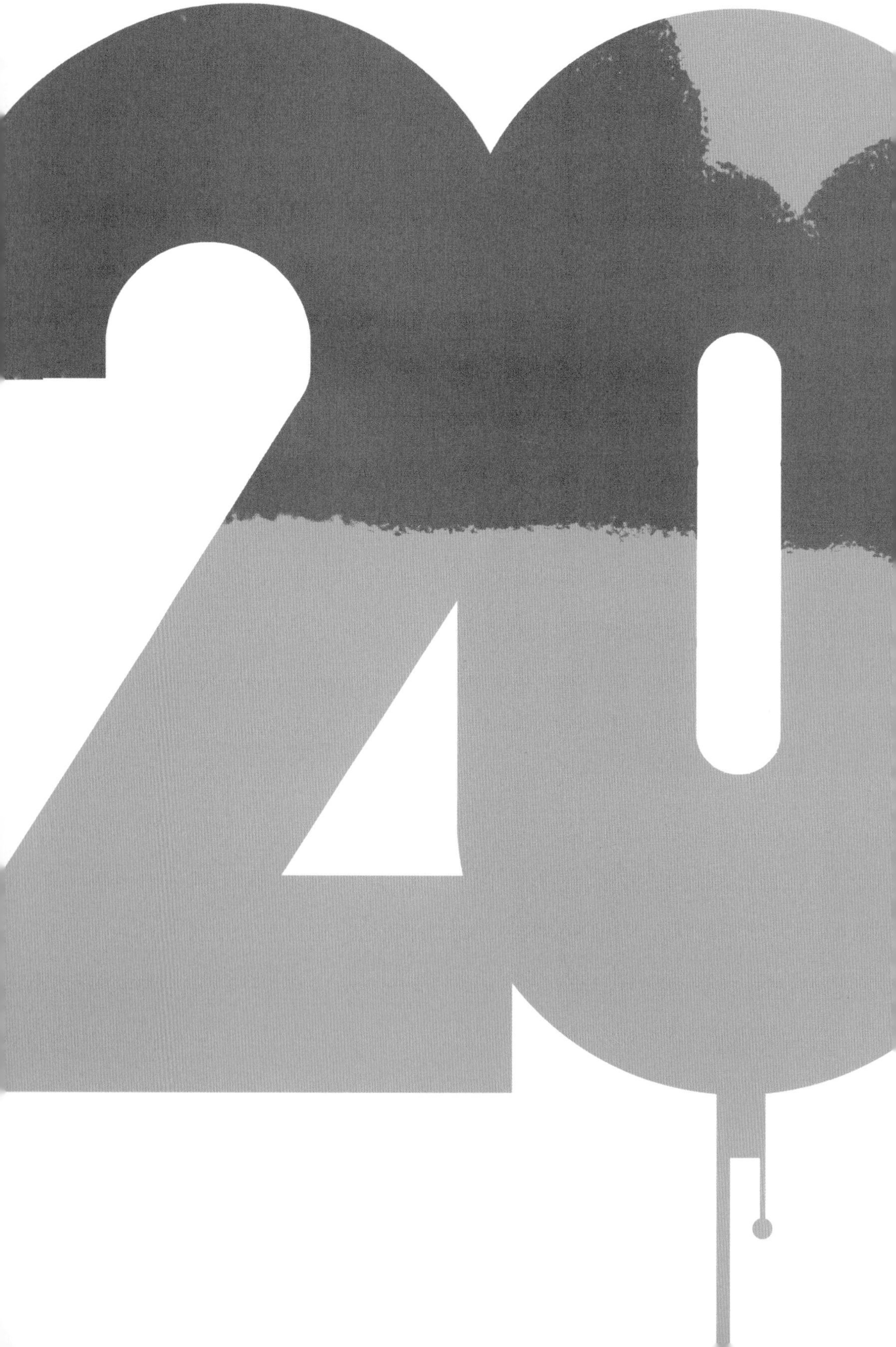

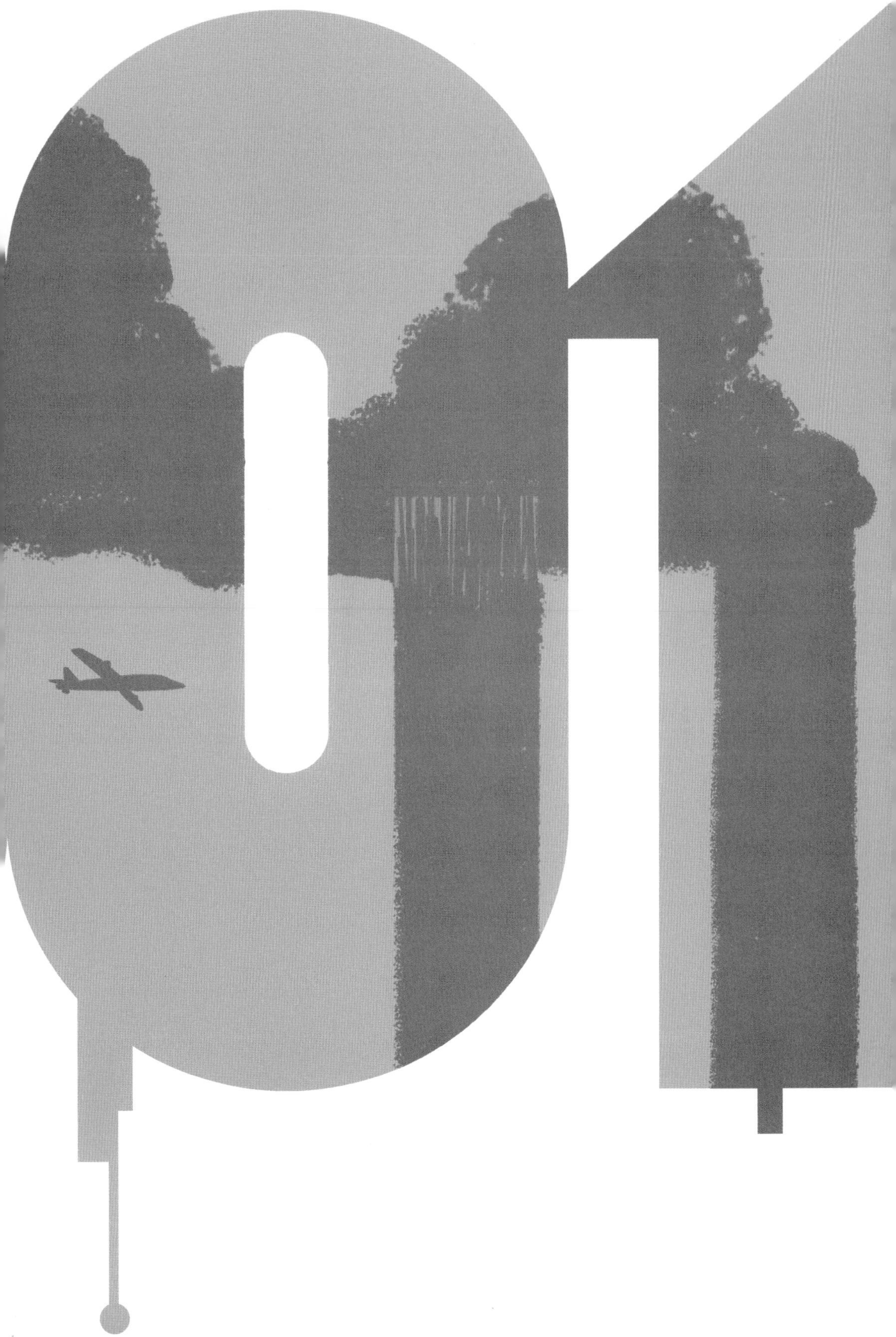

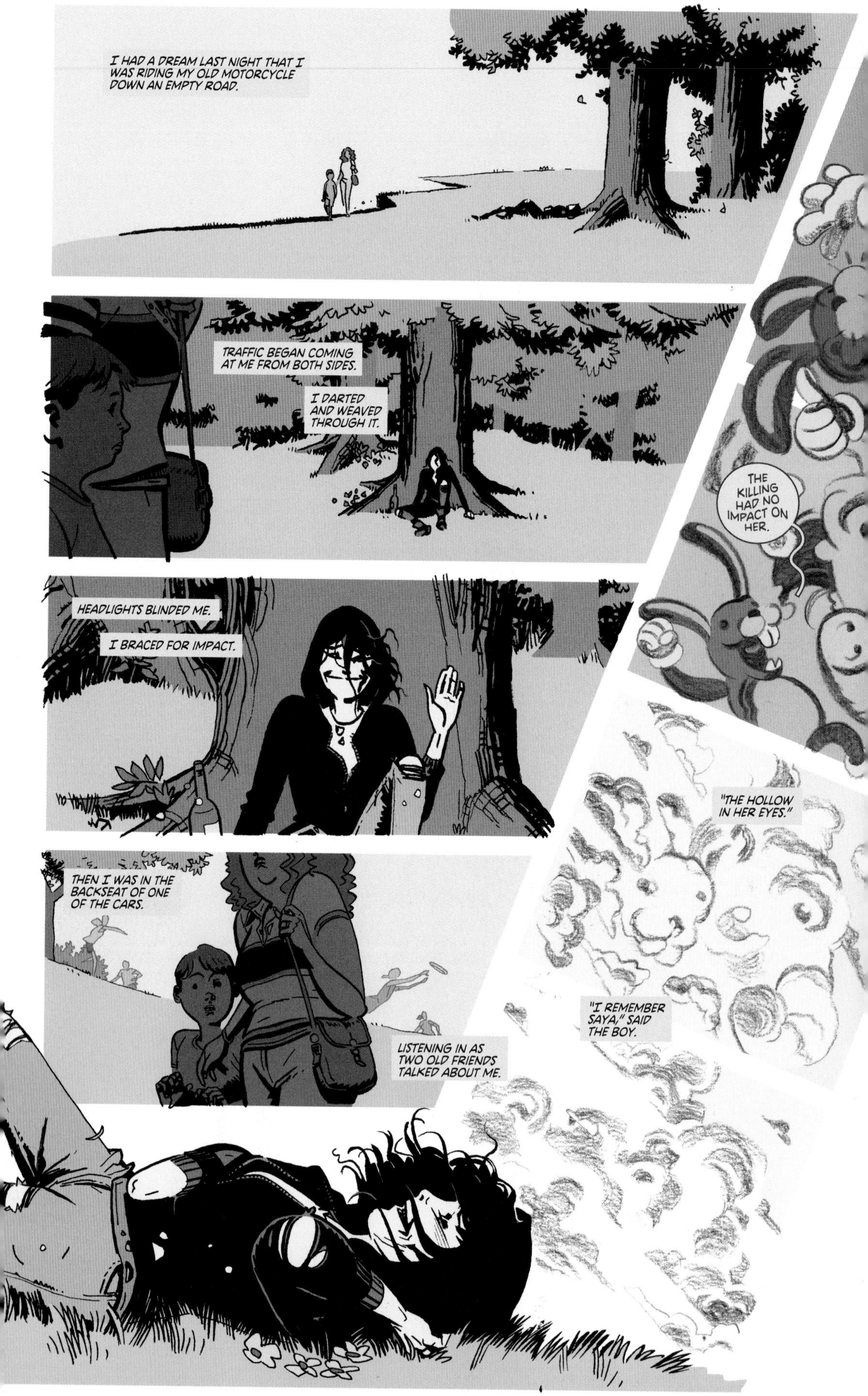
I HAD A DREAM LAST NIGHT THAT I WAS RIDING MY OLD MOTORCYCLE DOWN AN EMPTY ROAD.
TRAFFIC BEGAN COMING AT ME FROM BOTH SIDES.
I DARTED AND WEAVED THROUGH IT.
THE KILLING HAD NO IMPACT ON HER.
HEADLIGHTS BLINDED ME.
I BRACED FOR IMPACT.
"THE HOLLOW IN HER EYES."
THEN I WAS IN THE BACKSEAT OF ONE OF THE CARS.
"I REMEMBER SAYA," SAID THE BOY.
LISTENING IN AS TWO OLD FRIENDS TALKED ABOUT ME.

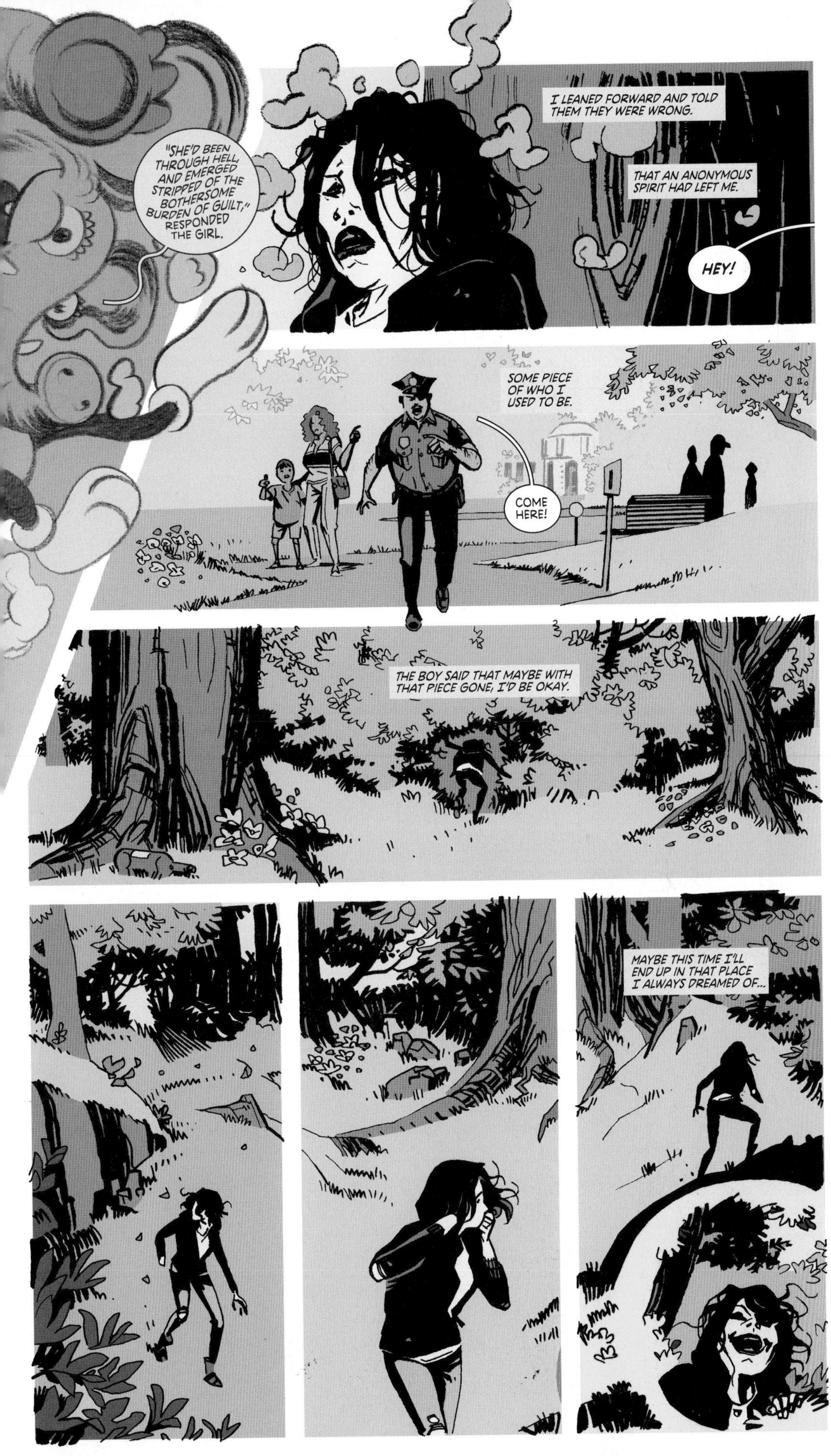
"SHE'D BEEN THROUGH HELL, AND EMERGED STRIPPED OF THE BOTHERSOME BURDEN OF GUILT," RESPONDED THE GIRL.
I LEANED FORWARD AND TOLD THEM THEY WERE WRONG.
THAT AN ANONYMOUS SPIRIT HAD LEFT ME.
HEY!
SOME PIECE OF WHO I USED TO BE.
COME HERE!
THE BOY SAID THAT MAYBE WITH THAT PIECE GONE, I'D BE OKAY.
MAYBE THIS TIME I'LL END UP IN THAT PLACE I ALWAYS DREAMED OF...

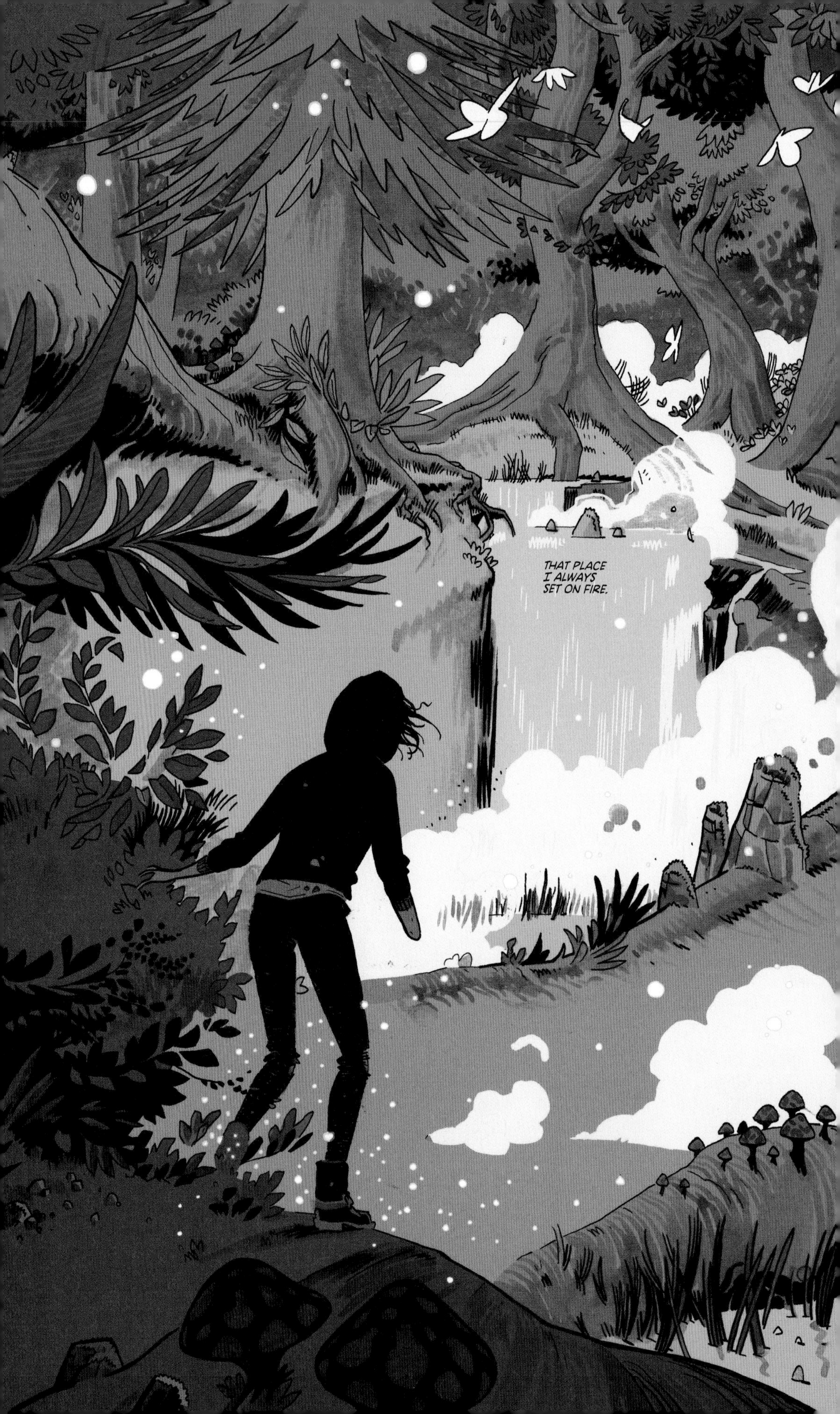
THAT PLACE I ALWAYS SET ON FIRE.

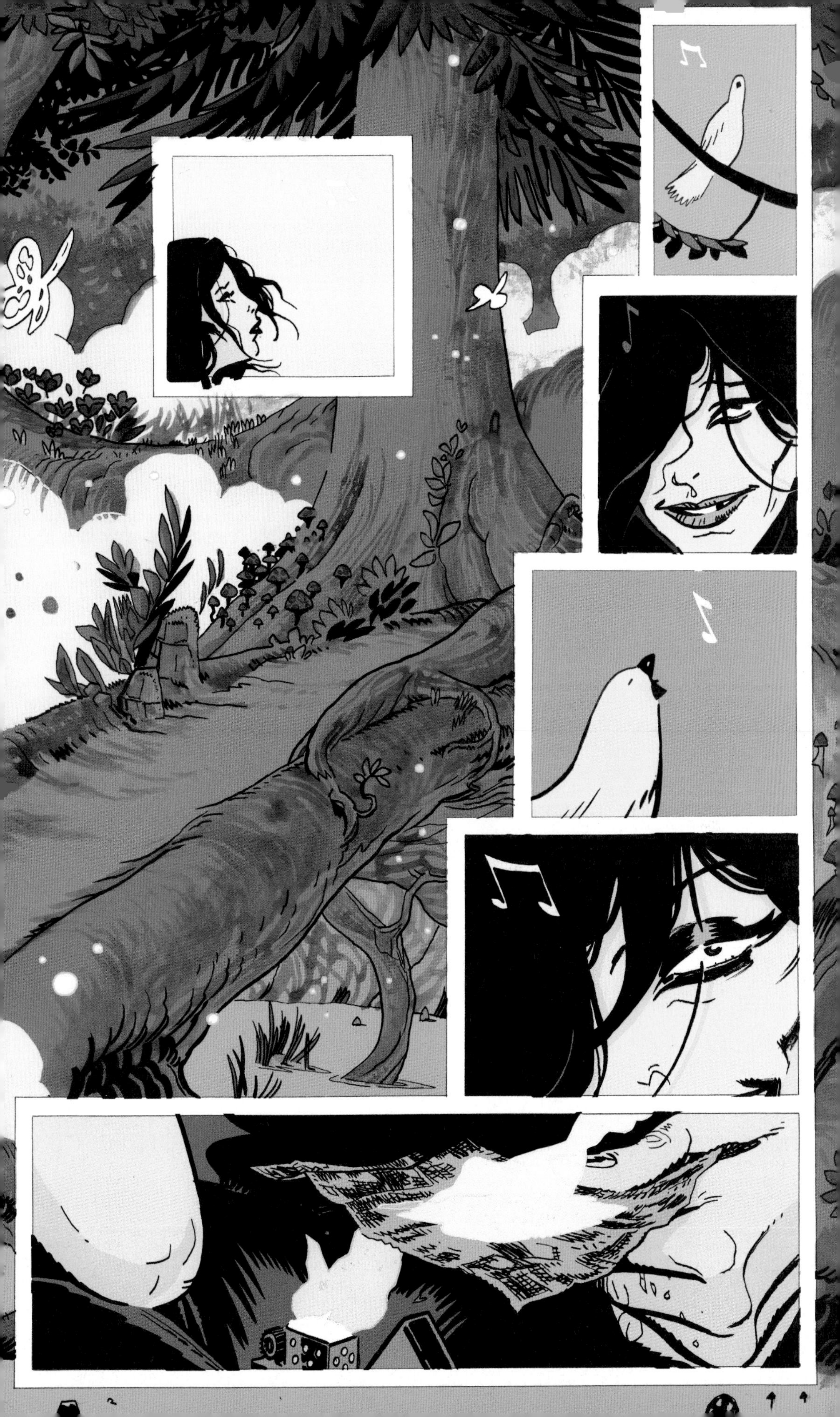

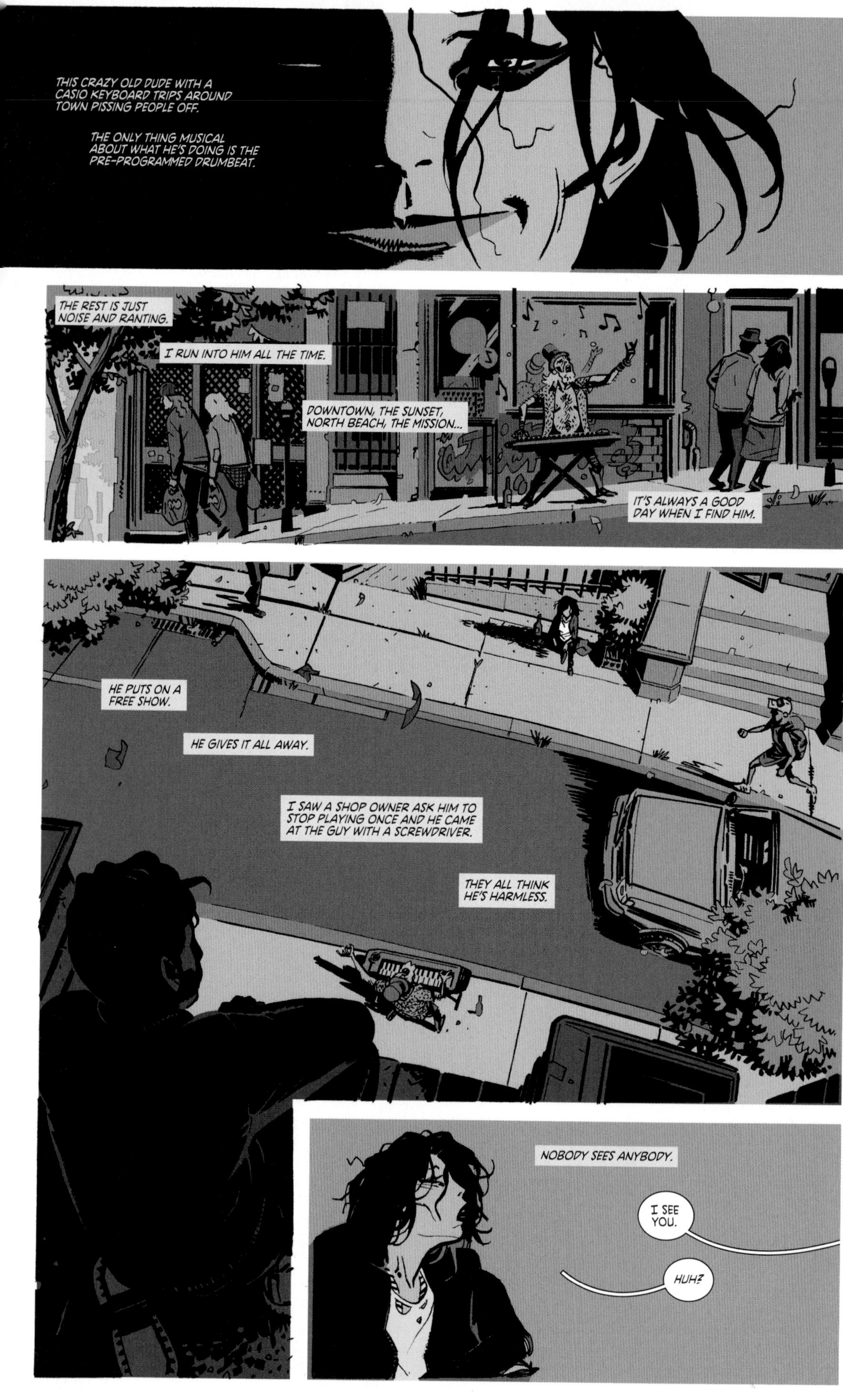

THIS CRAZY OLD DUDE WITH A CASIO KEYBOARD TRIPS AROUND TOWN PISSING PEOPLE OFF.
THE ONLY THING MUSICAL ABOUT WHAT HE'S DOING IS THE PRE-PROGRAMMED DRUMBEAT.
THE REST IS JUST NOISE AND RANTING.
I RUN INTO HIM ALL THE TIME.
DOWNTOWN, THE SUNSET, NORTH BEACH, THE MISSION...
IT'S ALWAYS A GOOD DAY WHEN I FIND HIM.
HE PUTS ON A FREE SHOW.
HE GIVES IT ALL AWAY.
I SAW A SHOP OWNER ASK HIM TO STOP PLAYING ONCE AND HE CAME AT THE GUY WITH A SCREWDRIVER.
THEY ALL THINK HE'S HARMLESS.
NOBODY SEES ANYBODY.
I SEE YOU.
HUH?

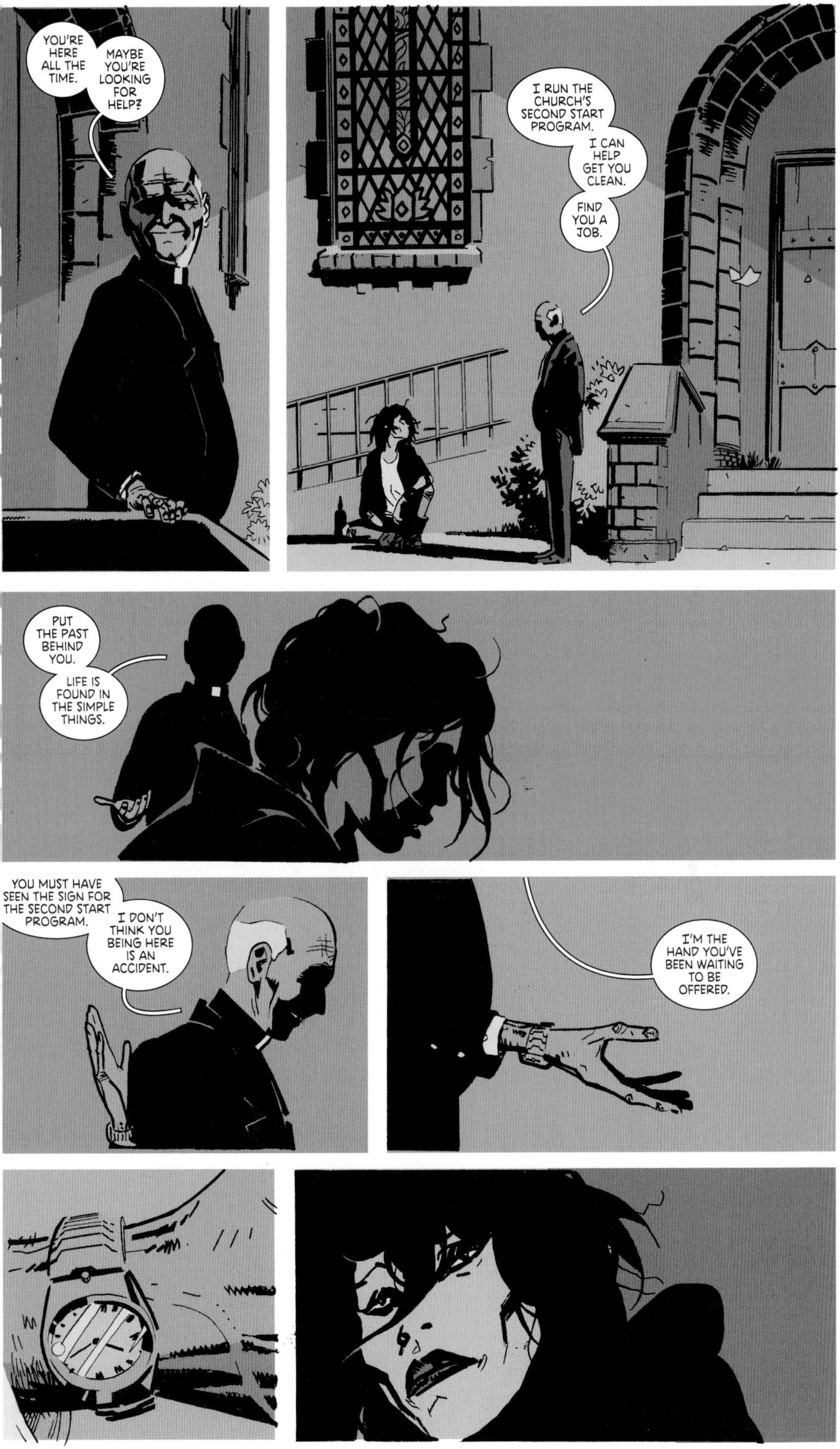
YOU'RE HERE ALL THE TIME.
MAYBE YOU'RE LOOKING FOR HELP?
I RUN THE CHURCH'S SECOND START PROGRAM.
I CAN HELP GET YOU CLEAN.
FIND YOU A JOB.
PUT THE PAST BEHIND YOU.
LIFE IS FOUND IN THE SIMPLE THINGS.
YOU MUST HAVE SEEN THE SIGN FOR THE SECOND START PROGRAM.
I DON'T THINK YOU BEING HERE IS AN ACCIDENT.
I'M THE HAND YOU'VE BEEN WAITING TO BE OFFERED.

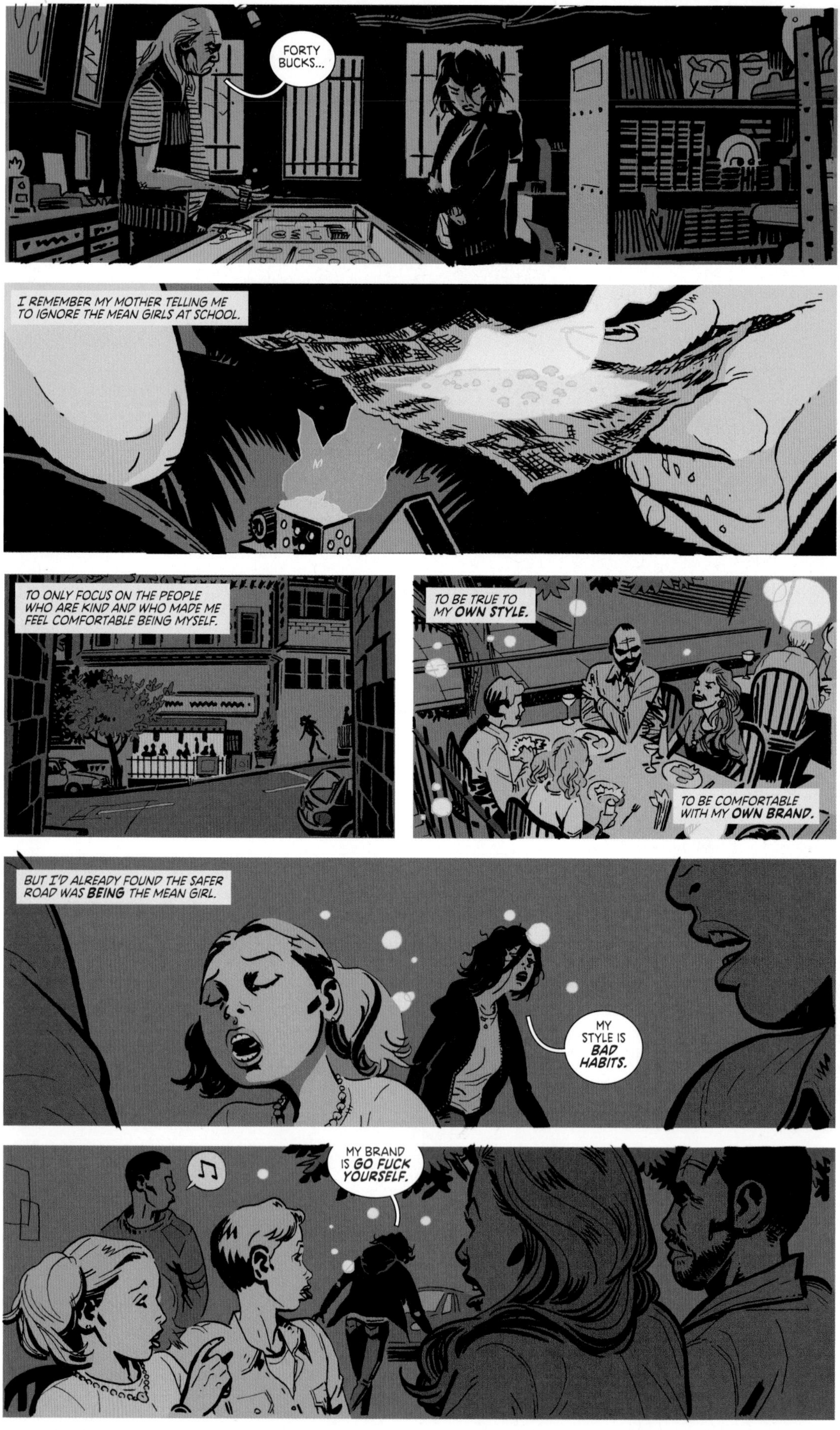
FORTY BUCKS...
I REMEMBER MY MOTHER TELLING ME TO IGNORE THE MEAN GIRLS AT SCHOOL.
TO ONLY FOCUS ON THE PEOPLE WHO ARE KIND AND WHO MADE ME FEEL COMFORTABLE BEING MYSELF.
TO BE TRUE TO MY **OWN STYLE.**
TO BE COMFORTABLE WITH MY **OWN BRAND.**
BUT I'D ALREADY FOUND THE SAFER ROAD WAS **BEING** THE MEAN GIRL.
MY STYLE IS **BAD HABITS.**
MY BRAND IS **GO FUCK YOURSELF.**

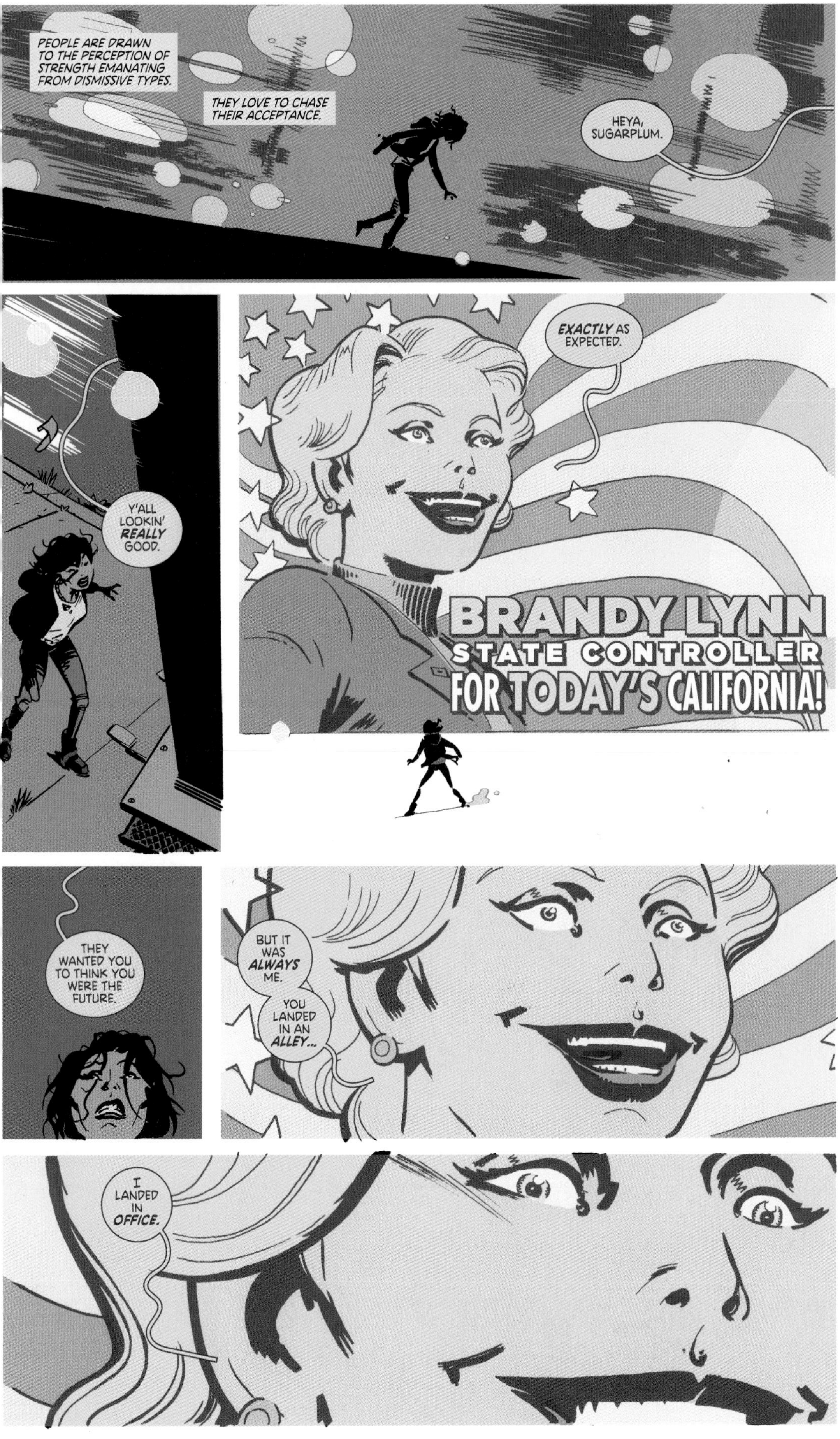
PEOPLE ARE DRAWN TO THE PERCEPTION OF STRENGTH EMANATING FROM DISMISSIVE TYPES.
THEY LOVE TO CHASE THEIR ACCEPTANCE.
HEYA, SUGARPLUM.
Y'ALL LOOKIN' REALLY GOOD.
EXACTLY AS EXPECTED.
BRANDY LYNN
STATE CONTROLLER
FOR TODAY'S CALIFORNIA!
THEY WANTED YOU TO THINK YOU WERE THE FUTURE.
BUT IT WAS ALWAYS ME.
YOU LANDED IN AN ALLEY...
I LANDED IN OFFICE.

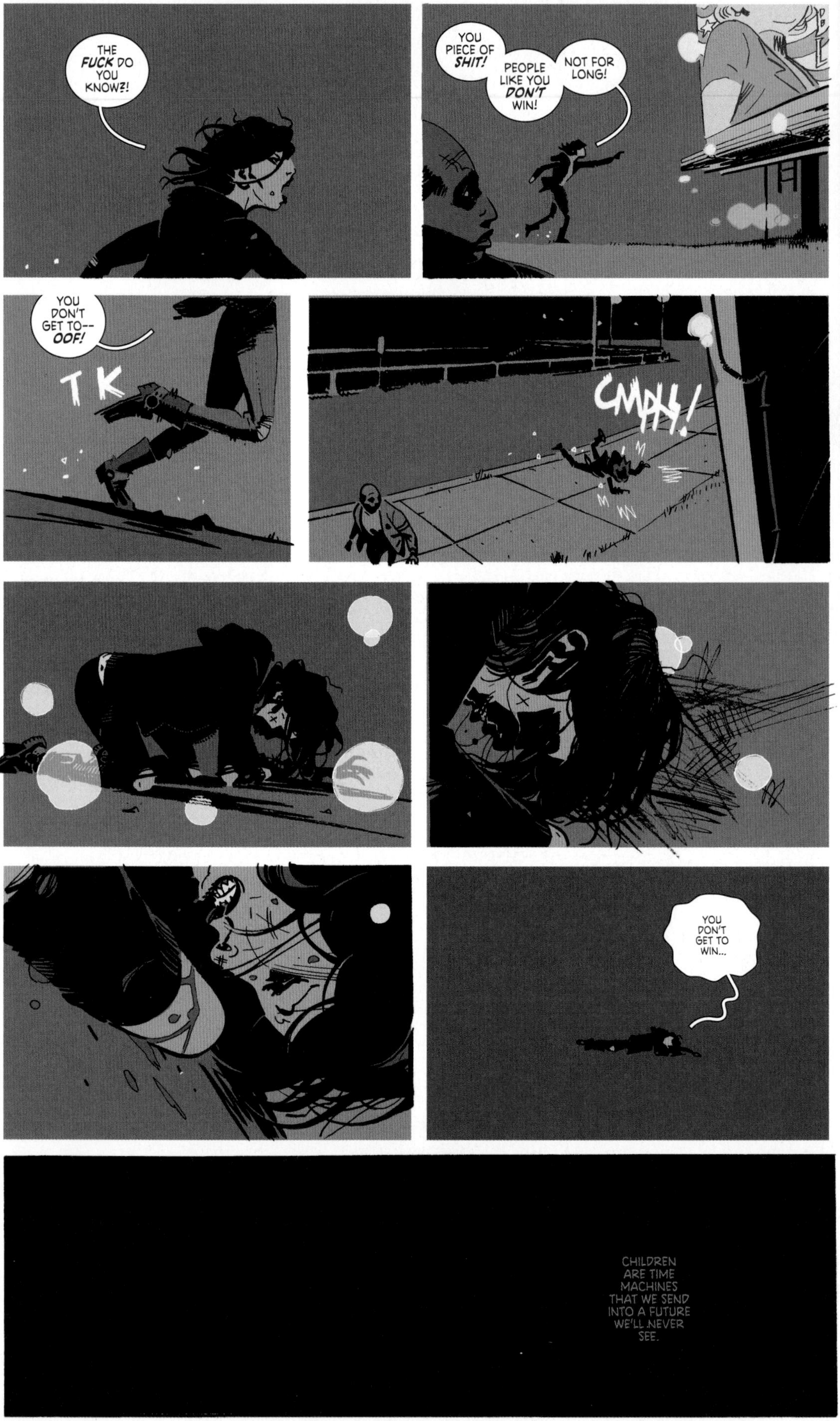
THE FUCK DO YOU KNOW?!
YOU PIECE OF SHIT!
PEOPLE LIKE YOU DON'T WIN!
NOT FOR LONG!
YOU DON'T GET TO-- OOF!
TK
CMPH!
YOU DON'T GET TO WIN...
CHILDREN ARE TIME MACHINES THAT WE SEND INTO A FUTURE WE'LL NEVER SEE.

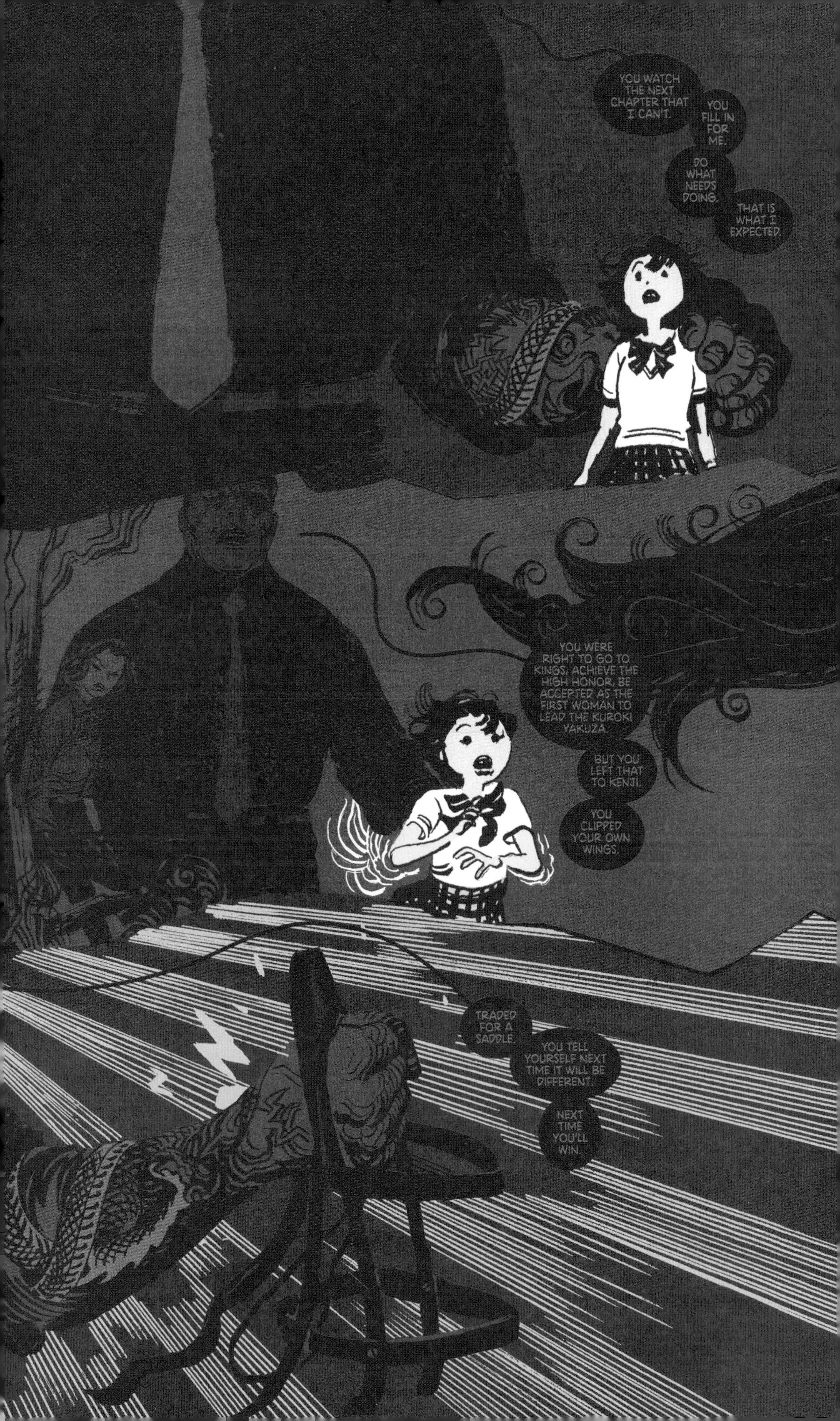

YOU WATCH THE NEXT CHAPTER THAT I CAN'T.
YOU FILL IN FOR ME.
DO WHAT NEEDS DOING.
THAT IS WHAT I EXPECTED.
YOU WERE RIGHT TO GO TO KINGS, ACHIEVE THE HIGH HONOR, BE ACCEPTED AS THE FIRST WOMAN TO LEAD THE KUROKI YAKUZA.
BUT YOU LEFT THAT TO KENJI.
YOU CLIPPED YOUR OWN WINGS.
TRADED FOR A SADDLE.
YOU TELL YOURSELF NEXT TIME IT WILL BE DIFFERENT.
NEXT TIME YOU'LL WIN.

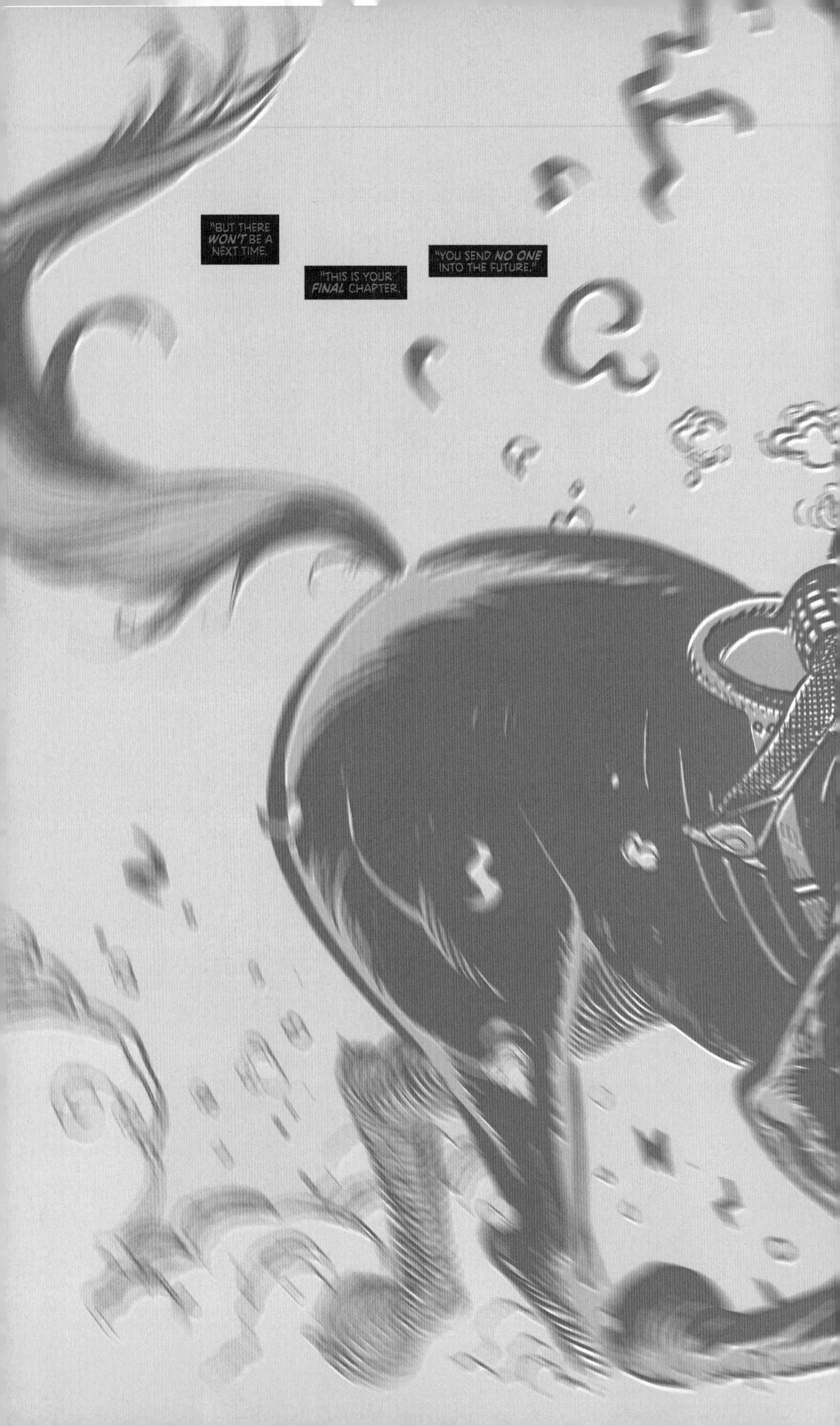
"BUT THERE WON'T BE A NEXT TIME.
"THIS IS YOUR FINAL CHAPTER.
"YOU SEND NO ONE INTO THE FUTURE."

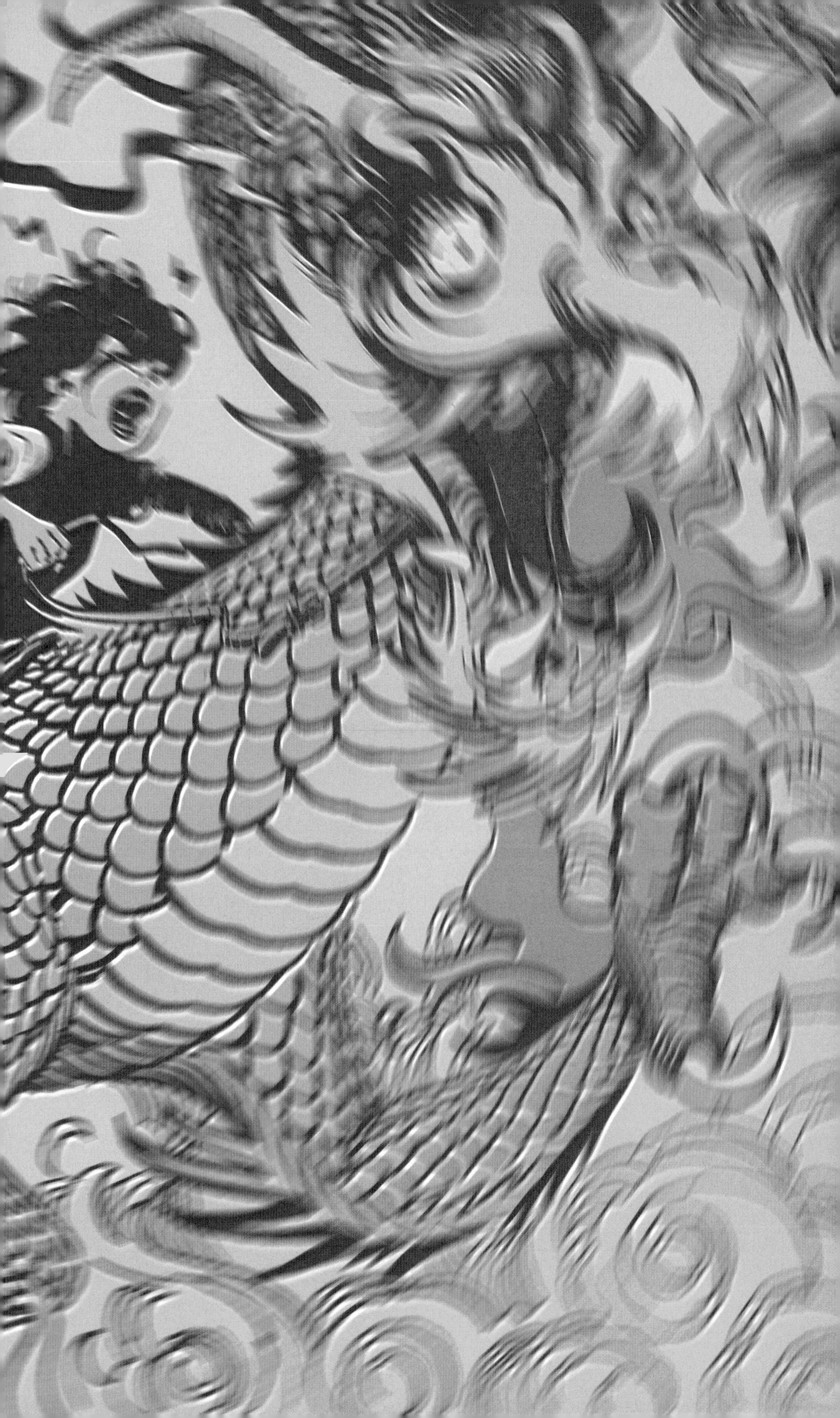

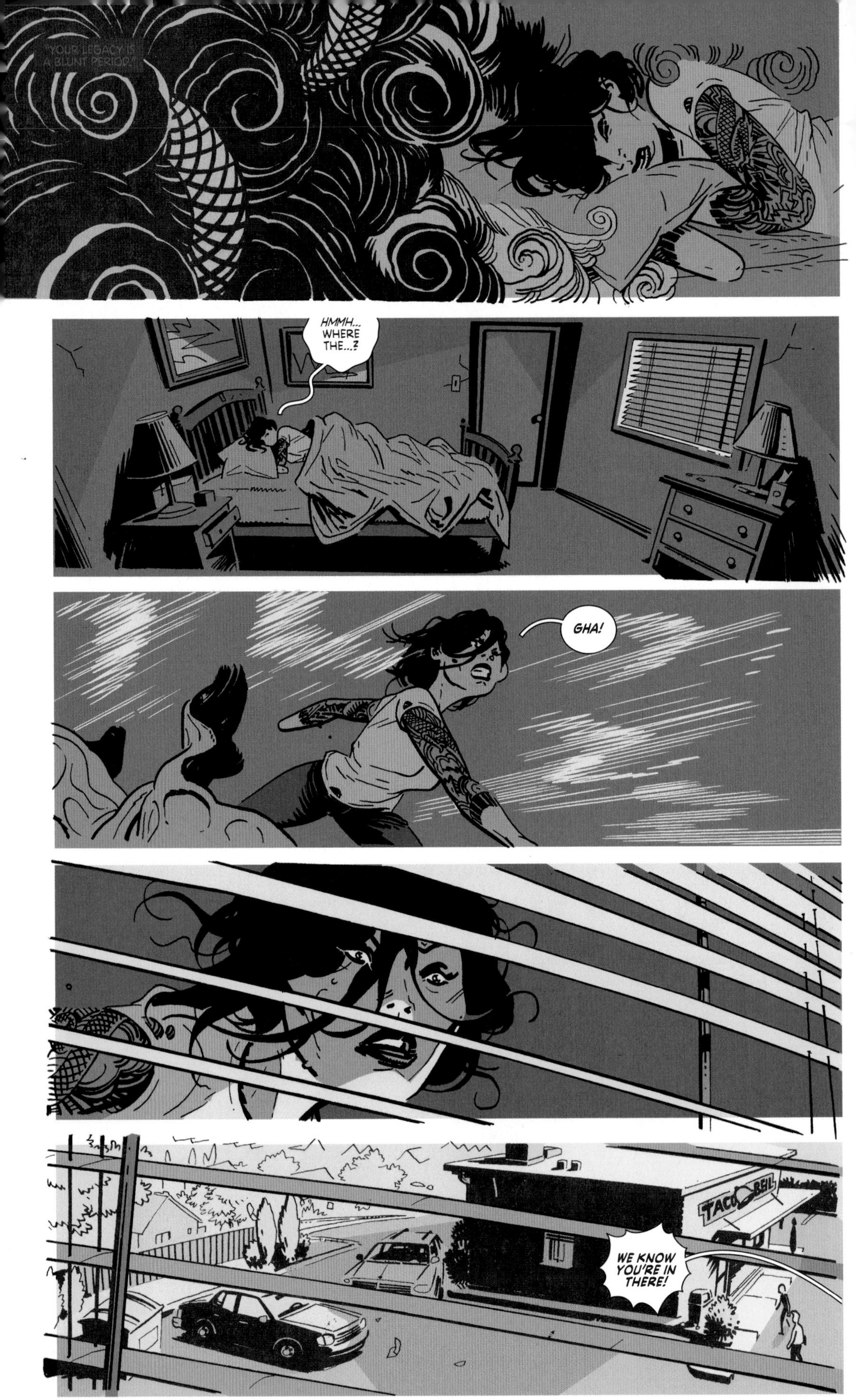
"YOUR LEGACY IS A BLUNT PERIOD."
HMMH... WHERE THE...?
GHA!
WE KNOW YOU'RE IN THERE!

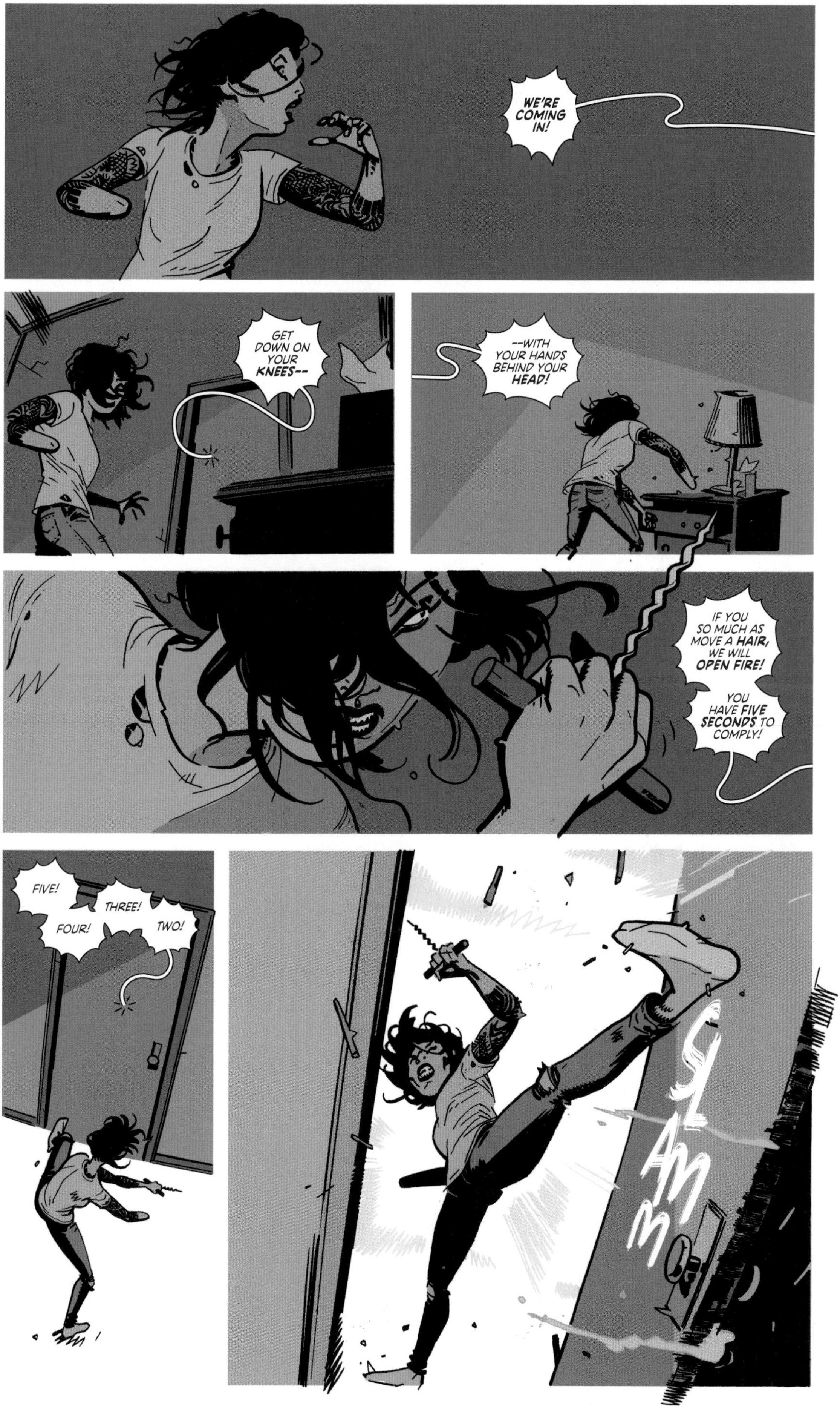
WE'RE COMING IN!
GET DOWN ON YOUR KNEES--
--WITH YOUR HANDS BEHIND YOUR HEAD!
IF YOU SO MUCH AS MOVE A HAIR, WE WILL OPEN FIRE!
YOU HAVE FIVE SECONDS TO COMPLY!
FIVE!
FOUR!
THREE!
TWO!
SLAMM

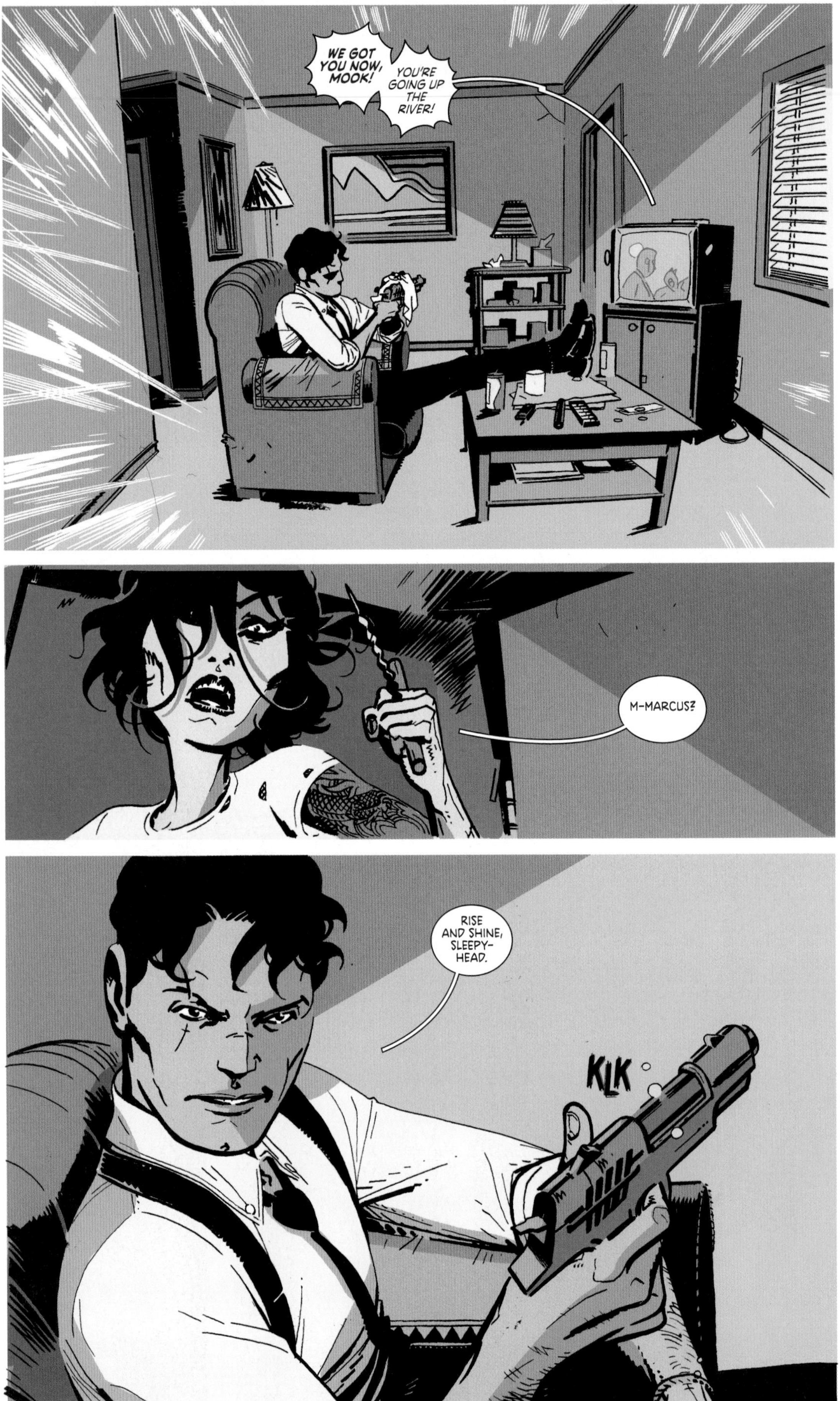
WE GOT YOU NOW, MOOK!
YOU'RE GOING UP THE RIVER!
M-MARCUS?
RISE AND SHINE, SLEEPY-HEAD.
KLK

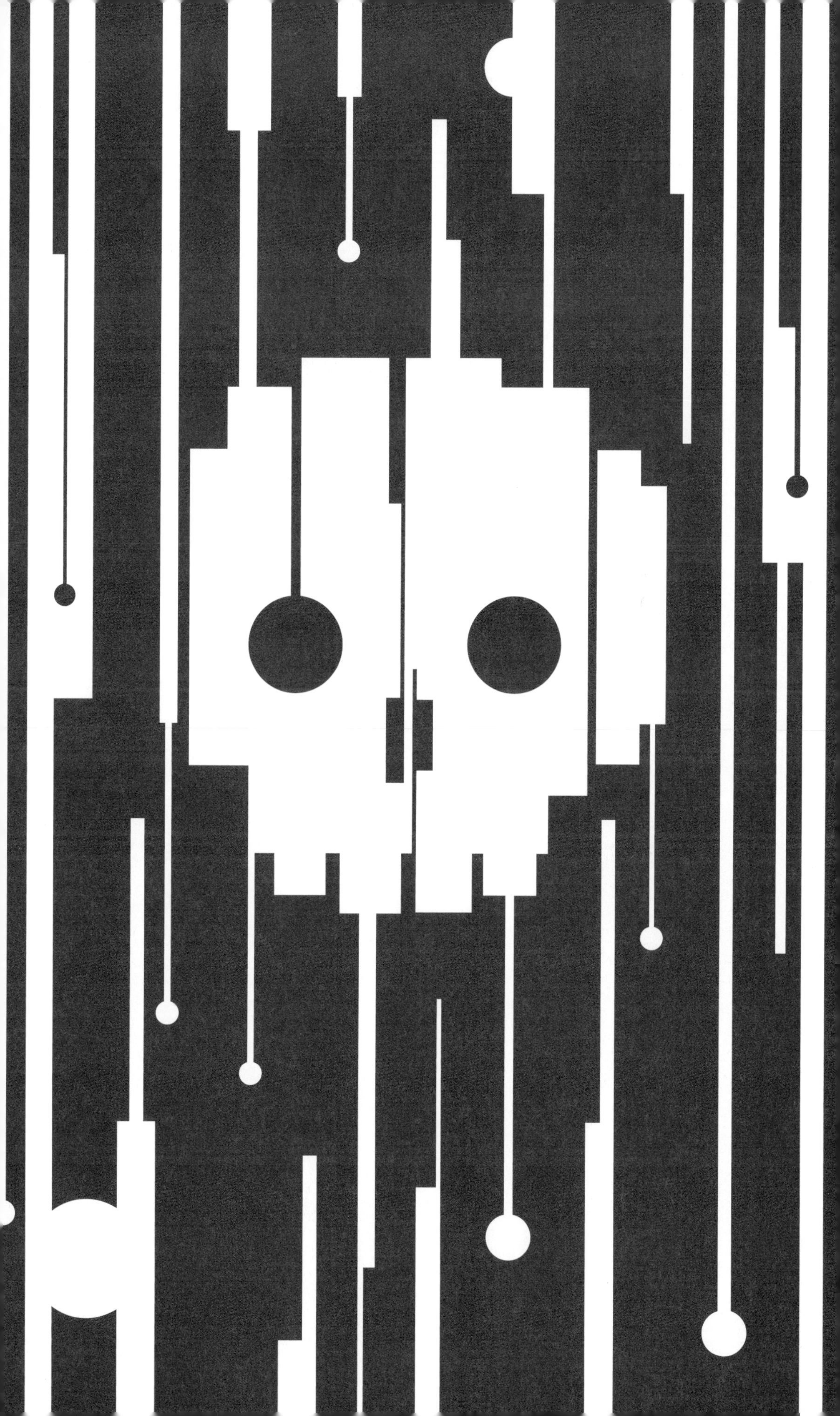

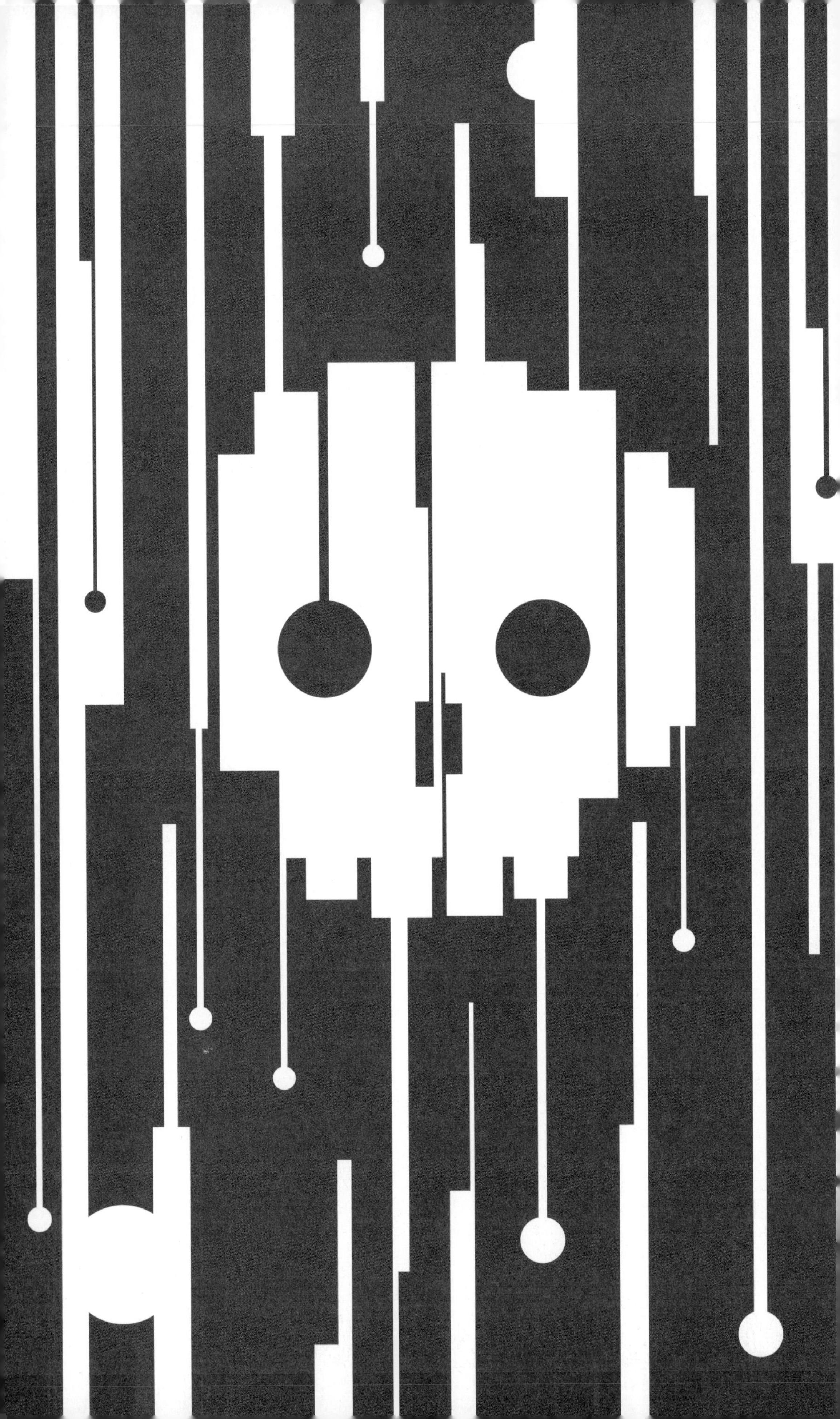

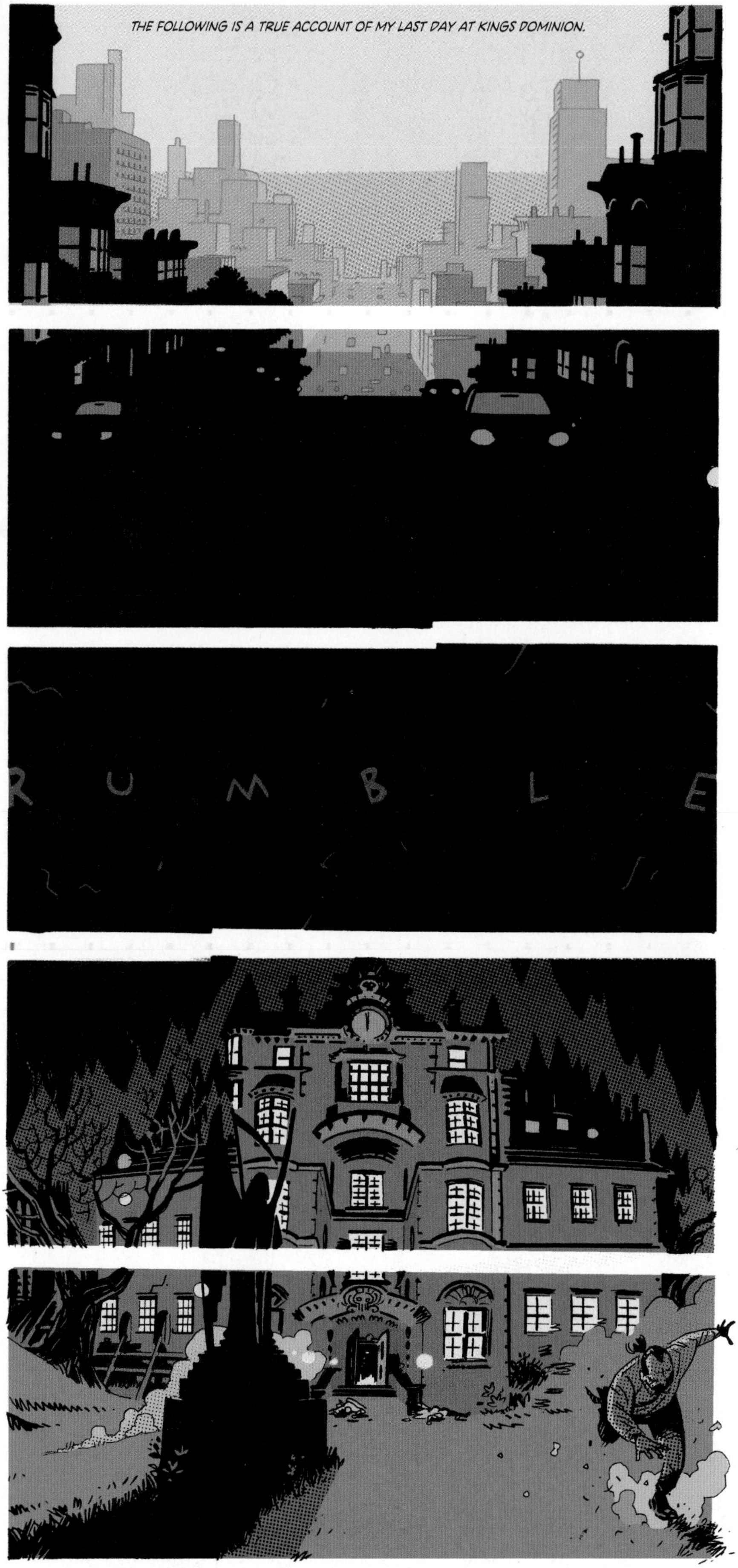
THE FOLLOWING IS A TRUE ACCOUNT OF MY LAST DAY AT KINGS DOMINION.
R U M B L E

A DAY I'D SPENT THE ENTIRE PREVIOUS YEAR PLANNING.

BUT, OF COURSE, NONE OF IT FOLLOWED MY BLUEPRINT.

LIKE DAD USED TO SAY, "MAN PLANS, GOD LAUGHS."

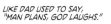

BUT, SOMEHOW, IT ALL ENDED THE WAY I'D EXPECTED.

I'D GO SO FAR AS TO SAY IT ENDED THE WAY I'D HOPED.

IT ENDED SAME AS IT BEGAN...

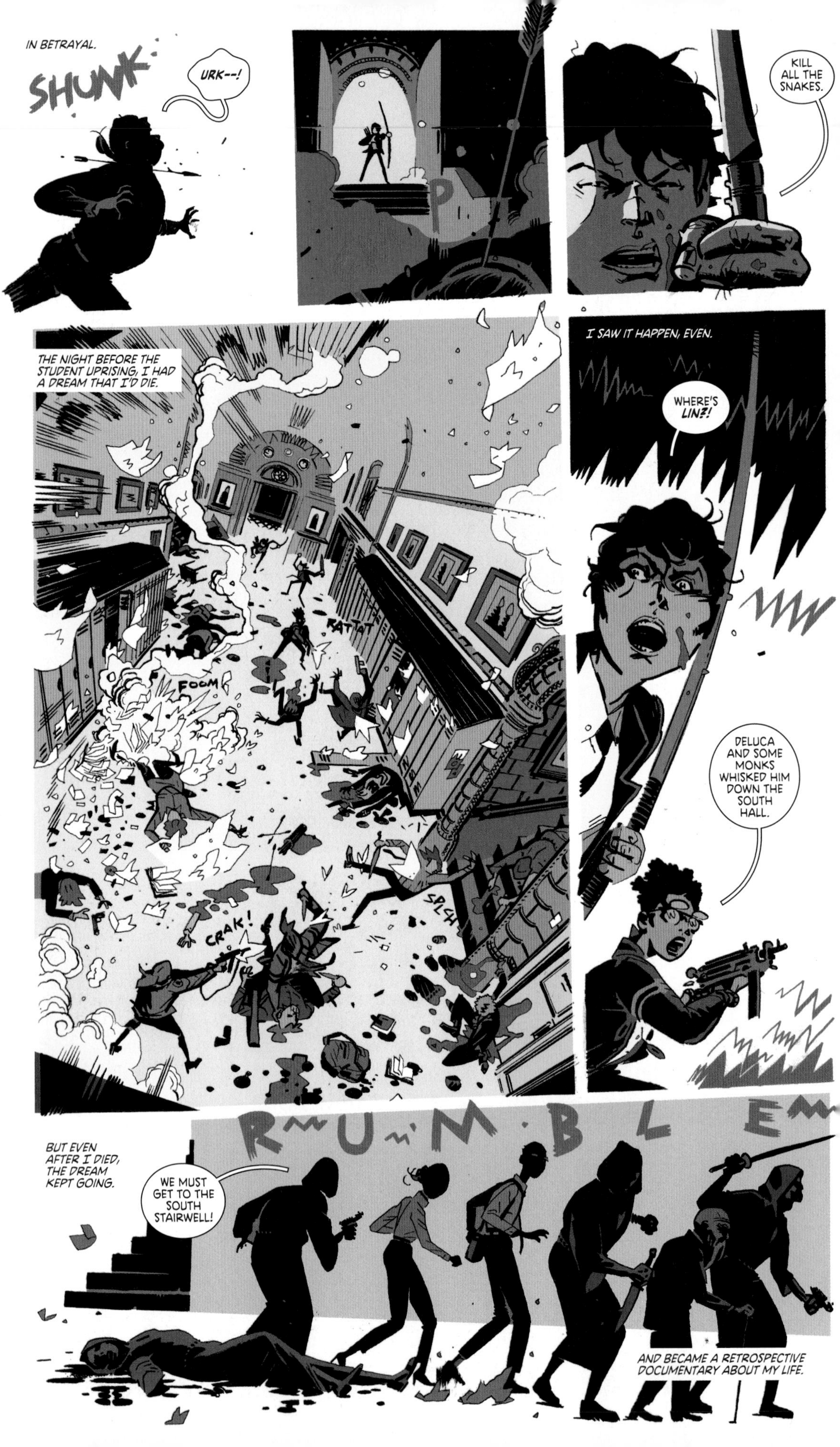
IN BETRAYAL.
SHUNK
URK--!
KILL ALL THE SNAKES.
THE NIGHT BEFORE THE STUDENT UPRISING, I HAD A DREAM THAT I'D DIE.
RATTAT
FOOM
CRAK!
SPLCH
I SAW IT HAPPEN, EVEN.
WHERE'S LIN?!
DELUCA AND SOME MONKS WHISKED HIM DOWN THE SOUTH HALL.
RUMBLE
BUT EVEN AFTER I DIED, THE DREAM KEPT GOING.
WE MUST GET TO THE SOUTH STAIRWELL!
AND BECAME A RETROSPECTIVE DOCUMENTARY ABOUT MY LIFE.

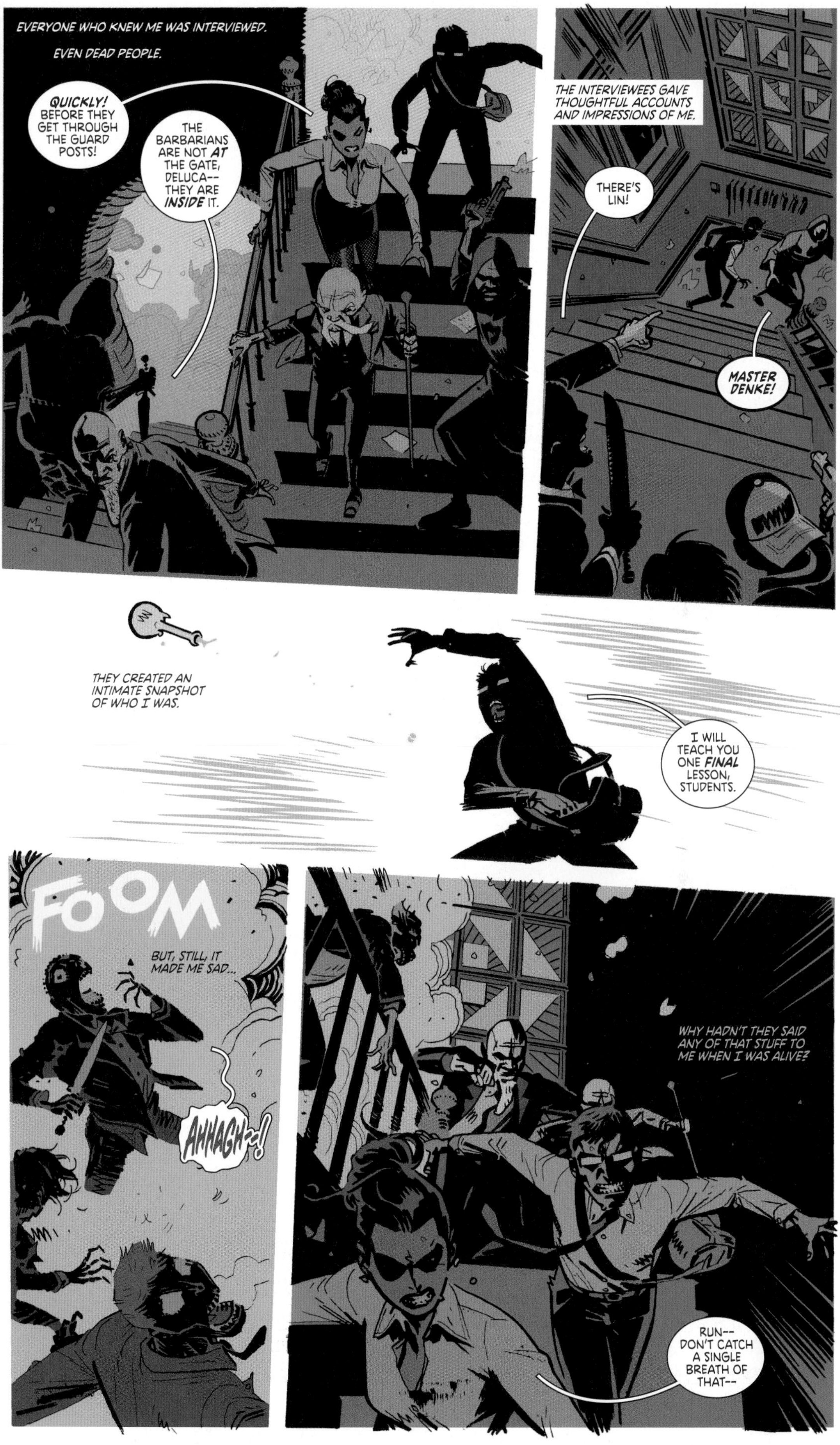
EVERYONE WHO KNEW ME WAS INTERVIEWED.
EVEN DEAD PEOPLE.
QUICKLY! BEFORE THEY GET THROUGH THE GUARD POSTS!
THE BARBARIANS ARE NOT AT THE GATE, DELUCA-- THEY ARE INSIDE IT.
THE INTERVIEWEES GAVE THOUGHTFUL ACCOUNTS AND IMPRESSIONS OF ME.
THERE'S LIN!
MASTER DENKE!
THEY CREATED AN INTIMATE SNAPSHOT OF WHO I WAS.
I WILL TEACH YOU ONE FINAL LESSON, STUDENTS.
FOOM
BUT, STILL, IT MADE ME SAD...
AHHAGH--!
WHY HADN'T THEY SAID ANY OF THAT STUFF TO ME WHEN I WAS ALIVE?
RUN-- DON'T CATCH A SINGLE BREATH OF THAT--

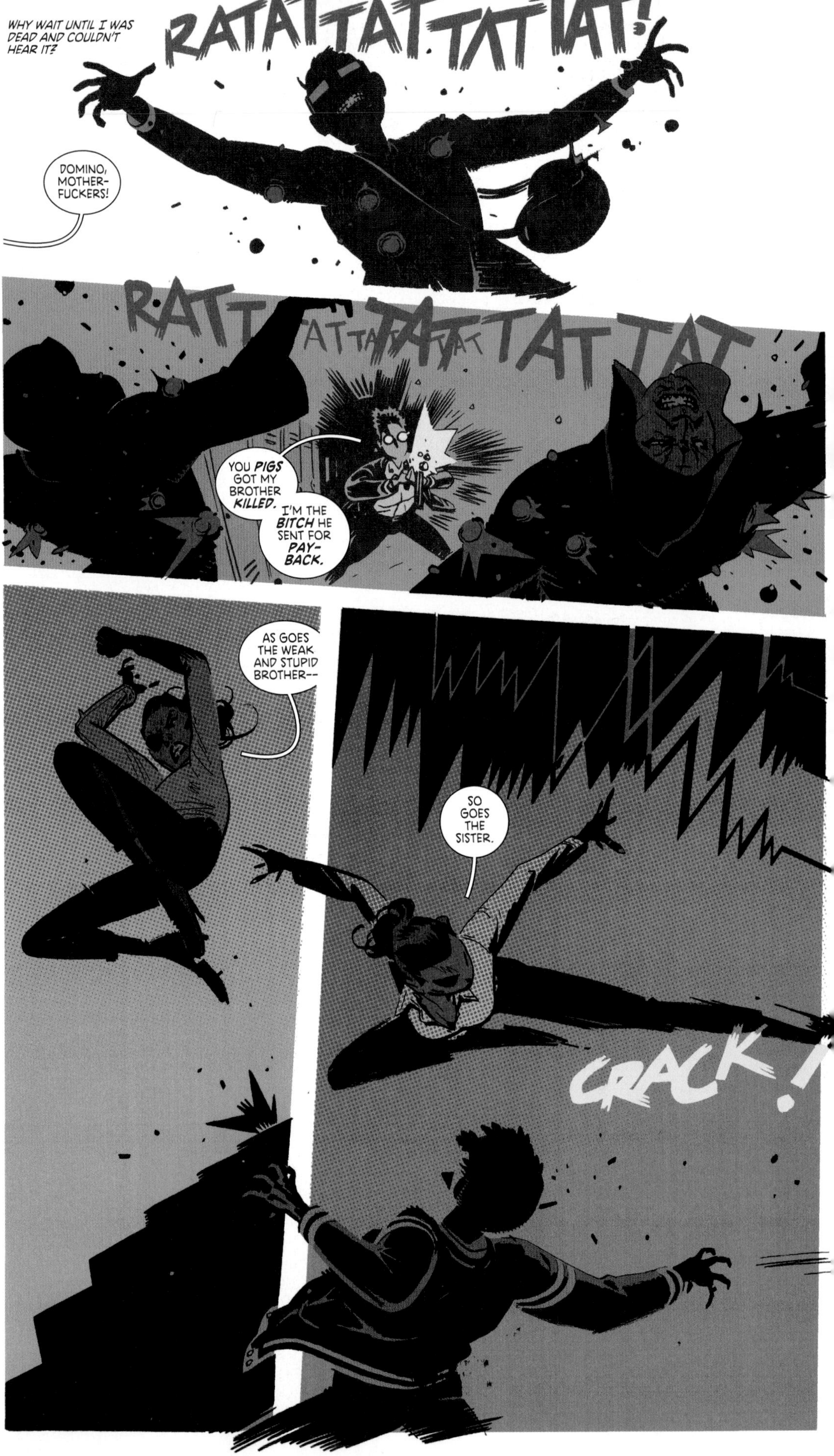
WHY WAIT UNTIL I WAS DEAD AND COULDN'T HEAR IT?
RATATTATTATTAT!
DOMINO, MOTHER-FUCKERS!
RATTATTATTATTATTAT
YOU PIGS GOT MY BROTHER KILLED.
I'M THE BITCH HE SENT FOR PAY-BACK.
AS GOES THE WEAK AND STUPID BROTHER--
SO GOES THE SISTER.
CRACK!

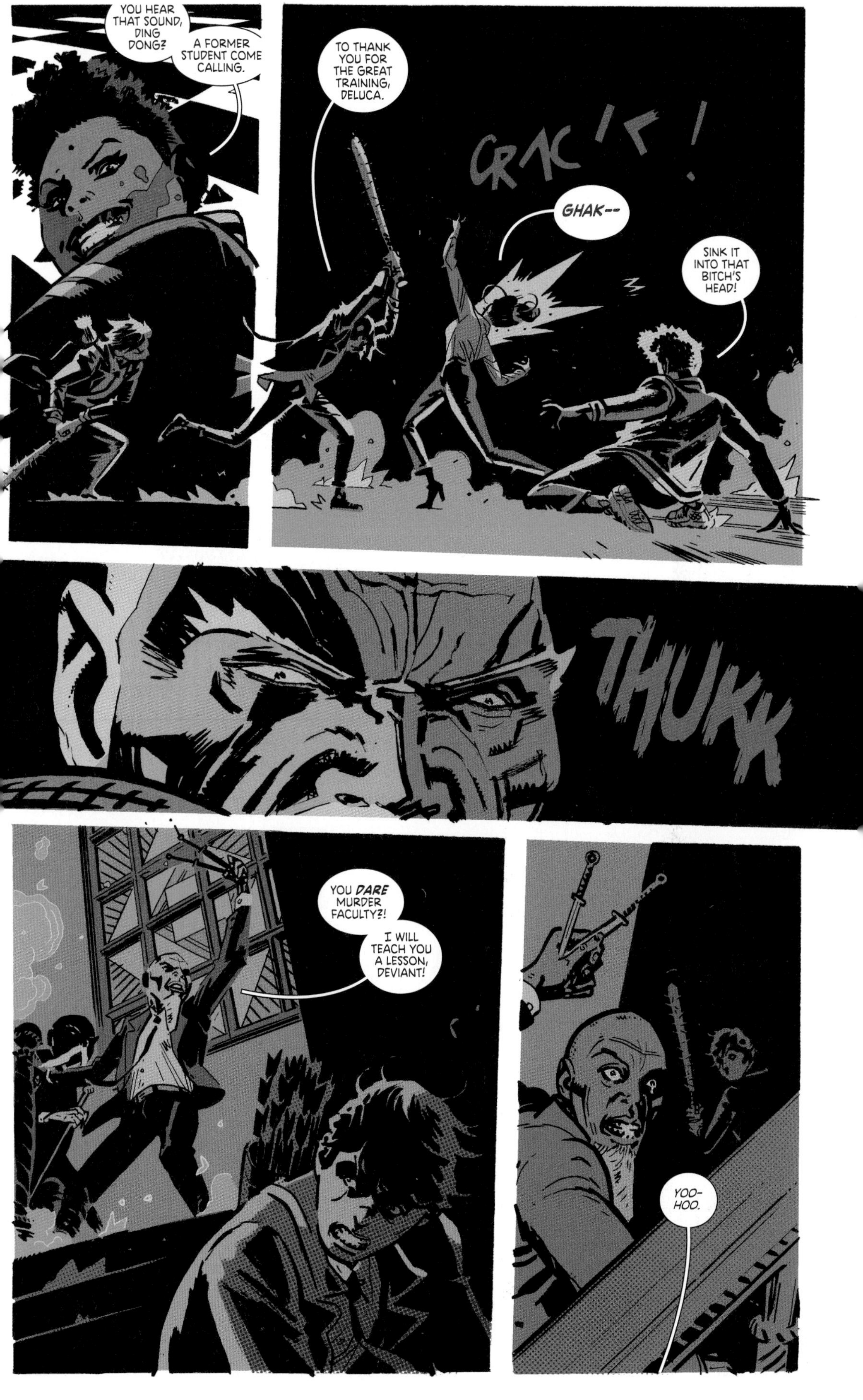
YOU HEAR THAT SOUND, DING DONG?
A FORMER STUDENT COME CALLING.
TO THANK YOU FOR THE GREAT TRAINING, DELUCA.
CRACK!
GHAK--
SINK IT INTO THAT BITCH'S HEAD!
THUKK
YOU DARE MURDER FACULTY?!
I WILL TEACH YOU A LESSON, DEVIANT!
YOO-HOO.

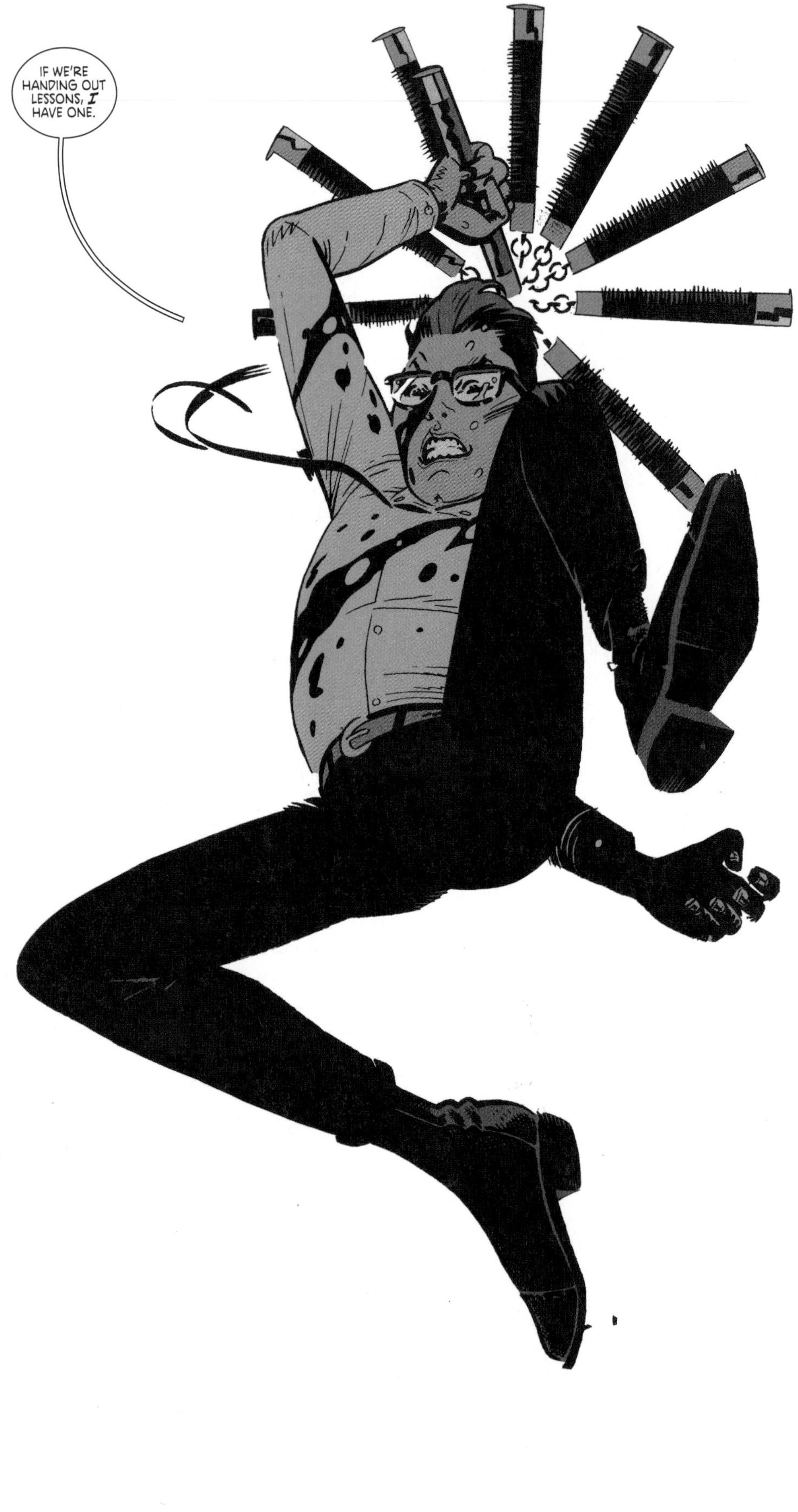
IF WE'RE HANDING OUT LESSONS, I HAVE ONE.

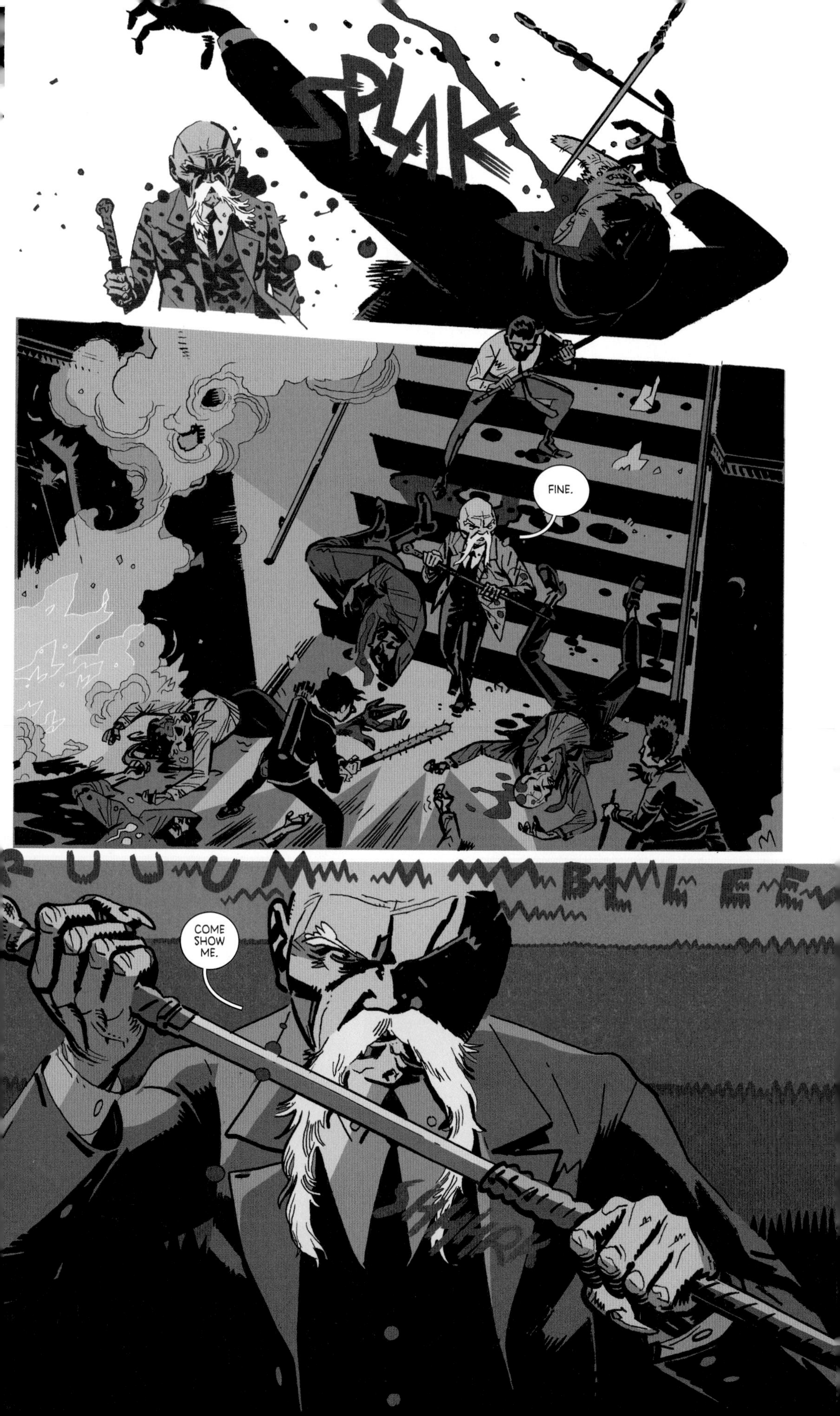
SPLAK
FINE.
COME SHOW ME.

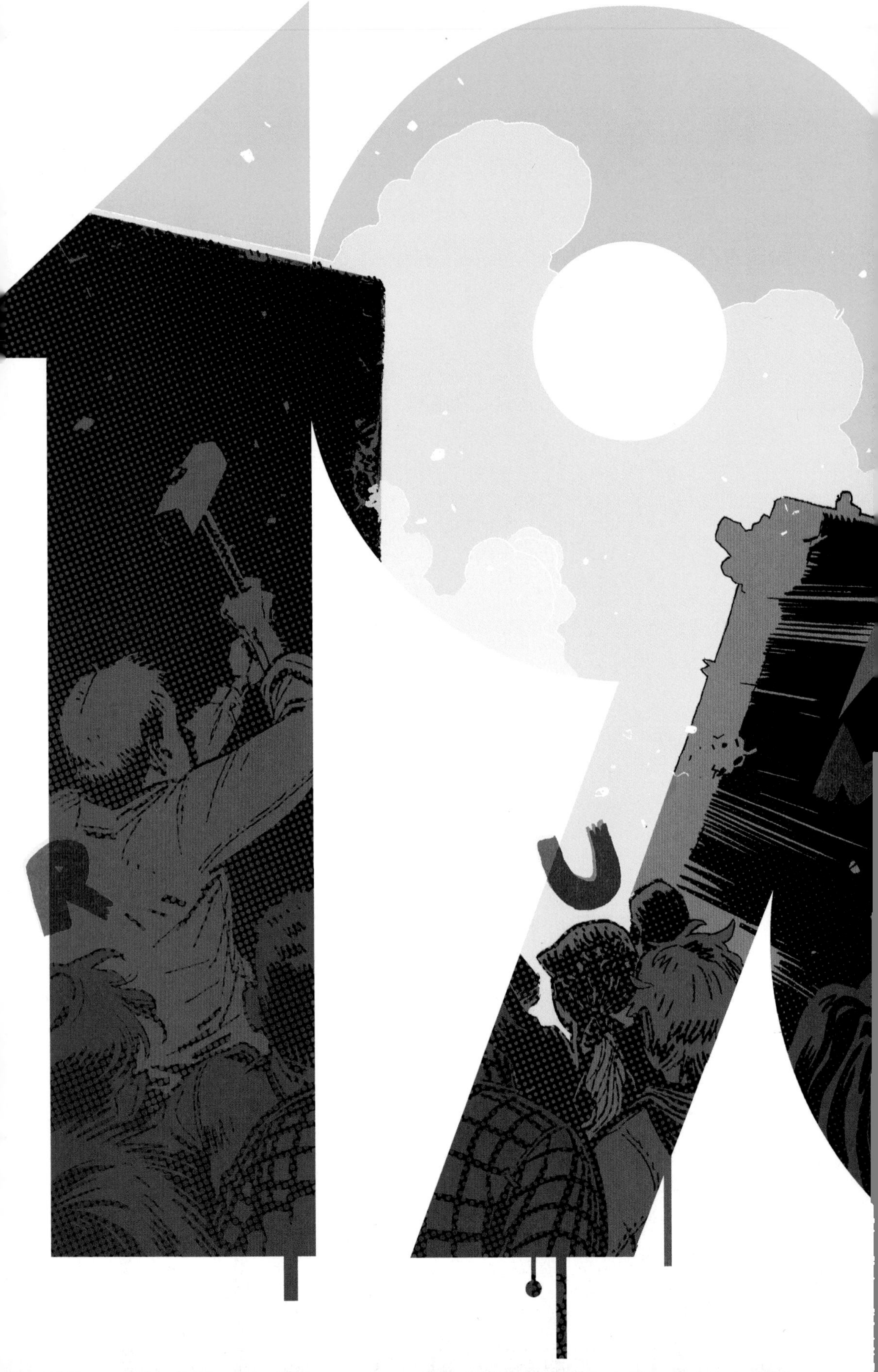
19

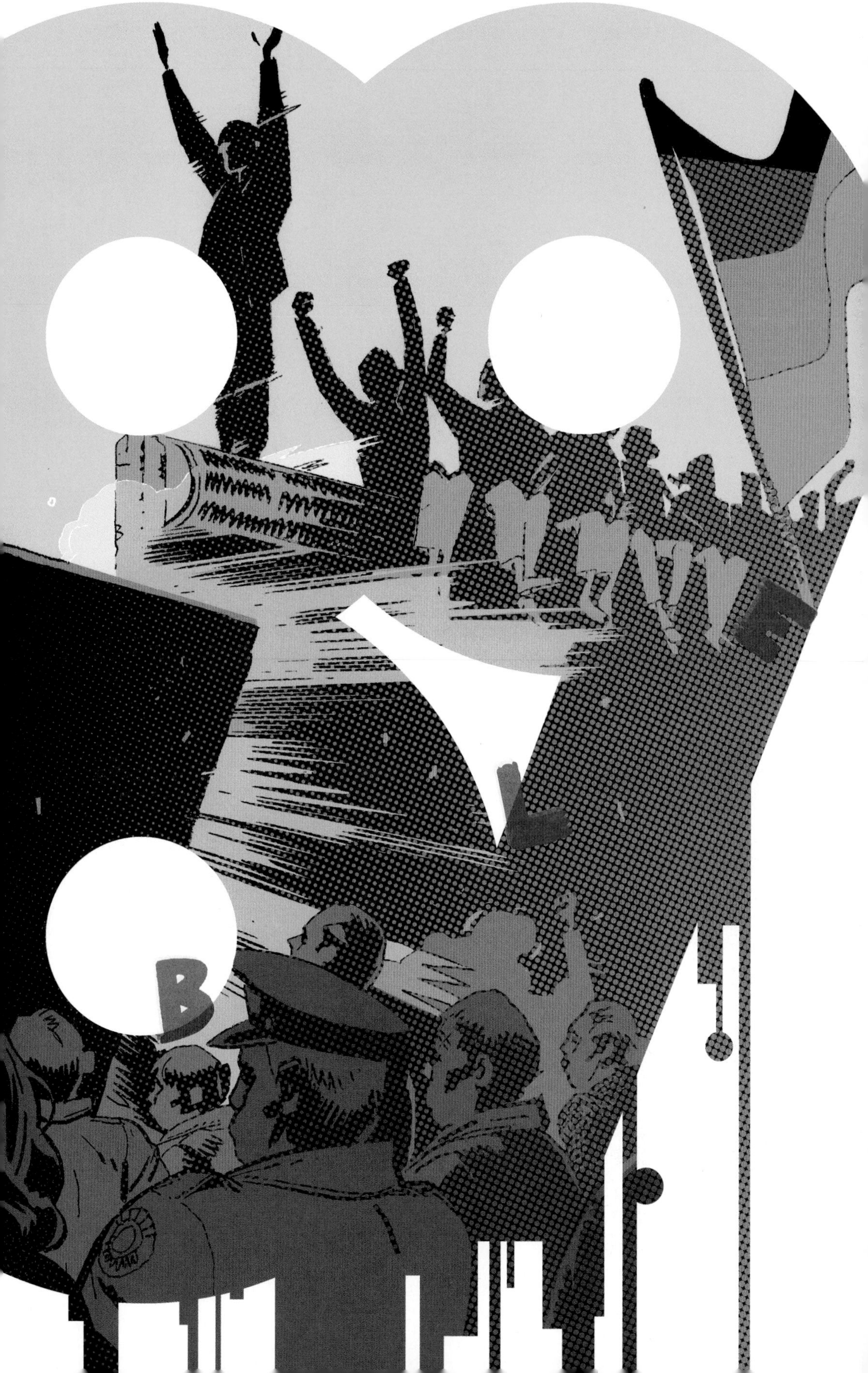

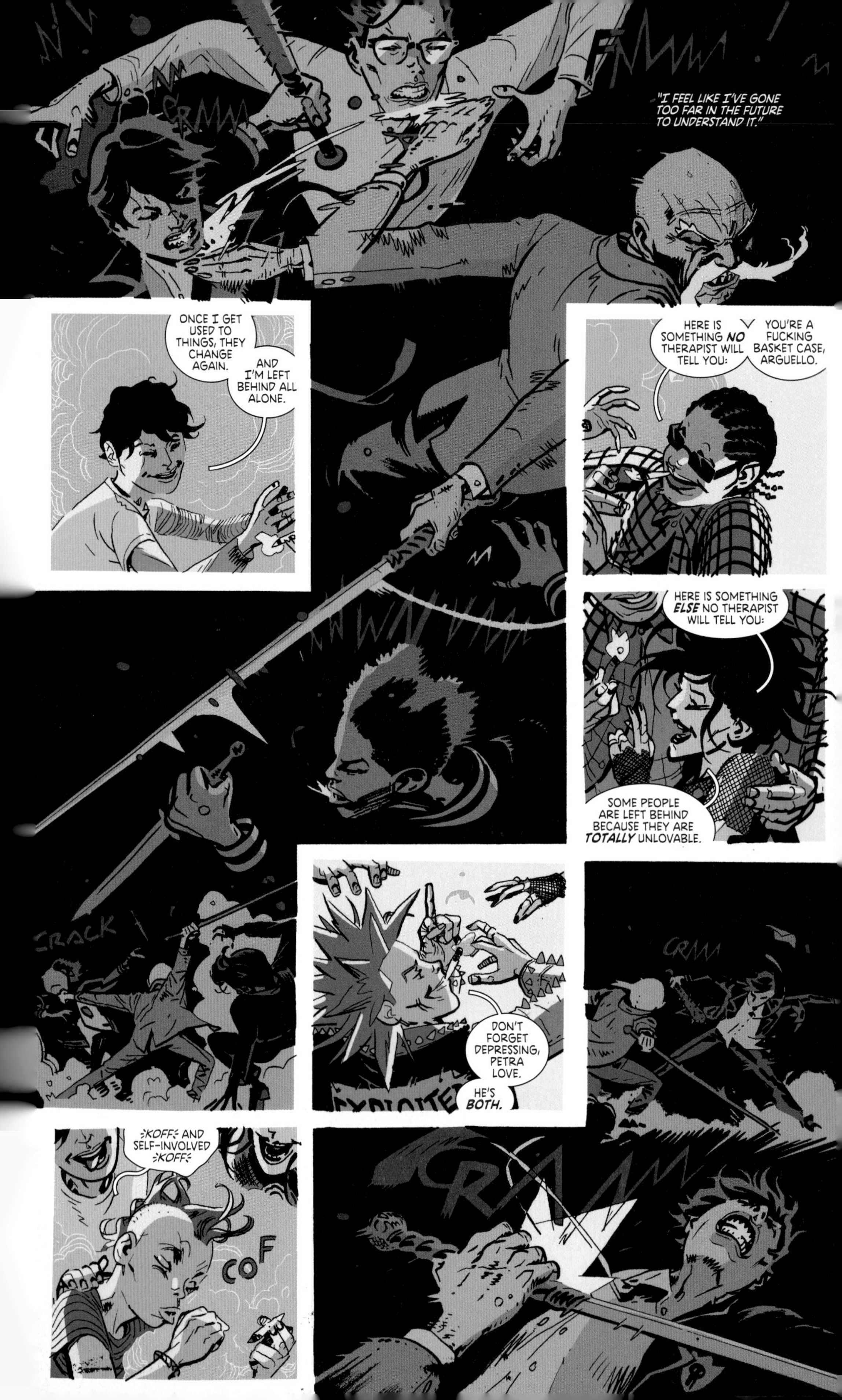
"I FEEL LIKE I'VE GONE TOO FAR IN THE FUTURE TO UNDERSTAND IT."
ONCE I GET USED TO THINGS, THEY CHANGE AGAIN.
AND I'M LEFT BEHIND ALL ALONE.
HERE IS SOMETHING NO THERAPIST WILL TELL YOU:
YOU'RE A FUCKING BASKET CASE, ARGUELLO.
HERE IS SOMETHING ELSE NO THERAPIST WILL TELL YOU:
SOME PEOPLE ARE LEFT BEHIND BECAUSE THEY ARE TOTALLY UNLOVABLE.
CRACK
DON'T FORGET DEPRESSING, PETRA LOVE.
HE'S BOTH.
CRAM
KOFF AND SELF-INVOLVED *KOFF*
COF
CRAM

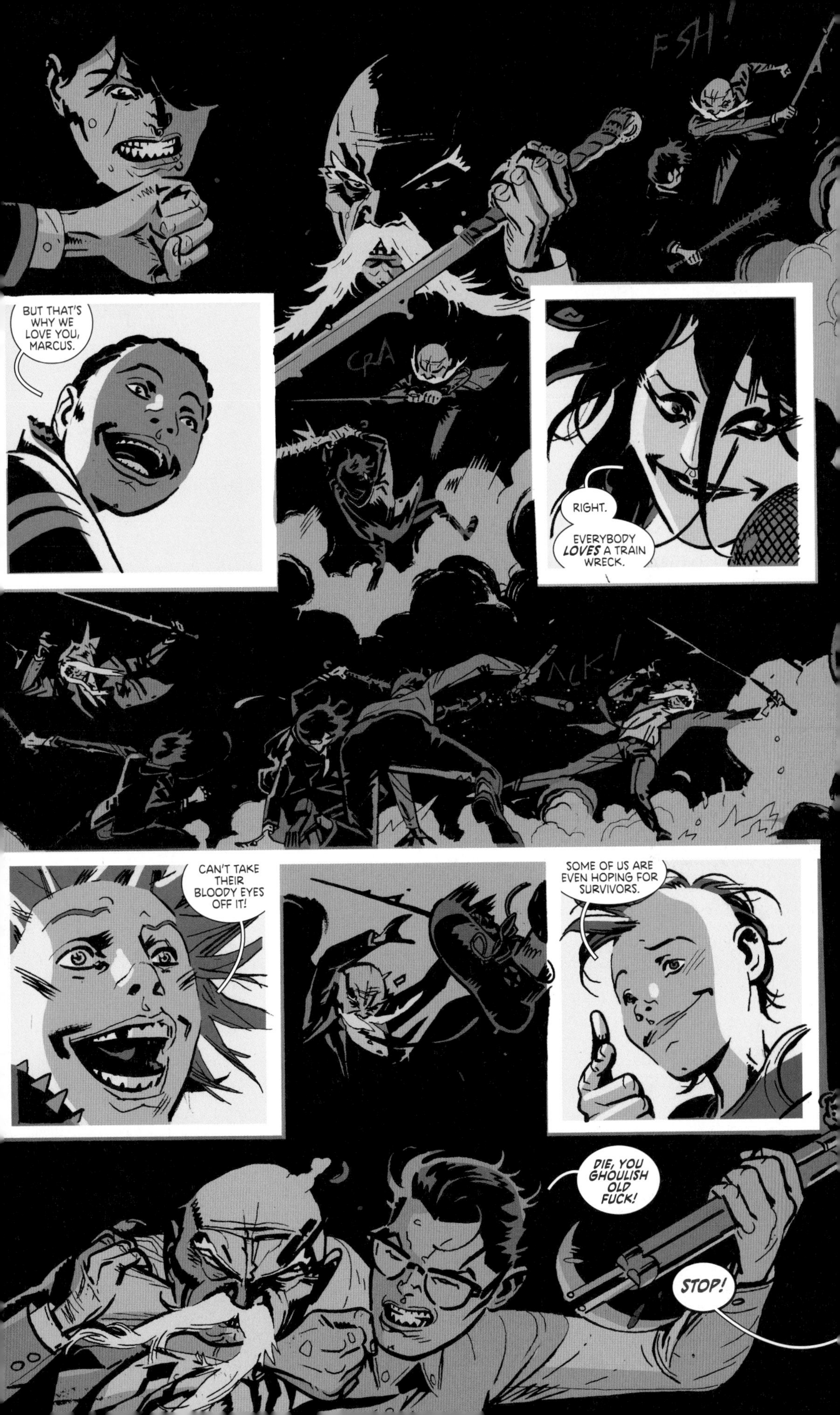
FSH!
BUT THAT'S WHY WE LOVE YOU, MARCUS.
CRA
RIGHT.
EVERYBODY *LOVES* A TRAIN WRECK.
ACK!
CAN'T TAKE THEIR BLOODY EYES OFF IT!
SOME OF US ARE EVEN HOPING FOR SURVIVORS.
DIE, YOU GHOULISH OLD FUCK!
STOP!

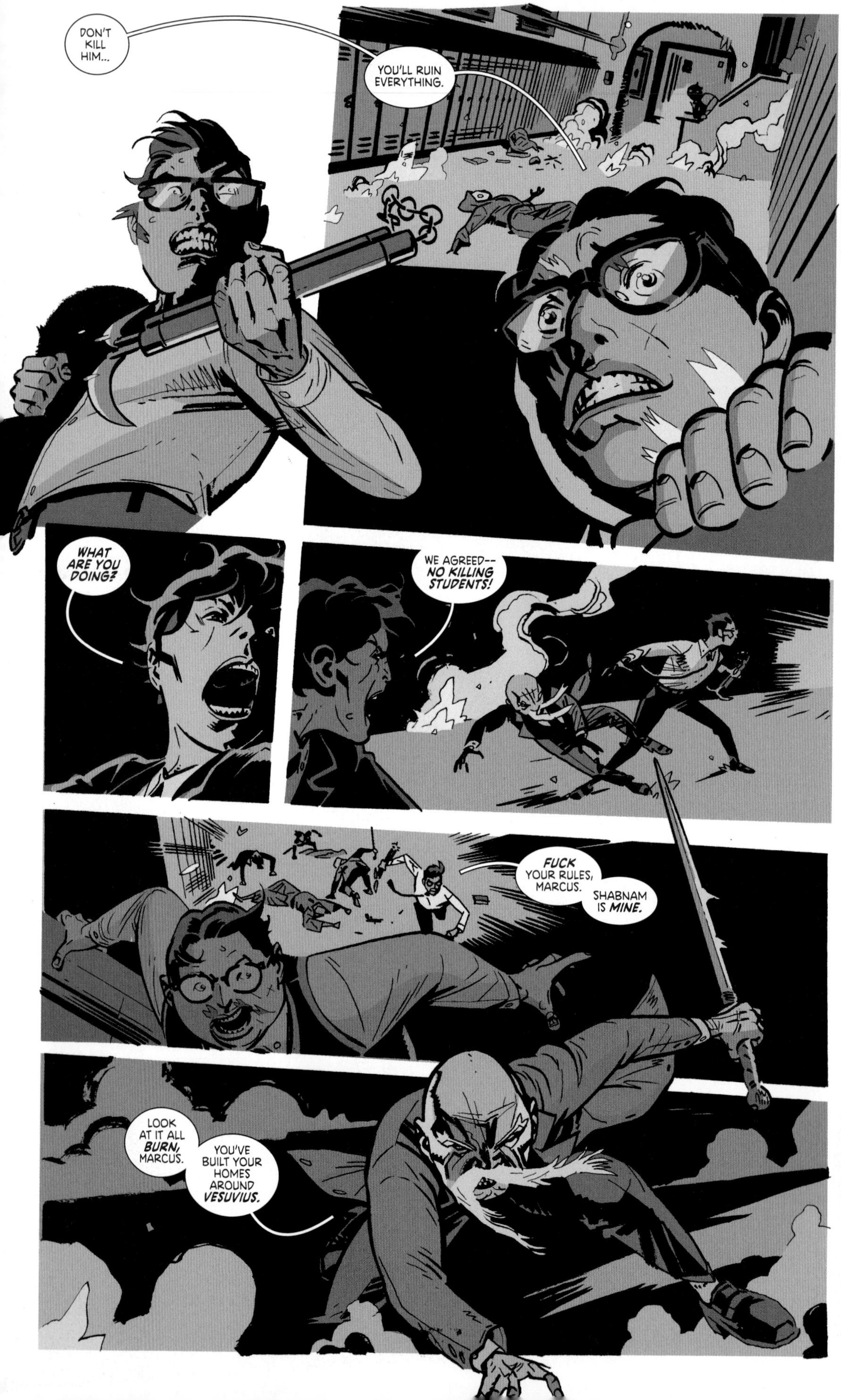
DON'T KILL HIM...
YOU'LL RUIN EVERYTHING.
WHAT ARE YOU DOING?
WE AGREED-- NO KILLING STUDENTS!
FUCK YOUR RULES, MARCUS.
SHABNAM IS MINE.
LOOK AT IT ALL BURN, MARCUS.
YOU'VE BUILT YOUR HOMES AROUND VESUVIUS.

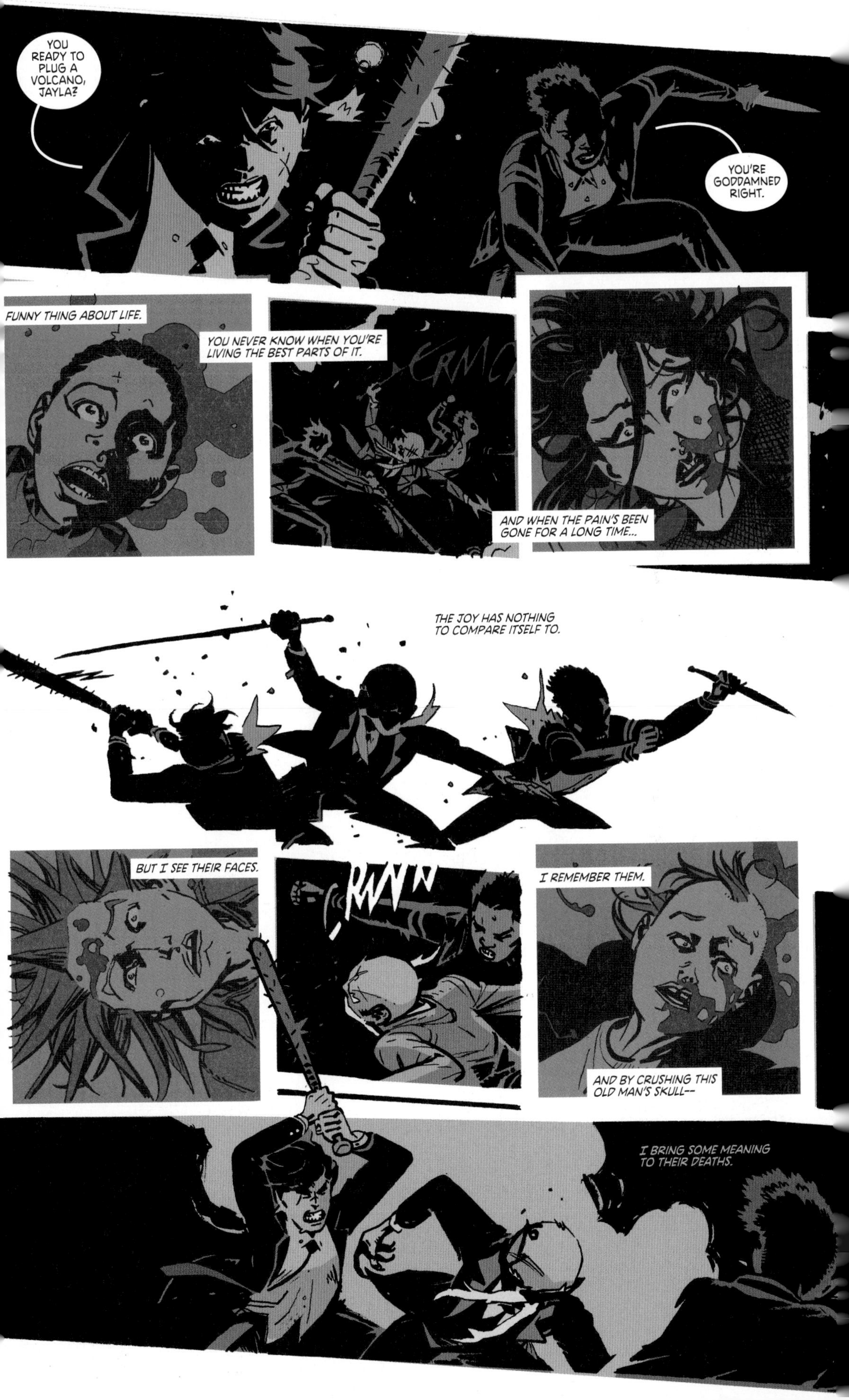
YOU READY TO PLUG A VOLCANO, JAYLA?
YOU'RE GODDAMNED RIGHT.
FUNNY THING ABOUT LIFE.
YOU NEVER KNOW WHEN YOU'RE LIVING THE BEST PARTS OF IT.
AND WHEN THE PAIN'S BEEN GONE FOR A LONG TIME...
THE JOY HAS NOTHING TO COMPARE ITSELF TO.
BUT I SEE THEIR FACES.
I REMEMBER THEM.
AND BY CRUSHING THIS OLD MAN'S SKULL--
I BRING SOME MEANING TO THEIR DEATHS.

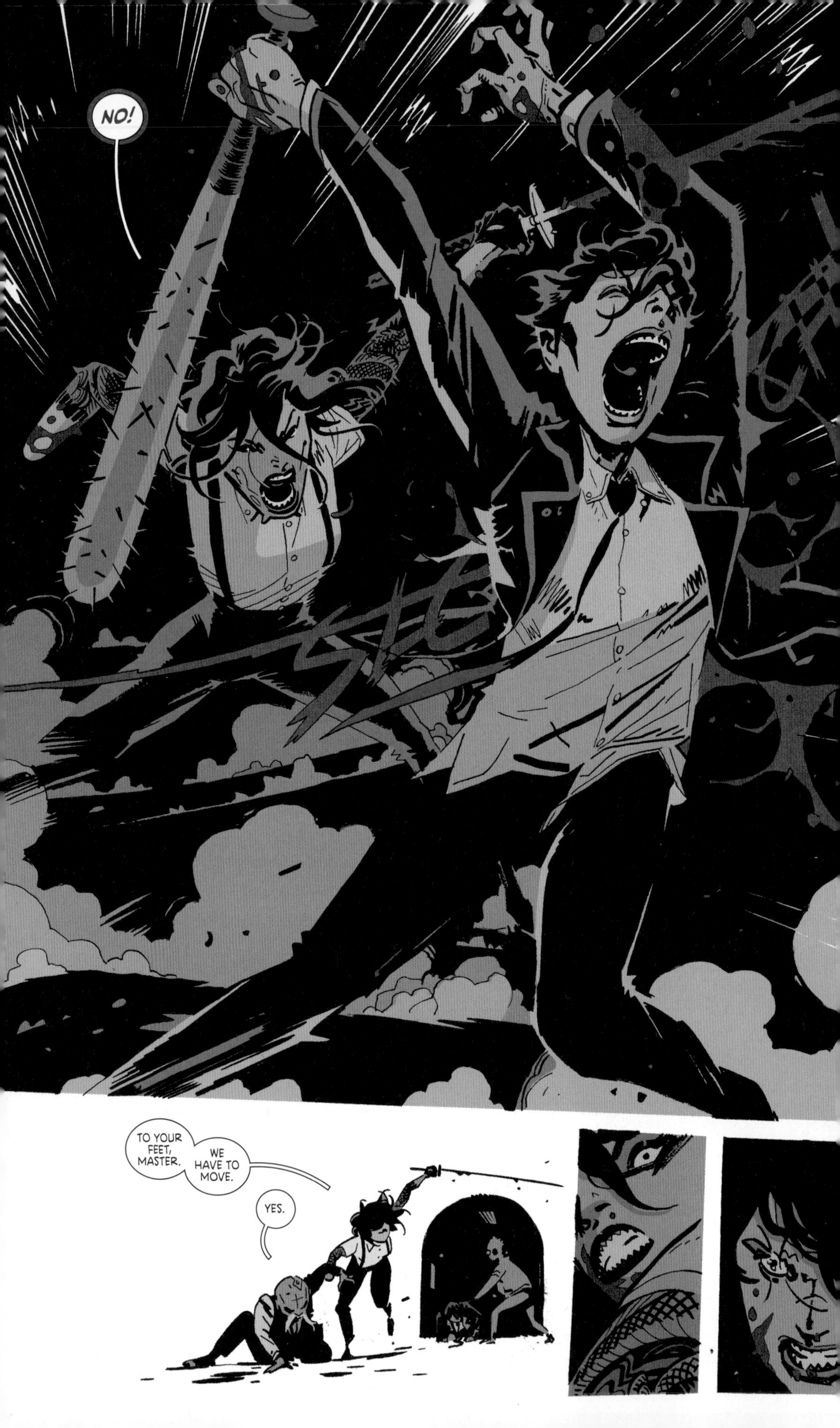
NO!
TO YOUR FEET, MASTER.
WE HAVE TO MOVE.
YES.

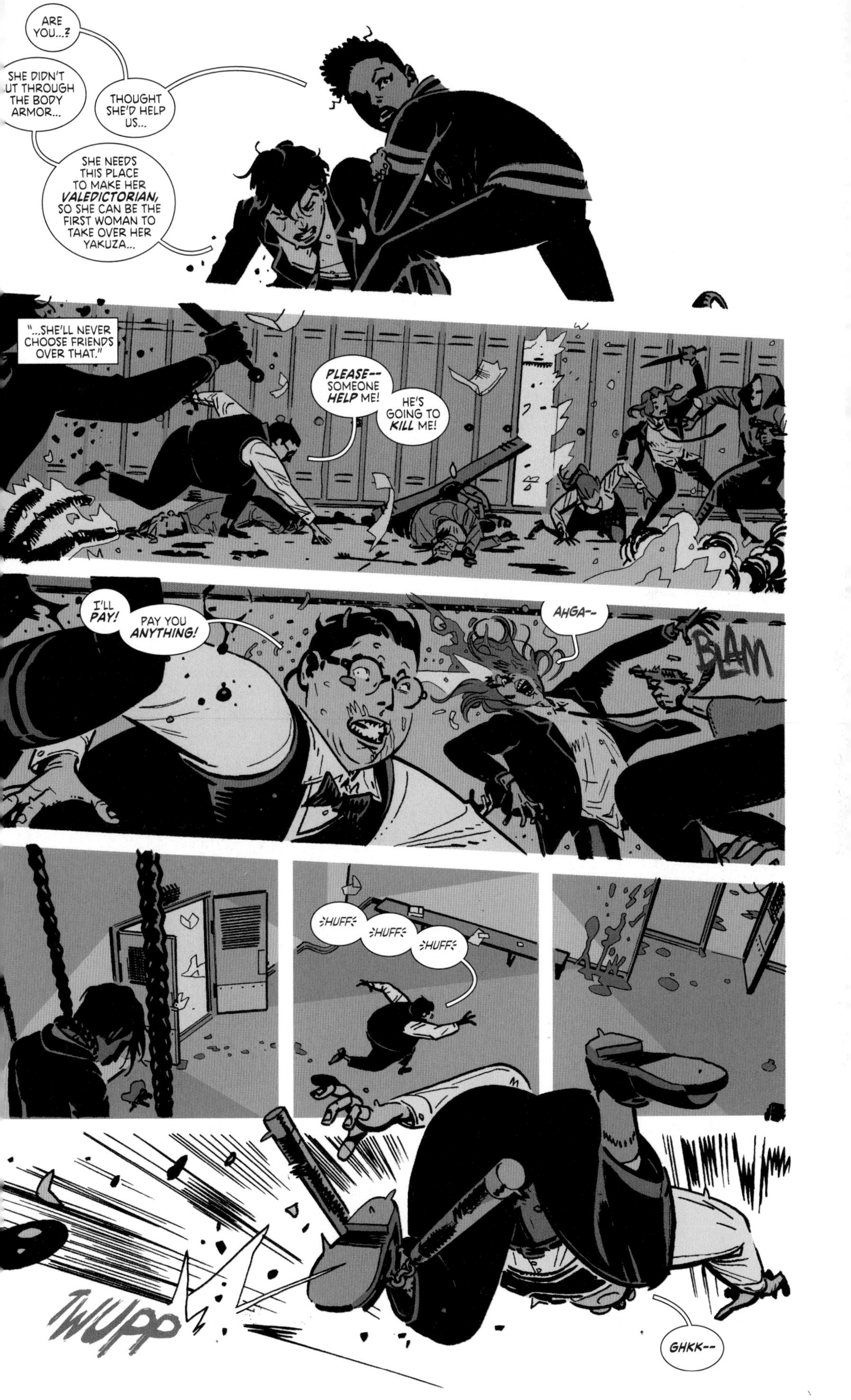
ARE YOU...?
SHE DIDN'T UT THROUGH THE BODY ARMOR...
THOUGHT SHE'D HELP US...
SHE NEEDS THIS PLACE TO MAKE HER VALEDICTORIAN, SO SHE CAN BE THE FIRST WOMAN TO TAKE OVER HER YAKUZA...
"...SHE'LL NEVER CHOOSE FRIENDS OVER THAT."
PLEASE-- SOMEONE HELP ME!
HE'S GOING TO KILL ME!
I'LL PAY!
PAY YOU ANYTHING!
AHGA--
BLAM
HUFF
HUFF
HUFF
TWUPP
GHKK--

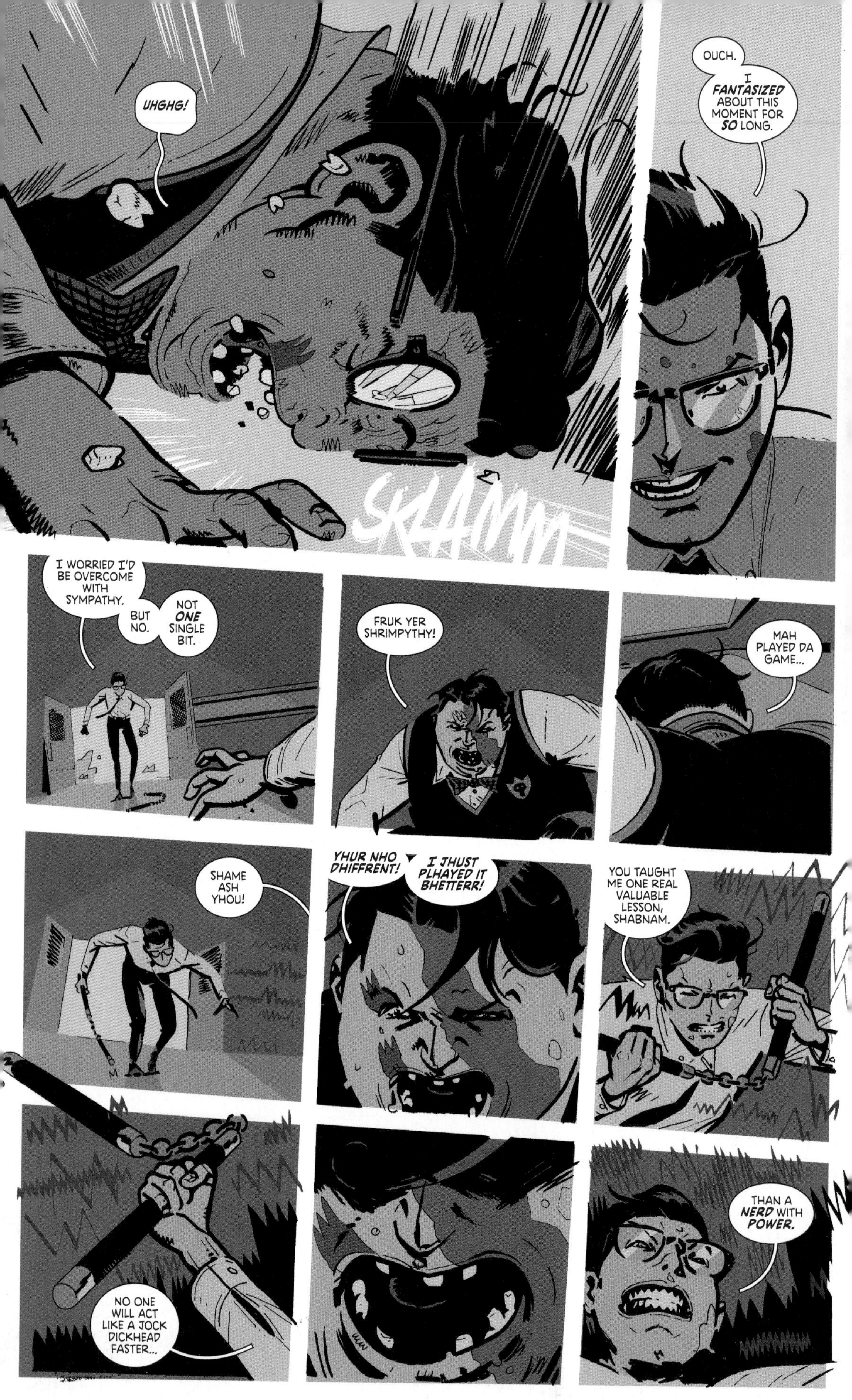
UHGHG!
SKLAMM
OUCH.
I FANTASIZED ABOUT THIS MOMENT FOR SO LONG.
I WORRIED I'D BE OVERCOME WITH SYMPATHY.
BUT NO.
NOT ONE SINGLE BIT.
FRUK YER SHRIMPYTHY!
MAH PLAYED DA GAME...
SHAME ASH YHOU!
YHUR NHO DHIFFRENT!
I JHUST PLHAYED IT BHETTERR!
YOU TAUGHT ME ONE REAL VALUABLE LESSON, SHABNAM.
NO ONE WILL ACT LIKE A JOCK DICKHEAD FASTER...
THAN A NERD WITH POWER.

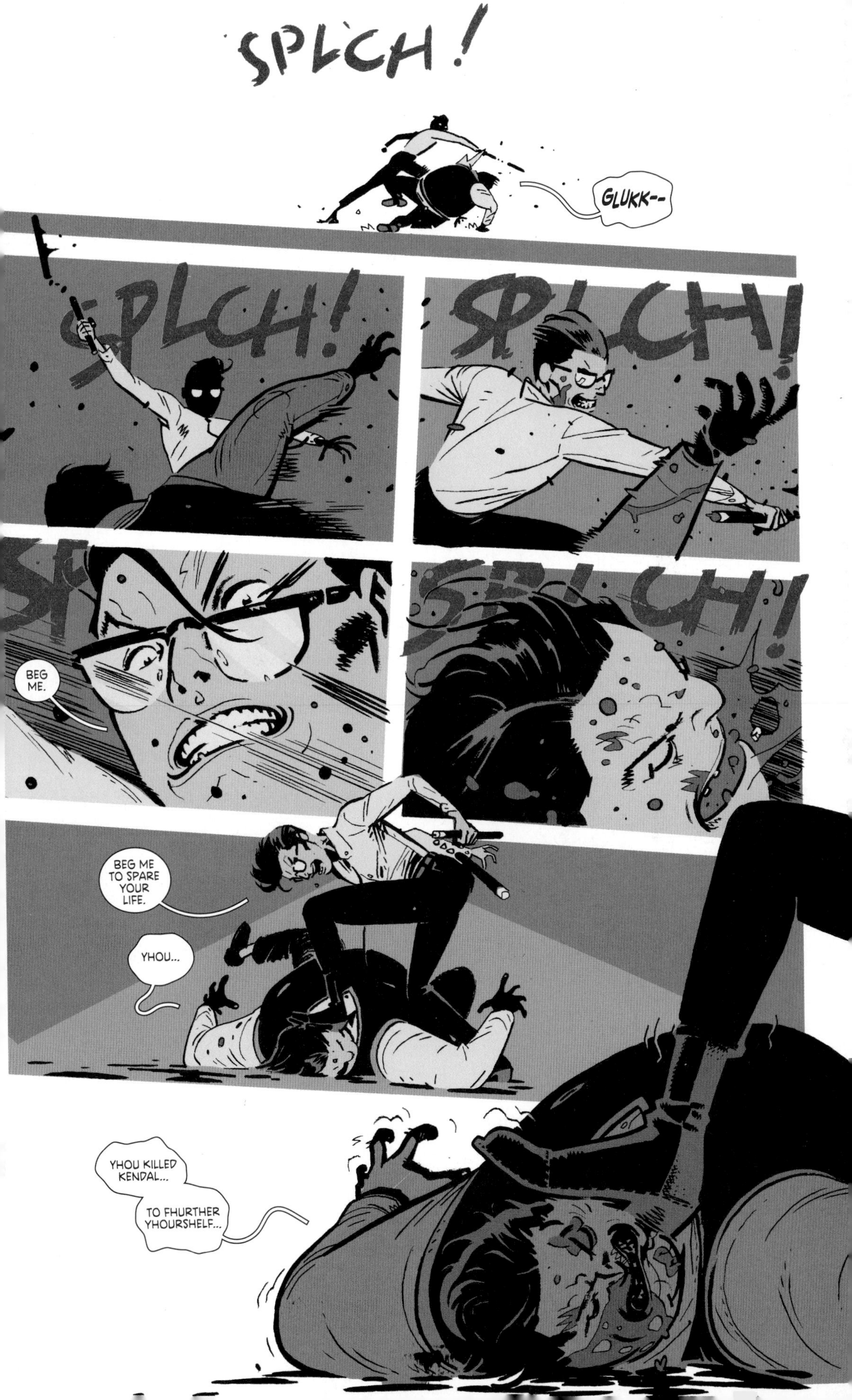
SPLCH!
GLUKK--
SPLCH!
SPLCH!
BEG ME.
SPLCH!
BEG ME TO SPARE YOUR LIFE.
YHOU...
YHOU KILLED KENDAL...
TO FHURTHER YHOURSHELF...

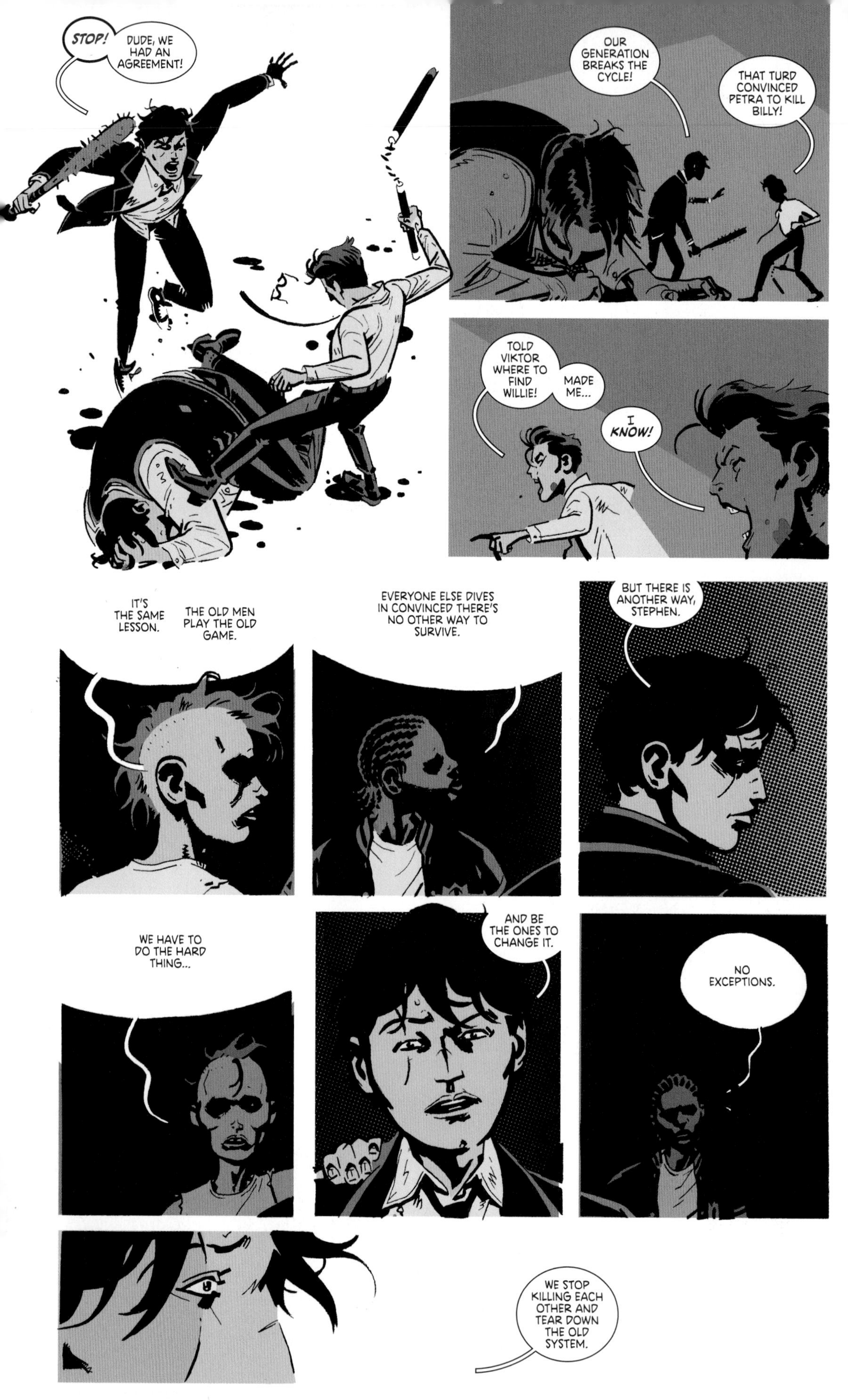
STOP!
DUDE, WE HAD AN AGREEMENT!
OUR GENERATION BREAKS THE CYCLE!
THAT TURD CONVINCED PETRA TO KILL BILLY!
TOLD VIKTOR WHERE TO FIND WILLIE!
MADE ME...
I KNOW!
IT'S THE SAME LESSON.
THE OLD MEN PLAY THE OLD GAME.
EVERYONE ELSE DIVES IN CONVINCED THERE'S NO OTHER WAY TO SURVIVE.
BUT THERE IS ANOTHER WAY, STEPHEN.
WE HAVE TO DO THE HARD THING...
AND BE THE ONES TO CHANGE IT.
NO EXCEPTIONS.
WE STOP KILLING EACH OTHER AND TEAR DOWN THE OLD SYSTEM.

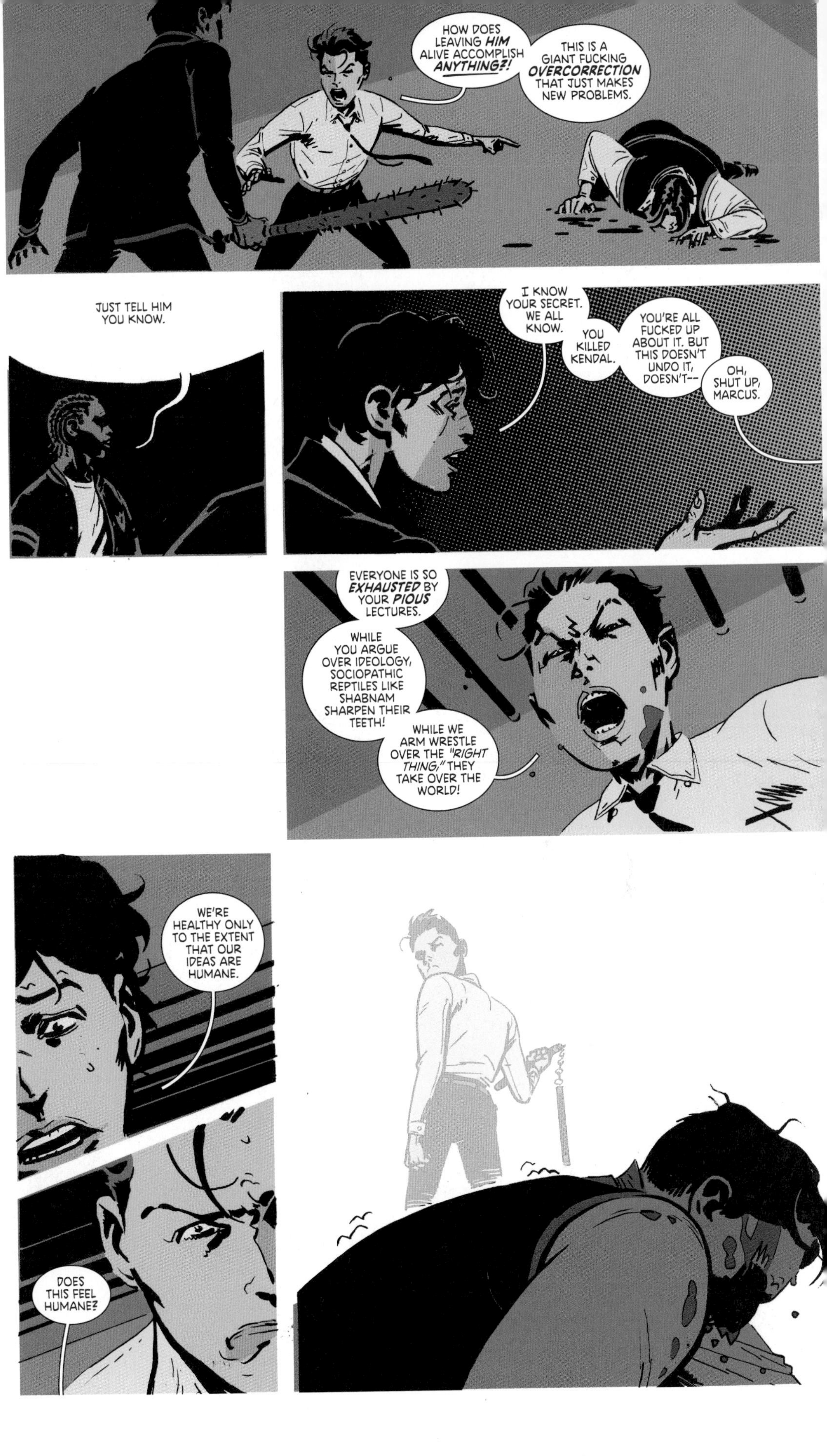
HOW DOES LEAVING HIM ALIVE ACCOMPLISH ANYTHING?!
THIS IS A GIANT FUCKING OVERCORRECTION THAT JUST MAKES NEW PROBLEMS.
JUST TELL HIM YOU KNOW.
I KNOW YOUR SECRET. WE ALL KNOW.
YOU KILLED KENDAL.
YOU'RE ALL FUCKED UP ABOUT IT. BUT THIS DOESN'T UNDO IT, DOESN'T--
OH, SHUT UP, MARCUS.
EVERYONE IS SO EXHAUSTED BY YOUR PIOUS LECTURES.
WHILE YOU ARGUE OVER IDEOLOGY, SOCIOPATHIC REPTILES LIKE SHABNAM SHARPEN THEIR TEETH!
WHILE WE ARM WRESTLE OVER THE "RIGHT THING," THEY TAKE OVER THE WORLD!
WE'RE HEALTHY ONLY TO THE EXTENT THAT OUR IDEAS ARE HUMANE.
DOES THIS FEEL HUMANE?

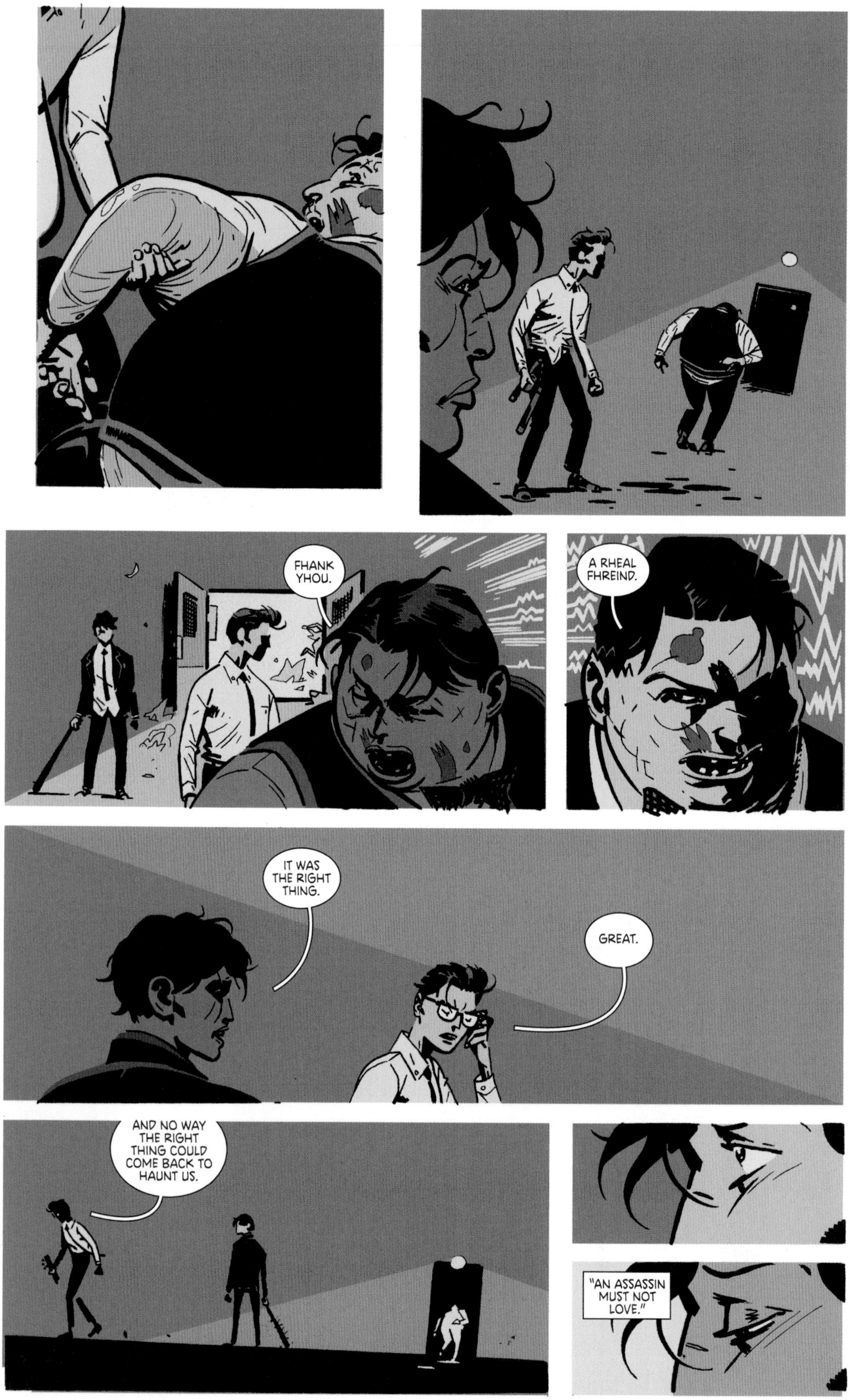
FHANK YHOU.
A RHEAL FHREIND.
IT WAS THE RIGHT THING.
GREAT.
AND NO WAY THE RIGHT THING COULD COME BACK TO HAUNT US.
"AN ASSASSIN MUST NOT LOVE."

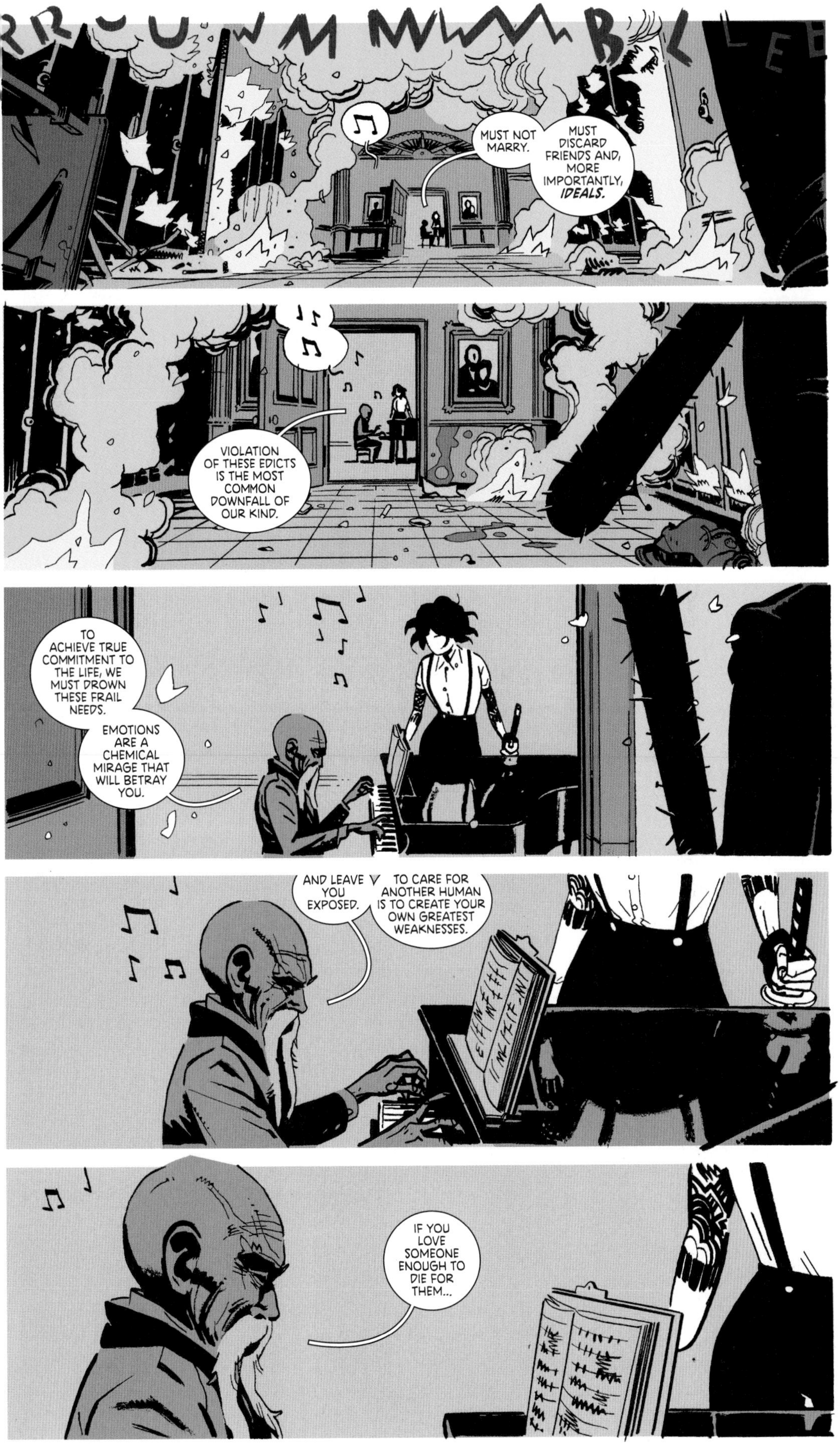
RRROUWMMMWMMBLLEB
MUST NOT MARRY.
MUST DISCARD FRIENDS AND, MORE IMPORTANTLY, *IDEALS.*
VIOLATION OF THESE EDICTS IS THE MOST COMMON DOWNFALL OF OUR KIND.
TO ACHIEVE TRUE COMMITMENT TO THE LIFE, WE MUST DROWN THESE FRAIL NEEDS.
EMOTIONS ARE A CHEMICAL MIRAGE THAT WILL BETRAY YOU.
AND LEAVE YOU EXPOSED.
TO CARE FOR ANOTHER HUMAN IS TO CREATE YOUR OWN GREATEST WEAKNESSES.
IF YOU LOVE SOMEONE ENOUGH TO DIE FOR THEM...

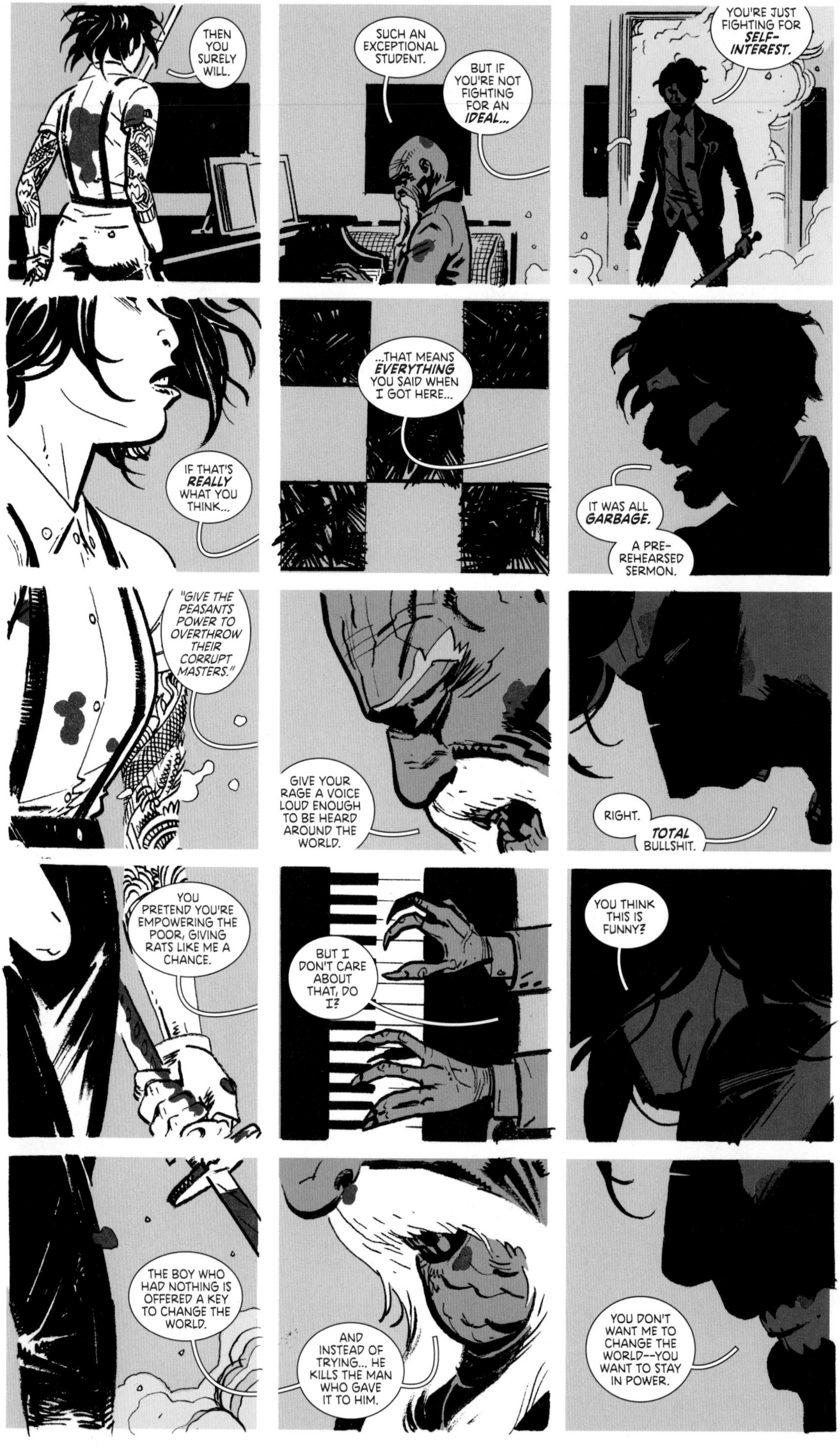
THEN YOU SURELY WILL.
SUCH AN EXCEPTIONAL STUDENT.
BUT IF YOU'RE NOT FIGHTING FOR AN IDEAL...
YOU'RE JUST FIGHTING FOR SELF-INTEREST.
IF THAT'S REALLY WHAT YOU THINK...
...THAT MEANS EVERYTHING YOU SAID WHEN I GOT HERE...
IT WAS ALL GARBAGE.
A PRE-REHEARSED SERMON.
"GIVE THE PEASANTS POWER TO OVERTHROW THEIR CORRUPT MASTERS."
GIVE YOUR RAGE A VOICE LOUD ENOUGH TO BE HEARD AROUND THE WORLD.
RIGHT.
TOTAL BULLSHIT.
YOU PRETEND YOU'RE EMPOWERING THE POOR, GIVING RATS LIKE ME A CHANCE.
BUT I DON'T CARE ABOUT THAT, DO I?
YOU THINK THIS IS FUNNY?
THE BOY WHO HAD NOTHING IS OFFERED A KEY TO CHANGE THE WORLD.
AND INSTEAD OF TRYING... HE KILLS THE MAN WHO GAVE IT TO HIM.
YOU DON'T WANT ME TO CHANGE THE WORLD--YOU WANT TO STAY IN POWER.

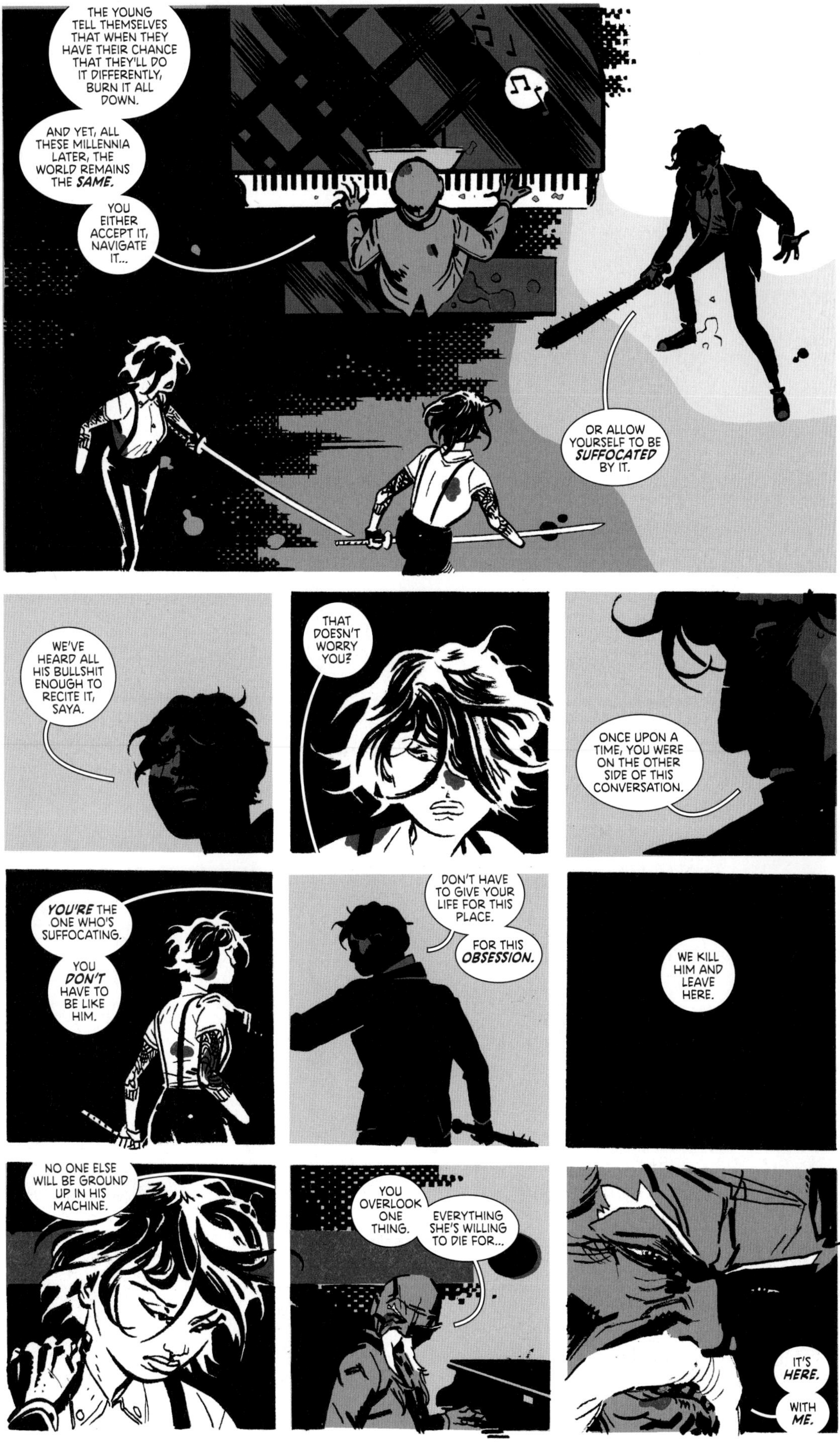
THE YOUNG TELL THEMSELVES THAT WHEN THEY HAVE THEIR CHANCE THAT THEY'LL DO IT DIFFERENTLY, BURN IT ALL DOWN.
AND YET, ALL THESE MILLENNIA LATER, THE WORLD REMAINS THE *SAME.*
YOU EITHER ACCEPT IT, NAVIGATE IT...
OR ALLOW YOURSELF TO BE *SUFFOCATED* BY IT.
WE'VE HEARD ALL HIS BULLSHIT ENOUGH TO RECITE IT, SAYA.
THAT DOESN'T WORRY YOU?
ONCE UPON A TIME, YOU WERE ON THE OTHER SIDE OF THIS CONVERSATION.
YOU'RE THE ONE WHO'S SUFFOCATING.
YOU *DON'T* HAVE TO BE LIKE HIM.
DON'T HAVE TO GIVE YOUR LIFE FOR THIS PLACE.
FOR THIS *OBSESSION.*
WE KILL HIM AND LEAVE HERE.
NO ONE ELSE WILL BE GROUND UP IN HIS MACHINE.
YOU OVERLOOK ONE THING.
EVERYTHING SHE'S WILLING TO DIE FOR...
IT'S *HERE.*
WITH *ME.*

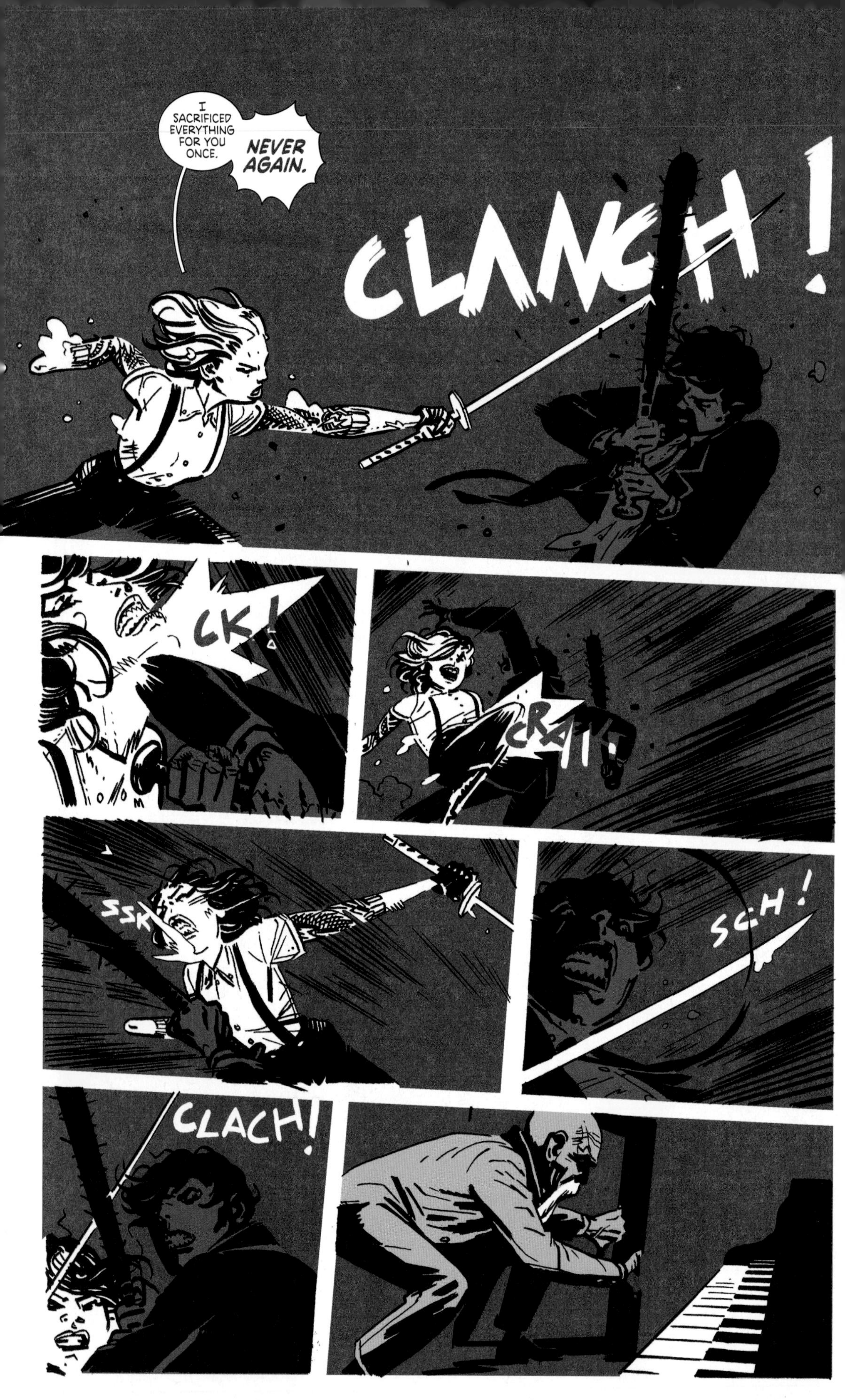
I SACRIFICED EVERYTHING FOR YOU ONCE.
NEVER AGAIN.
CLANCH!
CK!
CRAK!
SSK
SCH!
CLACH!

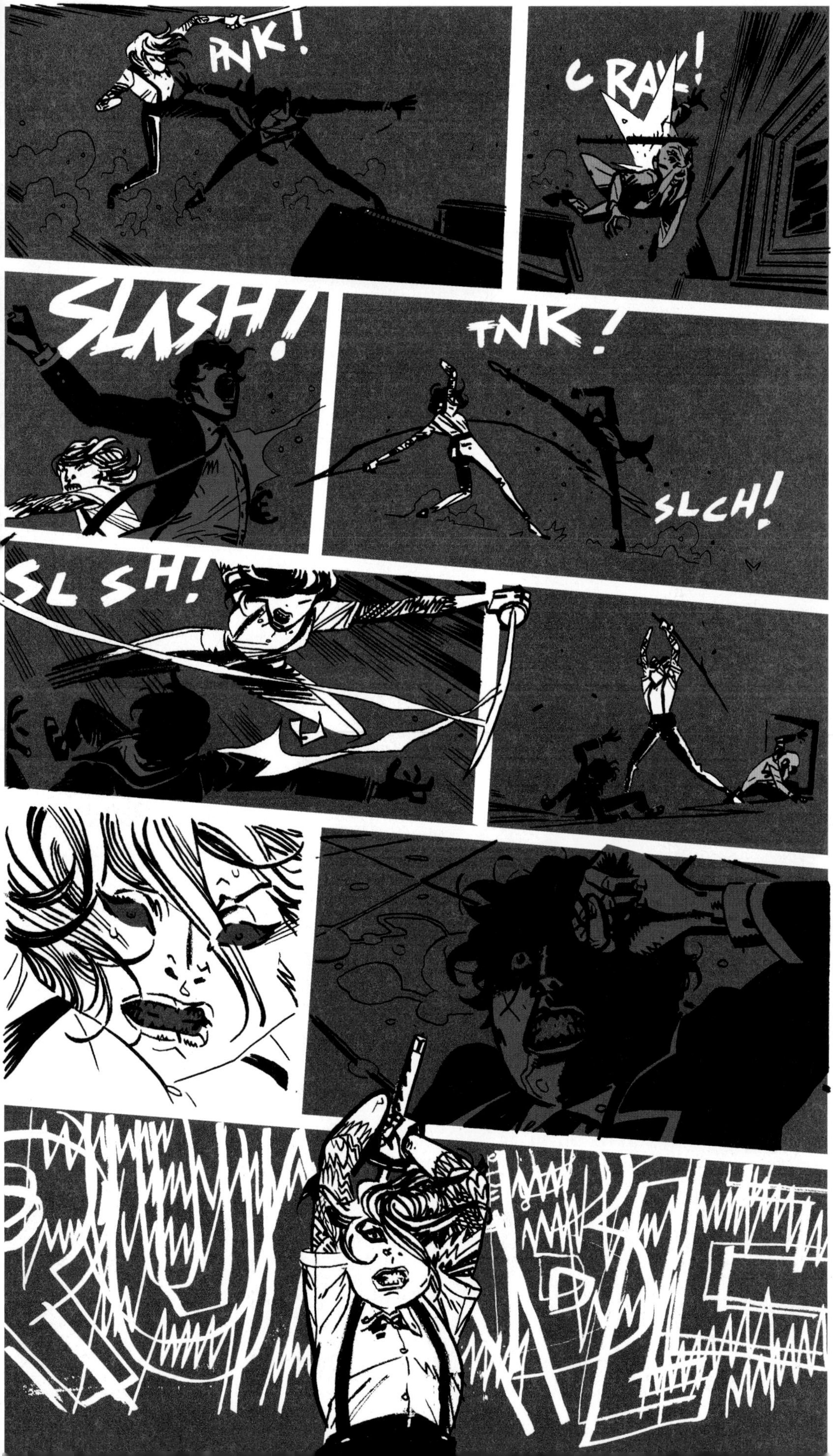
PNK!
CRAK!
SLASH!
TNK!
SLCH!
SLSH!

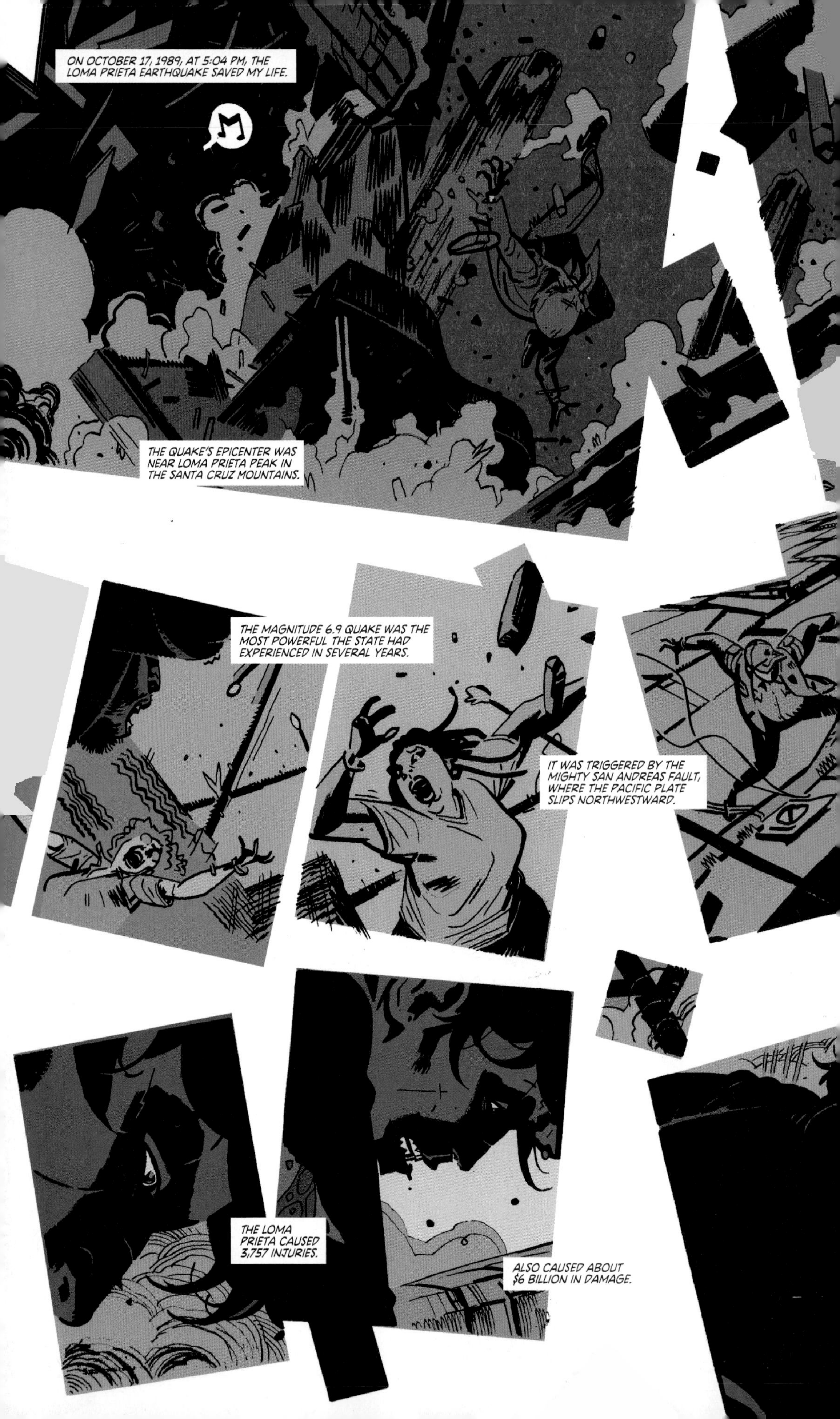
ON OCTOBER 17, 1989, AT 5:04 PM, THE LOMA PRIETA EARTHQUAKE SAVED MY LIFE.
THE QUAKE'S EPICENTER WAS NEAR LOMA PRIETA PEAK IN THE SANTA CRUZ MOUNTAINS.
THE MAGNITUDE 6.9 QUAKE WAS THE MOST POWERFUL THE STATE HAD EXPERIENCED IN SEVERAL YEARS.
IT WAS TRIGGERED BY THE MIGHTY SAN ANDREAS FAULT, WHERE THE PACIFIC PLATE SLIPS NORTHWESTWARD.
THE LOMA PRIETA CAUSED 3,757 INJURIES.
ALSO CAUSED ABOUT $6 BILLION IN DAMAGE.

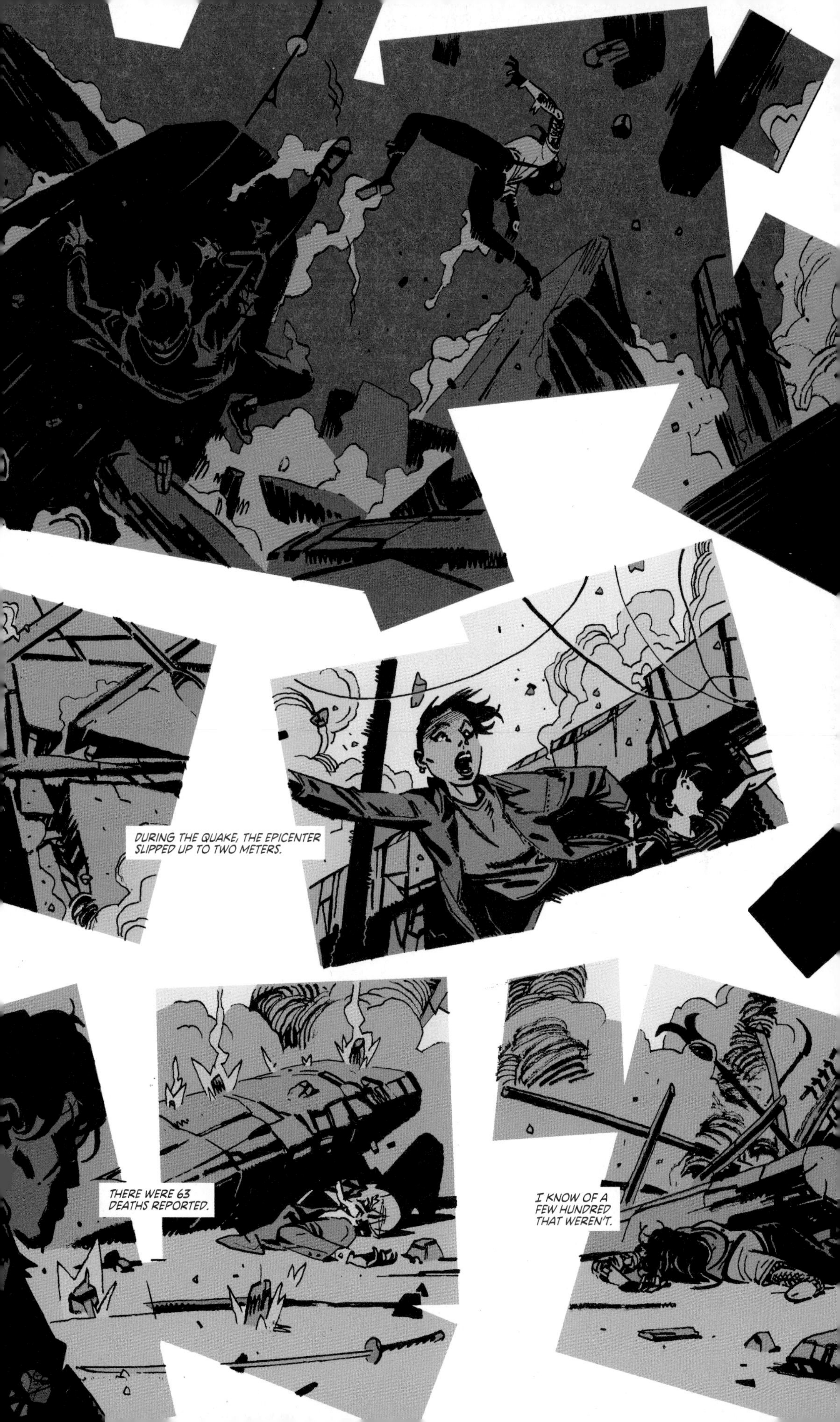
DURING THE QUAKE, THE EPICENTER SLIPPED UP TO TWO METERS.
THERE WERE 63 DEATHS REPORTED.
I KNOW OF A FEW HUNDRED THAT WEREN'T.

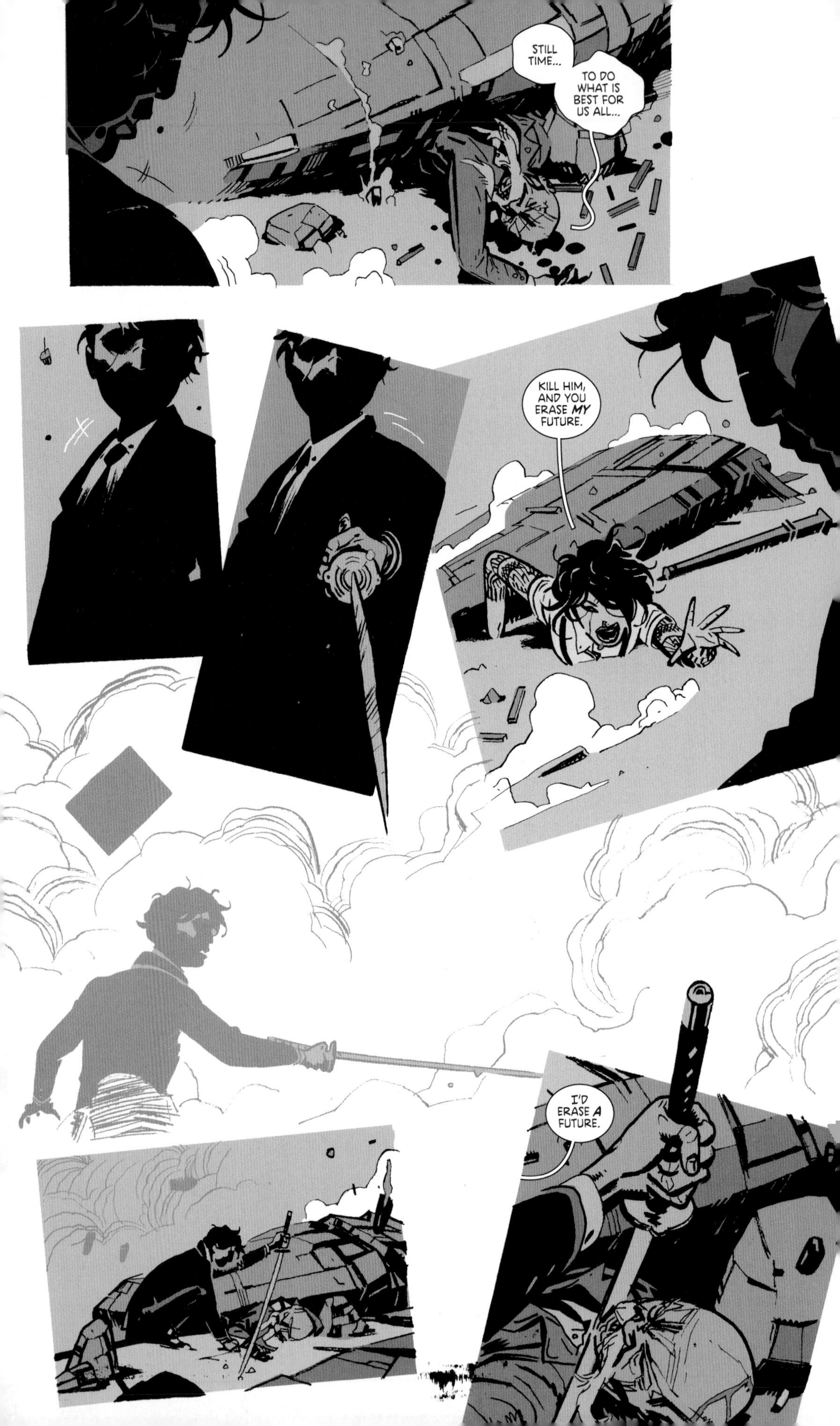
STILL TIME...
TO DO WHAT IS BEST FOR US ALL...
KILL HIM, AND YOU ERASE ***MY*** FUTURE.
I'D ERASE ***A*** FUTURE.

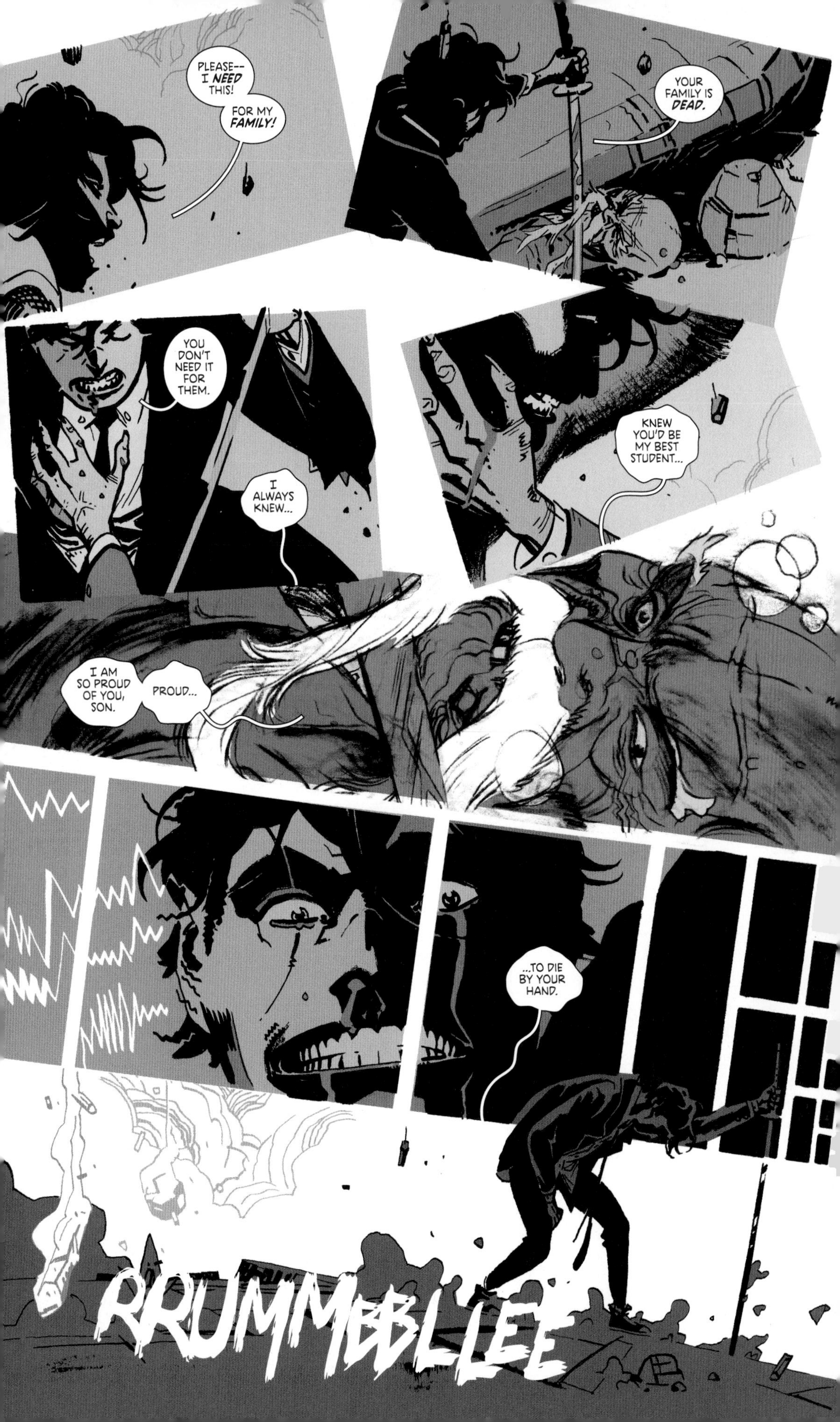
PLEASE-- I NEED THIS!
FOR MY FAMILY!
YOUR FAMILY IS DEAD.
YOU DON'T NEED IT FOR THEM.
I ALWAYS KNEW...
KNEW YOU'D BE MY BEST STUDENT...
I AM SO PROUD OF YOU, SON.
PROUD...
...TO DIE BY YOUR HAND.
RRUMMBBLLEE

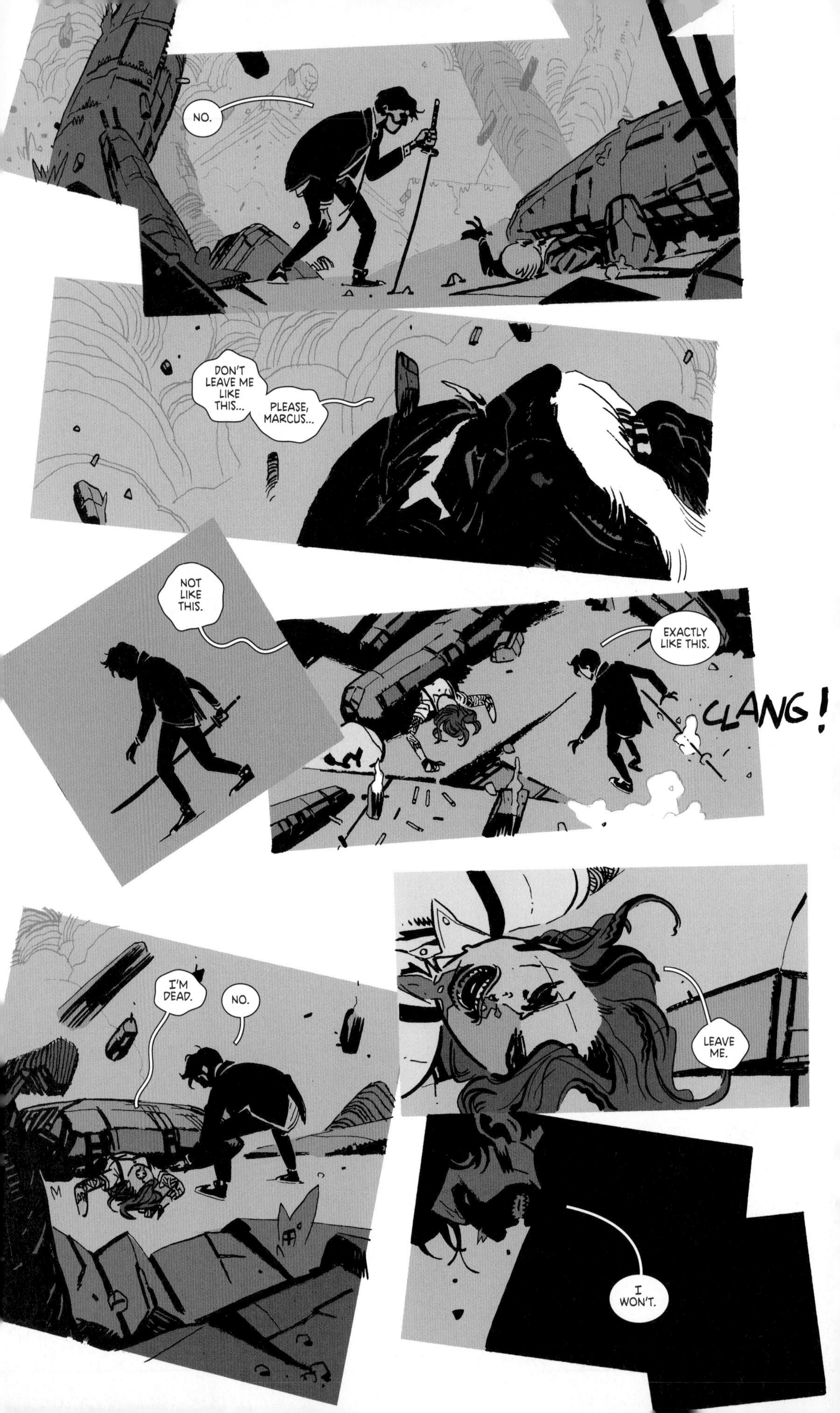
NO.
DON'T LEAVE ME LIKE THIS...
PLEASE, MARCUS...
NOT LIKE THIS.
EXACTLY LIKE THIS.
CLANG!
I'M DEAD.
NO.
LEAVE ME.
I WON'T.

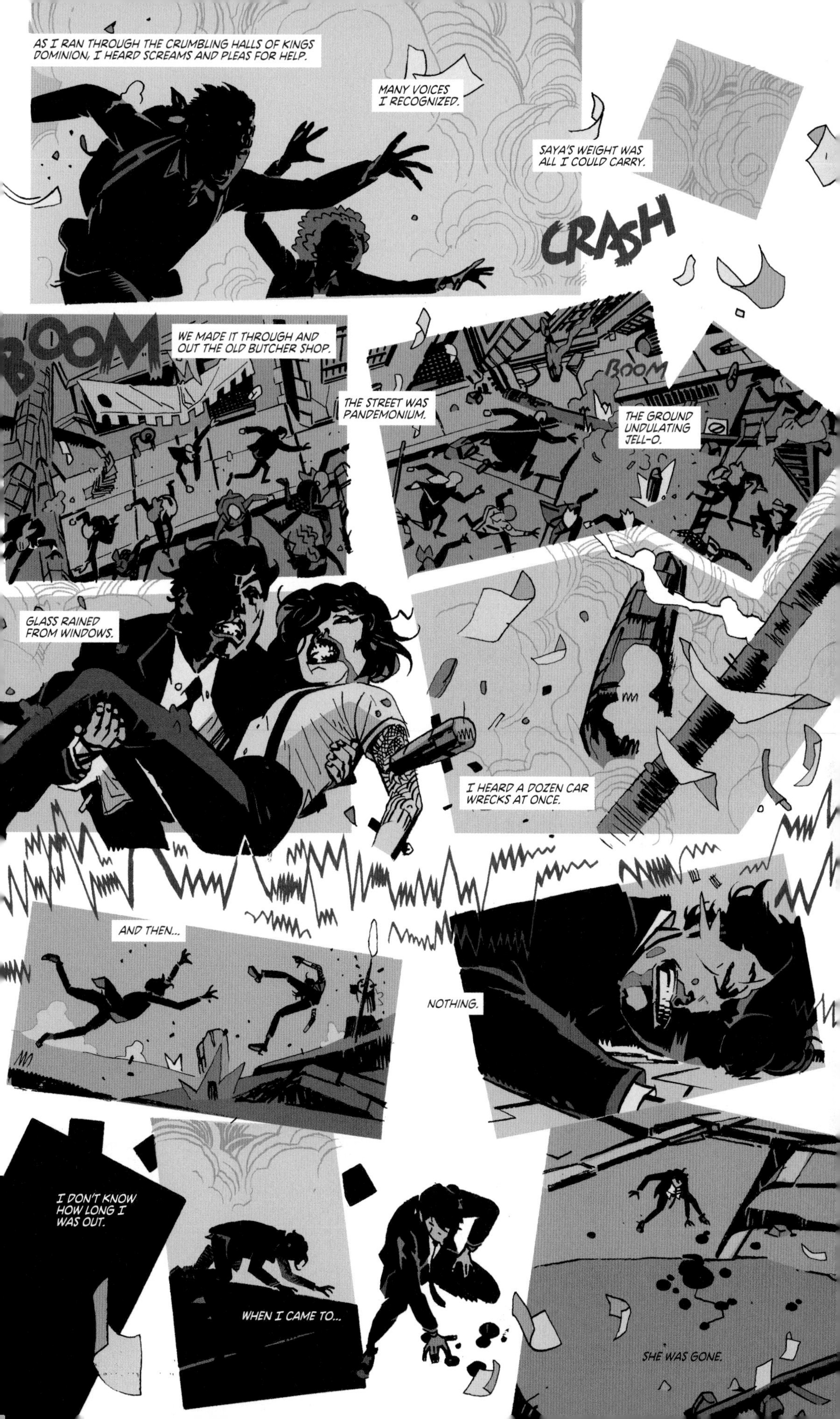
AS I RAN THROUGH THE CRUMBLING HALLS OF KINGS DOMINION, I HEARD SCREAMS AND PLEAS FOR HELP.
MANY VOICES I RECOGNIZED.
SAYA'S WEIGHT WAS ALL I COULD CARRY.
CRASH
BOOM
WE MADE IT THROUGH AND OUT THE OLD BUTCHER SHOP.
THE STREET WAS PANDEMONIUM.
BOOM
THE GROUND UNDULATING JELL-O.
GLASS RAINED FROM WINDOWS.
I HEARD A DOZEN CAR WRECKS AT ONCE.
AND THEN...
NOTHING.
I DON'T KNOW HOW LONG I WAS OUT.
WHEN I CAME TO...
SHE WAS GONE.

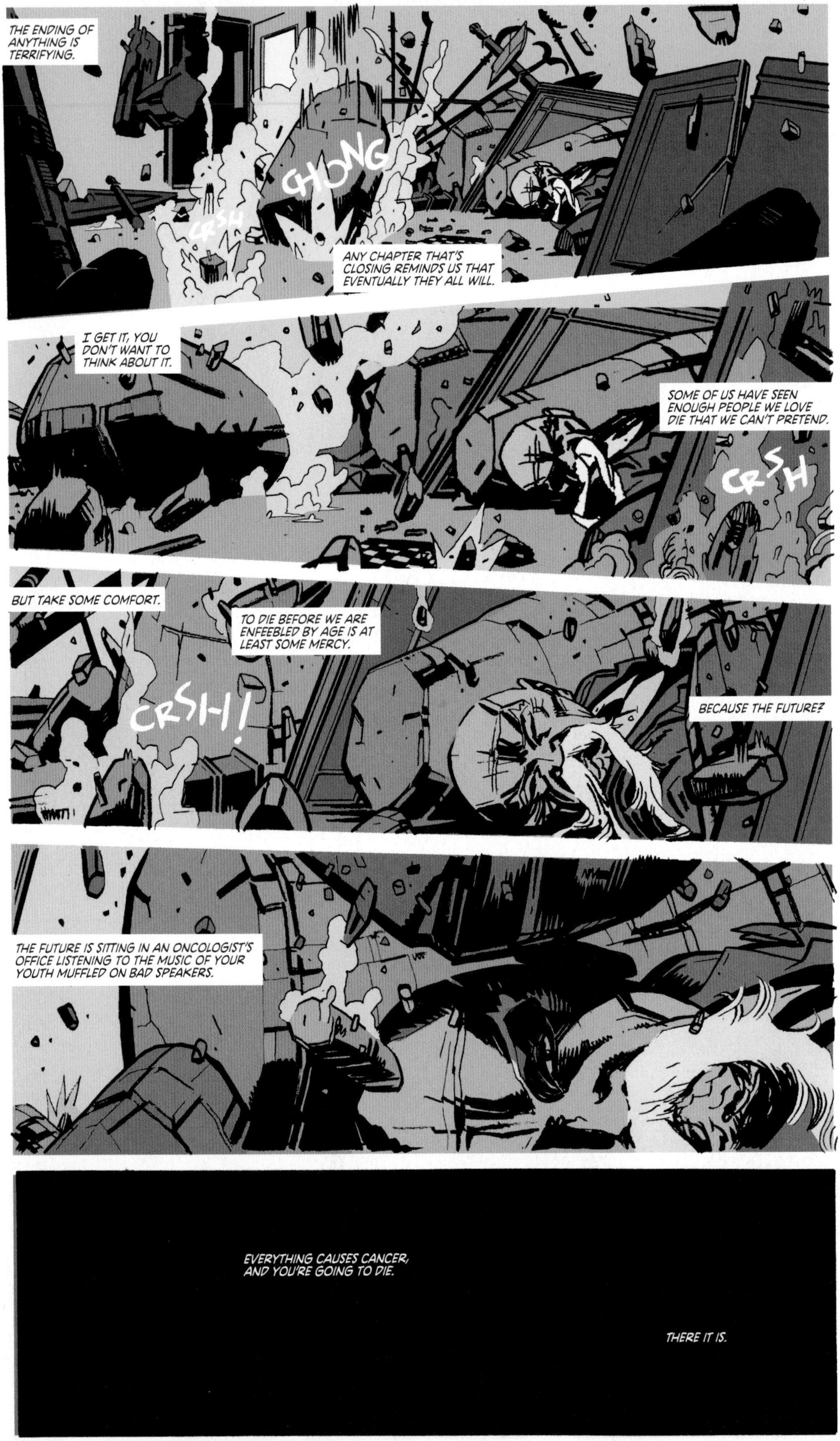
THE ENDING OF ANYTHING IS TERRIFYING.
CHONG
CRSH
ANY CHAPTER THAT'S CLOSING REMINDS US THAT EVENTUALLY THEY ALL WILL.
I GET IT, YOU DON'T WANT TO THINK ABOUT IT.
SOME OF US HAVE SEEN ENOUGH PEOPLE WE LOVE DIE THAT WE CAN'T PRETEND.
CRSH
BUT TAKE SOME COMFORT.
TO DIE BEFORE WE ARE ENFEEBLED BY AGE IS AT LEAST SOME MERCY.
CRSH!
BECAUSE THE FUTURE?
THE FUTURE IS SITTING IN AN ONCOLOGIST'S OFFICE LISTENING TO THE MUSIC OF YOUR YOUTH MUFFLED ON BAD SPEAKERS.
EVERYTHING CAUSES CANCER, AND YOU'RE GOING TO DIE.
THERE IT IS.

NOW, CAN WE JUST GET ON WITH THIS?

EST
1637
IN VITAM MORTEM

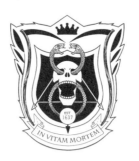

COVER GALLERY

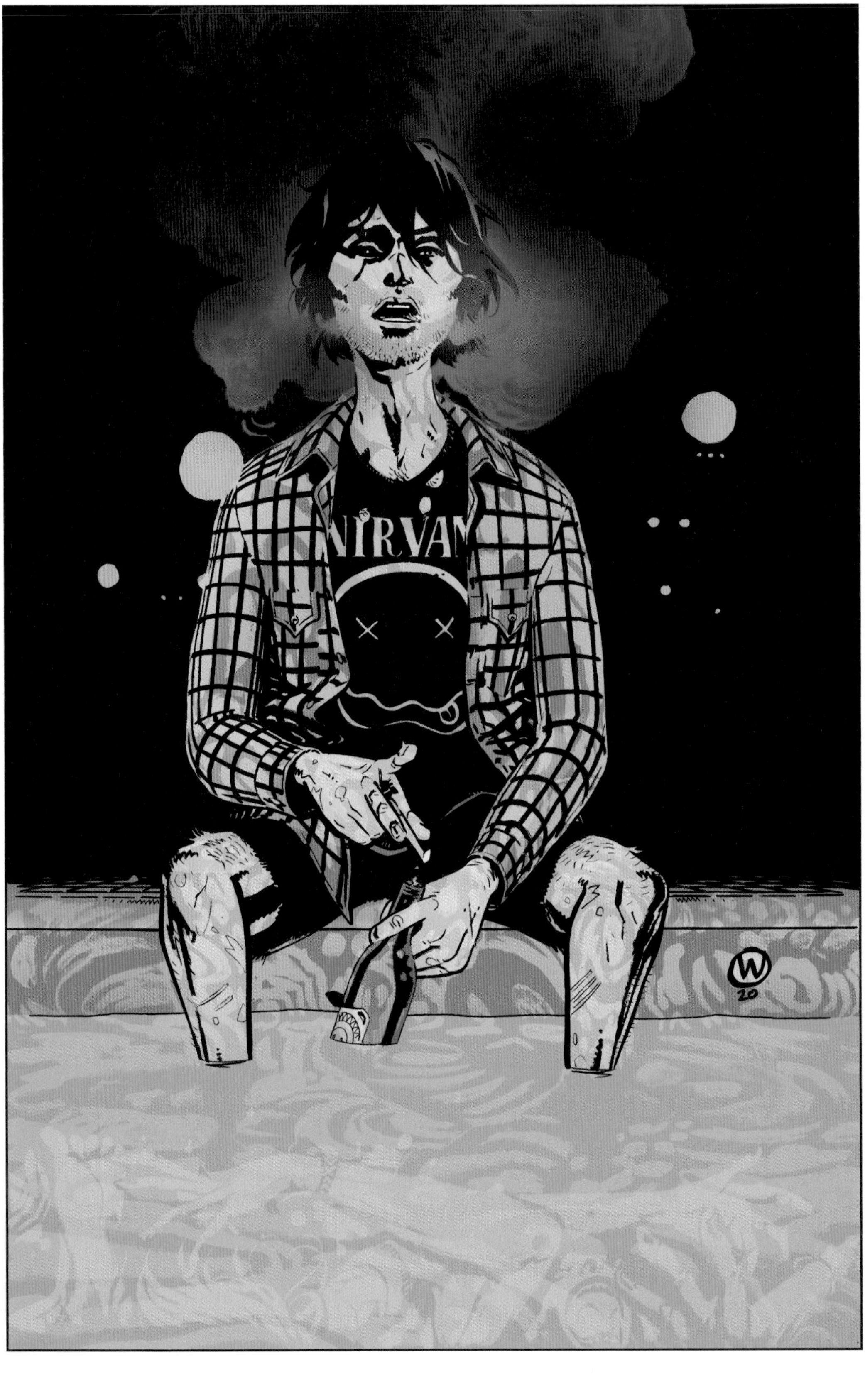
NIRVAN

#45 COVER BY **WES CRAIG**

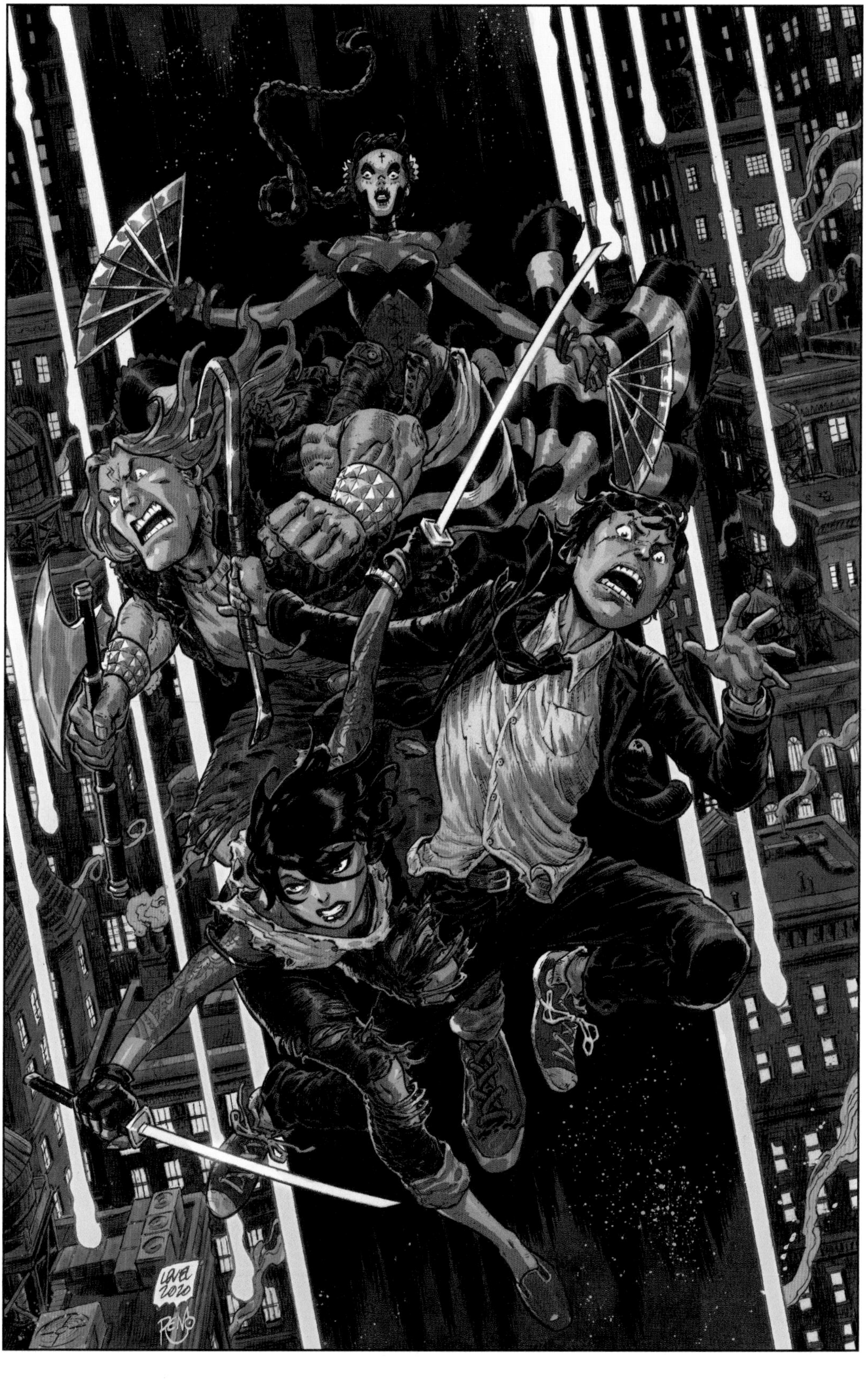

#45 VARIANT BY **BRIAN LEVEL & MORENO DINISIO**

#45 VARIANT BY **JIA**

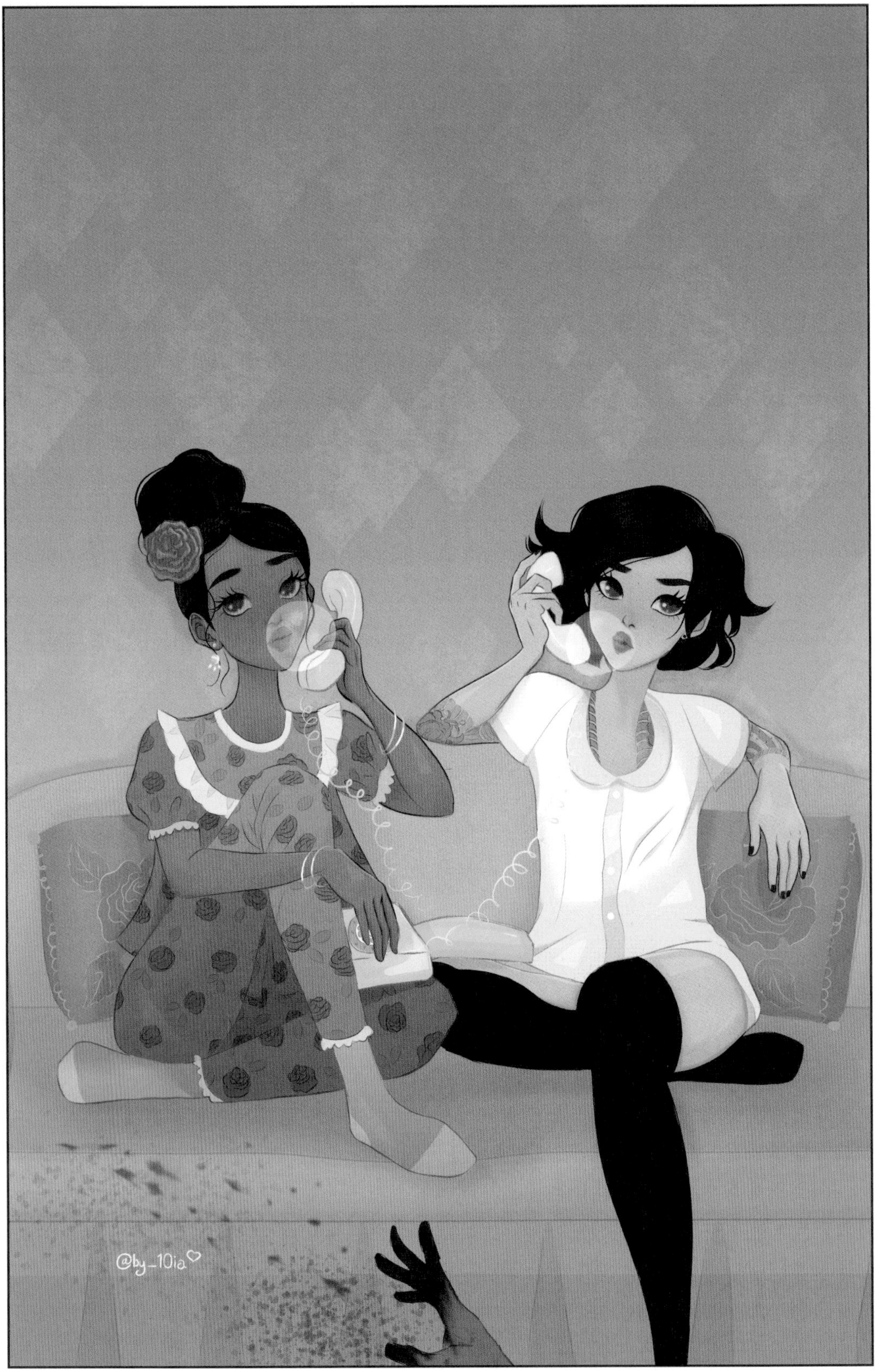
@by_10ia

#46 COVER BY **WES CRAIG**

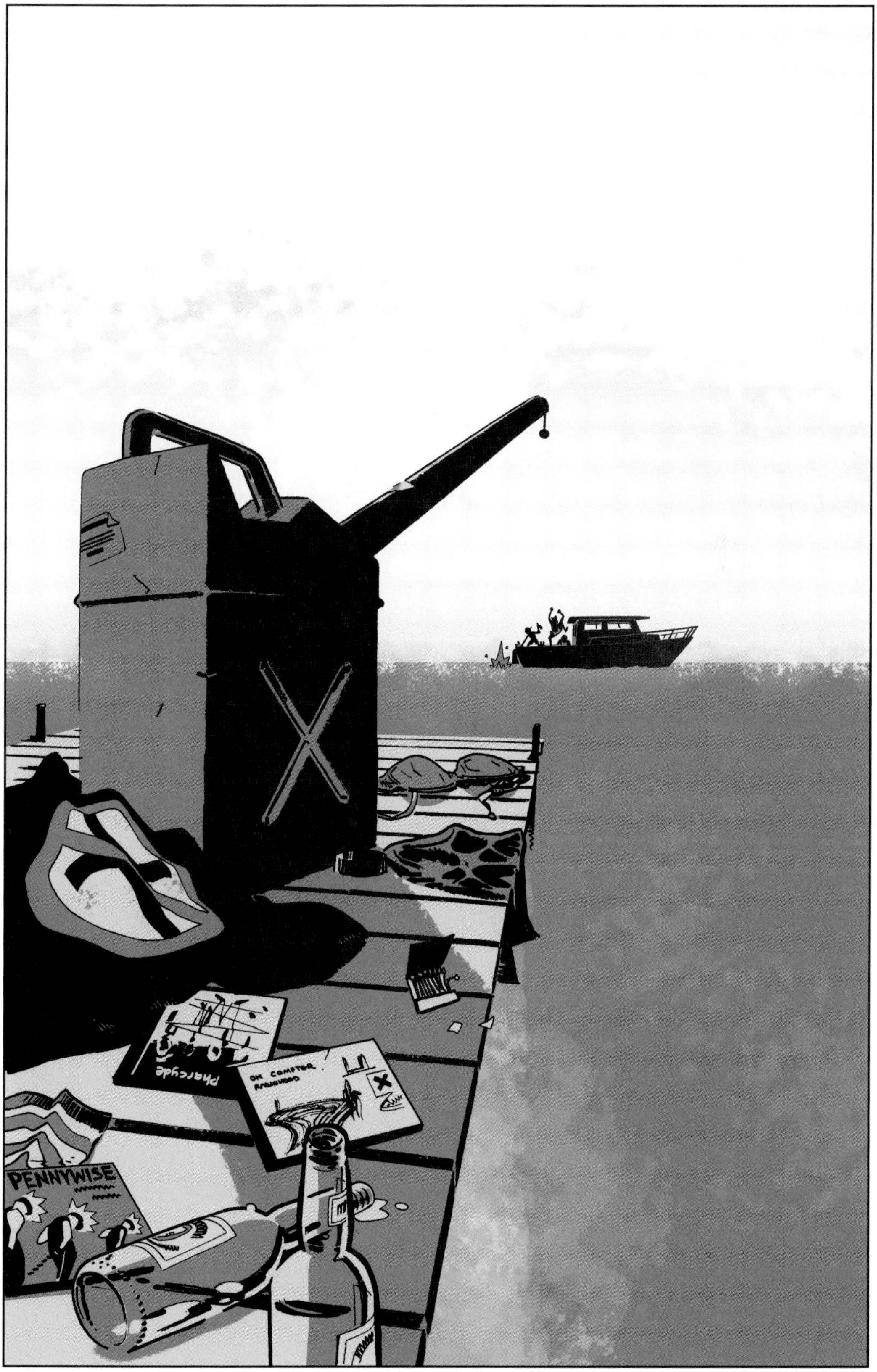
PENNYWISE

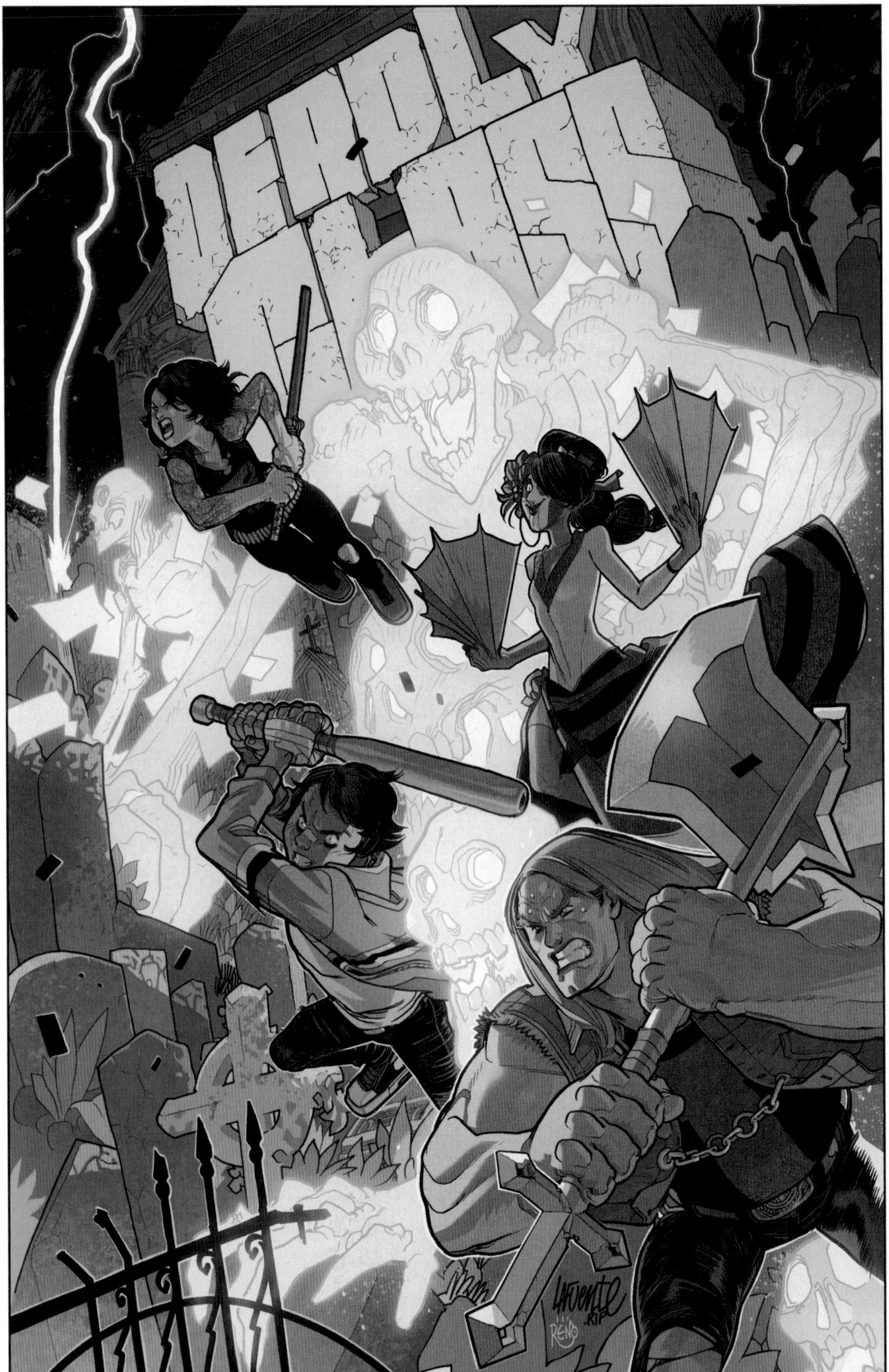
DEADLY CLASS

#46 VARIANT BY **DARKO LAFUENTE & MORENO DINISIO**

#47 COVER BY **WES CRAIG**

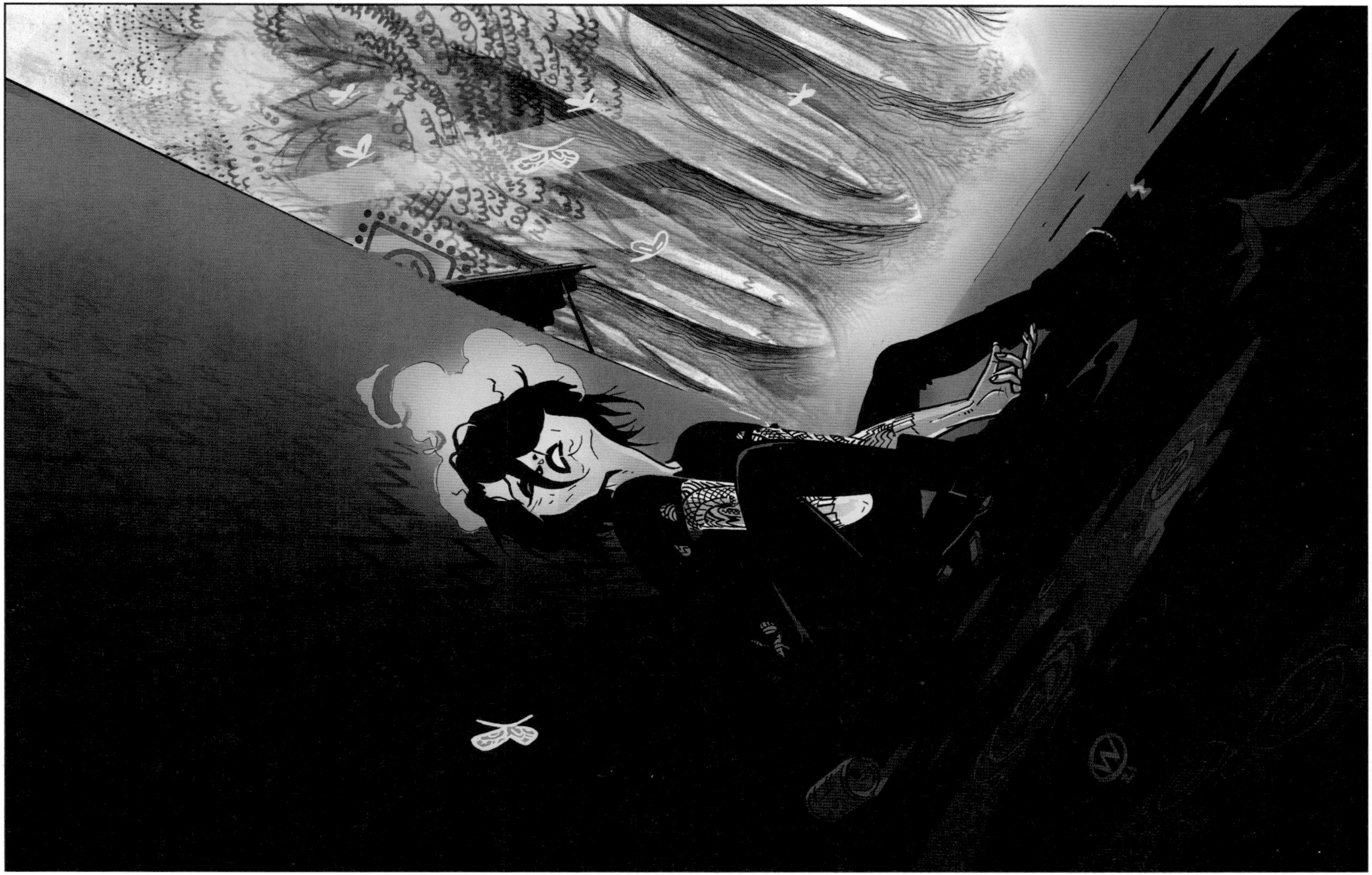

#47 VARIANT BY **JEFF DEKAL**

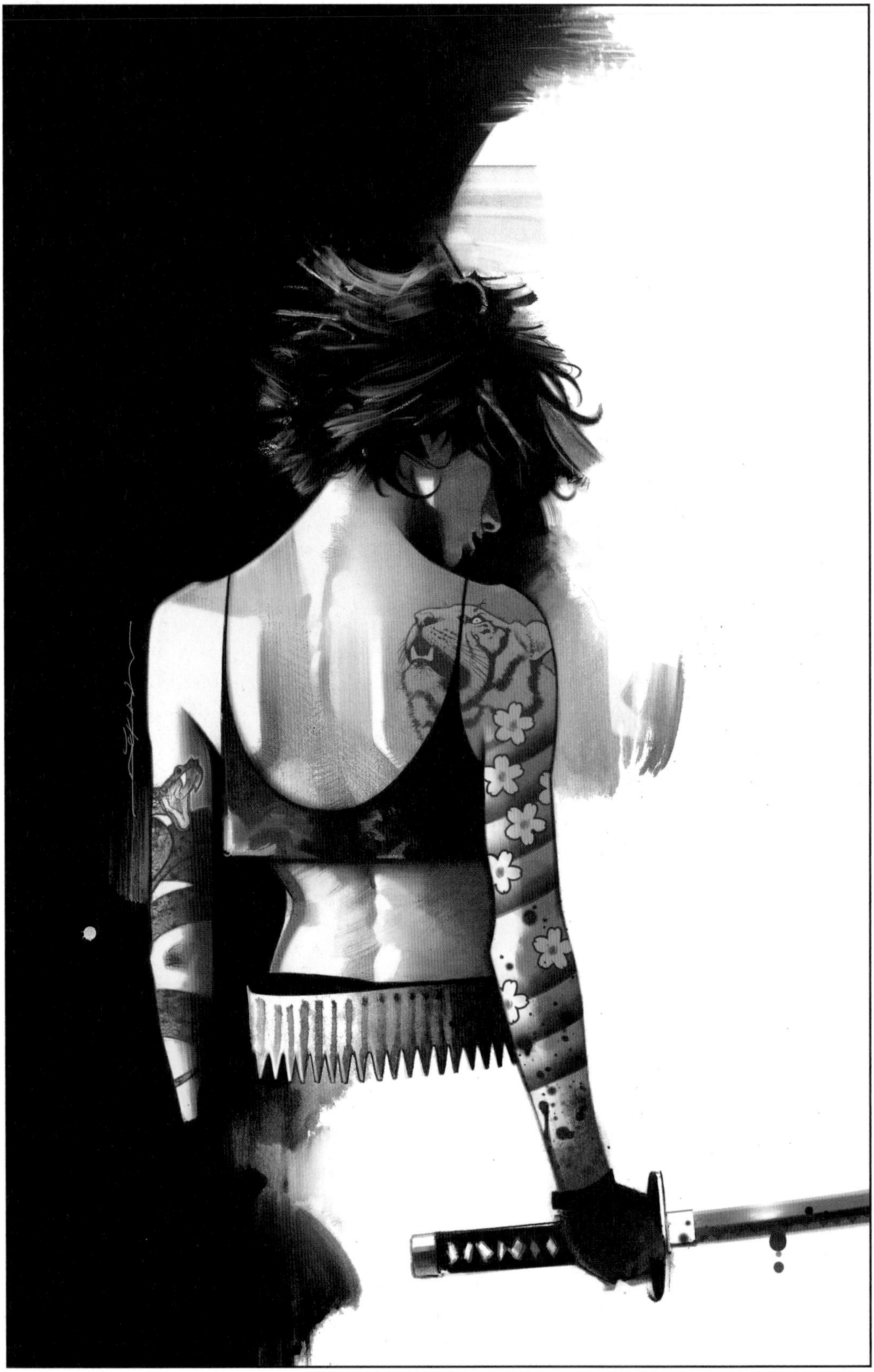

#48 COVER BY **WES CRAIG**

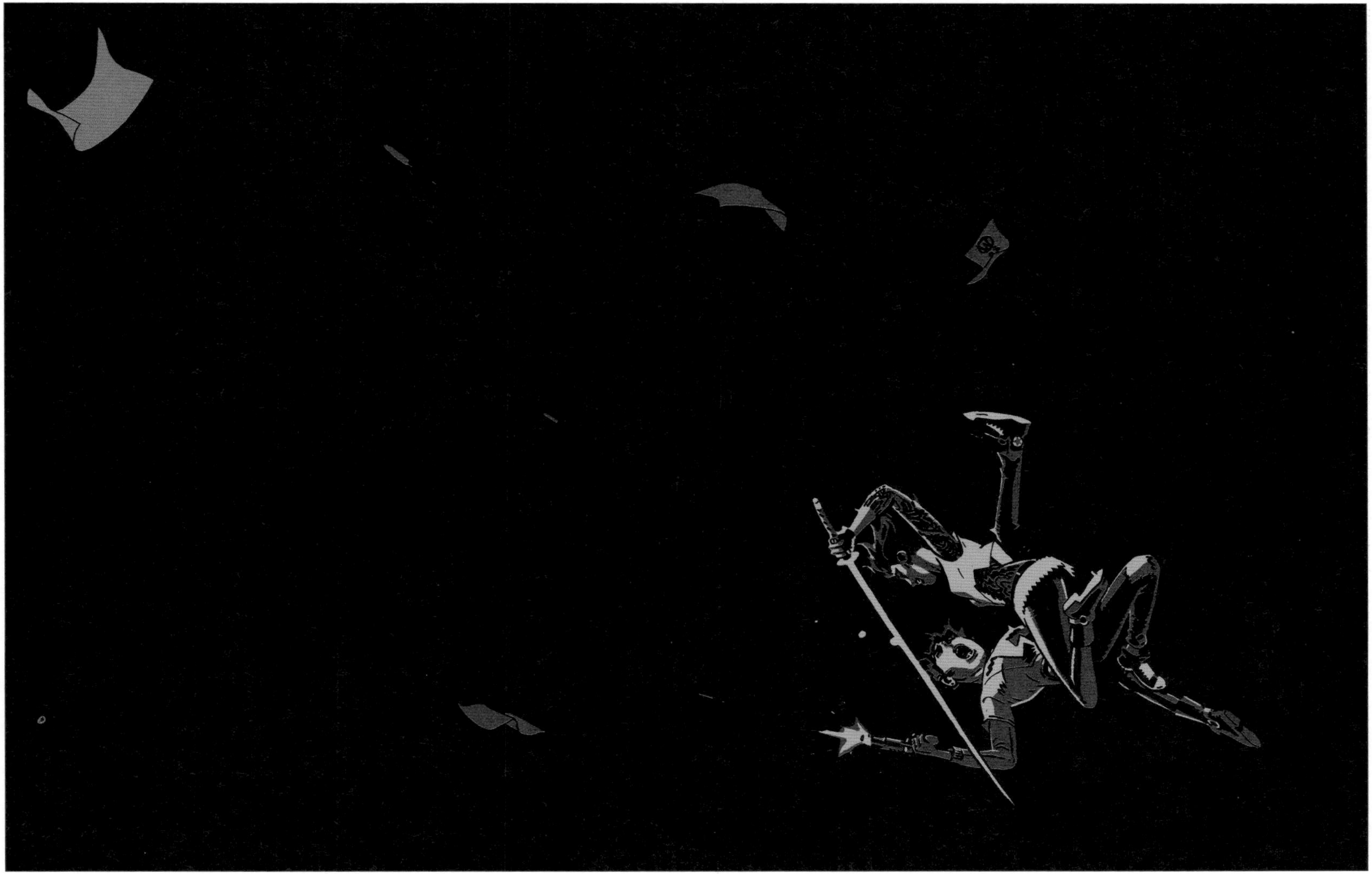

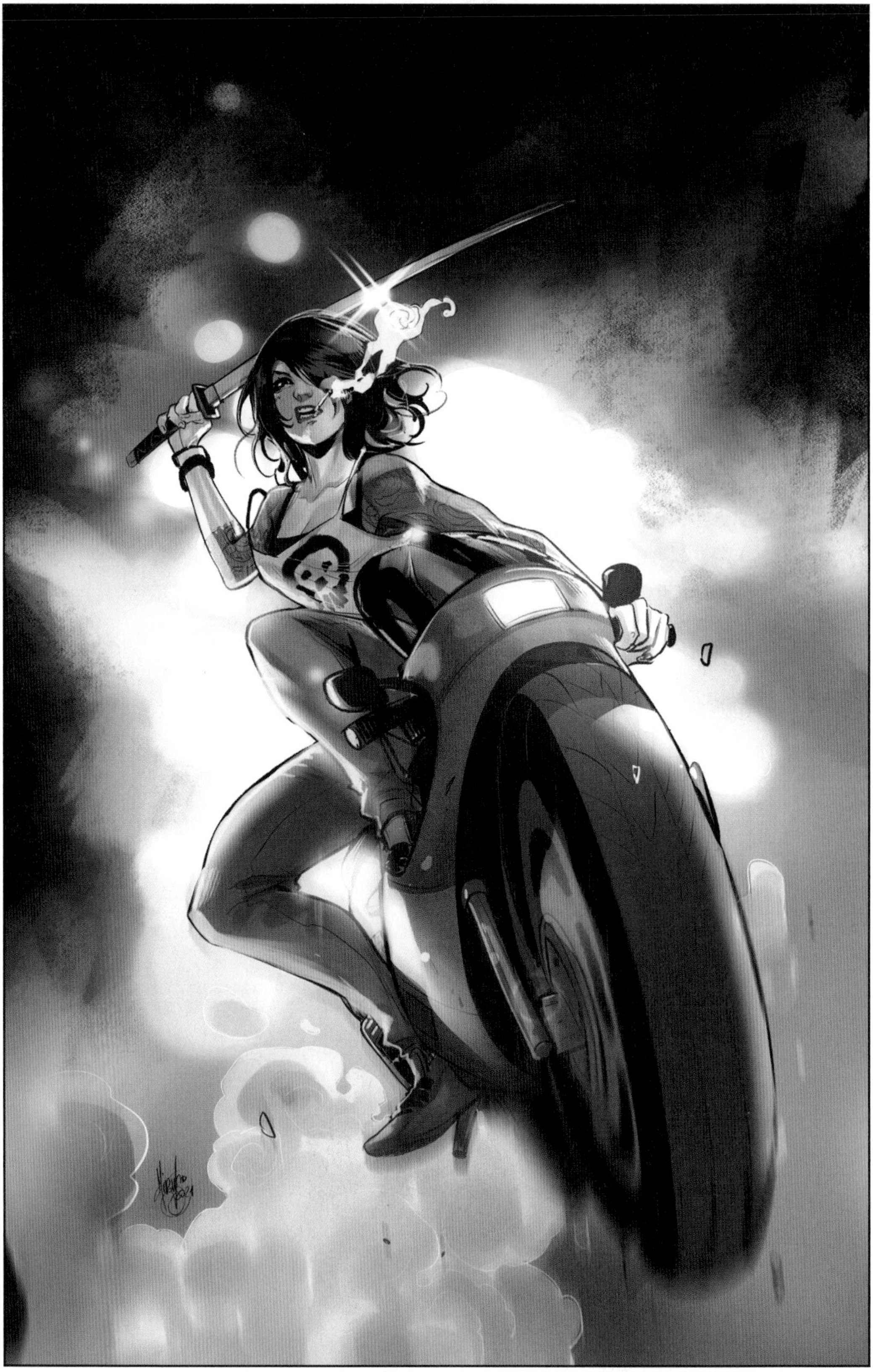

#48 VARIANT BY **MIRKA ANDOLFO**

#48 INTERIOR ROUGHS BY **WES CRAIG**

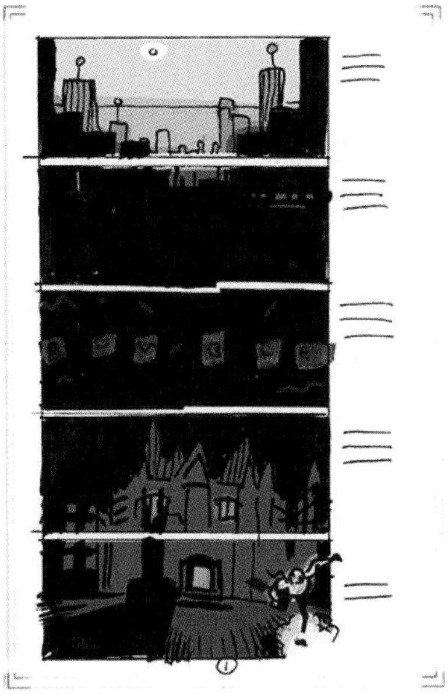
1

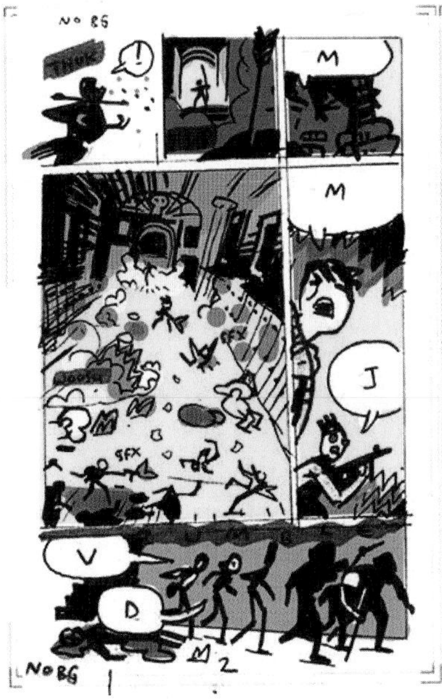
NO BG
THUK
!
M
M
SFX
SFX
J
V
D
NO BG
2

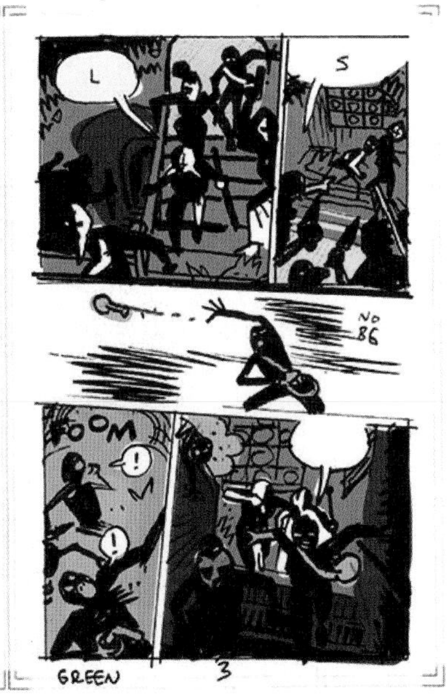
L
S
NO BG
OOM
!
!
GREEN
3

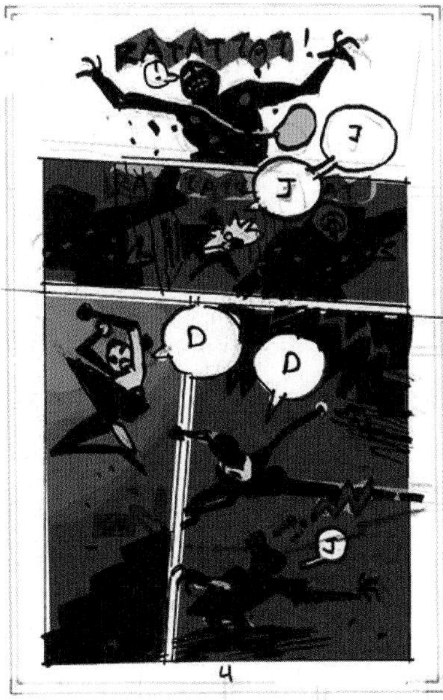
!
J
J
D
D
J
4

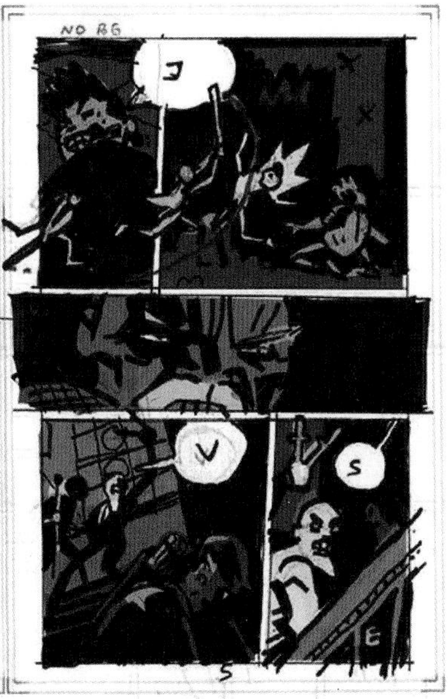
NO BG
J
V
S
5

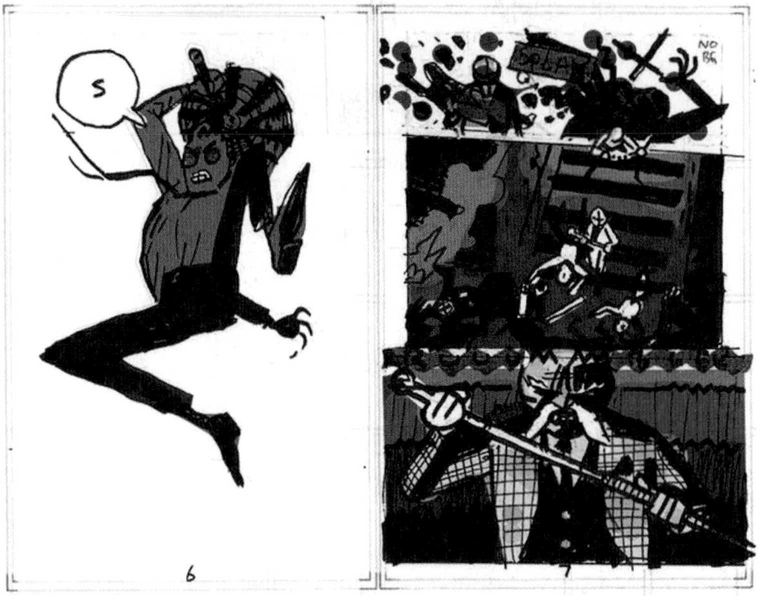
S
NO BG
6
7

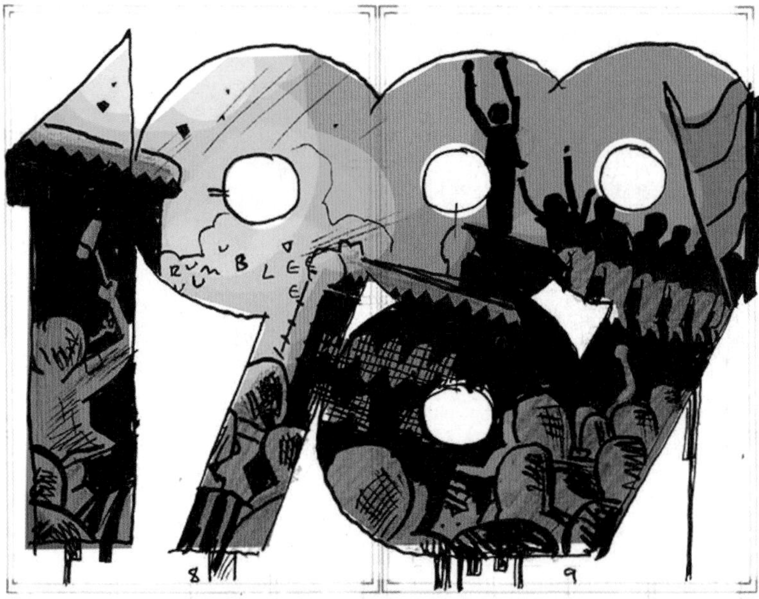
8
9

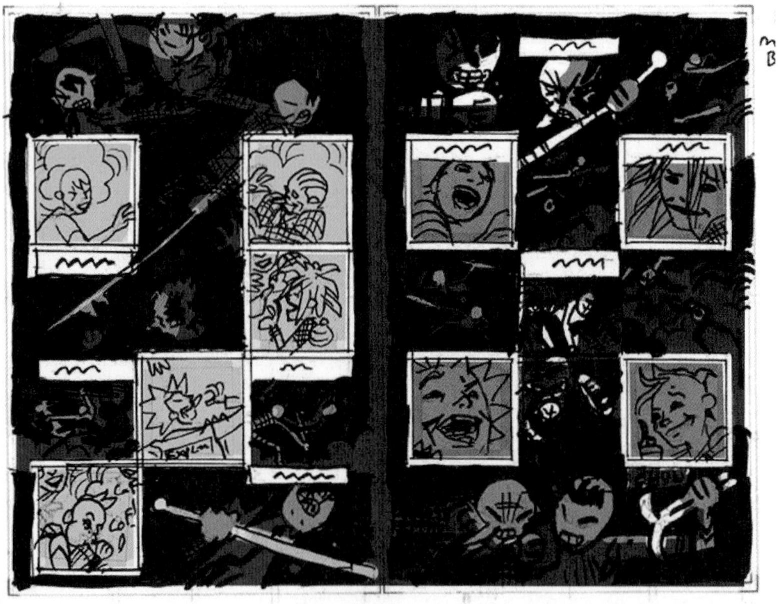

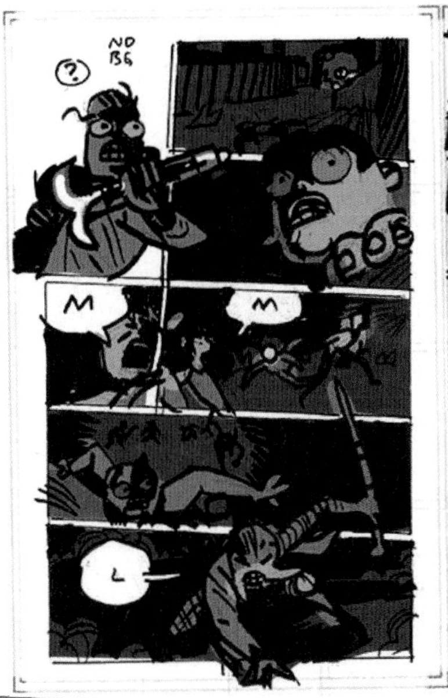
NO BG
?
M
M
L

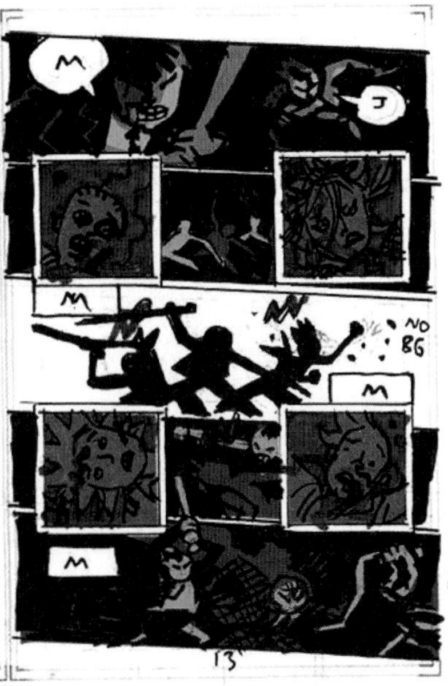
M
J
M
NO BG
M
M
13

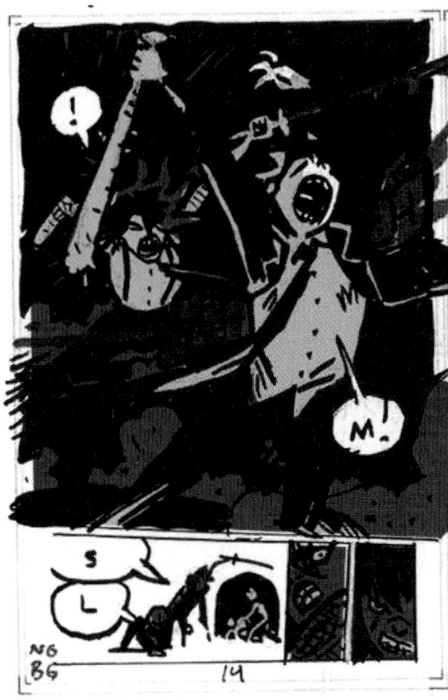
!
M!
S
L
NO BG
14

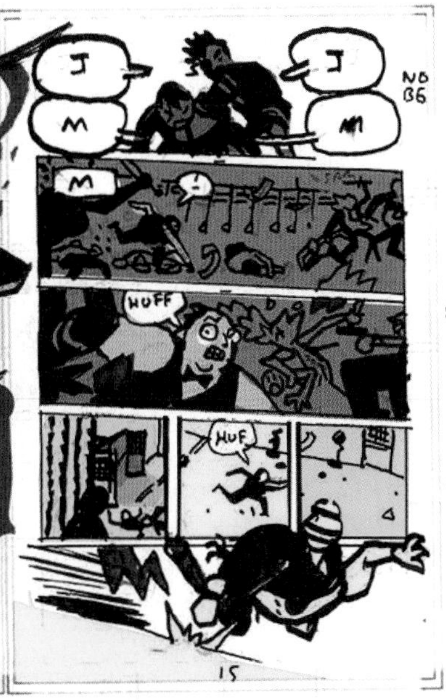
J
J
NO BG
M
M
M
HUFF
HUF
15

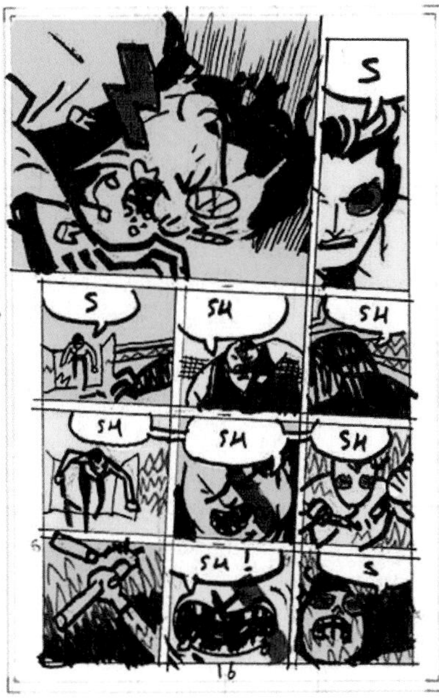
S
S
SH
SH
SH
SH
SH
SH!
S
16

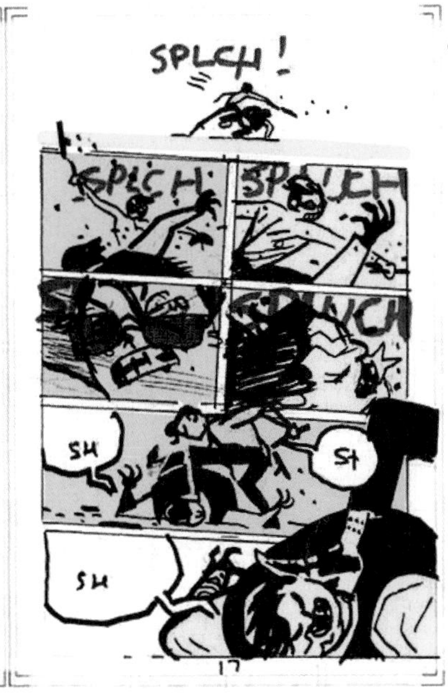
SPLCH!
SPLCH
SPLCH
SH
SH
17

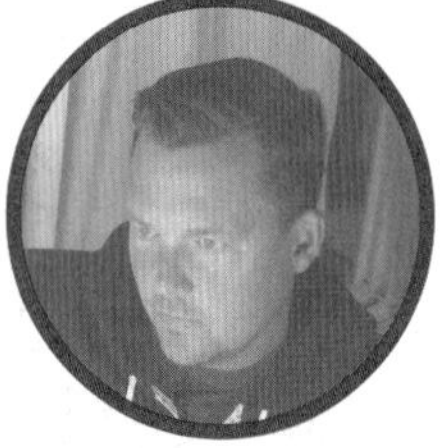

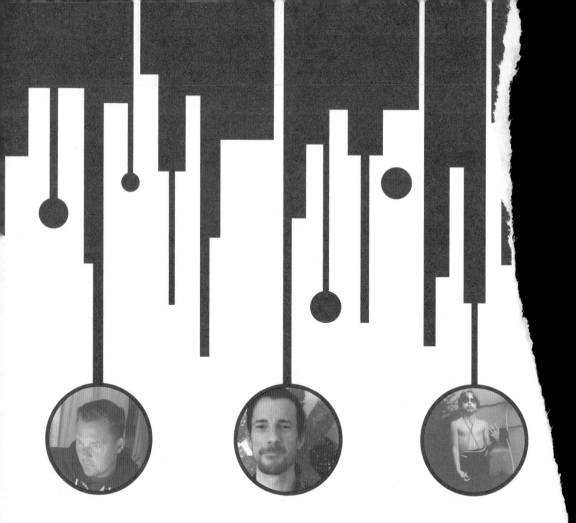

RICK REMENDER is the co-creator of *Deadly Class, Black Science, Seven to Eternity, LOW, The Scumbag, Fear Agent, Tokyo Ghost*, and more for Image Comics. His work at Marvel Comics is the basis for major elements of *Avengers: Endgame, The Falcon and the Winter Soldier*, and *Deadpool 2*. He's written and developed several sci-fi games for Electronic Arts, including the universally acclaimed survival horror title *Dead Space*, and he has worked alongside the Russo brothers as co-showrunner of *Deadly Class*'s Sony Pictures television adaptation. Currently, he's writing the film adaption of *Tokyo Ghost* for Cary Fukunaga and Legendary Entertainment and curating his publishing imprint, Giant Generator.

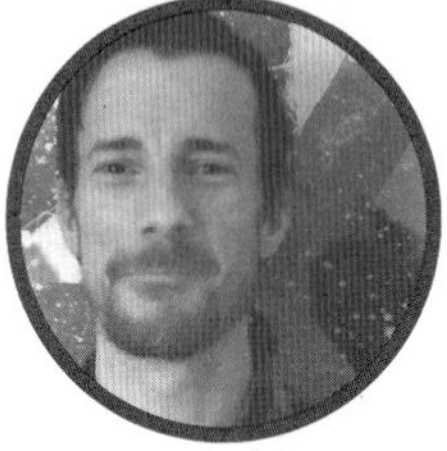

WES CRAIG is the artist and co-creator of *Deadly Class* with Rick Remender; the writer, co-creator, and cover artist of *The Gravediggers Union* with Toby Cypress; and the writer-artist of *Blackhand Comics*, published by Image. Working out of Montreal, Quebec, he has been drawing comic books professionally since 2004 on such titles as *Guardians of the Galaxy, Batman*, and *The Flash*.

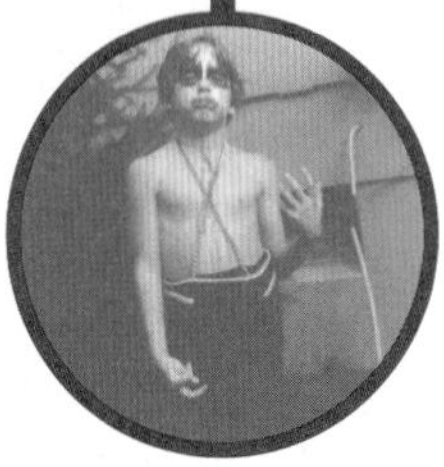

LEE LOUGHRIDGE has been in the comic industry for over 20 years working on hundreds of titles. Lee is far more handsome than any other member of the *Deadly Class* team. The last fact was the basis for his previous departure from the book. He resides in Southern California longing for the days when his testosterone count was considerably higher.